I0831171

Book One of Blackbird Hollow

Welcome to Blackbird Hollow

by

Allison Carr Waechter
&
Victoria Mier

Ebook ISBN: 978-1963134261

Paperback ISBN: 979-8-9930414-0-7

Hardcover ISBN: 979-8-9930414-1-4

Book Cover by Averil the Artist

Editing by Erin Larson-Burnett

Interior Illustrations by Annie Konst, Designed by Allison Carr Waechter

First edition 2025

Welcome To Blackbird Hollow

For everyone who is looking for a place to belong in this cruel world. Welcome to Blackbird Hollow. You're home now.

Content Guidelines

The stories in the Blackbird Hollow timeline take place on Earth, but in a speculative near future based on a similar, but not identical, past/present to our own, due to the fact that in our worldbuilding, the Fair Folk are real, and are a driving force for many governments' historical behavior.

This obviously makes the future we describe play out in a different way from the one that, in real life, we might experience in thirty to fifty years. We want to acknowledge before our journey begins that this is not meant to be a 1:1 representation of our timeline or Earth as we know it.

TWs:

Blackbird Hollow is written for an adult audience, and therefore includes adult content and a mature storyline. While this is, by no means, a "dark" book, there are some TWs we'd like you to heed before going in:

- A whole lotta fantasy violence and gore

- So much swearing
- Vivid descriptions of oppression, and violence related to that oppression
- Grandparent loss
- Parental death/murder
- Children who were parentified
- Explicit sex
- Alcohol consumption, including to the point of drunkenness

A note on terminology:

As two authors who have experienced a lot of marginalization regarding mental illness, we choose to use terminology around insanity in a colloquial way. This is an artistic choice and we understand that some might not find it palatable. If this use of terminology is upsetting for you, we want you to keep yourself safe.

PROLOGUE

Alice

It's not *my* fault Aston Devereux Wallingford the Third has such a punchable face. Maybe his parents should've been concerned about that instead of perfecting the bloodline, or whatever the fuck it is rich people care about anymore.

I barely suppress my eye-roll when his "not really a question, more of a comment" reply to Professor Achebe goes on for four whole minutes. She's tolerating him—she *has* to, with the amount of money the Wallingfords contribute to the university —but even her poker face is starting to crack.

"So that's why I don't really trust the Ranscuro Study," he finally concludes, settling back in his chair and shooting me a smug glance. I smile at him, baring my teeth. He knows as well as anyone else in this room that the Ranscuro Study provided groundbreaking information on extraterrestrial biology.

It's just that *I*—Alice Blythe, a twenty-nine-year-old second-term PhD student with a factory foreman dad and post office clerk mom—have authorship on the published paper and he doesn't.

"Must be hard to swallow when everything's been handed to you," I mutter under my breath, closing my notebook.

"Fantastic thoughts, Aston," Professor Achebe manages with a tight smile. "Thanks for sharing. Well, class, on that note, let's call it a day."

I'm sliding my notebook and planner back into my backpack before she's finished her sentence, eager to leave. The light slanting through the room's huge windows is already the glimmering gold of early evening, making all the antique wood sparkle like it's been freshly polished. I sigh. It'll be a late night in the lab. A fresh specimen delivery is coming in—the new, unnamed genus that collapses into dust twelve hours after harvesting—and it would be great to microwave some soup and get another cup of coffee before heading in. My stomach's been rumbling for two hours now, and I don't know the last time I slept for an appropriate amount of time. But such is the life of a fully funded PhD student with three classes to teach, thirty hours of lab work each week, and, of course, my own coursework to handle.

Which is a nice way of saying I'm hanging on by a fucking thread.

"Alice," calls a singsong voice just as I'm slipping through the door, out into the relative safety of the hallway. I don't even turn around, don't give any indication I've heard Aston at all. I just keep walking, hefting my backpack up my shoulder. The repair on the left strap is fraying again. I've already sewn it back up at least three times now.

Too late to do anything about it, I hear his rapidly approaching footsteps on the worn hardwood floors. The next second, fingers grip my arm and wrench me to a halt.

"What the fuck," I snap, turning on my heel to find Aston grinning at me, his blond hair in its perfect coif, leather loafers gleaming in the setting sun framed by the windows lining the hallway.

"No rebuttal?" he asks, pouting. "You know I love our debates."

"I'm not in the mood," I tell him, feeling the rubber band of my admittedly limited tolerance stretch further and further. Before it can snap, I yank my arm from his grasp and turn to leave.

"Is it because you can't keep up?" he wants to know, still in that teasing, singsong voice. "There's no shame in that. It was nice of the old man to include you in the study." Aston pauses, and my throat feels like it's closing off. Before I can reply, he continues, eyes narrowing.

"But I'm not nice, Alice, and I'm not afraid to tell you the truth," he says, stepping closer—*too* close. My blood pounds as my hands curl into fists. "People like you don't belong here."

Maybe if I'd slept more than three hours last night, I'd just keep walking. Maybe if I'd had time to eat lunch, or if I didn't have five texts from my landlord asking about the rent payment, or if there was more in my kitchenette than canned soup from the bodega, my better senses would prevail.

But instead, that rubber band inside me pulls taut and snaps. And then, of course, I wheel on Aston Deveraux Wallingford the Third and punch him in his stupid fucking face.

Chapter 1
Alice
One Month Later

My pager pings just as I settle into the scuffed plastic chair, the rich scent of coffee filling my nose. Out of instinct, I almost reach to snatch it off my belt until I remember there won't be any urgent communication from the lab or exciting test results.

Because I'm not a PhD student at OrthCon University of Technology and Sciences any longer. Punch the wrong guy, and everything disappears overnight, it turns out. Doesn't matter how incredible Professor Emilio Ranscuro thinks I am or how excited the Alien Biologies Department chairwoman is about my ideas. It only matters that the Wallingfords can't possibly send their baby boy to school with a girl who can (sort of) throw a punch.

I still find it annoying that no one wants to admit he *fucking deserved it*, but whatever. My pager pings again, and I realize it's probably just my parents, wanting to let me know they've safely arrived at their next destination. For now, I ignore it, shaking the computer mouse awake. The pad beneath it is peeling, the wrist pillow gummy with wear. I wrinkle my nose and pull the mouse off the pad entirely, placing it on the fake wood table instead. With a sigh, I plunk my backpack between my knees, digging past the eviction notice slips for a granola bar I swear I tossed in there a few weeks back and never ate.

Triumphant, I emerge from my quest with the bar in hand, though it's more like loose granola in a plastic sleeve at this point. Food is food, so I tear it open and begin to chew as I boot up the internet. Even all these years after the Reformation, connecting still takes a few minutes—though part of that's due to all the VPNs this internet café runs.

Out of habit, I heft my pockmarked, sticky-tabbed copy of *The Joy of Cooking* onto the table, rattling the mug and saucer of another customer a few computers down.

"Sorry," I mouth when they glare in my direction. I clear my throat and push the book away. I don't know why I brought it. I'm not going to look. I promised myself I wouldn't. Also, I promised the *government*, and there's no way they weren't made aware of my expulsion. Can't imagine another reason I've seen so many suits skulking around my apartment building.

I'm just here to email the bursar and get my tuition reimbursement. That's it. And I only came to the Halal Brothers' Café because it's close to my apartment and because I like Habib, the little orange cat. Amir and Ali, the owners, are nice, too, though I can tell they hold me at arm's length. Or, at least, they used to.

Back when I used to practically live here, before I started the program at OrthCon. Before the suits at Sector came to say hello and basically told me I could go legit and channel all my "boundless passion" into a not-so-covertly government-funded research program at the city's prestigious university...or I could go to jail. And by jail, I'm pretty sure they meant a black site. Stuff's plenty different now after the Reformation, sure—but some things never *really* change.

"Haven't seen you in a minute," comes a voice at my elbow. So lost in my thoughts, I nearly jump out of my skin. Occupational hazard, I guess.

"Been busy with school," I tell Amir, shoving *The Joy of Cooking* to the far side of the table so he can set my mug and saucer down. They don't match—a hefty, plain cream-colored mug with a dainty, Persian-patterned saucer. I like it, though.

This place feels homier than the coffee shops sprouting up as the city gets back on its feet. They're all white walls and chrome, minimal black lettering, a lot of information about where the coffee comes from and what notes you're supposed to be able to taste, but absolutely no soul. All catering to the influx of graduate students into OrthCon, no doubt, after the program's reopening a few years ago.

That's the weirdest thing about the Reformation. It's been almost thirty years—basically my whole lifetime. Will the history books assigned for some undergrad class a hundred years from now reflect just how long it *really* took for things to settle down? To reach some sort of normalcy? Because shit was pretty fucked for a while there.

"Good to see you," Amir replies. He turns to leave without any further conversation, the kind I've seen him launch into with other folks.

For a strained, weak moment, loneliness grasps at me with pleading hands. I ignore it, shoving the feeling deep down, as I always do. With a sigh, I pull the pager from the waistband of my jeans. When my parents left for their world travels, they splurged on the fancy kind of beepers that allow short text messages.

Made it to Barcelona. Going to eat tapas by the sea now! Love, mom & dad.

I don't know what tapas are, but I'm glad they're safe. I still think they're insane for taking all their savings and using them to see the world, particularly after a lifestyle so focused on practicality. I sure as shit didn't see it coming, but I guess the world's safer than it's ever really been in their lifetime, so it sort of makes sense.

Still seems extravagant to me. Whatever. I tuck a lock of long, dirty blonde hair that refuses to stay in my braid behind my ear and settle my elbows onto the slightly sticky tabletop. The internet finally connects, so I click to log into my email, sending a quick message to my parents before I forget.

I haven't told them about being expelled. There's not really a point. They won't be disappointed, but they also won't be surprised, not exactly. They're firm believers that people like us don't mingle with people like the Wallingfords. My dad might even be a little proud I punched someone.

I take a sip of my coffee—I have no idea why I can never brew it as good as Amir and Ali—and begin to draft my email to the bursar's office. The first version is probably too mean, so I add more begging. Habib jumps up onto the table, aggressively rubbing his head on my arm.

"Hey, bud," I murmur, scratching his head the way he likes.

Habib's the runt of some street cat's litter that Amir fell in love with a few years ago. Little guy's been here ever since, barely more than seven pounds fully grown. I scoop him up and lift him onto my shoulder. Purring, he wraps himself around my neck like a scarf. It's his favorite place, for some reason. He makes bread into my sweater—luckily thick enough that I'm safe from his sharp-ass claws—and then settles his head down atop his paws.

Before I know it, Habib is snoring softly in my ear and my coffee is gone. Refills are cheap, but I really shouldn't spend anything extra. Outside, dusk has fallen, casting the city into hues of gray and blue. The street's quiet, with only a few occasional pedestrians. Another way not too much has changed. We're free to be outside our homes whenever we'd like, and it's much safer to do so, but folks are stuck in their habits. It's too drilled into us to keep well away from the dark.

I finally reach some version of the email I consider passable and click send. It's only for one class; everything else was included in my program. I planned to cover the costs of the folklore course with part of my stipend, but naturally the university is making me jump through a hundred hoops to get a refund for a class I'm not even taking. Because expelling me wasn't enough, apparently.

I lean back in my chair, causing Habib to give a squeak of annoyance. "Sorry, bud," I murmur, reaching up to scratch his chin. Careful not to disturb him, I rub my eyes and start closing out of my tabs. I should go home. Sleep. Figure out what's next.

My gaze falls on *The Joy of Cooking*. My fingers itch and my heart lurches. I chew on my lower lip, shoving my hands into the pockets of my jacket.

I can't. Especially since I've been expelled. It'd be putting a target on my back. Making my shit situation even shittier.

"Doesn't really seem like it can get *that* much worse, though," I mutter. The next second, I'm grabbing for the book like it's the last loaf of bread in the supermarket back during the bad years. With shaking fingers, I open to the right page, the spine so familiar with the exact spot that it falls open easily. Then I'm frantically typing *booksandblueberrypies.com* into the browser, pulling up the blog I haven't looked at in nearly a year.

It's still up, which I'm sort of surprised by—until I realize it's probably a good way to root out other people like me. My hands tremble as I click around to navigate to the post with the creme brûlée recipe, scrolling to the third image. I click the word "joyful" in the caption's photo. When that takes me to an apple pie recipe, I check over my shoulder before scrolling to the second image in the blog post, clicking on "delightful" in the caption.

I follow that trail—the trail I designed, the one I have memorized by heart—until I reach the log-in page.

My fingers fly, the long, complicated passkeys still burned into my mind. When the back-end page loads, I pretend to stretch—to Habib's outrage—while taking a look around the café. Should be in the clear. Historically, Sector isn't great at blending in.

Electricity arcs through me when I see I have a message from love_cookies210 that's gone unread for six months. We've never exchanged real names, but we've traded plenty of other things—extremely sensitive information about our theories, our research, our movements. I don't trust a lot of folks—a side effect of growing up during the Reformation—but I *almost* trust Cookie. That's saying a lot.

I click on their message, my entire body hunched around the hulking desktop, my heart in my throat. It takes a few minutes to decode using *The Joy of Cooking*—the cipher for my online conspiracy board.

Ever heard of Blackbird Hollow? Cookie's message reads. *Not too far from you. Some really, really weird activity. Leaf peepers disappear every autumn as far back as the records go. Someone else just went missing a few days ago. And guess what? You bet your ass it's on a major ley line.*

My heart is hammering in my chest, and I'm suddenly way too warm in my dad's old duck-lined Carhartt jacket.

And there's more, Blue. Lots of good intel about the Wild Hunt moving through there. You should go.

I bite down on my tongue as I reread the message over and over again, my eyes beginning to burn from the screen's glow. A quick search shows that another couple just disappeared a few days ago. My blood absolutely *thrums*.

Because maybe I have my first real chance at proving that I'm right about the world. That everyone who laughed in my face was wrong. That my ex, who broke up with me when he found my stringboard of theories, is the real asshole, and also intellectually incurious as all hell.

"Blackbird Hollow," I say out loud, and something about it feels *right*. Like I'm finally going to show everyone the supposed existence of aliens is nothing more than a cover-up for something way, *way* worse. That there's a conspiracy so massive, even the government is hoodwinked.

We were stupid to think the otherworldly entities arrived from the vast void of space. No—non-human creatures were *already* here. In fact, they were here long before us, and something tells me they'll be here long after we're gone.

They're called the Fair Folk, and I'm going to be the one who tells everyone the truth about them.

Chapter 2
Wyatt

My watch isn't wrong—it's never wrong. Fallon's just late again. The smell of bacon sizzling and maple syrup fills my nose as I take a deep breath. I close my eyes and stifle the bone-deep sigh tangling with my lungs. It never helps to let myself get shitty about Fallon being Fallon.

There's only one way to solve this. I drain the last of my coffee and lay down a tenner for Janey, who just materialized out of the back. She makes eye contact with me, then shakes her head. Everybody knows how Fallon is. Hard to say if that makes it better or worse.

"You wanna take something to go?" She must have been washing her hands, because she's drying them on her crisp white apron.

I slide out of the ruby-red booth, my jeans snagging on a crack in the vinyl, shaking my head as I stand. "I'll come back after I find her and grab lunch."

Janey smiles, her freckles crinkling around her dark brown eyes. "The usual?"

I nod, then leave a twenty on top of the tenner. For lunch.

"And a turkey leg for Fern, if you wouldn't mind." Janey smiles. She likes my dog. I lean against the counter and lower my voice. "Fries extra crispy, if Mac can manage it."

Not low enough, apparently. Janey's husband grumbles from behind the window. She snickers, loving every minute of the gentle ribbing. As I head toward the door, she leans over the counter to tug on the sleeve of my old wool jacket. "Heard Barnes is headed back from the Groves. You know what that means." There's a twinkle in her eye. A few people look up, nudging each other.

I give Janey a grin I can't quite feel, nodding as I push out the diner door. Something about Fallon ghosting me this morning doesn't feel right. We're only a year apart, and Mama always said we acted like twins when we were little.

A cold, wet wind hits me in the face, bellowing down from the hills like old man winter. The weather turned a week ago, and the leaves in town are going all out, a riot of golds and reds. Heavy mist still hangs high in the pines, a promise that more rain's on the way.

There's cars I don't recognize everywhere on Main Street, the leafers blowing in for their annual peeping. I do my best not to mutter to myself. Caden says it makes me look unstable, and Fallon's enough instability for one family. I let out a low whistle as I approach the truck. Fern stretches, yawning sleepily as she pops up out of the bed.

A white woman in her mid-forties, dressed like she bought everything out of one of those town and country catalogs, gasps, literally clutching her chest. "Is that a *wolf?*"

Her pasty-looking husband, who's got beady little eyes and is wearing a matching quilted jacket, glares at Fern, then at me. I force a grin, ruffling Fern's ears as I approach. "Nah, husky-golden mix."

The man keeps glaring, but the woman nods, giving me a

tight little smile. They move on, and I can't help but roll my eyes. Fern gives me a stern look, as though she knows I just lied straight through my teeth to the leafers.

"C'mon," I urge her. "Let's go find Fallon."

Fern jumps down, bounding into the cab of my old pickup as I open my door. I only half-lied. She probably is golden, or maybe yellow lab, but definitely not a drop of husky in her. Whatever her other half is, there's no doubt she's mostly wolf.

I pull away from the curb, cutting off Jones McConnell's smooth-talking as I go. The local disc jockey will be pandering to the leafers for the next three weeks, playing practically ancient, pre-Reformation jazz and all that shit they like. I like it too, but the fact that it's *for* them irks me.

It was never like this when we were kids. Blackbird Hollow was barely a place back then. Just an old, abandoned town in the hills, the population wiped out by the pandemics. We were some of the first to move in, along with Janey and Mac, Jones McConnell, and the Foxglove Coven, who got the all-clear from the local tribe to move in. Everyone else came after, and we've been growing little by little for the past twenty years. Finally made the local atlas and everything.

Five years back, one of the big city publications ran a series on the "small town revival," as they termed it, and Blackbird Hollow made all sorts of lists. The leafers started showing up like clockwork in the fall after that, and then again in the spring for the damn lilacs. It's been a problem ever since. Outsiders don't know the way things work in these hills, and do stupid shit like go into the woods after dark, or play music by the lake.

There's more traffic than usual on Main Street, so I cut through the numbered streets to get out of town. Nearly everyone's steps boast jack-o'-lanterns and mums on the front porch, and big old rosemary bushes by every garden gate. The residents of Blackbird Hollow know better than to talk openly about what goes on around here, but no one takes unnecessary risks.

It's a good life, but it isn't for everyone. The leafers come and yap endlessly about how nice it must be to live here, but they never stay. Something in them senses that our quaint little traditions have darker origins, and when their week's up, they check out of the Archer Inn and go home. Most never come back.

I wave at a few of our neighbors on the way up the hill, and mouth "fuck you, forever," at Widow Harkness, who's shucking corn on her front porch, surrounded by a bevy of cats, singing a sardonic old song about a woman who ruined everything. I come to a stop at the corner to greet the old witch.

"You going up to the house?" she shouts from her rocking chair.

I nod, and Fern barks, affirming my plans.

"Fallon got any honeycrisps?" the old woman asks.

"Sure she does," I reply. "Want a bushel?"

Widow Harkness's wrinkled skin is a deep shade of umber, and rumor has it she was a high fashion model back in her day. I can still see it. "Bring me half a bushel of the honeycrisps and another half of whatever Fallon likes for pies, and I'll make you one."

I lean out the window, ready to wheedle a little. "You know I prefer a cobbler—with the crumble top. And vanilla ice cream."

"Freshly churned, no doubt," Widow Harkness replies with an arch of her eyebrow.

I grin for real this time.

She shakes her head. "Classic Wyatt Hayes." I snicker, and she makes the usual witch's hand motion to remind me that she sees all as I pull away, shouting after me, "Come by this afternoon. I'll be home."

Widow's voice fades away as I take the sharp turn up the switchback onto the familiar gravel of Blackbird Road. Fern whines when we pass our house, but only a little, like she's just saying hi to her food bowl. She leans against me, her giant head resting on my shoulder.

"Fallon'll get you something to eat," I promise her.

Fern growls a little in response, but it's a chatty noise, not a warning. Fallon is one of the few people the canine trusts. I take a right turn at the old mailbox shaped like a trout. Its mouth's gaping open for all the world to see. The monstrosity is at odds with the elegant loops of the wrought-iron gate. This far up in the hills, mist hangs everywhere, and though there are clusters of gold-leafed birches, the old place is fully in the pines.

The drapes of the rickety old Victorian are all thrown open, so I know my sister hasn't just slept in. Not that Fallon sleeps much to begin with. Fern tumbles out of the truck ahead of me when I open the door, shooting off after a squirrel. I head onto the porch and push open the kitchen door, calling out for Fallon.

She doesn't answer, but the coffee in the pot is still warm, though there's barely enough for me to have a cup. My heart slows, its thump all I hear as I stare at the kitchen stairs. They're painted a shade of light blue that feels like childhood. It was the first thing we did when we moved here. Paint was all we could afford, so we painted *everything*.

Just me, Caden, and Fallon.

I was twelve, Fallon thirteen, and Caden five. We weren't old enough to be alone by today's standards, but things were chaotic back then. Technically, we were fifteen years into Reformation, but shit was still wild. There weren't even public utilities out here 'til the tribe turned them on for us. We spent the first few weeks in the dark, since Fallon didn't know enough to fill out the right paperwork.

She figured things out, though. We all did. A familiar pit opens up in my gut. I try swallowing it down. Hoping it'll just go away—that the memories will all just stay put.

My heart beats slower, thumping hard as I call out Fallon's name again. *Where the hell is she?* Childhood panic takes over; a memory of coming downstairs one winter morning to a cold, empty kitchen and a fresh blanket of snow in the garden. Caden was sick, and Fallon was nowhere to be found. Her footprints went into the woods, but none came out.

I steady myself against the big old fridge, letting its familiar whirring hum wash over me. She'd just been out then, and she's probably just out now. I close my eyes, waiting for the panic to subside. It took years to get these episodes under control, but I'm better at it than I used to be.

Outside, Fern barks, bringing me out of the past. "You monster!" Fallon squeals. "Puppy paw prints all over my gown!"

Relief floods through me, a flush of heat inflaming my cheeks. I try to keep my footsteps slow, but I rush for the back door, almost knocking over the umbrella stand in the mudroom. The door flies open, but I barely remember touching it.

Fallon's in the garden, dressed only in a pair of wellies, a thin white nightgown, and a genuine Cowichan sweater our dad got years ago for bringing the Coast Salish a collection of banned books for their massive library. It's got orcas on it, and it's one of Fallon's favorite sweaters.

My sister looks just exactly like our mom. Long, dark brown hair. Tall, but not willowy. *Built like a volleyball player.* That's what our dad always said. *Strong and long.* And pretty enough to get herself into trouble. But unlike our mom, Fallon is covered in tattoos. And now paw prints. Fern leans against her thigh, grinning like a fool while Fallon scratches under her chin.

She looks up at the porch, her brows knitting under her messy bangs. "Why're you so pale?"

I shake my head, not able to speak just yet. That's when I notice the bruise purpling on my sister's left cheek. "We were supposed to meet an hour ago," I blurt out. "What the fuck have you been up to, Fallon Hayes?"

My infuriating sibling just holds up the basket she's got propped on her hip and grins. "Picking the last of the cherry tomatoes. Want an omelet?"

Chapter 3
Alice

"What do I have to lose?" I ask Habib, even though my hands are shaking above the keyboard. I mean, I've been expelled. I'm probably blacklisted at every graduate program worth attending. I can't go home—my parents took the landlord's enormous buyout to give up their rent-controlled apartment last year. And Angelica Wallingford, Aston's mother, already told me she'd do her best to poison any standing in the scientific community I have left.

"Habib," I say, gently extracting the cat from my sweater. He's still sleepy, back legs hanging limp. I give him a kiss on his forehead. "I gotta go, buddy. Thanks for the cuddles."

But I still hold him against my chest as I finish clearing my browser history and make sure I've logged out of everything. Then I stand, curling one arm around his little body, and gather up my things. I set him down on the seat of my chair—still warm, no doubt, which hopefully he appreciates. He curls up in an instant, looking like a creamsicle-swirl ice cream cone from old-timey photos of oceanside boardwalks. The ones that used to line the coasts, before all the climate change ravaged seaside communities.

Amir bustles by with a bin of used mugs, reaching for mine. I open my mouth to tell him I'm leaving and that I'll probably never see him again. But then I remember that's exactly what he's always expected of me—to stay for a few years and inevitably disappear back to wherever I came from. So, instead, I just zip up my jacket and sling my backpack over my shoulders.

"See ya, Amir," I say. He responds with something brief and noncommittal, and then I'm off, slipping out into the dark autumn evening.

It's only a few blocks to my apartment, and I keep my head down, eyes keen for anything sketchy but avoiding looking at anyone directly. Most of the shops—the ones that bothered to come back at all—are already closed up tight even though it's barely dinnertime. There's more loose trash on the streets than there are people.

As I round the corner onto my street, I notice a group of neighbors gathered in the side garden of one of the nicer houses—a big, old brownstone that's no doubt been sitting empty for years and sold for next to nothing. This neighborhood isn't fashionable, and it's far from any of the sophisticated ones that the magazines are starting to tout as a "must-visit" or a "can't-miss destination."

My heart does a strange thing in my chest as I walk by, looking in their direction to offer a nod. Five or six folks are gathered on the browning lawn around a small bonfire. They're wrapped in scarves and blankets, steaming mugs in their hands. Little lights strung along the side of the building dip across the narrow garden, creating a web of illumination.

Despite myself, my steps slow as I pass the garden gate, rusted and just barely hanging onto its hinges. A wild, genuine laugh bursts out of one woman's mouth, and I like the sound of it, like the look of her well-worn plaid jacket with elbow patches. Woodsmoke curls up from their bonfire, tickling my nose. The owner of the house—Tomas, I think it is—turns and looks my way.

"Oh, hey, there you are!" he calls, raising his mug. "Come on in, the gate's open."

I hesitate, a warmth I haven't felt in a very long time—not since those early days back on the farm—flooding my entire body. My shoulders relax, and suddenly the autumnal wind doesn't feel so biting anymore. I move toward the gate.

Maybe I can scale back my plans. Blackbird Hollow might not need to be more than a weekend trip, a brief investigation. Maybe I don't need my program's limited stipend to stay. Maybe there's jobs at those sterile coffee shops or downtown diners.

Maybe there is still something for me here.

"I hope you have a cider ready for me!" comes a voice over my shoulder. I freeze as a tall, sturdy person in painter's overalls and a giant sweatshirt breezes past me, slipping through the gate.

The group in the garden closes like a door, their backs to me now. I realize Tomas had never been speaking to me—of *course* he hadn't been speaking to me. Why would I even think something like that? We've said, what, ten words to each other in the time I've lived here?

The warmth seeps out of me, leaving me colder than before as I trudge the rest of the way to my building. The hallways are empty as I make my way to my apartment, tearing down the new notice on my door when I arrive.

"Can't evict me if I'm already leaving," I mutter as I slip inside. I should make something for dinner, sit down for a second, but there's a horrible kind of sadness building in me.

It's been building for a long time, I know, and if I give it an opening right now, I'm afraid it'll tear me apart.

So, instead, I set my jaw and flick the lights on, beginning to search the tiny space for my belongings. Ten minutes later, and it's kind of depressing how little is actually *mine*—or, at least, how little I really care about. There's my small collection of secondhand books, my limited wardrobe, the framed photo of my parents, my undergrad degree, and the stuffed rabbit I've had since I was a baby. And yeah, I'm a fully grown woman, but I absolutely still sleep with him every night.

"Your entire life fits in a backpack and an overnighter, Alice," I mutter to myself, beginning to pace the worn carpet. I stride from my door to the window, and then back again, and again, and then again. I pause, pulling my stuffed animal from my bag. His once-white fur is a worn-in cream these days.

"Mr. Rabbit," I say, addressing the plush by his full name, because this is serious. "Are we doing this?" I stare into his black button eyes as if he might actually give me an answer.

What I find there makes my stomach bottom out, sheer horror sweeping through me. No—I'm wrong. I'm seeing things. I've cracked under the pressure. I'm as crazy as Angelica Wallingford says I am.

My breath coming in short gasps, I stagger to the kitchenette and turn the big overhead light on. It flickers unpleasantly, humming all the while, as I lay Mr. Rabbit down on the counter like he's a specimen I'm dissecting. I dig through my drawer with trembling hands, grabbing a fork.

And then I lean low over the stuffed animal, using the prong of the utensil to pry at a tiny black bead in the middle of his left eye. It looks like it's been glued on, or maybe even fused, to the original button. I scrape at it again, but I can't get any traction.

I swallow hard and grab a pair of scissors. I hesitate, which I know is so stupid, but the last thing I want to do is maim the little plush. Mr. Rabbit might be my only friend, if I'm honest.

I let out a long breath and, with gritted teeth, force myself to snip the thread. The button comes loose, clattering onto the counter. I snatch it up and examine the small black dome, my heart beginning to race as I understand there's absolutely no mistaking what I'm looking at.

Sector bugged me. *Sector fucking bugged me.* This shit isn't supposed to happen anymore—not after the Reformation, not after everything we did to get society back on track. Entire cities drowned and half the countryside went up in flames and pandemics swept through unchecked and somehow we're still back to bugging civilians again.

All I want is to go home. Back to the farm before everything went to shit, with its creaky floorboards and chipped sink and the old, sunken-in sofa and the smell of my mom baking bread on the weekends. I want to come around the corner into the kitchen and see her on the landline, the thick, curly cord wrapped around her fingers as she exchanges hushed sentences, not wanting me to overhear. Things were worse then, objectively. And yet I wish for it all back so fervently that it makes me lightheaded.

But it's all gone. My parents are eating tapas next to the sea thousands of miles away. Some developer probably tore out all the wood trim in the farmhouse, or at the very least painted it white. That pink landline phone is surely rotting in a landfill somewhere. And my grandparents—

"Nope," I whisper so quietly I can barely hear my own words, squeezing my eyes shut. "We're not going there. Not right now. Get it together, Alice."

I shake my arms out, turning in a tight circle, trying to make my brain work. When I can finally manage a few thoughts, I nudge the button into the center of the counter—so if anyone checks up on me again, they'll know I found them out. That I'm so much smarter than they realize.

I snatch Mr. Rabbit off the counter, purposefully not looking at his poor little one-eyed face. I can be sad about a stuffed animal when I'm safely away from here. Gently tucking the plush back into my bag, I do another loop around the space, checking drawers and peering under the bed. But that's everything. That's really everything I have to my name that I can't bear to leave behind.

I welcome the numbness that settles over me as I slip my backpack on. There is no longer any doubt in my mind that I'm going straight to the bus station and buying a one-way ticket to the Upper Lakes Transportation Center. And then I'll figure out how to travel the final eight miles to Blackbird Hollow. Because the random little town that just got back on the map might hold the key to everything.

And it certainly doesn't hurt that Sector will have a much, *much* harder time finding me out there in the wild expanse of mist-damp hills and old-growth forests where faeries might just roam.

Chapter 4
Wyatt

There's this part of me that wants to yell at Fallon for whatever she did to get hit in the face. But my stomach growls, and that part goes quiet, like it always does. Fallon is a force of nature. Not something I can scold into better behavior. She's in charge, but sometimes it's hard to tell which of us is the elder sibling.

Without so much as a sigh, I reply, "Sure, an omelet sounds good."

Fallon smiles, but the expression stays on her mouth, never reaching her eyes. That's how Fallon smiles, unless she's talking to animals. I don't ever doubt that she loves me and Caden, but those dead eyes of hers are the reason I've always worried that someday she'll just be gone.

Fallon changed when our parents died.

"Let's get you some food, baby," she murmurs to Fern, who gallops ahead of her.

I catch my dog and use the towel by the back door to clean her paws before letting her in the house. Fallon makes her way up the steps, limping a little bit. She's got a bad hip and knee, but it's more than that. Whatever got her in the face did more, and she's hurting. She wouldn't have fought one of Them without telling me, so there's only one other option. "You went to the Roadhouse last night, didn't you?"

Fallon doesn't answer me, but she doesn't have to. The Roadhouse is about ten miles out of town, and the worst of "our types" end up out there, trading in illicit magic and other shitty substances. I've asked her not to go alone, but it's not like she listens to a damn thing I say.

I follow her into the kitchen, where she's already at the sink, washing the tomatoes and unloading eggs from her basket as well. Fern waits patiently until the tomatoes are drying in a colander. Fallon pulls a couple of random bowls from the drying rack and chirps, "Cat, you bastard, come and get it."

Fern's tail thumps heavily on the wide-planked wood floors as a giant black cat materializes out of thin air. Nobody knows when the cat-sìth showed up, or why it attached itself so firmly to my sister, but it's been coming around for about a decade now, and has never aged a bit.

Fallon dumps crunchies into the two bowls she has on hand, not caring who eats what, and then goes about making more coffee. "Make yourself useful, Wyatt. Those omelets aren't about to make themselves."

Only Fallon would offer you an omelet and expect you to make it in *her* house. If asked, she'd say it's *our* house. But we haven't lived together since Caden turned. I finally sigh, not wanting to think about that this morning. We lived here together long enough that we have a rhythm in the kitchen, and before I know it, we've managed to rustle up a pretty good breakfast.

By the time we're finished eating, the rain's set in and the morning's gone dark. Not so unusual for October, but the wind up here howls in an especially eerie way that doesn't sound the same, even a block away, at my house.

I lean back on the cushions in the alcove bench seat and take a long sip of my coffee. It's always better when Fallon makes it. Or maybe it's always better in the mugs she collected over the years. Mine has a great big 40 on it and says "Over the Hill" in orange and brown letters.

"What happened at the Roadhouse?" I ask when it becomes clear that she's never going to tell me.

She licks her lips, shrugging a bare shoulder back into her sweater and shaking her head. "Just got into it with a few pack members from Sunnyvale."

My molars grind together. That's down by the Groves. "Fuck, Fallon. What are they doing this far north?"

She shakes her head because I already know the answer. "They wouldn't take no for an answer and that damn Shelly just about gave them his address."

I let out a string of curses. "I *told* him not to sleep with her. Godsdamnit, I *told* him."

Fallon rolls her eyes. "Shelly's not the problem, Wyatt. Cade's gotta say no for himself at some point. If he wants to stay a lone wolf, he needs to declare it and move on, or they're just gonna keep coming for him."

She says that, and she means it, but her face is still turning black and blue. "What's the other guy look like?" I ask when my irritation with the both of them dies down.

Fallon's head falls back, but when she looks at me again, she's grinning. "So much worse." Her brown eyes, just the same as mine and Caden's, darken. "Lots of whispers about the Hunt coming over Big Hill this year."

I shake my head. "That's foolishness."

Fallon shrugs. "I'm just telling you what I heard. People were saying they've heard the hounds..."

"What people?" I scoff. The riders have never come within a hundred miles of town, and are unlikely to start now.

Fallon opens her mouth to answer me, but the phone rings. She gets it, untwisting the long curlicue cord as she says hello. There's a lot of hummed responses before Fallon says, "Sounds good, Wanda," and hangs up.

"Job?" I ask.

Fallon nods. "You better go get those apples for Widow Harkness while I get dressed. It's gonna be a long one. Leafers went missing two days ago out of Mill Creek. They were coming this way, and there's no trace of them."

I chew the thought over in my head, then frown. "How'd you know about the apples?"

Fallon laughs as she heads to the stairs. "She already told Wanda to remind you. You know how it goes with the damn coven phone tree."

That I do. I sigh and go to get my coat out of the mudroom. No sense in missing out on a good cobbler just because we've got a job.

Twenty minutes later, and we're rolling back down the hill. I send thanks to all gods that Fallon has deigned to wear pants today. The last thing I need is her biting some park ranger's head off for taking too long a gander at her legs. In fact, all things accounted for, Fallon is dressed like an adult about to go traipse around in the woods. Corduroys, a Nirvana t-shirt riddled with holes, the Cowichan sweater, and Fern draped over her lap like a blanket.

Wanda's out front with Widow Harkness, who's still shucking while Wanda makes a corn dolly. "You stay, girl," Fallon tells Fern as she slips out of the truck. Fern loves Cat, but isn't much for *actual* felines, and Widow Harkness is lousy with cats.

I fetch the apples out of the bed as Fallon gets to work pouring tea for everyone on the porch. This is what it's like to do the majority of our work with witches. You get good at making tea. Hedgeriders and witches go together like hell-hounds and the Hunt.

Wanda tells Fallon everything she knows about the missing leafers. They're a couple from the Coast, white, affluent, but not truly wealthy, and not much experience with the outdoors. They told the Mill Creek rangers that they were going to do the boardwalk tour at the visitors station three days ago and never returned. Apparently, they've missed three reservations for Mill Creek's fancy restaurants. Fallon looks like she wants to spit when Wanda says that.

Before she launches into a diatribe about Mill Creek selling out to rich tourists and the academics at Three Ravens College, I interrupt. "What makes the coven think this is our sort of thing?"

Wanda shakes her head, her ebony curls bouncing a little. She's a pretty Black witch in her late thirties and is the Foxglove Coven's leader. "To be honest, if there weren't so many rumors swirling about the Hunt coming this way, I wouldn't be worried. Leafers go missing every year... But with rumors about the Hunt..."

Wanda trails off, but Fallon finishes her thought. It's what we're all thinking. "Sector's bound to show up."

Widow Harkness spits like she always does when anyone mentions Sector. "Damn traitors."

I share her sentiment, and so does Fallon, who spits in solidarity, her hock traveling into the foxgloves by Widow Harkness's white picket fence. Wanda looks like she might lose her patience, but Widow Harkness smiles. Too many hedgeriders and witches went over to the government during the Dark Years, sharing secrets our people had kept well for thousands of years in the blink of an eye.

Fallon leans against the porch railing, squinting a little as she stares down the road toward town. "Better let the coven know. Batten down the hatches. If it is the Hunt, we'll need everyone prepared."

Wanda tips back in her chair. "Betty's making sure extra nails are going out to every household, and we've got the PTA phone tree working on sewing them into the kids' coats."

"You got enough help?" I ask. "For the kids whose parents work?"

Widow Harkness grins at me. "Nobody wants your help with sewing, boy." She pokes Fallon in the side. "Remember your senior pageant?"

Fallon snickers. "Who could forget?"

I glare at them both. "The dragon turned out alright."

Everyone laughs, and they get back to talking about rowan fences and salt bags. Fallon nods at me. "Marion's got the rest of the rock salt in storage at the Stardust. Can you go out and get it tomorrow?"

"Sure thing," I agree.

Fallon doesn't have to tell me to talk to Marion about who's been coming and going. I know the drill. I check my watch. It's just about time to pick up lunch from the diner, and then I've got errands that'll piss Fallon off.

"You good to get home?" I ask. "I've got a full afternoon."

My sister narrows her eyes at me, but nods. "I'll walk you out."

She follows me to the truck, scratches Fern's ears, and then leans against my door, blocking me from leaving. "You can't keep doing it all for him, Wyatt. He's had a year. I let it slide for this long because he's the baby, but he has to stand on his own two feet at some point."

We've had this argument dozens of times. Our views on Caden are decidedly different. "He's standing on them, Fallon. He just needs us."

She leans toward me, pushing off the truck. "What that kid needs is to get his ass kicked six ways from Sunday and to get real fucking brave."

I stare down at her boots and mine, both scuffed beyond fixing, resoled and worn. The two of us have always disagreed about how to raise Caden, and we might be adults now, but there's no doubt we're still raising him up.

"He *is* brave," I argue. "You know it as well as I do. He's been to hell and back this year, though. Cut him a little slack."

Fallon's jaw clenches tight. Her lashes brush her cheeks as she looks down, sharing my view of our boots. "Anybody ever cut *you* any slack, Wyatt?"

I cross my arms tight over my chest. "You sure as shit didn't."

My sister flashes me those dead eyes of hers and smiles. "You're doing just fine, and so am I."

She moves to go back to the house, but I grab her arm. I lean close to my sister, so the witches—the ever-loving gossips that they are—don't hear me. "Neither one of us is fine, Fallon. We're the walking wounded, and you fucking know it."

A breeze sends the shorter layers of her dark hair into her eyes. "You tell Caden Hayes I expect to see him at my table for Sunday dinner this week." I open my mouth to argue about Cade's agoraphobia, but Fallon shakes her head at me with a scowl. "No excuses. He doesn't show up, and I'll drag his ass out of that hovel in the woods myself."

Chapter 5
Alice

My head bangs onto something hard, and I jolt awake. For a moment, I have no idea where I am, and my heart nearly stops. My lungs tighten, thoughts of Sector's threats and black sites rattling around in my mind.

And then I remember I'm just on a bus—the one I very willingly climbed aboard a few hours ago, the third and final transfer in my journey. I admit I didn't realize just how far away Blackbird Hollow is or that I'd be signing myself up for an overnight bus trip. But I had to get out. I *had* to.

I stretch my legs, muscles cramping, and then double-check I still have all my shit. I do; my right arm rests on top of my backpack, my wrist looped through a strap. My duffel bag sits between my feet on the bus's sticky floor with one ankle slipped through the handles. I rub my eyes, the lull of sleep pulling at me.

But then, out the window, I see the sun peeking over the horizon. Something unfolds in me—something I don't have a name for—as I watch the golden light sweep across the landscape. It's nothing like the flat, even plains of the city, where most of the forest won't grow back anytime soon.

Here, trees grow so tall and thick that sometimes they blot out the sun entirely. Rolling hills covered in an autumnal carpet of fallen leaves undulate across the horizon like an ancient serpent. I press one hand to the cold window, my breath fogging up the glass. The bus climbs a hill, revealing a little valley laid out below, a lake—or maybe a large pond—glimmering like a diadem's jewel in the middle.

I've *never* felt so sure the Fair Folk are real. The ones with enough number, organization, and power to effectively create the illusion of extraterrestrial life—to keep us looking at the stars and the wide infinity above our heads, instead of the faerie halls right beneath our feet and the dark wood just outside our cities.

I pull my legs up onto the seat, resting my chin on my knees as I stare out the window, transfixed. But the closer I get to Blackbird Hollow, the more anxious I become. What if I've made an enormous mistake? What if there's nothing here for me, either? What if the real problem is that I just don't belong *anywhere*?

I spend the last forty-five minutes of my journey biting my nails and picking at my cuticles until they bleed. I try to stop myself a million times. It's a gross habit, sure, but even more importantly, for most of my life, there's been no guarantee of access to antibiotics if something gets infected. I slink lower in my seat, resisting the urge to tap my feet or pace the aisle or otherwise draw attention to myself. Instead, I watch the hills roll by as the bus—which is barely more than scrap metal, if we're being honest—drags itself along the narrow, winding road.

"Pulling into Blackbird Hollow," calls the driver, shifting down a gear. "Everybody off."

"Everybody" is me, an elderly man in a plaid flat cap who's barely moved for nearly an hour, and a bland middle-aged white woman who asked five or six times if she could smoke. Each time, the bus driver just tapped the "no smoking" sign above his head.

I gather my things and force myself to walk—not run—to the door. When I step off the bus, I slam to a stupefied halt that causes the elderly man to mutter something at me in a language I can't even identify, let alone understand.

Speechless, I scurry off to the side, realizing a little too late that I probably just marked myself as a wide-eyed, idiot tourist to anyone paying attention. But I can't help it. I'm *spellbound.*

The next breath I draw into my lungs is heavy with the scent of bonfires, rich soil, and fallen leaves. A wide cobblestone boulevard cuts straight up the hill, lined with sturdy streetlamps. The town is still sleepy; only a few businesses have lights on. It's early, though—about seven a.m., I think. The main drag is charming without being artificial or scrubbed clean of character. Toward the top of the hill, businesses give way to pretty houses that remind me of storybooks and gingerbread.

But it's what lies beyond the commercial corridor that makes my heart do a strange flip in my chest. Thin ribbons of roads wind into the forested hills, porch lights twinkling like tiny stars. Everything is crowned by the gray velvet swathe of mist, which grows thicker the higher it climbs into the hills.

I let out a long exhale, the cold morning turning my breath to smoke. Blackbird Hollow sits in the palm of a forest, sprawling and impossibly wild, thicket-dark and utterly primordial. Excitement thuds in my chest, and, despite my exhaustion, I pick up a quick pace and head into town.

I pull a folded note from my pocket as I walk. It's a basic sketch of Blackbird Hollow's cross streets, enough to get me to the Stardust Motel. According to the travel magazine I stumbled upon at one of the bus stations, the Archer Inn is the more popular choice. But the Stardust Motel is "perfectly adequate for those who appreciate vintage charm."

It's also a hell of a lot cheaper, which is really what sealed the deal. I make my way up the hill, mostly alone on the sidewalk. I pass a fantastic-looking diner, the smell of pancakes and syrup making my stomach rumble.

"I'll be back," I promise in a whisper as I walk by, longingly eyeing the laminated menu plastered to the front door. Even "adequate" accommodations can fill up fast here during leaf peeping season, and from what I saw on the ride in, Blackbird Hollow wears October like a couture gown. So, as hungry as I am, I'd like to make sure I have a place to lay my head tonight first.

The motel is off the main drag, past a few quiet residential buildings and what looks like an old brick mansion. I see it the second I turn the corner, thanks to a large sign spelling out "STARDUST MOTEL" in neon lettering. The building itself is neat and low-slung, stretching toward the dark overhang of the forest.

The woman at the counter eyes me for a long second—like there's something she knows about me that I haven't figured out for myself yet—before exchanging cash for a key to Room 11. To be honest, I barely look at the room beyond noticing that it's cozy and wood-paneled with lots of botanical art hanging on one wall, the space above the bed decorated with a gorgeous blanket that reminds me of Indigenous folk art. I make a mental note to find out what tribe's land Blackbird Hollow resides on. Unsurprisingly, the sleek travel magazine's article mentioned nothing of the sort.

For the moment, the siren song of pancakes is stronger than anything else. I chuck my bags onto a chair, stow my roll of cash

—already much thinner than when I set out—and head back into town. Everything except the tiny newsstand is still rolled up tight, so I let my stomach lead the way, even though my curiosity wants to stop and examine everything. I'm one of the only people on the street, anyway, so that's a better activity for when there's more folks around. It'll give me more cover.

The day is overcast, threatening to drizzle, as I make my way through the mist back to the diner. From further up the hill, I can see the glow of its neon red sign atop the building: "PINE CONE CAFÉ." I stuff my hands in my pockets to ward off the chill, and, for a reason I can't explain, my shoulders relax.

The door chimes when I walk in thanks to a collection of vintage brass bells strung on tattered ribbons hanging from the handle. A worn letterboard sign tells me to seat myself, and I do, sliding into a cherry-red leatherette booth. The walls are clad in dark wood paneling. Along a long ledge, dusty fake plants intermix with worn knick-knacks. Slender pendant lights made of swirling amber glass provide a warm glow in contrast to the cool gray-blue pressing against the windows. Oceanscape paintings of all kinds cover the walls.

I snuggle into the collar of my coat, still a little cold from my walk, as I pick up the menu. I already know what I want—a giant stack of pancakes and about twelve cups of coffee—so it's hard for my gaze not to stray around the cozy space. Across the aisle from me, there's a large, curving counter with red stools. It's busier than the booths, filled with people who seem like locals: worn coats similar to mine, heavy work boots, faded baseball caps, an easy familiarity.

I made sure to sit on the far end of the booth so I could keep my eye on the door, which appears to be the only entrance and exit. When the bells jingle again, I glance up to find a white, middle-aged couple walking into the diner. The woman's perfect copper hair and the man's brand-new Barbour jacket seem like dead giveaways that they're tourists. Ignoring the sign, they call out for a hostess. I frown and look back down at the menu.

"What can I get you, baby?" comes a voice from my elbow. I startle slightly, turning to find a short Black woman in a spotless apron with scalloped edges. Her dark brown eyes are kind, and there's something deeply endearing about the freckles scattered across her cheekbones. The nametag on her apron reads "Janey."

"Breakfast combo number two, please," I ask, sliding the menu to the end of the table.

"Plain pancakes okay?" she asks, pulling a pad from her apron.

"Perfect," I say. "Thank you."

"Of course," Janey says with another smile, making eye contact with me as she grabs the menu. "You new around here?"

My mouth goes dry, and suspicion creeps into my chest. "Just visiting," I say, chewing on my lower lip. "Needed a break from work."

Janey eyes me with that sharp, quick intelligence I normally appreciate in people, though in this situation, I admit it makes me a little nervous.

"Well, welcome to Blackbird Hollow," she says with a big smile, one eyebrow arching. "I'll have your food out in just a minute."

I thank Janey again, and she turns to go, spotting the couple at the door who apparently can't read. She huffs so theatrically that I have to choke back a laugh, and then makes her way down the aisle toward the front of the diner.

By the time she slides a carafe of coffee and a plate of perfect, golden, fluffy pancakes in front of me, a lot of the local-seeming folks at the counter have finished their meals, and more customers like the middle-aged couple have arrived. In the booth next to me, a group of people a few years younger than me who dress like Aston and his friends are discussing how excited they are to experience something so "authentic."

I slather my pancakes in butter and syrup and fix myself a cup of coffee from the carafe. I'm surprised when it's almost as good as Amir's brew. It's a little different—more molasses, less spice, with a deep note of chocolate. There's part of me that wants to stay and soak in the atmosphere, but the diner's starting to get a bit crowded. I don't want to hold up an entire booth, and all the different sounds and voices are flustering me a little, anyway. I leave cash on the end of the table—with a generous tip for Janey, of course—and slip through the door.

The sun seems to have burnt off some of the mist, and it's markedly warmer now. I barely need my coat and unwind my scarf from my neck, throwing it over my arm instead. The streets are busier, too—lots of people in expensive hiking gear stopping to take photos on disposable cameras. I try my best to blend in with them so I can have a better look around.

A few doors down, there's a fancier café with a little outdoor eating area. There's even a tiny dog in someone's purse set atop a curling wrought-iron table. I pass by a laundromat, which is busy, and then an admittedly charming general store. It's the kind of place that my parents—well, the people my parents turned into—would spend a stupid amount of money on a special kind of maple syrup or something.

It's becoming apparent that Blackbird Hollow is not a town where it's hard to tell who belongs and who doesn't. There's a fairly marked difference between locals and visitors. Conveniently, I'm dressed like a local, which hopefully gives me a little more cover. I have no idea if Sector is even looking for me, but better safe than sorry, I suppose.

My steps slow as I pass a botanica—a real one, by my estimation, with herbs hung to dry in the windows. Faded gold lettering on the glass spells out "Lúna & Daughters." My curiosity wins, and I step closer, peering into the shop. I find dark hardwoods, heavy cabinets, and a towering back wall filled with apothecary jars.

"Interesting," I murmur before continuing my way up the hill, my gaze catching on a strange symbol etched into the bottom of the botanica's dark green door. No, not *that* strange—not to someone like me.

My heart climbs into my throat, my chest tight with anticipation. The deep breath I force into my lungs smells like incoming rain and last night's bonfires.

I've seen the symbol before. A few times before, actually. I've seen it in photos of a stone circle the government says never existed—probably because they destroyed it—where it was carved into one of the altar stones. In the grainy photographs from a national park, chiseled into the trunk of a towering oak tree where a six-year-old child was found *two years* after she disappeared in the woods, well-fed and in perfect health, talking about the pretty winged person who took care of her. And once, etched into a set of stairs to nowhere, smack-dab in the middle of a massive swamp outside the city OrthCon calls home.

I found those stairs right before Sector found me, I think.

I swallow. My heart thuds against my ribs. Trying my best to look like I'm moseying, I move across the sidewalk to one of the large trees that line the pathway. Leaning against its trunk, I pull my map of Blackbird Hollow from my pocket, turning it over. I dig around in my pockets for a short stub of a pencil, and then copy down the symbol, my fingers trembling all the while.

And then I'm gone, shoving the crumpled paper back into my pocket. I tail the end of a large group of undergrad-aged kids, keeping my head down. To my advantage, the sun seems to have lost its battle, and the mist is beginning to creep back in. Even the quiet residential blocks near the hotel are busier now, people wandering around, pointing out architectural details. I weave through them, hands in my pockets, doing everything in my power to stop myself from breaking into a full-out sprint.

Cookie was right. I was right.

There *is* something here.

Chapter 6
Wyatt

Dawn might come a little later as the year dies, but Fern runs things on a tight schedule. Bleary-eyed, I stumble through the house letting her out, the back door in the kitchen open to the cold morning air. It's still dark outside, and there's a few of Them lazing about in the center of Their ring of toadstools as I grind the coffee.

Fern's gone into pounce mode, and as I start the coffee maker, I scold her. "Leave Them be, girl."

She sneezes purposely at the vicious little creatures, but They all laugh, still drunk on Their revelry. Fern turns her nose up at them, does her business right outside Their circle, and then trots back into the house. If she thinks she's offended the pixies, she's wrong. They cackle even harder. The noise is infectious, and I laugh along with Them, scratching the wolf-dog's ears as she leans against me.

I scramble some eggs for us both, then give Caden a ring as I wash the dishes. He doesn't answer, so I leave a message on his machine, letting him know I have his mail and groceries both, and that I'll bring them out before lunchtime.

He answers before I hang up, his voice slow with sleep. "Jesus fuck," my little brother says in greeting. "Sun's not even up."

It's a task to keep my molars from grinding together. Doc asked me to cut it out at my last checkup, and I'm trying. "You hear me about bringing your stuff by?"

"Yeah," Cade answers with a yawn. "Come by after lunch, though."

I pause, gathering myself. I've given Caden the benefit of every doubt for a year, since the wolf bit him. I've locked him up every month. I've done all his shopping, gotten all his mail. I've run around after him like a damn servant because he's my kid brother, and being turned did a number on him.

"Why's that? You got something big going down today?" I ask.

"Don't give me a hard time about this," Caden replies, an edge of irritation in his voice. In the background, a voice says, "Who's calling so early, baby?"

"Caden Wesley Hayes," I growl. "Is that Shelly Marie I hear?"

"Wyatt," he says, drawing my name out into several beats. "Calm down."

Fallon was right. She's always right.

"If you've got the energy to fuck Roadhouse tail," I growl, "you've got energy to come get your own damn food and mail. I'm sure as shit not bringing it to you."

There's a long pause. "I can't, Wyatt. You know that."

"You should see Fallon's face, Caden. She walking worse than ever because some shit from Sunnyvale wouldn't let things alone. Shelly tell you that?"

Another long pause. "I didn't ask Fallon to get involved."

If I could reach through the phone and shake him silly, I would. As though anyone's ever had to ask Fallon to protect us, to stand up for us. Caden doesn't remember what Mama and Pa were like. He doesn't remember the ways we got by before Blackbird Hollow. He doesn't get it. He never has.

"You'll come get your groceries today before sundown, and you'll be at the house on time for Sunday dinner." Caden tries to break in, but I don't let him. "I'm not fucking around. I'm not gonna push you too hard, but you can come here, and you can come home. We'll start there and see how it goes."

I can hear the gears in his head turning all the way across town. He's always been a wheedler, and the kid's such a looker that he nearly always gets his way. "I mean it, Cade. It's time. This isn't a request."

"Fallon says jump and you say—"

"I say how damn high. *Just. Like. You.*" I slam the phone down before Caden pokes me into saying something I'll regret.

Fern whines, leaning against me harder than ever. "Never get born the middle child," I advise her. "Or you'll spend your whole life navigating between tyrants."

She chortles a little in response, stretches, then wags her tail at me. The coffee maker beeps, and I pour myself a full cuppa. My mug for the day has pastel bears from the 1980s on it. When I moved in here, Fallon gave me a third of her massive collection of mugs.

I pad out to the back porch and sink into one of the four Adirondack chairs I built last year, right after moving in. The sun'll be up soon. I pull a quilt from the basket over my legs and sip my coffee in silence as Fern flops onto her side with a dull thump. I smile at her, and her big tail pounds the wood porch.

It's tempting to ruminate over my conversation with Caden, but, rough as she can be about things, Fallon's usually right. Our sister sees things sharper than just about anyone I know. Caden acts like I follow her without question, but the kid doesn't see us fight. We've always kept it like that, more his parents than his siblings in so many ways.

To him, she's just the hard-ass who never lets him get away with shit, and because the kid barely remembers what it was like to be out there before Blackbird Hollow, he can't appreciate the magnitude of what she's done for us, but especially for him. Caden is a good man, and someday, if he can get this wolf thing under control, he might be a great one. It's time for him to stop sulking and get back to life. I'm not willing to rush him on the how, but he's gotta take a few steps forward, or he's bound to get stuck.

The sun peeks up over Big Hill and hits the river, setting it ablaze with the golden fire of morning's first light. Three deep breaths, and I've got the family drama settled to a dull roar inside my head. Each of us is hardheaded in our own way, and I learned long ago not to let being in the middle fuck me up too hard. The light sinks into me as it creeps across town.

This view is the reason I took this house on. It's needed a lot of work, but I've been more than happy to do it to have a place of my own in the world. I'm proud of how things have turned out so far, and there's nothing more satisfying than spending a quiet morning on the porch with my dog. But even without delivery duty on the docket, today's going to be full.

I may not need to make the trip to Cade's, but I need to get up the hill before I do anything else. If I know my sister, she's going to spend the day scouring the woods for clues about the missing leafers. She can more than handle things alone, but Fern'll be better off with her than me today.

"C'mon, girl," I say to my pup as I push out of my chair. "Let's get you to Auntie Fallon's Doggy Daycare."

Marion Roanhorse glances up from her copy of *Miniatures Monthly* as I walk in. Not *because* I walked into the front office of the Stardust Motel, but just as a matter of coincidence. Nothing but whatever goes on inside her brilliant mind can interrupt Marion when she's focused on something.

The woman's a certified mathematical genius, but this year she's committed to miniatures, and there is a massive village of dollhouses behind the desk that she's tending to for an art installation. She pushes back her reading glasses, her long black hair swishing around her shoulders. Her eyes crinkle as she smiles.

Marion and I have been friends since high school, but we don't get together enough these days. When things are sorted with Caden, I'll invite her and Betty up for Sunday dinners again. Everything in my life got smaller when Caden turned, but if I'm going to force him into moving forward, I should do the same.

"You here for the salt?" she asks. "Or a decent cuppa and a bit of gossip?"

I laugh. "I'll take all three, if you're offering."

She pours me a cup of coffee, and I lean against the counter. "What's shaking?"

Marion snorts. "Who says 'what's shaking' anymore?"

I shrug. "Just giving it a try."

"You sound like a fogey," she says through a peal of laughter.

I let my mouth fall open in mock offense. "What kind of word is 'fogey,' then?"

"Write it down, Hayes," she replies. "You need to beef up your vocab for our next game night."

I raise my cup to her and nod. "That I do."

She tilts her head at me, her smile wistful and her dark brown eyes sparkling. It's like no time has passed, even though it's been a few weeks since I got out this way. It's always like that with us; we just pick up wherever we left off, giving each other shit and swapping tales.

"Well," she says, tucking her tiny hands into her oversized alpaca sweater. "I heard that Rebecca Jackson caught Michael cheating on her."

I let out a low whistle, even though that's not news. Mike's been cheating on Rebecca since they were homecoming king and queen. But leaning into the drama is more fun, so I play up my scandalized act a little.

Marion's cheeks pink up a little, as though she's a bit excited. This is gonna be good. "With Marcie Cavendish."

"No shit," I breathe, *actually* scandalized now. This is a juicy bit of news. Marcie Cavendish has been a pain in Rebecca Jackson's ass for nigh on three decades now. Fallon used to call them the Warring Barbies. "Is Becks pitching a fit?"

Marion's cheeks puff up with pure smugness. "Keyed both their cars last night while they were bumping uglies in Room 23. Wrote '*whore*' on hers and '*cheating filth*' on his." Marion leans back in her chair, shaking her head, pleased as punch. "I almost considered liking her."

"Almost," I quip, before taking a long drink of coffee. Everyone makes better coffee than me. "Anybody else interesting staying over?"

The mirth drains out of Marion's face. "This about the missing leafers?"

I nod.

Marion shakes her head. "Any chance you might just sit this one out, bud?"

Marion's tribe has very particular ideas about what's weird in the woods. They're not wrong about any of them. The things she knows are real. They're just not the things hedgeriders are tasked with handling.

We originated in the British Isles, long before they were called that. Historically, hedgeriders deal primarily with Them, like our ancestors. They have a long history of traveling far beyond Their land of origin to make trouble. The entities the Indigenous peoples of this land recognize are not ours to care for, only to respect. We don't talk about these things much, but Marion's always known what I am.

Though Fallon's always been stubborn about making sure Caden and I know the difference between Them and the entities indigenous to the land, it's possible we've got this one wrong. "Is there a reason for me to?"

Marion shrugs. "It's your kind of thing. Reeks of Them. Just some wishful thinking that maybe you'd just...y'know..."

"Butt out?" I suggest.

"Yeah," she agrees. "Any chance of that?"

Marion's a good friend. I always appreciate that she gets concerned about me. I shake my head and take another sip of coffee. "Nope."

Before Marion can fire off another volley, the bell on the front door tinkles. A white woman walks in, a gust of cold wind behind her, sending wet leaves swirling inside. My heart slows, thumping so hard in my ears I could swear I hear drums beating.

Her wavy blonde hair is the color of wildflower honey, and with the rain coming in, it's curled up a bit more around her face. Her frame is swallowed by a canvas barn jacket that looks about two sizes too big for her. Nice enough body, I suppose, but it's her face that gets me.

She's got one of those mouths that probably turns downward naturally, and cheekbones that make me wish I could paint, just to capture the way the light hits them. But her eyes. Her eyes are avid, filled with an intensity I can't rip my gaze away from.

I'm staring. It's rude. But I can't stop. Marion's eyes flick between me and the woman a few times before she saves my awkward ass. "Hey there. Room 11, right?"

The woman nods, giving me a wide berth as she steps around me to speak to Marion. *Couldn't have been the staring that did it.* I wonder if the universe might do me a favor and swallow me whole.

"I'll just load the salt, then," I say when it becomes obvious the woman isn't going to say a word with me leaning on the counter.

Marion just closes her eyes and nods, so full of secondhand embarrassment for me that *she* might blush. As I push my way out the door, I let out a hiss of air, feeling for all the world like someone's smashed me over the head with something.

Chapter 7
Alice

When I reach the parking lot of the motel, I break into a jog, my boots thudding on the pavement. I shoulder through the heavy glass door, tumbling into the lobby. I don't know why, but I'm expecting it'll be empty save for the woman at the desk. My mouth is almost open to begin questioning her, but then I notice there's someone else in the dim, carpeted room.

He's tall and well-built, his worn-in wool jacket taut across muscular shoulders as he leans against the counter. His treacle-dark hair is cut short, and when he turns to look at me, the warm glow of the desk's lamp traces his strong jaw with golden fingers. My pulse thuds. He's handsome, no doubt—a tanned face with crow's feet around his eyes from gazing into the sun his whole life, a soft-looking mouth that could probably curl into something meaner without much trouble.

I find my gaze dropping to his hands—large, a few white scars here and there, his veins and tendons standing out beneath his skin. My pulse slips lower, down into my belly. But then my fingers curl around the paper with the strange symbol in my pocket, and I look away, moving off to the side. I *should* want him to leave so I can speak with the woman at the desk, so I can get to a computer and the internet, so I can find my next breadcrumb.

But I don't. I want to know what his thick flannel shirt smells like, if his voice is as worn-in and comfortable as the rest of him, if his name suits him and if it feels nice in my mouth.

And I want to know why, of all the people who could possibly be standing in this lobby in this tiny town right as I rush in looking like a madwoman, it's *him*.

"I'll just load the salt," the man says as his gaze dips away from me. His voice *is* perfect—rough around the edges like old leather, but deep and warm at its center. He strides past me and out into the parking lot. The door swings shut behind him, and the lobby suddenly feels cooler, as if he's taken the sun with him.

I stand there for a long moment, frazzled and undone, a thousand thoughts running through my mind all at once. With a huff, I look down, gaze catching on the paper scrap clutched in my fingers.

The strange symbol. The tip from Cookie. Whatever's happening to those hikers, and whatever that means for the conspiracy that I feel like I was born to unravel. *That's* why I'm here. Not to be inevitably spurned by another boyfriend. Not to have another man talk down to me about something I've spent years researching. Not to be distracted from my literal life's work by a cute boy.

No matter how muscular his shoulders might be beneath that plaid jacket or how tingly his voice makes me feel. It's irrelevant. Fuck, for all I know, Sector has a file on my usual type and sent him my way.

I set my jaw and close the distance to the desk. The woman

—Marion, I think—somehow looks both deeply amused and like she wants to disappear into the floor at the same time.

"Hi again," I say, my voice trembling. She settles her expression and looks at me deadpan, though one eyebrow arches. "I'm a graduate student at OrthCon specializing in extraterrestrial studies. I'm currently working on a grant project about connecting folklore to alien activity. So I was wondering, if you're local, maybe you could tell me a little about the Fey and—"

"Oh, absolutely not," Marion says with a laugh that isn't mean-natured, though it makes me feel foolish all the same. "I don't touch that white people shit with a ten-foot pole."

I freeze, heat rising to my face. At the same moment, I notice the big sticker on the counter's plexiglass surround that reads "you're on Indigenous land!" in curly retro font. The heat intensifies as mortification sweeps through me.

"Oh my god," I mutter, smacking my forehead with my palm. "I'm an idiot. I'm so sorry."

Amusement twinkles in Marion's dark eyes, and the corner of her mouth curves up. "Well, you could go talk to your fellow idiot in the parking lot," she offers, gesturing to where the admittedly hot guy went just a few minutes ago. "He's probably still loading up salt."

"Salt," I echo, understanding turning slow wheels in my head.

"Yep," Marion replies, and then turns away, pulling the lid off a teapot on her desk and frowning at the color of the steeping brew.

Salt. I'm a hell of a lot closer to the mountains here than I was at university, but it's a bit early for snow in this climate. There's only rain in the forecast. I checked. But salt has been used as a protective tool for millennia. Its usefulness is heavily debated in conspiracy circles, but still—that's a breadcrumb if I've ever seen one.

"Thank you," I manage in something that sounds too much like a squeak. I turn, trip over my own feet, and leave all my dignity on the worn carpet of the Stardust Motel as I jog out into the parking lot.

He's down around the side of the low-slung building, loading sacks of something heavy into the back of his pickup truck. I take a deep breath and make my way over, absolutely not distracted by the way he's since removed his jacket and rolled the sleeves of his flannel to his forearms, revealing corded muscle.

"Hey," I say as I approach, my stomach roiling, nervous energy making my hands tremble. "Marion told me I should talk to you about...about my research project."

He pauses, leaning against one of the bags he just loaded, fingers drumming on the tailgate of his truck. "She did?" he asks, and maybe I'm imagining it, but a hint of a blush creeps across his cheekbones.

"I'm Alice," I offer, sticking out my hand. "Alice Blythe."

He looks at my hand like it might be a snake. After a long, stilted moment, he returns the handshake. "Wyatt," he replies. "Wyatt Hayes." His hand is warm, callused, fingers engulfing my much smaller palm. "So, uh. Your project?"

It's not a question, not exactly, but his words tilt up like it is. My mouth goes dry as I try to find words. Wyatt—of *course* his name is Wyatt—grabs another bag and hauls it into the truck bed. I look away from his hands, from the flexed muscles in his forearms.

"I'm a graduate researcher in the extraterrestrial studies department at OrthCon," I say, the words well-worn and familiar in my mouth. "And I'm—uhm, I'm here on a project.

I'm connecting alien activities to regional folklore. Fey folklore, to be specific."

Wyatt freezes, the line of his shoulders turned rigid. It reminds me of a dog's hackles going up. I watch his gaze swivel through the parking lot, as if a monster is going to jump out from a muddied Subaru.

"Don't know if I can help you with that," he finally says. He stalks toward the side of the building to snatch up another bag, but his movements aren't so easy and fluid now. He looks distracted, almost jumpy.

Interesting.

"Maybe you could just help me with this symbol," I say, digging into my pocket for the scrap of paper. All six-feet-two-inches of this plaid-shirt-wearing, 100-pound-salt-bag-hauling man slams to a halt. The entirety of his attention falls on my hand in my pocket, like I'm going for a gun and not a somewhat soggy scrap of paper.

"Nope," he says, exploding back into movement and throwing his hands up. With a loud clang, Wyatt slams the gate of his truck closed, even though I can see there's still a few more salt bags sagging against the building, and his bed's only half-full.

Frustration builds in me. I threw away whatever scrap of a life I had left. Sector is probably sniffing around my apartment right now. God only knows if they're going to trail me here, if they're going to make some deal with Marion to bug my room, if I'm destined for a black site in a matter of days.

I have to *know*. Even if I can't blow this whole conspiracy wide open, I at the very least need to know I'm right before I spend the rest of my life rotting in some damp cell. I bolt forward, toward Wyatt, grabbing the sleeve of his flannel.

"You obviously know something," I snap, that rubber band

inside me stretching, my body *always* choosing to fight when flight would be so much smarter. "Tell me."

He looks at me with equal parts horror and surprise before yanking his sleeve out of my grasp. "I don't know anything about good wineries," Wyatt says, too loudly, the words overly enunciated.

"What the fuck," I reply, throwing my hands up. "I didn't say shit about a winery. Could you *please* just look at this and tell me what you think, or at least help me find an internet café—"

I'm talking, but Wyatt's attention is trained over my head, his eyes narrowed, lips pursed with concentration. I don't know what he's looking at, and I don't care. I just need this *one* thing, just *one* more breadcrumb. I don't need him to do me some big favor or do more than give me the simple shred of my next stepping stone. It would take him two goddamn seconds.

All at once, Wyatt sweeps around me in a surprisingly lithe movement, considering his size. Suddenly, I'm pinned between the side of his truck and the muscular frame of a strange man I just yelled at.

Good job, Alice. Blackbird Hollow is going great.

"Get in the truck," he hisses, gesturing wildly at the passenger door with one hand.

I stare at him, my heart beginning to race. "Are you insane?"

"Get. In. The. Truck," Wyatt repeats in a low whisper. I stare at him, and slowly—too slowly—realize he's not threatening me.

He's *begging* me.

Alarm sweeps through me, and I shift my weight to peer around his side. "No, don't *look* at them," Wyatt pleads, sounding exasperated more than anything. "For fuck's sake. Just get in the truck."

I stop, looking up at him. I have to tilt my head back to meet his gaze, his eyes a distracting deep brown, the shade of tree bark gone damp with rain. I just met this man a few moments ago. I've only been in this town for a few hours. No one knows I'm here, except maybe Sector. No one who cares about me even knows I left the city, which means no one knows to look for me if I go missing.

"Okay," I find myself saying, because nothing matters more to me than a chance to unravel the government's biggest lie. I'll risk anything. I've already given up nearly everything, haven't I? "*Fine.*"

I reach for the handle, yank the door open, and climb into the truck.

Chapter 8
Wyatt

From the second she came hightailing it out of the office, I knew she was going to be trouble. Nobody on Earth walks with that kind of purpose who isn't a bushel and ten of vexation. Fallon and Caden both walk like that. Hell, I probably walk like that, but I've never given much thought to it before now.

When the black sedan pulls into the parking lot, I clock them, but Little Miss Has a Question doesn't, despite knowing a whole load of shit she probably shouldn't. Now I've gotta wonder why that is and get her the hell out of here before she does more harm than good. Two agents get out of the sedan, both dressed like agents. Cheap suits. Ugly black ties. They look like they've been cast in a pre-Reformation sci-fi flick. This is why it's hard to take Sector seriously.

Ye Gods, she is still blathering on. "I don't know anything about good wineries," I say, trying to inflect some intention into my words so she'll take a damn hint.

"What the fuck," she screeches, throwing her hands up. "I didn't say shit about a winery. Could you *please* just look at this and tell me what you think, or at least help me find an internet café—"

She's gonna talk forever, I realize. The Sector goons haven't looked over here yet, but they're gonna, and I'm here loading up salt while she talks about Them. Using the F-word and everything. My mind goes blank as I move. Typically, I like to ask before touching anyone I don't know, but we'll be in a cell before anyone can snap if she keeps this up, so I compromise my morals and pin her against the truck.

This makes her mad as a hornet, and I can't say as I blame her. If we get out of this, I'll apologize. To her and myself, because fuck all if she's not the most beautiful creature I've ever seen get so flustered. I feel none of my usual awkwardness. Instead, my heart thumps, sticky and hot, threatening something I don't like to think about much.

And then the agent looks our way, and that mind-bending flip my stomach was about to do stops and something near panic sets in. "Get in the truck."

She stares up at me, eyes wide with rage. "Are you insane?"

"Get in the truck," I whisper, slowing down my words so she'll really take my meaning.

Finally, she seems to understand what's happening. Seems to realize I'm not trying to kidnap her and that more is going on in this parking lot than her yammering on about aliens and Them.

"No, don't *look* at them," I hiss as she tries to crane her body around me. Trouble, trouble, all the way down. *Why can't one godsdamn woman in my life be easy?* "For fuck's sake. Just get in the truck."

She stares up at me like she's assessing how likely I am to murder her and then says words that send a flood of relief through me—"Okay. Fine."—and climbs in.

By the time I get around to the driver's side, she's got her seatbelt buckled and she's very casually putting her feet up on my dash, like it's something she always does. Both of the agents are watching us now. I hold up a hand. It's not like they don't know who I am. They always know. Hedgeriders have an uneasy truce with Sector. They're bastards, but we try to stay out of each other's way as much as possible.

Some things you just can't keep fighting, no matter how hard they are to swallow. As I open the door, I tell this slip of a woman, "This'll be more than enough for the water softener at Burt's. We can get lunch after, if you want."

We have exactly one water softener in town, in Burt Markle's gym, and we keep it going for just this purpose. Blackbird Hollow uses a lot of salt, and though Sector doesn't make its way through here very often, Fallon and the coven believe in being proactive. Since we've been spotted, the only answer is Burt's.

The woman nods. "Sure. But you're making me something. No getting around it, bud."

She waves to the Sector agents too, as I hop in, casual and cool as a cucumber. She sounds like she knows me, and not only that, like she likes me. So she does know something about what she's doing.

I try to attribute the return of my stomach flipping to the staring agents, rather than the sweet way her words wash over me. I wait until we're out of the parking lot and on our way back to town before saying anything. I reason that maybe she'd like to explain herself before I just jump in. But she doesn't.

I can't read her emotions, but she seems tense. Then I remember that she's in a strange truck, with a strange man. I take a deep breath and keep my hands on the wheel where she can see them. Ten and two, just like Fallon taught me.

Best I can do now is keep my word. "Normally, I'd pull over and let you out, but you made a pretty good show of things on the way out. We do actually have to go to Burt's and drop the salt off. But I'll answer what questions of yours that I can."

She nods once, but doesn't relax. Not that I expected her to. I know what the world is like, and who the fuck knows what she's been through. She still doesn't say anything.

"I am sorry for the rough treatment back there. But you can't talk about Them that way. Not in public."

Now she moves, curiosity getting the better of her, I suppose. She angles her body toward me a little, and though she's not exactly relaxed, some of the fear has gone out of the tension in her shoulders. "The Fae?"

"Fuck," I swear, not caring about the presence of a lady or any other such proprieties. "Don't just throw that word around."

She frowns. I can feel it in the small cab of my truck. I can *feel* her frowning. I glance over at her, only to find that there's so much puzzlement on her face that I nearly pull over. "You... Believe me? About the Fa—Them?"

I laugh. "'Course. Hard not to believe in something I've spent my whole life dealing with." Still that look of puzzlement, now mixed with wide-eyed amazement. "But what's all this about aliens? Surely someone who's worked this much out doesn't believe in that hooey."

"That *hooey*?" She snorts, laughing right at me, but I don't take a lick of offense. Something about that laugh sinks into me. It's not mean. It's sweet, familiar. Like she's already woven some bit of her threads into the fabric of my life.

"Well, it *is* hooey," I reply, laughing along with her. "*Aliens*." Burt's is up ahead. "This is where we'll drop the salt for now."

"What's it for?" she asks. "Does this have something to do with the missing hikers?"

Shit. She's gotta get some ground rules down right away. I

don't know why I'm considering helping her, answering even one of her godsdamn questions. I've lost my mind, and Fallon will have my head for this. "Look, I get that you're in a big hurry to know what's going on, but you could be anyone."

Now, she appears relieved. She lets out this huge sigh as I pull into Burt's parking lot, like she's been holding her breath this whole time. "I told you, I'm Alice Blythe."

"Sure," I agree. "And you're studying the folkloric origins of alien theories. I get it. You toe the line."

"The line?" she asks, frowning again. She'll give herself wrinkles frowning like that.

"The party line about Them," I clarify. What about this isn't she getting? Back at the Stardust, it felt like she knew something, and now she's more confused than ever. She looks irked as hell, her face all twisted up. I feel bad about making her feel bad. "Come on. Help me with the salt, and then I'll take you back to mine and make you lunch. Answer your questions."

Alice Blythe doesn't answer me. Her face is still twisted into that horrible knot, and I have to assume she's working something out for herself.

"Unless you want me to take you back to the Stardust. Happy to do that too."

She shakes her head, but still doesn't move. Alice is a funny little thing. Something about her oddness is endearing. Not sweet. But likable.

"Come on," I urge her. "Moving your body'll help you work out whatever's going on up there."

Alice frowns again, but she gets out of the car. We get the salt into Burt's shed, and I throw her the keys. "Go ahead and start the truck. I've gotta make a quick call about my dog."

She shrugs, but does as I ask. Cade would say it was a risk to give her the keys. Fallon would know it's a test. If Alice is afraid of me, she'll take my truck to get away. And truly, I don't care about that. I don't want her afraid, and I don't want her feeling like she can't trust me.

It's possible she's Sector. I know that. But if she's Sector, she's gotta be deep in because she's not setting off even one red flag for me. Fallon will know, and I'll have to test her, but before I cross any of those burning bridges, I want to see what else I can ferret out about Alice Blythe. But I've got to do my due diligence first.

No getting distracted by a braid and those eyes. I walk to Burt's back door and drop a coin from my pocket into the pay phone, dialing up Wanda. She answers on the third ring, sounding a little out of breath. "Hiya," she says, voice bright. "Was picking pumpkins, what's up?"

Wanda always answers the phone like she knows who it is already, and maybe she does, but I identify myself anyway. "It's Wyatt. Sector's in town. Saw me at the Stardust loading salt, so I dropped it at Burt's."

"Got it," she replies. "I'll activate the phone tree. On about your business, sir."

I chuckle and hang up, waving to Burt, who's come to the back door of the gym. He stares long and hard at my truck, appraising the newcomer inside. In about an hour, the whole town's gonna know about Alice. In under three minutes, Fallon's gonna know.

I have maybe thirty minutes before she intervenes. More if she and Fern are still out. Less if they're having lunch. I raise a hand to Burt and get back in the truck.

Alice stares at my kitchen like it's a three-headed dog. Or maybe it's me, making BLTs, that's got her panties in a twist. A mistake. It was a mistake to think about her panties. Now all I can think about is her panties. Fuck.

Only one way to stop this train of thought. "So, you had questions for me?"

She stays quiet for a second, chewing on what to ask, I assume. "Are there not aliens, then?"

I shrug. "Who knows? There might be. But the prevalent thought that alien life has been causing all the recent troubles? Nah. It's Them. You're right about that."

That seems to stun the curiosity right out of her. In fact, it looks like she might burst into tears. I have the odd urge to hug her. I keep to the stove, flipping the bacon. "Why're you here?"

Her eyes are empty and lost. "The missing hikers... Following a lead."

I already miss the firecracker from the parking lot. That sad look in her eyes is too tempting. Fallon always says I'll bring home any stray that makes eyes at me, and she's not wrong. It's how I got Fern, after all.

I plop a BLT down in front of Alice. "For school? Did you say you're a grad student?"

"Sort of," she says.

My phone rings. Then it stops. Then it rings once more. I get up before it rings again. "Hey," I say as I pick up halfway through the next ring. "I'm handling this."

"Who the fuck is she?" Fallon asks, her voice quiet. "She showed up at the same time as Sector."

I turn away from Alice, who is most definitely listening to every word I say. "Yes, and either that means something or nothing. Let me handle this."

"You have 'til dinner," Fallon agrees. "I expect to see her at my table by sundown. With explanations at the ready."

I am about to hang up when she adds, "Check her, Wyatt. You check her for it or I will."

There's no need to respond; Fallon's already hung up. I try not to slam the phone down. When I turn back to the table, Alice has finished her sandwich.

"Are you going to explain what that was about?" she asks.

I shake my head. Everyone's so direct today, and usually that wouldn't bother me, but right now it feels a little overwhelming. "Let me get straight to the point. Are you Sector?"

Her eyes practically bug out of her head, and then she laughs. "No. Are you?"

"No," I reply, feeling irritated all of a sudden.

"Not as though I'd answer truthfully if I was," she adds.

I pluck my plate off the table, no longer hungry for my BLT. "What do you know about hedgeriders?"

Alice frowns as I put my sandwich in the fridge. "Isn't that an old word for a witch?"

Either she's very good at pretending, or she's not Sector. I'm still gonna have to check, but we can talk first. "Follow me."

Her footsteps are soft behind me as I take her down the back hall to my office. I push the door open and let her through. My hope is that if I tell her something about me that Sector would already know, she might reveal something about herself.

"Hedgeriding is a little like witchery, but has a more defined purpose," I explain.

She's staring at my books, at the knives in the armory, the herbs on the shelves. This isn't anything compared to the stores we have up at the house, but it keeps me from having to go up there if I need to leave on short notice.

I let her look and keep talking. "Hedgeriders are medial. We walk between worlds. Keep the balance. Deal with Them, if They pose a threat. We keep humans out of things as much as possible, but since Reformation, it's been getting harder and harder. They're busier, somehow."

"This is your...job?" she asks. That empty look still haunts her pretty face, and while I long to know what it means, I don't ask.

I laugh. "I guess it is. More like the family business."

Now she laughs, her spark back. It's not a particularly nice laugh. In fact, she looks more guarded than ever as she leans against one of my built-in bookcases. "So, did your daddy teach you the family business?"

Sarcasm. I can't tell if she doesn't quite believe me, or if she's working on some other theory. That was the point of telling her all this. So she'd reveal something of herself to me. Fallon's way of getting things out of people sucks, and something tells me that Alice has been through enough.

If she wants to play the guarded game, we can do it. I snap back, "Hedgeriding is matriarchal."

I pick up the photo on my desk and take three steps across the room to hand it to her. It's a little worse for wear. Fallon carried it, and our small trove of family photos, in her backpack for months getting here. But the photo's still clear. Alice's eyes soften as she looks at it.

I tap the photo. Fallon was a head shorter than me at twelve, but her chin is jutted out, brave and fierce, her braid flipped over her squared-up shoulders. She's got Cade on her hip and her arm slung around my waist.

The little bungalow in New Big Sur is in the background. Mama took this the month before she died, developed the roll in our basement, like she always did when she could find film. Most of the photos wouldn't turn out, but the ones that did, she cherished. It's one of the few nice things I remember about her.

I don't let myself linger on those thoughts. "That's my little brother, Cade, and my sister Fallon. Our Mama taught us everything we needed to know about hedgeriding."

Alice stares at the photo. "Did she take the photo? Your mother, I mean."

I nod slowly. "She did. It was one of the last she ever took. Our parents are dead."

"Oh," Alice says, some flicker of complex emotion crossing her face before she remembers to add, "I'm sorry to hear that."

I take the photo from her. "Thanks. Fallon's in charge now. That was her on the phone. She'd like to meet you this evening, if you're up to it."

Chapter 9
Alice

"Fallon," I echo, still looking at the small girl in the photo. I try to imagine what she might be like all grown up, if that fierceness in her eyes has mellowed with age or been sharpened into a terrifying weapon by the whetstone of this world.

Probably the latter. "Must be nice to have siblings," I offer. I glance up from the photo just as Wyatt shrugs.

"I love them," he says, "but they're a lot of work. You an only child?"

"Yeah," I reply, trying to read the expression on his face. It's encouraging, almost kind, but he's seeking—attempting to understand something about me. Surely a Sector agent this deep would have a fully fleshed-out backstory, so that makes me wonder if he genuinely wants to know about *me*. "I always wanted a big sister."

Wyatt's expression softens, and he lets out a husky laugh. "They're a commitment," he says with a wry smile. "Be careful what you wish for."

I don't answer, turning everything over in my head as I look around the room. Twenty or so knives line the wall with military-like precision. The bone handle of a particularly large one is stained with blood. About a hundred sigils are carved into the fresh paint of the big bay window's casing. An alarming number of them are completely new to me, but I recognize the same one that I spied on the herbal shop and the stairs in the forest. My heart thumps hard against my chest. This all *means* something—these threads tie together into something greater. Bigger.

I finally meet Wyatt's gaze, and to his credit, he's just watching me patiently. Waiting. Probably expecting me to run screaming or something. There's nothing predatory in his gaze, though. I was a teen girl during the worst parts of the Reformation, which means I can usually spot that shit a mile away. But I'm still in a strange man's house in a strange town. I remind myself that I *should* feel unsafe, even if my better judgment is betraying me.

"Do I have a choice?" I finally ask. In the wan, misty light leaking through the window, I watch the skin around his eyes crinkle, his dark brows drawing together. "About dinner, I mean? Like...what happens if I say no?"

Wyatt steps back as if I've startled him, examining me with an expression that almost looks hurt. "Blythe, what do I look like to you?" he demands with an arch laugh.

He spreads his hands away from his hips, holding both palms up like I've just ordered he drop a weapon. The hem of his shirt pulls away from his waistband for a second, and I'm treated to a peek at scarred skin pulled taut over impressive muscles. Heat rises to my face, and I cross my arms.

"You look like a strange man with a bunch of knives in his house," I say, because it's the truth. Even if he does make a pretty mean BLT.

"Fair enough. But absolutely *nothing's* gonna happen to you if you don't come to dinner," Wyatt says, shoving one hand into his pocket, the other rubbing his stubbled jaw. "You just might not get all those questions of yours answered. If anything, not coming to dinner is the safer thing. Fallon is...well, you'll see, maybe."

I uncross my arms and glance down at the photo again, this time looking at little Wyatt. He's got a heaviness to him, a serious slant to the set of his mouth that no kid his age should have. I don't want him to think I'm afraid of him—because I'm not, to be honest, and because something tells me his biggest concern is keeping people safe. It's weird. I'll punch a different man right in the goddamn face with no remorse. But this one? I don't know. I don't wanna hurt him, I guess.

So, with a long exhale, I hand the framed photo back to Wyatt, my arm reaching over the space he created between us. Our fingers brush as he takes the photo, and I fight to shove away the sudden fluttering in my belly.

"I'll come," I say, forcing myself to meet his eyes. "But you were worried I was Sector just a few minutes ago. Now I'm getting invited to Sunday dinner?"

Wyatt's mouth—fuck, I have got to stop looking at this man's mouth—moves into a resigned sort of frown. "Yeah," he says, ducking his chin for a moment before meeting my gaze again. "Pretty sure you're not. But the thing is, I gotta check you for a Sector tracker before the dinner invite's official."

My mouth goes dry as I think about the bug on Mr. Rabbit's button eye. What if I missed something from my apartment? What if there's something sewn into the collar of my coat or tacked to the bottom of my boots, and this man's rough warmth turns into something else entirely when he finds it?

"A tracker?" I ask, feigning ignorance, though the last bit of his phone call with Fallon replays in my mind.

"Sector tags its agents," he says. "Always in the same place, though. Left forearm. It's not particularly comfortable to have someone digging around for it, but I promise it'll be a hell of a lot better for me to do it than Fallon."

I resist the urge to wrap my arms around my torso. Wyatt doesn't think I'm insane. If anything, he's *more* insane than me. Not only does he subscribe to my fringe conspiracy theory, but he's also apparently a hedgerider. I didn't realize that sort of thing existed outside of folklore. In my circles, I've occasionally seen people make this sort of claim, but it's always folks who seem more interested in pretending they're something they're not than exposing government lies with cold, hard science.

I swallow, pulling the collar of my jacket tighter. Wyatt's not pretending. Those sigils on the window are the real deal. The titles on the bookshelves are mostly anthropological and folkloric, plus a few worn medical texts. Those knives are well-used.

And he's...dangerous. Not in the way I'm used to, all cheap suits and tinted sunglasses. Not even dangerous with too much wealth, too much privilege—dangerous like Aston and all the men of his ilk are, because they think the world is theirs to plunder.

Wyatt's dangerous in another way entirely. One I haven't quite figured out. One that excites me for reasons I'm absolutely *not* going to investigate.

"Do you have to, like, slice me open or anything?" I ask with a choked laugh. I try to sound cool, blasé, as if such a thing wouldn't even bother me.

I absolutely don't sound that way.

I half-expect Wyatt to mock me, but instead he gives me this little smile that I don't understand. I like it anyway. "Nah," he says with a shake of his head. "Why don't you sit down, Miss Blythe?" He pulls out an overstuffed chair clad in chestnut-brown leather and gestures toward it. "You just gotta hold out your left arm, palm up. I'm gonna press real hard to feel around for the tag."

This is insane. I'm in a stranger's house. He just made me a BLT. A really fucking good one, to be specific, and now he's talking about Sector and implants and the Fey. Or Them, apparently.

For once, I'm not the craziest person in the room.

"Okay," I say, sliding out of my jacket and tossing it across the back of the chair. Then I settle down onto the worn leather, swallowing hard.

He gets down on one knee in front of me, his muscular thighs straining against his jeans, and I promptly blush so hard that my face feels a thousand degrees hotter than the rest of my body. "You know, if I *were* Sector, it would be really easy to kick you in the face right now."

"Well, Miss Blythe," Wyatt says, looking at me as I roll up my sleeve, "I'm sincerely hoping you make better choices." Something glitters in his eyes. My stupid, traitorous stomach flops.

"Good choices are not really in my repertoire lately," I admit, holding my hand out. I steady my elbow against the arm of the chair.

"That much is obvious," Wyatt says with a gruff laugh. "Sorta like that about you, though."

He wraps one large hand around the top of my forearm before I've prepared myself. His palm is callused, warm, his fingers strong, and I fail to stop myself from thinking about what his hands might feel like on other parts of my body.

Luckily, pain cuts that daydream short. I let out a gasp, going rigid, as Wyatt presses his thumb into the middle of my forearm with what I assume is a good portion of his considerable strength.

"Fuck," I mutter.

"You alright?" he asks, his gaze sliding to mine. It's too much, the way he's taken a knee at my feet, how his head is bowed over my body, how I barely remember the last time I slept with somebody sober and actually had a good time. How I barely remember the last time I felt like I actually had a *body*, not just a vessel for my brain and all its machinations.

"Fine," I say through clenched teeth as he pushes deeper, sliding his thumb up my tendons. I'm caught somewhere between the pleasure of an attractive man's bare skin on mine and the sharp pain digging its teeth into me. It feels like this search for a Sector tag takes forever, but then it's done and Wyatt's no longer touching me.

For a too-long moment I'm not proud of, I wonder if I'd suffer the pain to feel his skin against mine again.

"Well, not Sector," he says, straightening to his full height.

"That's great to hear, because it would've been news to me," I reply, shooting to my feet. "Okay. Your turn."

I smile and point at the chair. Wyatt looks at me, one brow arching. We just met, so I'm probably wrong, but it almost seems like he's trying very hard to avoid showing that he's amused.

"My turn, Miss Blythe?" he asks in a drawl that's thick and sweet, just like molasses. "You're in *my* home. Invited to *my* sister's dinner. In *my* town. On land *my* family protects."

"That's a shame," I say with a fake pout. "Kinda pegged you as a feminist, you know? Thought you'd be about equality. Seems only fair I make sure you're not Sector, either."

Wyatt smiles then, and I like the look of it. It's strange, though—it's almost as though he's unused to smiling, or if it's been a long time since he smiled and actually meant it. I'm probably projecting, looking for further kinship in one of the few people I've ever met who doesn't think I'm absolutely bonkers.

"I suppose fair is fair," he says with a shrug. Then he's sliding out of his jacket, and I realize I've made a grave mistake. Because it's much harder to keep my attention on my actual goals when I'm assailed by the way his flannel clings to his broad shoulders, how his t-shirt—bearing some vintage advertisement so faded I can no longer read it—stretches across his muscular chest.

Wyatt lays his jacket down on the edge of a big vintage desk and then takes up residence in the seat I've just vacated. I chew on my lower lip, tossing my braid over my shoulder.

"Well, don't keep me waiting, Blythe," he murmurs as he rolls up the sleeve of his flannel. I swallow, my mouth gone dry. Christ, I didn't realize how pathetically lonely I was. That's a lie; I knew it, I think, somewhere in the back of my head. I just didn't realize what a *weakness* it is.

"What exactly am I looking for?" I ask, stepping forward. I don't need to kneel; with him seated, I'm only a head or so taller than him. Instead, I lean over the arm of the chair, desperately trying to keep my legs from bumping into his.

"Feels almost like a coin under the skin," he tells me, offering me his forearm. "It's good for you to know this, considering you're going 'round like a dog on a bone."

"I've been called worse things," I tell him, reaching forward to wrap my hand around the top of his forearm, like he did to me. My fingers aren't long enough to meet on either side like his did, though.

"Wasn't an insult," he says. I can feel his eyes on me, but I refuse to meet his gaze, instead keeping mine trained on the expanse of his forearm—a map of thick veins and tendons, tan skin and white scars. "You'll need to press down harder than you think. Try to almost get your thumb between my tendons, if you can."

I do as he instructs, but it feels like trying to dig my fingertips into a rock.

"Harder than that, Miss Blythe," Wyatt says. "You won't hurt me. Promise."

"Not more than you've been hurt before, I'm sure," I reply, eyeing two long scars that bisect his forearm.

Wyatt recoils like I've burned him, yanking his arm out of my grasp.

I stumble back, head snapping up to look at him. "I'm sorry," I stammer, bumping into his desk. "What did I do?"

I'm surprised and slightly terrified by how much I actually care about his answer.

"Nothing," he says, dragging a hand through his hair, leaving it mussed in a way Aston and his friends would've paid an unseemly amount of money to achieve. "Static shock, maybe. Just wasn't expecting it."

I frown. I didn't feel any static. I almost open my mouth to tell him so, but there's something in his eyes—something desperate—and I decide to let it go. All at once, there *is* some kind of a charge, like electricity coursing between us, so strong that my fingers and toes seem to tingle.

"Let's try that again," Wyatt says, business-like now, and the charge disappears in a moment, a storm passing through. "Like I said, good thing for you to know. Unless you're willing to bury that bone and run home."

I smile at him, though I suppose it's more baring my teeth than anything. "Not gonna happen," I reply. "So, tell me exactly how to do this again. Also, how the hell do you get close enough to a possible Sector agent to even look for a tag?"

"Oh," Wyatt says with a mischievous smile. "That's usually

Fallon's territory." He pauses, his mouth parted, his gaze capturing mine.

All of a sudden, I can feel the collar of my sweater brushing the nape of my neck, the stitching on the waistband of my jeans, the weight of my braid down my back. My breath catches.

"I suppose," he continues, "that I got pretty close to *you* real quick, now didn't I?"

Chapter 10
Wyatt

The words are out of my mouth before I can stop them. Alice's cheeks pink up, and something base stirs in me. I draw my arm back. I overcompensated when she commented on the scars. Went too far in one direction, and now we're both backed into corners we'll have to fight our way out of if someone doesn't turn this boat around.

This isn't the kind of thing I'm any good at, but since I'm the one who took things too far, I'll have to shift direction. I clear my throat. "By which I mean, you should be a little more careful. I'm guessing you've had run-ins with Sector before?"

The wheels in her head are turning. That much is clear. She's trying to get her footing back, too. Finally, after a long moment, she nods. "Yeah. I have a baking blog they don't like."

I've heard plenty about this kind of thing, but never had occasion to make use of it myself. That's more Cade's area—computers and codes, people using the internet to bring back old-style blogs that communicate secret messages with out-of-print books as a key. Still, I'm pleased I know *something* about what she's talking about. "*Joy of Cooking* or *The Candy Cookbook*?"

Alice's left eyebrow quirks upward, a glimmer in her eyes. "*Joy of Cooking*. *The Candy Cookbook's* rare."

I feel the smirk crawl over my face as I reach for the bookshelf without looking. I know right where it is and pull a stained copy of the 1924 edition of *The Candy Cookbook* from my shelf.

Alice's eyes light up like a Solstice tree. "Can I see it?"

"Sure." I hand it over to her, not sure what she can do with it. Cade's got the only internet connection around here, except at the Archer Inn's fancy coffee shop. We don't broadcast that type of information, though, and I'm sure not gonna tell her.

But she just flips through it, smiling faintly like she's seen an old friend. When she closes it, she offers it back to me. "Sector confiscated mine a while back."

Not a few years back, or a few months. A while. Purposely vague. She knows what she's doing, but she's missing pieces. Forbidden hope flickers in my chest, but I push it back.

The woman's a conspiracy theorist, a grad student. She could be useful, but that's it. That has to be it. Hardly anybody gets drawn into Blackbird Hollow's web of magic. Expecting Alice Blythe to be one of the few who might stay is foolishness.

With that bit of depressing practicality, I blow out a breath. "Couple of goons in bad suits?"

"Yep." She bites her lower lip, those kaleidoscope eyes of hers glimmering with amusement. "Do they get them at the same place?"

She doesn't laugh at her own joke, but I do. "Fallon's got words about that, too. Something about how they all fit poorly."

Alice goes ahead and laughs. "They do."

It's nice to see her relaxing a little. "Well, that's one version of Sector. They're a bit of misdirection most of the time."

Alice's eyes are avid now, and she hands the book back to me. I shelve it and gesture for her to join me in the kitchen, grabbing a couple of beers from the fridge. She takes them from me, expertly popping the tops off both as we head out to the back porch.

Alice settles into one of my chairs with a contented sigh, looking out toward the river and Big Hill. "What a view." I nod, glad she likes the view—and the chairs I built—for reasons I won't name. "A bit of misdirection?"

I hum in the affirmative. "The ones you've gotta watch out for are nobody. Unnoticeable folk that no one pays attention to. Or sometimes they're annoying. The type that makes mundane trouble wherever they go."

To her credit, Alice stays quiet, absorbing the information I offer her. When she leaves Blackbird Hollow, I want her to take something useful away from all this. Because she *will* leave. They all leave, eventually. But she's worked out this much on her own, and that's a lot. With Caden's current level of unreliability, we could use some help from someone with a formal background in research. It's inconvenient to have to drive out to the university for help.

You keep telling yourself that's why you want her to stay, a voice in my head says in that acerbic tone that sounds like Mama. Best to ignore that shit. "You've been right about a lot, Blythe." And suddenly I'm calling her by her last name, like she's one of us, just to spite the leftovers of Mama in my head. "If you and Fallon get on alright, we could use an extra hand with what's going on here. You up for that?"

Alice Blythe's grin is like the sun coming up on a bright spring morning. "Absolutely," she says, clinking her bottle against mine.

Luckily, Fallon had all the supplies for making chili in her fridge, because she sure as shit wasn't here to make it when we arrived. Alice and I are halfway through a bottle of one of Fallon's best reds when she and Fern blow in. My sister's eyes narrow when she spots the bottle, but she swipes it off the table and heads for the stairs.

"Clean the pupper's paws off," she calls from the top of the stairs. "She's muddy."

I wait for a count of ten and clean off Fern's paws—letting the depths of my frustration with my sister rise and fall. But it's something deeper than irritation building in me as I listen to the sound of Fallon's footsteps moving around upstairs. Most everyone in Blackbird Hollow tolerates her moods because she's the one you call when there's a problem with Them, and there's never been an instance where she hasn't solved said problem. I've failed plenty of times, and so has Cade, but Fallon's a sure thing, and it gets her pretty far around here.

It's been years since I had to introduce her to anyone new, to anyone that mattered, and it feels like this might matter. A glance across the kitchen table reveals that Alice is positively unbothered...by Fallon, at least. She's dealing with the fact that Fern has placed her muddy paws directly into her lap and is currently licking Alice's face. Every muscle in my body freezes.

Fern is not a friendly dog. She's not aggressive by any means, but she takes a while to warm up to new folks. When Alice grabs her by the face to tell her she's the cutest baby puppy in the whole world, my mouth falls open into a gaping void. My sister, of course, reappears in the kitchen at just that moment, dressed in old sweatpants and the Nirvana T-shirt with all the holes.

Fallon lets out a low whistle. "Well, you're right at home here, aren't you, Ms. Blythe?"

I've heard Fallon use nastier tones—this one's just dry—but

inwardly I wince, waiting for Alice to snap back. She's got a tongue like a knife, and if there was ever going to be a clash between women, it would be between these two.

But Alice surprises me. Something in her eyes softens as she watches Fallon cross her arms over her chest. It's a subtle enough change in her demeanor, but Fallon sees it too, and her shoulders hunch up tighter. Alice lets out a slow breath, stares up at the ceiling, and lets out the weirdest non sequitur I've ever heard: "I got kicked out of grad school for punching a rich douche-canoe."

Fallon nods once, her mouth turning down in a stalwart fashion. "Most excellent. Red or white next?"

"Red, I think," Alice replies, draining the rest of her glass.

Fern lies on the floor at Alice's feet, her tail thumping three times as she smiles at me. Damn dog probably thinks she brokered a genuine peace treaty here in the kitchen. And, fuck, what do I know? Maybe she did—whatever happened, Alice is up from her chair, tasting the chili, and the two of them have pushed me aside, moving around one another like they've known each other for years.

Something fragile and warm sinks deep within me. I take down another bottle of red from the rack above the ancient fridge and get to work opening it and pouring everyone another glass. By the time I get that done, the chili's served. The three of us eat in relative quiet, Fern flopping heavily on the floor under the old walnut table.

When our bowls are clean, Fallon pours us each another glass of wine. "So what's your story, Alice?"

Alice takes a long drink, then shrugs. "The usual. Mom's a postal worker, dad's a factory foreman. They went on a retirement trip around the world and I went to grad school—I've got an MA in folklore already, and I was in for a PhD in extraterrestrial biology."

She's playing things close to the vest, which I like. Not too many details, but enough that it's easy to see she's being earnest. I clear my throat. "And you have a theory that They are conspiring to make it look as though Their activities are of extraterrestrial origin, correct?"

Alice swallows a bit hard, the only crack in her armor. "Yeah. I do. That's why I'm here."

Fallon raises an eyebrow, and to my sister's credit, she doesn't so much as smirk. It hits me: she thinks it's a smart theory. And I do too. Alice is so close to the truth, but since she's only ever read about Them, as far as I know, she's got it turned wrong-side-down. Though I've got things to say, I let Fallon handle this. It'll save time in the end to let her lead.

"What made you think that?" Fallon asks, her voice soft and young-sounding. "What about Their biology suggests extraterrestrial life?"

Alice's mouth screws up at one corner. "How much biology have you had?"

Fallon and I both shrug, but I answer, "High school. Neither of us went to college."

"And I don't remember a godsdamn thing," Fallon says before taking a drink of her wine. She pulls her legs up in her chair, and it strikes me how young she looks. There's a vulnerability in my sister's eyes that pulls at my heartstrings. I hadn't realized she felt insecure about the fact that she didn't go to college 'til now. We sent Cade, because the kid was so book-smart from the beginning, but neither of us ever saw it as an option for ourselves.

Alice's eyes do that softening routine again. She likes Fallon, I realize. My heart does a triple flip. Almost nobody likes Fallon the first time they meet her. When Alice continues, her voice is even. "Well, the particulars don't really matter much, but there are plenty. The bottom line is that any organic matter we've found of..." She pauses—rethinking her words, I guess. "Of Theirs isn't consistent with anything we've concretely identified from Earth."

Fallon and I nod at the same time. She gives me a half-grin, then turns a full-watt smile on Alice, her head falling back in laughter. "That's fucking amazing," she says when she's done having a chuckle. "I'd love to hear more about that later."

Slowly, Alice smiles. "You would?"

It occurs to me that she got sort of thrilled when I didn't think she'd emptied out her drawer o' marbles earlier. Has no one ever taken her seriously before? I shift in my seat, suddenly uncomfortable in the old wood chair.

"Yeah," Fallon says. "If you can be patient with me, I'd love to know what some of the particulars are." Alice nods, but there's a question in her wide eyes. She wants to know if she's right. Fallon sighs. "You're almost there. Like ninety-nine percent right."

Alice throws herself back in the chair in mock frustration, but there's a smile on her face, those pretty eyes sparkling with curiosity. "What'd I miss?"

Fallon looks at me and gestures, *go ahead*. I lean back in my chair a little. "I doubt They care much one way or another about what we think of Them—besides, They're not organized enough to coordinate any kind of conspiracy."

Alice leans forward now, shaking her head. "Of course. Sector?"

Fallon does finger guns at Alice. "You got it."

Alice bites her bottom lip, then stares at the ceiling for a moment. "Not organized enough... What level of intelligence are we talking about?"

My mouth just about gapes. She's not missing a beat. It's as though she's been waiting to have this conversation for years.

And then it hits me: she has. She's been looking for the answers we can give her for a long time.

"A lot of Them are about as smart as a mundane dog or cat," Fallon answers. "But others—"

"Are They as smart as humans?" Alice asks, her entire posture alight with interest now.

"Lots are probably smarter," I offer. "But none of Them think the same as us." Alice frowns, clearly confused. If she stays, she'll see soon enough. "It's like they have the most intense case of ADHD you've ever seen."

Fallon nods. "That's a good way to explain it. It's like they can't remember where they put their favorite unicorn mug for the life of 'em. Or they're so hyper-focused they haven't peed in eight hours."

"Not that she has personal experience or anything," I say.

"Fuckable or not?" Alice shoots.

Fallon points at her with one spindly finger. "Mostly not, but if you could, you shouldn't."

Alice blows out a breath. "All those romantasy books I read were wrong then."

The kitchen goes dead silent for a second, and then Fallon and Alice laugh the exact same laugh. Which makes them both laugh harder. For fuck's sake, it's like a pair of soulmates.

For a moment, I'm filled with envy—but I can't tell if I'm jealous that Alice isn't on *my* exact wavelength or if it suddenly feels like I'm not my sister's best friend anymore. Maybe it's both, but I don't have time to tell. The feeling dissolves as quickly as it came, replaced by the odd sensation that we're all exactly where we're supposed to be.

So I laugh with them. And it feels so good, I don't want it to stop. I wish Cade were here, but maybe we'll do this again on Sunday. An ache in my chest peeks out from the shadows. I didn't even know I wanted this, for our little trio to grow.

For there to be more family—more love. I'm getting ahead of myself again. Alice has been here three seconds, and I've turned her into family. *What in the world is wrong with me?*

Fallon goes suddenly serious as our laughter dies down. "We've got a big problem." The smile falls off Alice's face. "The Wild Hunt is almost certainly headed our way."

"How do you know?" Alice breathes.

Fallon's eyes slide to mine. "Hellhounds in the woods today."

I push a hand through my hair, closing my eyes. "Well, fuck. That's gonna ruin trick-or-treating."

Chapter 11
Alice

I don't need my master's in folklore to see that the Wild Hunt is dangerous—that They're *real*, They're here, and They're just as deadly as I always suspected.

I should probably be scared as I sit at the table, listening to Fallon and Wyatt trade information back and forth that I only partly understand. But it's like there's this big ball of warmth inside of me, tingling across my skin, and it won't let me be properly afraid. Like maybe I'm finally where I belong, finally with the people I belong to—have always belonged to and just never realized it.

Or maybe it's just the four—five?—glasses of wine I've had.

"Hellhounds," Wyatt echoes again, his voice dropping down into something serious and a little unsettling. His gaze goes far away for a second, and it makes my heart pang.

"What does this mean, exactly?" I ask, folding my hands on the table so I don't reach out for Wyatt, which would be absurd. "I mean, I have a folkloric understanding of the Wild Hunt. But what's it actually like?"

Fallon and Wyatt exchange a long look. Fallon mutters

something under her breath and twists in her chair, popping open the enormous, battered hutch hulking against the kitchen's shadowy wall. When she retrieves a bottle of something molasses-dark and definitely stronger than wine, my heart climbs into my throat.

"Well," Wyatt offers, folding his hands in a mirror of my movement. He looks like he's carefully considering his words, picking the ones that'll help me understand best. I appreciate that. I appreciate it so much, apparently, that my face decides to blush. "It's nothing pretty."

"They don't usually come through these parts," Fallon adds, pouring a concerning amount of whisky—I think—into her empty tumbler. I don't know her very well, but she seems completely sober, her big, dark eyes still clear, no flush creeping across her tanned skin.

Fallon's the kind of pretty that normally intimidates me. The kind that just doesn't even have to try, putting the rest of us to shame in worn jeans and an oversized sweater. But we just...clicked. Easy. I don't know the last time I felt anything like that.

My eyes slide to Wyatt, who's watching his sister, the crow's feet around his eyes crinkling. I guess I felt something like that with him, too. But...different. I want to drink wine and talk shit with Fallon for the rest of my life. There's this instant sweep of comfort with her, cozy as a worn blanket—because I'm pretty sure she's just as insane as me. Actually, crazier. Feral, even. And there's something so soothing about that when everyone you've ever loved thinks you've completely lost your marbles.

Wyatt, though? I force myself to look away from him, back to Fallon as she chugs whisky, apparently some kind of preparation for telling the uninitiated about the Wild Hunt. With Wyatt, it's...I want a lot more than wine and shit-talk.

I stop myself from considering that train of thought further. Fallon speaks up just in time. "The Wild Hunt is kind of fucked," she says with a shrug. "They'll come straight through the town, taking anyone They can get a hold of. And Main Street's right on the ley line..." She pauses, her mouth screwing into a frown. "Alice, if you stay..."

"You're gonna see some unholy shit," Wyatt finishes for his sister, leaning back in his chair to consider me with those nebula-brown eyes.

"Alright," I say with a shrug. "I mean, if you think I'm a liability—"

"Definitely not," Wyatt says with unusual fervor, leaning toward me, his forearms coming to rest on the table. In my peripheral vision, I see Fallon smile into her glass. As if he knows what his older sister is going to say before she even opens her mouth, he whirls toward her. "I just mean, it sure would be nice to cut out those drives up to the university, yeah? And with Cade...going through it, it'd be good to have someone around with his kind of knowledge."

"Sure thing," Fallon agrees, grinning wildly, though there's nothing malicious in her expression—not as far as I can tell. She downs the rest of her whisky and pushes up to her feet, not even swaying a little bit. "You're down at the Stardust, I imagine?"

"Yep," I say, reaching to gather up my dirty dishes, but Wyatt tucks my empty bowl into his before I can do so.

"You can stay here," Fallon says, letting her brother pick up her dishes, too. He looks at her pointedly as he does it, and I have the strong sense the bowl and spoon might sit there for a day or two if he weren't cleaning up after her. "In Wyatt's old room."

Wyatt freezes and turns a color I didn't even think him capable of: a deep, dark red, his entire face overtaken by the hue. Fallon takes one look at him and lets out a cackle, sashaying toward the fridge, her stockinged feet gliding across the antique wood floors.

"Why're you so godsdamn red?" she demands, digging her arm into the freezer, her expression obscured by the fridge door. "You think she's gonna find your dirty magazines stuffed underneath the mattress? Worried she's gonna think you're a little perv?"

Even though I'm sure my face has flushed to a shade that rivals Wyatt's, I can't help but laugh at the sibling ribbing—the kind I never had and always sort of wanted. Someone to call my own, someone who had to put up with my rants and theories. Somebody who couldn't leave, I guess.

"You two can't be here *alone*," Wyatt sputters as though there's absolutely nothing more insane in the entire world. He's frozen to the spot, the cool, calm, and self-assured man I met this morning reduced to pure panic.

Over *me*. Over me sleeping in his old bed, poking around in his childhood room. My heart does a somersault in my chest, and an absurd number of butterflies takes flight in my belly.

"Why not?" Fallon demands, a shit-eating grin spread wide across her face. She closes the freezer, one arm curled around a giant tub of ice cream. "We'll have a girls' night! You're always telling me to make more friends."

Wyatt lets out a long huff, rubbing the back of his neck. "Yeah, but not—"

"Oh," Fallon near-shouts, pouncing on her little brother with more glee than I've ever felt in my entire life, "but not *her*? Not with the pretty girl you've got a crush on?"

"Okay, maybe my estimation of having an older sister was off," I say to save poor Wyatt, turning toward him—even though, in truth, I'm eating this up with a spoon. It's sweeter and richer than the ice cream Fallon's got tucked under her arm, I have no doubt. "They *are* kinda rough."

"Yeah," Wyatt says, meeting my gaze, one eyebrow arched, the blush across his cheeks making my own face heat again. "And they apparently can't make their own damn friends, either."

"The Hayes are an acquired taste," Fallon announces, slamming the giant tub of ice cream down onto the table. She's got a fistful of spoons in her other hand, the metal gleaming in the low light as she pries off the lid. "And also a package deal."

"Think you're up for that, Blythe?" Wyatt asks, leaning his hip onto the side of the old farmhouse table. He says my last name like it's more than that—like it's a nickname, some sign of intimacy between us. His mouth moves into a smile that makes me want to slam my lips into his. Okay, that's probably the wine.

At least, I'm definitely going to *blame* it on the wine.

"I like you guys," I say with a shrug, reaching for a spoon even though I'm not sure if my stomach can handle chili, four glasses of red, and dairy. "And you don't think I'm insane."

"Your standards," Fallon announces, leveling her spoon at me like it's an arrow, "are entirely too low."

"I mean, clearly," I reply, gesturing at the two of them. The Hayes siblings break into laughter, exchanging glances. The glance isn't meant for me, but I still catch it, and for a moment, I think I see something there that makes my entire body feel like the first warm day after a long winter.

Acceptance.

"What flavor is this?" I ask instead of saying something stupid, leaning over the table.

"Pumpkin," Wyatt says, opening the hutch and retrieving adorable sherbert glasses that make me think of an idyllic childhood I never had, all frosted glass and old-fashioned scalloped edges. "Sally only makes one batch every year. I'm not one for the pumpkin everything, 'least not the way some of the tourists are, but this shit is *unbelievable*." He pauses, looking at his sister. "Why don't you have an ice cream scoop?"

Fallon scoffs. "Do I look like Martha fuckin' Stewart to you?"

Wyatt, clearly used to his sister's antics, just shrugs and digs into the ice cream, nearly bending the spoon as he doles out the frozen treat into one of the sherbert glasses. I try to stop myself from watching his hands as he does it, the way his fingers curl around the spoon, the flex of his tendons.

You'd think I've never seen a fucking man before today.

"For you," Wyatt says, startling me. I manage to tear my brain away from his hands to notice that he's offering me a sherbert glass filled with ice cream—before he even scooped some for himself.

"Oh, ar—are you sure?" I ask, stumbling over my words like I'm in the sixth grade with my first crush. I reach for the glass, and our fingers brush. My entire body goes tingly, my heart lighter than it's felt in years.

Wyatt doffs an imaginary hat. "Quite sure, Blythe."

Across the kitchen, Fallon pulls a giant quilt from an ancient-looking trunk and settles back into her chair at the head of the table, wrapping herself up in the patterned cloth. "Wyatt," she says, more serious now, her gaze sharpening. "Grab Alice's stuff from the Stardust. I want her with us if the Hunt's coming through."

Out of nowhere, tears prick at the backs of my eyes. It's the wine, it's the wine, *it's the wine*. It's certainly not the way that these people I just blundered into—following a six-month-old lead that should've been long stale—are taking better care of me than the people I've known all my life ever have. More than the university administration that called me "brilliant" when it suited them and "disruptive" when it didn't.

I stare down into the sherbert glass, toying with my spoon. Have I ever *let* people care for me? Have I always been too afraid? Because, god forbid, what happens if I let someone care for me, and then I *need* them?

What if I let Wyatt Hayes get my things from the Stardust and tuck me into his old bed and keep me safe from the Wild Hunt, and then I can't imagine living without his care? What then?

I let out a long breath. "Will Marion be alright with that?" I ask. "I can come with you if it's easier."

"Marion would probably let Wyatt burglarize half the rooms if the people renting them annoyed her enough," Fallon says with a fond laugh. Her gaze slides to Wyatt, who's still standing, not doling out any pumpkin ice cream for himself.

"Well," he begins, his eyebrows lifted, "I'd be much more likely to nick a thing or two from the folks staying at the Archer Inn, truth be told. But nah. As long as everything's still more or less packed up, I'll just go. It's better that way—just in case I run into trouble."

"Okay," I say, pulling the sleeves of my sweater over my hands. It's too cold for ice cream, but, like Fallon, I'm willing to bundle up for the sake of a delicious treat. "I pretty much threw everything down and left."

"You mean, 'came barreling out into the parking lot to accost a local with ten thousand rapid-fire questions,'" he corrects in such a playful tone that I turn bright red again.

"Something like that," I agree. "I got lucky that the local wasn't Sector. Or one of Them. And that he makes a damn good BLT."

"Stop flirting," Fallon says, digging in for another big spoonful of ice cream. "*Hellhounds*, kiddos. The Wild Hunt's on the prowl. Shit's gonna get real and it's gonna happen fast." She pauses, checking under the table, where Fern is sprawled out on the old, faded rug, half asleep. "Fern can stay here while you run to the Stardust."

Wyatt acquiesces almost immediately, and it makes me remember he said hedgerider tradition is matrilineal. With his mom gone, does that make Fallon his sister *and* his boss, sort of?

"It's been a long time since I hung out with anybody other than my shithead brothers," Fallon says, leaning forward on the table. I barely manage to tear my eyes from Wyatt as he slides into his jacket. "What do you think about drinking more, telling each other secrets, and seeing if any of the old goddesses will answer our violent pleas?"

"You make a compelling argument," I admit, not wanting to be too eager, not wanting to give in to this warm, wonderful fuzziness that's enveloping me. I bring a spoonful of ice cream to my mouth, and shit, Wyatt's right—this stuff is incredible.

"Say a prayer for me, Fern," Wyatt calls from where he's standing near the door. "Because these two are gonna make each other so much *worse*."

Fallon and I burst into laughter, the sound of it so loud and rich and perfect that I barely hear the door close behind him. But even sitting here with someone who could become the only close friend I've ever had, there's still a part of me that goes a little cool in his absence.

As if I've already decided to let Wyatt Hayes help keep me warm.

Chapter 12
Wyatt

As I walk through the kitchen, the two of them stay at the table, cackling like old biddies. Honestly don't think either one noticed or cared that I'm headed out. I pull the phone tree off its designated corner of the pinboard by the phone, moving it to front and center. Fallon has some calls to make later. Or, from the sounds of things, tomorrow morning.

Fern lifts her head to give me a long, steady look that tells me she's got my girls under her watchful eye before tucking herself back in under my sister's chair.

My girls.

I've got to get the hell out of here.

Now.

When I've got my feet solid on the front porch, I take a couple of shallow breaths, then one deep one. My mind's gone topsy-turvy, and I need to get it right before I head out. When I don't feel like I'm about to do something rash—like ask Alice Blythe to go steady with me after fifth period—I reach underneath the big bent-willow couch. There's three Winchester rifles strapped underneath, just in case. I take one.

I flip the radio on as soon as I get back in the truck and switch over to the college station. It's just about Johnny Cash hour over there, and I could use a little of the Man in Black. When the first few notes of "Ghost Riders in the Sky" play, I shut the radio off. I don't need even a vague reference to the Hunt right now. It's a long ride to the Stardust in silence, but I should keep my eyes on the road anyway.

The front office is dark when I pull up, and I'm glad to see Marion's gone home. I pull a key from the butthole of one of Marion's plastic flamingos and step inside. Before I touch a thing, I dial the proprietress herself at home.

She answers on the first ring. "Wyatt Hayes, what are you up to?"

It takes me a split second to remember that all members of the tribe have more advanced security than the rest of us before I turn and wave at the camera in the far corner. "Hey, wanted to tell you what Fallon spotted out in the woods."

"Wanda just called," she interjects.

"Fallon's on the horn, then," I reply.

"On the horn?" Marion sighs. "Criminy, Wyatt. Are you a ninety-year-old man, or what?"

I chuckle. "At least I'm not throwing 'criminy' around."

"Touché, big dog," she replies. We could go on all night, but Marion adds, "Don't worry about us—we're already on it."

Relief floods me. Not that I expected anything different, but I always worry 'til we have our bases covered. "Glad to hear it. I'm here to pick up Alice Blythe's things."

"That's what Wanda told me." Sometimes that damn phone tree is a curse, not a blessing. "You can grab the keys. Thanks for not jimmying the lock."

"No problem." I laugh, but there's not much joy in the sound. My feelings are all twisted up at the moment.

Marion hangs up without saying goodbye, which she's done

since we were in seventh grade. She saw it in an old movie or something and has done it ever since. Sometimes it's a kindness. I grab the master key from behind Marion's desk and lock the office up on my way out.

The air in the parking lot has the kind of deep, damp cold to it that seeps straight into your bones. A thick mist crawls out of the forest, which isn't unusual this time of year, but neither is it welcome. I move slowly, scanning the woods for anything out of place. The neon sign in the parking lot pulses erratically, and I take a sidestep toward my truck.

When the High Courts walk, They disturb electricity—it's one of the things that modern folk attribute to the dead that actually has a far more sinister origin. I grab the rifle from under my front seat and slide the old leather strap over my chest. Silver bullets won't kill one of the High, but they'll sting enough to let me escape.

I soften my footfalls as I approach Alice's hotel room. The air is far too quiet. The night's usual symphony has gone silent since I stepped into the office. Yet another bad sign. It isn't that I don't trust Fallon's perception of the evidence, but my training kicking in. The hedgerider way is to double—if not triple—confirm all signs of Them before acting. Fallon made the sighting, but Cade or I will confirm.

When I'm across the parking lot, the sound of a car coming toward me from up the highway has me hustling into Alice's room. When I've got the door locked, I don't turn the lights on, but watch and wait. Sure enough, headlights from the black sedan swing into the parking lot. I sit down on the bed, next to Alice's bags, which are right where she said they'd be. Might as well see what can be seen of the Sector goons.

The sedan's headlights shut off, and the agents get out of the car. One is chattering on about the spaghetti at the diner being the best he's ever had, while the other nods. Neither spares a glance for the sign, nor the mist. These two have the observational skills of a pair of bowling balls.

Fucking Sector. Half of their so-called agents couldn't fight their way out of a soaking wet cardboard box. Anything comes out of the woods to snatch them, and I swear I'm gonna let them get gobbled up. But nothing jumps out as they make it safely to their pair of rooms and exchange a brisk good-night. The lights on the front of the building flicker, going a pale green.

That's not great, but we're in the thick of it now and I can't afford to slow down. The tension leaves my shoulders—somehow, I'm always calmest in what Wanda calls "one of our *situations*." I get to checking the drawers and under the bed. Alice said she didn't do any unpacking, but I like to be sure.

I also want to be sure that Sector didn't stick their fingers into her business while she was out. I know how they like to drop little devices here and there. As I pass the desk, the phone catches my eye. I pick it up and call Cade. He answers after a few rings, and I'm happy to hear him sounding sober and alone. "Did Fallon call?"

"Hello, Caden—how ya doin', kid? Well, good evening, Wyatt, I'm rather disturbed by the news of hellhounds in the forest. How about you?"

My brother, the smartass. "Glad you've been informed of our situation. See you Sunday."

"Wyatt, hang on..." Cade pauses.

"What?" I ask, impatient to be gone. I stretch the long cord into the bathroom, where I check the sink and the medicine cabinet.

"Oh, nothing." My little brother laughs. "I just didn't want you to hang up on me."

I laugh along with him, not because it's particularly funny, but because it's good to hear him sound so normal. I shut the medicine cabinet, catching three pairs of glowing red eyes in the reflection.

"Fuck," I swear under my breath. "*Fuck.*"

Cade sucks in a breath on the other end of the phone. We've worked together our whole lives. I trained him. He doesn't need specifics to know when shit's gone bad. "You got silver on you?"

"Yeah," I growl, cradling the receiver between my ear and shoulder to pull my rifle into position, aiming through the thin glass of the bathroom window.

I get a good look at the thing now. Hellhounds are rangy, sleek things, with six fiery eyes and a mouthful of razor-sharp teeth. Bit like a wolf, a lot like something else nobody's ever seen walk this Earth. I stare back at the otherworldly being that has its sights set on me, but then it turns and lopes off into the trees, a white scar flashing on its shoulder.

"It saw me," I breathe, "and then just...left."

Caden hums a little, and there's the sound of ruffling paper that's likely his notebook. "Yeah, I've been picking up some chatter about that on the darknet. Hedgeriders all over have reported that when they've encountered the Hunt lately, it seems like They almost purposely avoid them. Like They're hiding something."

I let out a dismissive hiss. "That's attributing too much to Them, don't you think?"

Caden grumbles a little before reasoning, "The Hunt is an instrument of the High Courts, Wyatt. We don't have any clue what They're up to."

They're up to nothing more than planning macabre parties and fucking each other's brains out, but I'm not gonna dissuade Caden from this particular notion. Some scholar amongst the hedgeriders always has a thesis going about the High Courts and Their shenanigans, but it pans out the same each time.

"The High are planning a fête and need human eyeballs to freeze for ice cubes"—or some other gruesome thing.

Undoubtedly, there's something deeper brewing somewhere under the hill, but I doubt very much that the Courts care one way or another about it past Their endless, spiteful politicking. Caden and I stand on opposite sides of this debate, and that is as it should be. Disagreeing helps us see the full potential in any situation we get into with Them.

It's kept us alive all these years, and we're a pretty good team. In my mind, Alice slips neatly into things, somewhere between Fallon's ability with strategy and Cade's with research, and I can see how she just might fill in all the cracks that the three of us can't quite manage on our own.

"Earth to Wyatt," my brother practically shouts. "I asked if you were okay."

"Yeah," I answer. "Just fine. Headed out now. Stay in tonight, alright?"

"I'm not so foolish as to think I can take a hellhound on my own, big brother," Cade replies, before adding, "Careful on your way home."

"Yep," I agree and hang up.

When I pull up to the house, Fern's lying on the couch in the front room, her chin perched on the back so she can see outside. She woofs softly a couple of times as I get out. A greeting, not a warning, thankfully.

When I push open the front door, Fallon waves at me from the kitchen, where she's got her old wooden stool pulled up under the phone. She's yapping away to Widow Harkness about some town gossip, which I can only take to mean she's done with her phone tree chores.

Before I can wonder where Alice got off to, she's half tumbling down the front stairs. I drop her bags and catch her in my arms, just in time to see that she's wearing a pair of my sweatpants and one of my old faded blue football jerseys. It has the words "Blackbird Hollow Football" printed across the chest in collegiate letters, with a giant raven on it, and a couple of white stripes on the sleeves.

I swallow hard, knowing that the back says "Hayes" on it. Alice Blythe is wearing my jersey—and it just about sends me over an edge I didn't know I had.

"Sorry, I took your clothes. I spilled wine on myself," she mutters into my shirt. Her hair is damp and curling at her temples. She laughs into my chest. Fallon got her shitfaced while I was gone.

"Careful there," I murmur. "There's a trick step—third one from the bottom."

She smiles up at me, so unguarded that I know I've got to go. I've only known Alice for a few hours, but I am certain she'll hate herself tomorrow if she reveals something too personal to me tonight. She can say whatever she likes to Fallon. My sister is a vault. It's one of her best qualities.

"You smell good," Alice says.

"So do you," I reply with a smile, setting her steady back on her feet.

"I had a shower," she informs me.

I'm not touching that one with a ten-foot pole. "You need a snack?"

Alice shakes her head. "I'm stuffed."

"Wanna watch a movie?" I ask, feeling like I'm interviewing her with all these questions. "I think Fallon got *The Goonies* this week."

"With you?" Alice asks, a little too brightly.

My heart thumps, slow and heavy and far too hard. But a

vision imposes itself on me: her snuggled up next to me on the couch, wearing my clothes...and I shake my head, firm in my resolve. "No, I've gotta keep watch tonight. But I could put it on for you."

Alice looks like she might pout for a second, and if she does, I'm a goner. But then she blinks, and it's like a sober light flicks on in her head. She blinks a couple more times, then yawns. "I think I'm going to get a big glass of water and go to bed."

I sigh with relief, watching her bare feet pad into the kitchen of the house I grew up in, open the correct cabinet for cups, and run water into one with a cartoon bear on it, like she's always been here. Fallon raises an eyebrow at me from her stool, twisting the phone cord around her index finger with a mischievous glint in her eye. The two of them are having a wretched effect on one another already.

Fern bumps my hip with her big head, and I scratch behind her ears, a bittersweet ache forming in my chest. My dog watches Alice carefully as she walks back toward us. "Go on with her," I urge Fern, stepping back from the foot of the staircase.

"Really?" Alice asks, picking up her backpack. "Can she sleep in the bed with me?"

There's hesitation in her voice that cracks me in two. Like she's never had a pet to cuddle with in her life. "Just try and stop her," I reply with a grin. "I'll bring your duffel up in a bit."

Gonna wait 'til I'm good and sure she's asleep for that. Alice doesn't say another word—she just takes each step on the grand old staircase extra slow. She's obviously tired. It's hard to believe we've only known her for a few hours. It feels like we grew up together.

Fallon hangs up the phone as Fern and Alice make it to the top step and disappear into my room. I cannot possibly think about her climbing into bed, wearing my jersey, while she and

Fern snuggle up. That's one stop too far down the optimist track for me.

To nip this train of thought in the bud, I walk into the kitchen and lean against the sink. Nothing kills a buzz like Fallon on a mission. "Well?"

"All done," Fallon says. "Word's out."

"That's good," I say, dread curling up in my gut like it's there to stay. "I saw one of the hellhounds lurking outside the Stardust—stared right at me. Ran off when it spotted the Winchester."

Fallon's eyes narrow. She's always taken an agnostic view on the Courts, the Hunt, and all Their antics. I'm sure Caden's run his theories by her dozens of times. She has more patience for that kind of talk than I do.

"You gonna take first watch?" she asks, not addressing any aspect of that. "Fern'll keep an eye on Alice."

I nod, grateful for the fact that with all her teasing, my sister knows when to be serious. "Get some sleep."

Fallon yawns, slipping off her stool. "Wake me at three, 'kay?"

"Sure," I agree. "I'm gonna go salt."

Fallon pauses on the stairs. We don't usually go so far. They don't usually come so close to the house. There's too much iron buried in the yard. When she nods, I know she's wondering the same thing I am—if there was a reason the hellhound was hanging around near the Stardust.

If Alice is one of the Hunt's Chosen, They will have a fight on Their hands. They're not leaving with her. If I have to shove every leafer in three counties in Their path to take her place, I will.

Chapter 13
Alice

Sometime the next morning, I awake in an unfamiliar bed. I'm curled up on my side, hair loose and tangled, and there's a pleasant warmth pressed against my back. I blink slowly into the misty sunlight leaking through the two tall windows, trying to get my thoughts together. My head throbs painfully, a punishment for too much wine.

Movement stirs in the bed next to me, and my heart races into my throat. Beneath the old, handmade quilt, I'm fully dressed, but in someone else's clothes: a football jersey with an unfamiliar mascot and soft, wash-worn sweatpants. A faint memory trickles into my mind, something about stairs and *The Goonies*, my face pressed into Wyatt Hayes's chest, the smell of him indescribably wonderful.

I don't think a man with a jawline like *that* and such easy, worn-in confidence has much interest in the strange drunk girl at his sister's kitchen table, but I admit that hope still pounds in the hollow of my throat as I gather myself and roll over slowly.

A long tail thumps happily on the top of the quilt as Fern

greets me with an excited yip. "Hey, girl," I murmur, stroking the top of her head as she gives me several kisses. "You know, you're so big, I almost thought you were your dad for a second."

I regret the words the second they leave my mouth. My face reddens as I consider what Wyatt's long, lean body might feel like tucked into bed next to mine. What kind of weird, old-timey greeting he'd offer in the morning. What his brown eyes would look like in the misty light.

As if she can read my thoughts, Fern pulls away and cants her head to one side, looking at me with what I can only describe as canine judgment.

"Sorry," I tell her, reaching out and giving the huge, wolfish dog a hug before I think better of it. I'm lucky she's decided I'm alright, because I feel her relax into me, placing her chin on my shoulder. "Thanks for cuddling with me. I always wanted a dog."

Fern decides that the best course of action in this tender moment is to turn her head and shove her damp nose into my ear. I cry out her name with a laugh and push her away. With a low, playful bark, she leaps off the bed and trots toward the door, turning to look at me expectantly.

"Alright, alright," I murmur, pushing my hair out of my eyes. My head is gonna hurt so much worse when I stand. Slowly, I swing my legs over the side of the bed and pull myself up, hoping all the while that my hangover is a mild one.

Because the Wild Hunt is coming *here*. Hikers are missing. Hellhounds stalk the woods. And I'm in the thick of it, hiding from Sector and running toward the truth. I have shit to do. I cannot be stopped by a blistering hangover, nor a raging crush.

I shuffle across the creaking hardwoods and pull the bedroom door open all the way, discovering two things in quick succession: the full force of daylight sending my headache into a screeching crescendo, and Wyatt Hayes standing at the top of the stairs, wearing jeans and a fitted white t-shirt.

Perhaps I *will* be stopped by the hangover and the crush if they gang up on me like this.

"Sorry," he murmurs, as if *he*'s the random outsider who showed up yesterday. "Fallon forgot to wipe Fern's paws when she came in. Got mud all over my shirt. Wanted to see if I had anything in my old dresser."

My mouth goes dry. The hangover drives nails into my eyeballs. "But her feet are clean," is all I can say, my words coming out stilted and uneven.

"Sure are." He smiles at me, one of those damn eyebrows lifting. "Wouldn't let her get in bed with you all muddy. My shirt was a necessary sacrifice."

I shove Wyatt Hayes saying the words "in bed with you" out of my mind before they can sink into memory and come barreling into my thoughts at the worst time possible. "Well, then the least I can do is permit you into your own room for a spare shirt, sir," I reply, doing a weird bow and scuttling away from his door.

I want to die. But he just laughs, all autumn sunshine and crystal-clear creek water. "You have my thanks, milady," he replies in a funny accent, striding past me.

I hold my breath, waiting for him to cross the threshold.

"Oh," he says, turning toward me, his muscular shoulder resting on the doorjamb. "Not sure if you saw, but your bags are at the foot of the bed. In case you want to get changed."

I blink, struggling to keep up. Hangovers at twenty-nine are a whole different beast than at twenty-one. "Sorry," I manage, realizing distantly that I'm turning red. I gesture to his borrowed clothes on my frame. "Your sister said it was fine—"

"'Course it's fine," he replies with something that seems like panic, of all things—though I must be wrong. Just because it *feels* like I've known him for years doesn't mean I can read him like a book. "Just thought you'd be wanting your own clothes."

And then he slips into the room I slept in, leaving the door cracked only a few inches. I hear a drawer pull out, antique wood scraping, before I realize I'm standing there like an absolute weirdo.

"Fern," I say to the wolfdog, who's sitting at the top of the stairs, almost like she's waiting for me. "Could you please take me to the coffee?"

With the help of ibuprofen, sunglasses borrowed from Fallon, and a giant mug of coffee, I'm dressed and pulling myself into the passenger seat of Wyatt's pickup truck at a respectable hour.

"Not quite there yet, huh?" he asks as he slides into the driver's seat, gesturing toward the still-wrapped burrito sitting in my lap. He'd swung by the diner instead of "subjecting anyone to Fallon's piss-poor breakfast fare."

"Nope," I reply in a croak, remembering what the smell of scrambled egg, peppers, and cheese did to me just a few minutes ago when Wyatt unwrapped his own breakfast. "Not yet."

"Want me to put it in the back? I have a cooler," he offers, turning the key in the ignition.

"No," I say, curling over the burrito. "It's mine. My *precious*."

He laughs, putting his arm on the back of my seat as he reverses out of the driveway. "Easy there, Gollum," he replies, shifting into drive.

Fern settles into the space between us, which is admittedly not large enough for what is essentially a wolf. But she's very polite about not nosing into my burrito or begging. Granted, Wyatt already told me she couldn't have any more "people food"—apparently, in my drunken stupor, I'd given her some ice cream the night before. In my defense, she is very cute, which weakens my ability to say no.

I swallow, glancing over at Wyatt. I could've stayed at Fallon's, slept off more of the hangover. But he asked me to come with him to the town hall, where the local coven of witches is preparing for the arrival of the Wild Hunt. I mean, how the fuck does anyone say no to an invitation like that? As an academic, these kinds of primary sources are positively irresistible.

And then, of course, there's Wyatt Hayes himself. He's got one hand on the wheel and the other scratching Fern's head, dressed in what I suspect is his typical attire: charcoal flannel button-down over his t-shirt, worn jeans, and a dark plaid wool coat with some kind of thick, fleecy lining. His stubble's grown a little longer, like he hasn't had the chance to shave, and there's more tension in his brow than yesterday. Or maybe I'm just noticing it now.

I look out the window as we wind down the hill, admiring the pretty houses still shrouded in morning mist. All the vegetation is damp with rain and dew, turning ordinary autumn leaves into glistening garnet and shimmering topaz gems. A comfortable silence stretches between us, the kind I don't even have with people I've known for much, much longer.

At some point, Fern's resolve breaks, and I feel her wet nose brush my wrist as she investigates my still-wrapped burrito.

"Ah-ah," Wyatt chides.

Fern pulls away from me and turns to stare at him, looking absolutely miserable, her eyes full of accusation. I find myself laughing at her expression.

"What's so funny?" he asks, taking a hard turn onto what seems like a main road that heads straight down the hill.

"The way she just looked at you," I explain, gesturing to Fern. "Like you're starving her to death." He isn't. I saw the hearty breakfast Fern got this morning.

A soft smile takes over Wyatt's features, illuminated by the yellow glow of the streetlamps that line the road. "Did you have a dog growing up?" he asks. I shake my head no. "I'm surprised you can read her that well, then."

Contentment warms in my chest like a good cup of coffee on a rainy day, and I smile, looking down at my hands. "She's an expressive lady," I say instead of something more complicated and raw. I reach over and scratch Fern between her shoulders.

"Got a lot of those around here," Wyatt returns dryly. He looks like he wants to say something else, but then his expression shifts—more stoic, removed. Flipping on the windshield wipers, he clears his throat. "I figure I can introduce you to some folks and we can see what we might be able to dig up about the missing hikers."

A thrill races through me. "So am I an official consultant for the investigation?" I ask, turning in my seat to look at him.

He glances toward me and smiles. My heart flutters in my throat. "Something like that," he replies as we pull onto the town's main drag. Off in the distance, I can see the diner's neon sign flickering like an omen. The mist isn't as thick here, but the wind picks up, sweeping leaves back and forth across the streets like a brightly colored tide. "As long as that's what you want, Blythe."

I startle at that, pulling my attention away from Blackbird Hollow's undeniable charm to turn back toward him. "I thought my annoying enthusiasm made it obvious," I tell him, thankful he's driving so I don't have to look into his eyes as I say it. "I'm so in."

"Who made you think your enthusiasm was annoying?" Wyatt asks me abruptly, his gaze abandoning the road. His eyes are intense, his jaw tight, almost like his hackles have gone up. Like he's *mad* at some nameless, faceless person from my past. My stomach flips, and I feel my face redden.

He turns back toward the road, his shoulders rounding, something sheepish about his posture. "Sorry," he says with a wave of his hand. "You were probably just joking."

"I'm not that funny," I admit, pulling my canvas coat closer. "Usually I just try to make fun of myself before someone else gets the chance. Then the joke's stale, you know?"

"I wouldn't make fun at your expense, Blythe," Wyatt says with an echo of that previous intensity. I watch his hands tighten around the wheel, a muscle in his jaw jumping.

"Thanks," I say brightly, poking at the wrapping around my breakfast burrito. "If you ever want to take a trip to the city, you can break the kneecaps of everyone who's ever wronged me."

Laughter bursts out of him like sunshine through a cloud. "You're a violent little thing," he says, pulling off the main drag. As we pass the side of a large building covered in pale stucco, accented with carved wood that's painted a deep green, I wonder if we're flirting. I mean, I *want* this to be flirting.

"Is that a yes?" I ask with little idea of where such boldness came from.

Wyatt pulls up alongside the stuccoed building and slows the truck to a halt. He considers my question, putting the gear into park.

"If you help me with preparations for the Wild Hunt," he finally says, looking up at me with a mischievous smile that makes me aware of every single stitch of clothing on my body, "I'll return the favor by breaking some kneecaps."

He reaches over Fern to offer me his hand. To shake on it. Before I can think too much about it, I extend my palm, and then his fingers are closed around mine—strong, warm, callused.

I take a deep breath, heat unspooling low in my belly. "Deal," I agree. "Guess it's better to be making bargains with you instead of *Them*."

I intend it to be flirtatious, I guess, but I'm clearly shit at that sort of thing because Wyatt startles, looking over at me with concern. "That's not..." He trails off, narrowing his eyes. "Blythe, that's not something you've done before, is it?"

"Jesus Christ," I sputter with a laugh. "No. Definitely not. They've always been...an abstract thing to me, you know? Theoretical. Academic."

Something in his expression darkens as he pushes open his door, letting Fern bound over his lap and into the street. She takes off for a nearby field where a group of kids is playing. One of them notices her and starts calling her name excitedly, quickly joined by the rest.

"It would be wise for you to keep it that way," Wyatt warns, like following him out of the truck is some kind of point of no return. "Theoretical. Academic."

But I'm long past that. I think I have been for a while, even before Cookie's message and Mr. Rabbit's bugged eye. "Luckily, I'm an idiot," I say with glee, pushing my door open and slipping down from the passenger's seat, my burrito still in tow. I'm not abandoning it anytime soon. Even as my stomach roils at the thought of eating, I tuck it into my coat pocket and follow Wyatt as he heads for a side door: tall, narrow, also painted that deep, pretty green.

The mist sits over everything like a soft blanket, dampening the sound of tires through puddles and far-off dog barks and shops starting to open up for the day. But the second Wyatt pushes through the side door, sound thunders into my delicate, hungover senses.

I set my jaw against the loud music and cross the threshold into the stuccoed building. He reaches past me, pulling the door closed tight. I blink, looking around the large, vaulted room and trying to get my bearings. Pale morning light pours through three arched windows at either end of the space. The floors are old, battered pine in a herringbone pattern, creaking with every movement. A rich, earthy, herbaceous scent fills the air—like a bunch of fresh plants mixed together. I would normally find it pleasant, but my stomach still feels queasy.

Even worse is the thumping bass of someone's boombox blasting the oldies—"Zombie" by the Cranberries, I think. My mom loves that band, even though they were old news by the time she first heard 'em on the radio.

Long folding tables are lined up with military precision across the floor, heaped with petals and leaves and nails and salt and things I can't identify. A pretty Black woman in jeans and a delightful cardigan with candy corn appliques stands at the head of the tables with a small throng of folks around her. She's holding a clipboard and gesturing, so I assume she's in charge.

"That's Wanda," Wyatt tells me, following my gaze. "She's the Foxglove Coven's leader."

"So she's actually a witch?" I ask with delight. Much like Them, the mere thought of witchcraft—or hedgeriding, for that matter—is brushed off as utter nonsense in academic circles. To be honest, I brushed it all off, too, but I guess I still always hoped. Because a world with magic is just better than one without, even if that magic is wild and strange and dangerous—just like it seems to be here in Blackbird Hollow.

Wyatt nods, watching me closely. "Witches are human, like us, but they've got Changeling blood," he explains, raising a hand in greeting to an older woman with incredible bone structure. She's dressed in jeans, boots, and a field coat like everybody else, but somehow she looks like she stepped off a magazine spread. It's exactly the way the tourists here *wished* they looked in their brand-new gear.

"Wait, humans with Changeling blood? And Changelings are Fey?" I demand over the music as my mind catches up, dragging my gaze away from the attention-commanding woman to look at him with wide eyes. He just nods solemnly. "So that means somebody *did* fuck one of The—"

"But we don't do that anymore!" Wyatt protests, though I can see he's holding back a laugh. It must be the dim lamplight of the room that makes me think he's blushing. "Besides, there's a lot of older hedgerider texts that indicate Changelings are something more complicated than just the ol' switcheroo you see in folklore."

I don't know why I find a six-foot-two man who looks like he does a lot of manual labor blushing and saying things like "ol' switcheroo" so delightful, but I absolutely do.

"Is everybody here a witch?" I want to know, not trying to sound too excited but definitely failing. Wyatt scans the room, and it's at that moment I notice quite a few people are glancing my way with lingering interest. That's normal, I guess—I am an outsider, after all.

"Most of the coven's here," he answers, shoving his hands in his pocket and leaning closer to me so I can hear him over the music. "But the table with the nails? That's just townsfolk."

"And this is preparation for the Hunt?" I ask, itching to wander closer and examine everything. I have to remind myself that I'm actually here to help, to participate—not just to observe. For once, I'm actually part of something.

"We're usually pretty prepared for this time of year," he replies, his shoulder bumping mine. Heat floods my entire body. "But with hellhounds in the woods and the Hunt coming right for us, we're taking extra precautions."

He explains that most of the town's little ones have iron sewn into their coats and backpacks year-round. Everybody's got rosemary at their garden gate and rowan near their back door. What I'm looking at is extra, drawing from the town's collective reserves, to make sure everybody's safe.

I nod, wishing I'd brought a notebook or something. He's just finishing up his explanation when the striking older woman I saw earlier makes her way over. "Morning, Wyatt," she says as she draws closer. "Who's this you've got here?"

Her playful, singsong voice tells me she knows *exactly* who I am. I mean, I saw enough of Fallon's phone tree action to assume that everyone in this building probably has my full name and birth date, plus a snapshot of my spiritual weaknesses.

"You know damn well, Harkness," Wyatt shoots back without any venom, a kind of worn-in, well-practiced teasing—like he has with Fallon. "Or is that memory of yours starting to fail?"

Harkness cackles. Like, actually cackles. "Sharp as ever," she replies, tapping her temple with one slightly bowed finger. Her gaze moves to mine, and I'm unprepared. Meeting her eyes feels like peering into the cosmos or the night itself. Her attention makes me slightly woozy, and the air seems to throb for a long moment.

"Lovely to meet you, Alice Blythe," she says with a feline grin. There's something about this woman that makes me love her immediately, even though she's also kind of terrifying. "Wyatt doesn't bring many beaus around, you see. Thanks for taking one for the team."

Wyatt turns red, which makes me blush in turn. "And this is precisely why," he protests. "You all can't let a man just *live*."

Harkness winks at me and levels her gaze at Wyatt. She's tall, I realize—probably only a little shorter than Wyatt. "You two up for distributing iron reserves and making sure all the kids' coats are ready to go trick-or-treating?" she asks with a sly little smile.

"Alice was looking forward to getting to see the coven work," Wyatt replies, rubbing the back of his neck. I bite the inside of my cheek, trying to stop myself from wondering if he's just trying to avoid being alone with me. If it's painfully obvious that I'm developing a hell of a crush and he doesn't want to encourage something like that with a city girl who doesn't know the first thing about actually dealing with Them.

"Willa Proctor and Sally Laveau'll be out doing the garlands," Harkness says with a wave of her hand. "Besides, with the Hunt on its way, there won't be any shortage of getting to see what we're up to here."

"That okay with you?" Wyatt asks, turning toward me. I will my face not to flush further when I meet his gaze, tilting my chin up to look at him.

"Sure," I say with a shrug. "Might be easier to ask some folks about the missing hikers, anyways." I wouldn't normally be so loose-tongued, but Harkness practically oozes authority, so I think it's alright.

"Nikhil waited on the two that went missing most recently," she offers like a consolation prize. From a nearby table, she scoops up a burlap sack and hands it to Wyatt. His shoulders unpin from his ears as they exchange a long glance.

"Fine," he relents with a heavy, theatrical sigh. Then he turns to me and gestures toward the front of the building. "Let's go out the front door."

I make my way across the antique hardwoods, taking in the gleaming wood paneling. Wyatt leads me through an impressive set of double doors, which are held open by a very large garden gnome and a children's wagon, and into a smaller chamber. Two hallways branch off from either side, the cream-colored walls covered in framed art. I glance closer at one as we walk by, intrigued when I realize I'm looking at scientific sketches of the region's flora and fauna.

We reach a plain vestibule with plastic chairs and fliers about things to do in Blackbird Hollow, and then we're back out on the street. The sun's starting to burn through the mist and rain. At the base of the hill, the valleys spill out like an embroidered tapestry, accented with silver threads of dew. I pull in a deep breath of damp leaves, wet pavement, and woodsmoke.

"What are you gonna do with all the tourists?" I ask, thinking about the fliers we just passed. "I mean, it seems like the full-time residents...understand what it's like out here. But what about the leaf peepers?"

Wyatt leads me down the hill, taking the first left to abandon the main street and head into what looks like a residential area with tall, narrow houses and small front yards lined by what I suspect is iron fencing. He glances at me over his shoulder, the sun turning his dark hair bronze.

"What about 'em?" he asks, his brow creasing.

"Well," I say, jumping across a puddle, the cool air fresh and energizing against my skin. "How do you keep them safe?"

Wyatt snorts, swinging the burlap sack. It's a few more seconds before he speaks again. "We *don't*, Alice."

I halt abruptly on the sidewalk in front of a cottage with mossy stepping stones leading to its front door, painted a bright blue. "So you're just gonna hope they don't get taken?" I demand, unease curling in my belly where heat bloomed only a few moments ago.

He stops and turns to face me, his broad shoulders blocking out the sun as he considers me, saying nothing. The unease becomes a stab of fear.

"You aren't hoping they don't get taken," I say slowly, measuring the words. "You're hoping they *do*. That strangers who come here just to look at leaves and drink cider get taken and your people don't."

Wyatt looks away from me, but it's not with shame. He's stalwart, resolute, though his jaw works back and forth. When he finally meets my gaze, his mouth parts and his shoulders shrug. "What exactly would you have me do, Alice?"

Chapter 14
Wyatt

Alice makes this terrible disapproving face, and for half a second I feel a little bad. But then I realize that while she's wise to a lot of what's happening here, it's all just theory to her. She's never seen one of Them. When she comes close to one—and she will sooner than she'd probably prefer—I think she'll get it.

Besides, there's no use sugarcoating much of anything for Alice Blythe. I want her to know exactly who we are and what we do here. I saw her getting comfy with me in the truck, and I'm not ashamed to admit that I liked it. But if there's even a hair's breadth of a chance that she won't run off at the first redcap sighting, she has to know the truth of things.

Nikhil jogs toward us as we head out, his long legs swishing with the sound of his track pants. He's got his hair in a bun, and he looks a little like a romance hero. For the first time in my life, I feel a little nervous about what a woman might think about another man. The deep voice, with which he booms, "Widow Harkness said you wanted to talk?" doesn't make me feel any better.

Alice stands next to me, stony-faced, not sparing even a glance for Nik. I try not to smile. She's obviously still mad at me. Instead, I clear my throat. "You were one of the last to see the most recent missing hikers, weren't you? Can you tell us anything about them?"

Nik frowns. "Were they white people dressed up like equestrians?"

I shrug. There's a touch of a smile on Alice's lips. Either she's warming up in general, or to Nik. I try not to wonder which.

Nik shakes his head. "They all look alike to me. Sorry."

Alice snickers as Nik jogs back the way he came. *Does he have to run everywhere like he's in an episode of* Baywatch*?* I think to myself.

"C'mon," I finally say. "We can pass out the iron while you decide how much you're gonna hate me for letting innocent leafers get snatched by the Hunt."

She makes a hateful little face at me, and I can't help but think that if she'd just eaten the burrito, she might be in a better mood by now, but a hangover's a hangover. I whistle for Fern, who's refereeing a game of stickball with a bunch of kids in the field out back. The kids all groan when they hear me, and my little girl takes a victory lap around the bases before she trots up to us and shoves her head right under Alice's hand.

Alice's eyes soften for a moment, until she remembers she's supposed to be angry with me. She glares again to strengthen her resolve, I reckon, but when I walk, she walks. We're quiet as we skirt up and down the streets, following the list we were given.

She doesn't say much, but I notice with each house we go to, with each door that opens with welcome and thanks, that she mellows more and more. She sees what I hoped she would —that Blackbird Hollow is special. It's not that we don't have our troubles and petty grievances. We do, but in times like this, we sure as shit pull together and take care of our own. We always have, and as long as I have something to say about it, as long as Cade and Fallon and the coven do, we always will.

Lizzie Bishop comes walking towards us, a redheaded witch of about sixteen. She waves at me and blushes, giving Alice a bit of the stink-eye. Someone's already been out to hang the rowan boughs on all the fences on Whitethorn Drive, but Lizzie's job is to activate them.

I nudge Alice with my elbow. "You wanted to see magic. Watch Lizzie work."

Alice glares at me again, reminding me so much of Fallon flirting that I almost laugh. But that might hurt her dignity, and I might be wrong and that would hurt mine, so I don't tease her. At any rate, she does as I ask, watching as Lizzie trails a hand through the dried rowan as she walks, humming an arcane folk song as she goes.

The boughs green up. They don't exactly come alive again, but their faded colors glow with vibrancy, with magic. But I don't watch that. I've seen it before, and I'll see it again. I watch Alice's hazel eyes get big, and her pretty mouth falls open. She's got a young look to her face, countered by those old-soul kaleidoscope eyes, but at this moment, she could be the same age as Lizzie. Something in my heart aches for her.

She looks up at me and shakes her head a little, clearly working through some complicated shit in her head. "I think I get it." Fern sits on her foot, pushing her big old head into Alice's hip, grinning like a fool. Alice scratches her chin, almost absently, repeating, "Yeah, I think I get it."

Lizzie nears us, sticking her tongue out at Alice rather pointedly as she approaches. She stops near me, blushing again. "Are you going to the Hallows party?"

I smile as gently as I can. "Probably, but you're not old enough for that shindig."

"I will be soon," Lizzie replies. "Just two more years."

"That you will. You bring your beau with you then, and I'll drink a beer with 'em and give all the standard warnings about breaking your heart."

Disappointment shines in Lizzie Bishop's eyes, but she nods. "Good enough, then." She glares again at Alice, saying, "Are *you* staying for that, or are you too Big City for such nonsense?"

Alice raises an eyebrow. "I haven't been invited to any parties, so I guess not."

Lizzie smiles like the cat who swallowed a whole damn flock of canaries and sidesteps Alice deftly, humming happily as she continues on.

"Well," Alice breathes. "I think I know where I stand with *her*."

I snicker a little. She doesn't actually sound too put out. "You can come to the party," I say as we turn back toward the town hall and my truck. "It's a dress-up affair, out in the woods. Big bonfire. Lots to drink." Alice grimaces, and I add, "You'll probably lose the headache by then, Blythe. Take heart."

Alice Blythe sticks her tongue out at me, just like Lizzie did to her, and she and Fern march ahead, leaving me in their dust.

When we get back to the truck, Alice ravages her burrito while I check in with the coven. As expected, when I return, she seems to have regained some equilibrium. She's got the truck windows rolled down. She and Fern look to be communing with the breeze, their chins tipped into the autumn air as I walk up. There's a faint smell of caramel apples on the wind.

"Better?" I ask, feeling tentative as I lean against the side of the truck to peer in at her.

Alice nods, but there's no quick joke. She actually looks a little sick, and I wonder for a moment if the burrito went wrong in her stomach. But then she speaks. "My parents check in every few days, and they'll worry if I don't respond," she says, her eyes shining with worry. "Should I use the café at the Archer Inn?"

I do a couple of quick calculations in my head. We're a little close to the full moon for my comfort, but it's high noon—and I'd rather she not use the internet at the Archer this time of year. After every tourist season, Cade has to go through a whole rigamarole of debugging the internet café.

Whether it's Sector or some corporate goofball trying to track spending habits in small towns, there's always some issue I don't want Alice tied up in. Especially not now that she's "all in," as she says.

"You up for meeting the last Hayes spawn?" I ask. "My little brother's got the only other internet in town outside of tribal lands."

Alice gives me a surprisingly sweet smile for the morning we've had, but I've lived with Fallon Hayes my whole damn life. I know better than to trust sweet smiles. "That sounds great."

I want to ask what she's thinking as I climb in the truck, but I also know better than to ask questions that I'll get lies for answers in response. Alice is allowed to be mad that I'd let tourists die, rather than my own people. If I were her, I'd probably be mad too.

There's not much reason to go this way, but I take Main Street out of town on a whim. Maybe I just want to remind

Alice that Blackbird Hollow is special again. This time of year, downtown is especially charming. All the shops have their front windows decorated with seasonal wares, window boxes overflowing with bright chrysanthemums and sweet potato vine.

There's little kids everywhere as we make our way down Main Street. The rush on Halloween costumes has begun, so everyone's out settling theirs, and between that and the leafers, downtown is crowded. I keep my eyes locked on the road, thinking this was probably a mistake.

But then Alice leans forward, right as I slow for the last stop sign before the turnoff to Cade's. She makes this terrible little noise, and before I know it, she's out of the truck, Fern following close behind with a displeased growl that's not about Alice leaving the vehicle.

"Shit," I swear, throwing the truck into park, despite the fact that in exactly thirty seconds, traffic's gonna pile up behind me. As I push my door open, I see what's got both Alice and Fern all riled up.

Five-year-old Belle Laveau is slumped over on the sidewalk, clutching a skinned knee, weeping silently, her angelic obsidian ringlets practically vibrating with her quiet sobs. Fern growls again, and Alice points half a block up the sidewalk. Even through her pain, little Belle knows better. She grabs onto Alice's arm and shakes her head.

"We don't point," the little witch says as I jog over, shaking her head in a schoolmarmish fashion that makes her look about thirty-five. "Outsiders think it's cursing."

Alice puts her hand down immediately, but the glare she shoots at the couple walking away is venomous. "They didn't even notice that they knocked her over," she hisses.

From half a block away, I clock the expensive, quilted outerwear. The oversized rock on the woman's left finger. The leather hiking boots that have never been worn. They look just like Nik described. All the same, all assholes. "Stay here," I warn under my breath. "Wait for her mama."

Sally Laveau is very likely dropping off eggs at the bodega, and will be out for her babe in a second. I'd like for Alice to meet her anyway. She and Belle are newer to town, migrating up after the Last Flood in New Orleans, and she can give Alice a better picture of Black southern craft.

I catch up with the couple in a matter of moments, falling into step with them easily. They're probably just another couple of rich white folks, dime a dozen this time of year, but it's always possible they're Sector. I plan to keep things as civil as possible, since we're all full up on trouble at this juncture.

"This town's not your playground," I say, keeping my voice soft as I grip the man's elbow. He's gym-fit but not much else, that much is clear as he slows, an edge of both defiance and fear in his eyes.

"What the hell is your problem?" the wife asks, swinging her bleach-blonde hair away from the slick of sticky-looking gloss on her unnaturally puffy lips.

Her nails are painted the same color as her skin, but sparkly, and I notice her big rock is on the wrong finger. Maybe she's just the girlfriend. I don't really give a shit. The way they're dressed—hell, even the way they smell—tells me that they're the type who come to places like this to use us up and take stories of how they "roughed it" in the country for the weekend back to their big-city burbs. As though a stay at a boutique hotel like the Archer Inn is roughing it.

They stop, waiting for me to explain why I'm accosting them in the street. I gesture back at Belle, Alice, Fern, and now Sally, who has her little girl cuddled into her arms. Elena Fernandez, the store manager at the bodega, is hurrying toward them with a first aid kit.

Alice gives the couple one of the most toxic mean-mugs I've ever seen in my life, and I grew up with Fallon. Who is, at this very moment, due to nothing more than bad luck, coming down the sidewalk in the opposite direction. We're about to have a good old-fashioned shitshow, right here in the street at high noon.

"The fuck is this?" Fallon asks in a syrupy sweet tone as she approaches. "Why's that precious little one crying, Wyatt?"

My sister, who has thankfully decided on normal human attire for the second day in a row, crosses her arms over her chest, making a menacing nest out of the florals on her prairie-style dress.

I smile at Fallon. Keeping things civil is no longer an option with her here, but I'm sure as shit gonna try. "These two didn't notice that they knocked Belle down."

"Oh," Fallon says with a smile that should sour the city folks' stomachs. "Please let me handle this, Wyatt. You're causing a traffic jam, and people need to get to *work*."

At the very least, I can let Fallon run her mouth at them and warn them off treating Blackbird Hollow's residents like side characters in some dime-store novel. I block out as much as I can of what Fallon's saying, just to let myself get going. Things are about to get ugly, I'm afraid, and I'd rather Alice weren't here when it happens.

As I turn, the girlfriend calls Fallon a "dumb hick," and I spin back in the other direction, but Alice is already ahead of me, so fast I can't even grab her sleeve. And I'll be damned by the old gods and the new, but she's slapped that woman across the face so hard I can see a handprint on her pale cheek.

The woman lunges for Alice. Fallon grabs her by the hair, and the boyfriend just stands there looking perplexed. No way they're Sector. Sector's inept as can be in a fight, but they're never surprised about being hit. They're assholes who know they're assholes, at least. Unlike these two yuppie shits. I move as quickly as I can, yanking the woman out from between my sister and Alice Blythe before real harm can be done.

I shove her at her man, but he jerks back from her, causing her to stumble and fall, twisting her ankle in her ridiculously high-heeled boots.

"Get out of this town, if you know what's good for you," I sneer at the two of them. "We don't tolerate that kind of behavior here."

The woman spits at Fallon, and I have to push my sister behind me to keep her from skinning the bitch alive. "You're ruining my *vacation*," the woman wails.

And then Fallon starts laughing, which is apparently contagious, because Alice laughs too, in exactly the same unhinged way that tells me they're about to descend upon her like a mob of Maenads.

"Get in the truck," I growl, pushing them both toward the street before someone draws blood.

Elena Fernandez is laughing her ass off as Sally scoops Belle into her arms, smiling a wicked smile.

"You think your vacation's ruined *now*?" Sally says as she shakes her head, her twin ringlets to her little girl's shaking with fury. She practically shimmers in the golden light of the afternoon, a sure sign that her words are laced with magic. "Good luck to you both."

Belle sniffles, saying, "Can we go home, Mama?"

"Yes, my sweet." She hugs the little girl tight, and they turn away.

I breathe a small sigh of relief and order Fern into the cab of the truck. Fallon was right that people are backing up behind me, but not one person honks. They're all watching the outsiders as they walk away. A couple of folks shake their heads, but everyone has the same brand of satisfied smirk on their faces.

They all heard Sally Laveau. It wasn't exactly a curse, but it's not a thing you'd want a witch to say to you, if you knew what was good for your health.

When I slide back into the truck, Fallon is complimenting Alice's strategy with the open-hand slap, rather than a nose-breaking punch.

I shake my head, waving thanks to the line of folks behind us as I take the turn toward Cade's. Alice leans around Fallon, who has Fern on her lap like a child, to say, "I really do get it now, Wyatt. The two of them can be the first to go."

Fallon smiles and bumps me in the shoulder. "Don't worry, baby," she says to Alice. "I'll be the first to push 'em straight into the Hunt's path."

Alice nods once, appearing confident in her evaluation of the situation, I suppose, and leans back.

"Guess we got that solved," I mutter under my breath. "Can we get through the rest of this day without incident, *please*?"

The two of them will be the death of me, and I know it because they devolve into giggles as I drive deep into the forest.

Chapter 15
Alice

The woods are dark and deep. We're only a few minutes up the road, but it feels like we've left all the sunlight back in the downtown area, towering trees swallowing up the brightness of high noon. Mist creeps along the ground, reaching toward the truck with pale gray fingers.

"I'm dropping you off at the house, Fallon," Wyatt says, flipping on the fog lights. "We're running over to Cade's and I'm not taking the chance you get him all riled up this close to the full moon."

"The full moon?" I echo, lurching forward to peer at the siblings. "What's *that* got to do with anything?"

"You're gonna find out real soon," Fallon tells me with a wild grin, patting my shoulder. Then she turns to Wyatt and asks, "What would make you think I'd get our dear little brother wound up?"

"Yeah, come on, it's not like she's ever done anything insane, Wyatt," I add, fighting to keep my expression neutral.

He cruises the truck to a stop sign and then presses his forehead into the steering wheel as if we've defeated him entirely.

"I can handle one of you," he says, his gaze fixed straight ahead. "Not both of you. Not with everything else going on."

"I thought you were a stronger man than that." Fallon sniffs, scratching Fern's ears in a precise spot that makes the big dog thump her foot happily.

"A weaker man," Wyatt mutters, turning off the road onto a familiar drive, "would've throttled you both by now. You slapped somebody right on Main Street, Alice. And Fallon, you had her by her goddamn *hair*. In the middle of the damn day."

"She deserved it!" Fallon and I shout at the same time. Fern apparently agrees, because she throws her head back and howls. All of us—even Wyatt—dissolve into laughter. We fall into a comfortable silence, Fallon's shoulder pressed into mine, Fern's legs splayed across my lap as she settles in for the ride.

I lean my head against the window, feeling better thanks to the burrito and the fact that I'll get to let my parents know I'm alive. If they don't hear from me, they might contact the university, and I just don't feel like explaining it all to them right now. I mean—I don't know how to explain *any* of it to them. I guess I'll tell them I'm safe, taking a weekend trip with some friends. I don't have any friends besides the people (and dog) in this truck, but they might be so happy at the prospect I've made some that they'll buy the rest of it.

The cab of the truck is still warm from sitting in the sun next to the town hall, so I crank a window down. Wyatt's catching Fallon up on everything we did this morning, and my attention wanders. I stare out the window, appreciating the beauty unfolding all around me.

A copse of silver birches catches my attention, and I take them in with delight as we draw closer. The meager sunlight that manages to pierce the thick tree canopy coats the slim, pretty trees like molasses, turning them into bronze sculptures. Except for one, I think—it's a strange hue of spring-green, moving in some unseen breeze. I open my mouth to point it out, but then a horrible stench overtakes my senses, and I retch.

"What in the fuck?" Fallon asks just before Wyatt slams on the brakes. My head glances off the truck's frame—that's what I get for hanging out the window like a damn dog, I guess. I blink, trying to get my bearings, and then I realize the movement I see up ahead isn't just the mist.

It's a sleek black creature, all taut muscle and long limbs, utterly otherworldly. I lean forward onto the dash, peering closer. My brain protests what I'm seeing, trying to convince me the pitch-colored hound doesn't have its jaws unhinged at an impossible, snake-like angle.

"Shh," Wyatt hushes when Fern lets out a quiet whine.

Fallon comes to life all at once, reaching over me to pull a pistol out of the glovebox. The creature takes no notice of us, shaking its head violently before tearing a limb from its victim.

Biting down my tongue, I force myself to look closer through the writhing fog. For a moment, I'm terrified it's a person, but then I understand it's only vaguely humanoid. It's a little smaller than me, I think, and its skin is an impossible gray hue, patchy and scarred. A bright slash of red catches my attention, and I squint, academic curiosity overcoming any sort of self-preservation or disgust.

A decapitated head lolls on the dirt road. Its features are almost human, but not quite. Its eyes are open corpse-wide, the pupils and irises an impossible black. Pointed ears knife through stringy hair. On its head is a red hat, made of a strange fabric.

Oh. Not fabric, I realize, the nausea rising up my throat now. *Skin*. "A redcap," I breathe.

"I'll be damned," Fallon murmurs.

"I am begging you," Wyatt pleads in a barely-there whisper. "Shut. *Up*."

The dirt road is damp with dew and viscera, a trail of red-black blood trickling down into the grass like run-off during a summer storm. The feasting creature—it's a hellhound, I realize all at once—pays us no mind, biting into the redcap's head. Gore bursts forth like fountain, gray brain matter dribbling down the hellhound's chin.

Its maw isn't any kind of canine mouth. Instead, its entire jaw is lined with razor-sharp teeth, and the way it moves is *wrong*. Or at least my brain tells me—screams at me—that it's wrong, wrong, *wrong*. My entire body buzzes, and my heart thrashes like a living thing caged by my ribs. Distantly, I realize I've never felt flight or fight quite like this before, as if there's always been a bottomless well of primal fear inside me waiting for the right moment to activate.

The hellhound finishes off the redcap's head and then fastens its teeth around a torn-off limb—an arm, maybe? All at once, it straightens and turns toward the truck, its eyes gleaming like a predator's in the dark, even though daylight still leaks through the treetops. I notice an interruption in its sleek, black coat—a white scar on its shoulder, like a half-moon, almost. And then it's gone. Not the way a dog runs away, bounding off into a field. The hellhound is there, and then it just melts away, leaving nothing more than a smear of gore on the abandoned dirt road.

All four of us breathe out in a collective exhale. As the adrenaline fades, the stench overpowers me and I retch again, reaching over to crank the window back up.

"Shouldn't be any redcaps this close to town," Fallon says, an edge in her voice.

"No," Wyatt agrees, beginning to slowly inch the truck forward. "No, there damn well shouldn't be."

THE FIRST THING I do in the yard of Caden Hayes's surprisingly cute cottage is vomit.

"Well," Wyatt says as he kneels beside me, "least it's not in my truck." I would probably laugh at his dry tone were I not puking my guts up, trying to avoid the potted mums and the porch steps.

Fingertips brush the nape of my neck—Wyatt's, I realize, as he gathers my hair back. Despite the nausea, despite the fact I'm literally on my fucking knees in damp grass, dry-heaving on a stranger's lawn, something bright and warm flutters beneath my breastbone.

More contradictory feelings flood my body as I lurch forward again and throw up whatever was left of my poor, beautiful burrito. A hand ghosts up and down my back in a comforting stroke. I want to melt into it, into *him*, but I'm preoccupied at the moment. And it's so stupid, I know, but I hope he's not judging me for tossing my breakfast at my first sight of Them.

I rock back on my heels and shiver. It's way colder up in the hills, particularly with this weird, midday mist. Wyatt stays next to me, reaching into his coat pocket for a square of fabric. It's Black Watch plaid, I think, forever unable to turn my brain off, as he offers it to me.

"Oh my god," I say in a strained voice. "You carry around a fucking handkerchief."

"Do you want to wipe your mouth off or not?" he demands, one eyebrow arching.

"Whatever," I grumble, taking the handkerchief and doing exactly that. My mouth is sour as he helps me to my feet. Despite the projectile vomiting, I'm pretty steady, but I'm not gonna ruin the moment.

I drag the back of my hand across my forehead and glance at Caden's door. To my utter delight, a group of tiny winged creatures is lined up on the porch railing. They shimmer with some kind of iridescence or maybe even bioluminescence, blue-tinged and lovely. Their wings are gossamer-thin, and maybe I'm seeing things, but I swear They're dressed in little outfits that look like flower petals.

"See!" I near-shout, whipping around to stare at Wyatt as I point toward the porch. "*That's* what I thought They were gonna look like! Cute little guys! In little flower dresses! Not decapitated corpses!"

Wyatt looks between me and the pixies. "They're laughing at you, I think," he says.

"Rude," I reply, pulling my coat closer as I shiver again. "Can you tell Them I've just been through something very traumatic and also deeply gross?"

He shoves his hands in his pockets and shakes his head. "We can't speak to most of Them, pixies included," he explains. "We don't know Their language, and They've no interest in learning ours. Most of the witches can communicate with Them due to their Changeling blood, and there's some hedgerider records of Them occasionally choosing to speak with us, but it's always on Their terms and usually temporary."

"Huh," I say, watching one of the pixies dive off the porch railing and zip around the yard. "Do They have any written records? And if so, has anyone tried translating?"

Wyatt stays close, one hand on the small of my back, as we make our way up the porch steps. "Even if They did," he says carefully, his gaze slipping toward the pixies, who are absolutely watching us with Their beady, black eyes, "I imagine They wouldn't take kindly to that."

He lifts his arm and knocks on the door—three quick knocks, a long pause, then three more, followed by one final knock. "Cade, it's me," he calls. "Let us in."

There's no answer. Wyatt grumbles and knocks again while

I look at the pixies. But as magical and earth-shattering as They are, it's the completely mortal and mostly normal human man I find my attention going toward, no matter how much I fight it. I can't stop thinking about the way he handled that couple on Main Street. The way he saw that little girl crying and didn't *hesitate*. I don't know him that well, but I have no doubt in my mind that Wyatt Hayes can and would absolutely throw the fuck down if push came to shove.

I swallow hard when warmth blooms low in my belly as I recall the way the autumnal midday light sharpened his deeply distracting features. I know he said something to the man—I saw his lips move—but it must've been really low, and a strange part of me yearns to hear him speak in that dark, threatening tone, barely more than a growl from the back of his throat.

I hear the door creak open, at which point I get my shit together. "Inside, Blythe," Wyatt says, gesturing for me to go first, his gaze sweeping the yard and the border of the forest a little ways off.

I oblige, stepping over the threshold and into the front room of the little stone cottage. It's surprisingly cute, considering a boy lives here. Caden's got a few framed family photos, a really cool vintage banner with decorative embroidery spelling out "Blackbird Hollow," and some posters from old horror movies.

A cozy lamp with a fringe-trimmed, bell-shaped shade flicks on, and I find myself looking at Caden Hayes. The youngest Hayes sibling is built like a goddamn linebacker, but with the face of a hero from a gothic romance. He's got the same dark, gorgeous eyes as his siblings, but his features are a little less rugged than Wyatt's—like he got more of his mom, maybe.

"What the fuck is with this family?" I mutter under my breath.

"Hey," Caden greets with an awkward wave. He's tense, I

realize, all those powerful muscles standing out from beneath his thin sweatshirt. "Nice to meet you, Alice. Fallon called me from the house. Would love to let you use the internet. Just a little frazzled. You know. The moon."

"You're all good, Cade," Wyatt says in a soothing tone, coming to stand next to me. "I know you aren't gonna hurt us."

"Ha, well," Caden replies, rubbing the back of his neck in exactly the same way his older brother does. "I'm glad one of us is confident about that." He pauses, that absurd jawline flexing, his gaze darting to me. "I'm just gonna get the dial-up going. Be right back." Then he turns and strides down a shadowed hallway, moving like a goddamn Greek god.

"What the *fuck* is in your genes?" I demand, turning on my heel to look up at Wyatt. He's closer—closer than I realized—so I see every moment of his confusion as he looks down at his pants and then at mine.

"What's in *your* jeans, Blythe?" he asks, his admittedly very kissable lips curving into an expression that I like very, very much.

I, an adult turning thirty in a few months, turn bright red. I pray fiercely that the cottage's low light hides the fact. "Wouldn't you like to know," I reply. I mean it to come out like a joke, like maybe I'd stick my tongue out after I say it, but it sounds insanely flirtatious.

Anxiety climbs up my throat, and I quickly add, "No, *genes*, Wyatt." Then I gesticulate wildly for some reason. "Like, why is everyone in the Hayes family hot? Your little brother looks like he could be on the cover of one of those historical romance novels."

Wyatt considers this, though his eyes linger down by my hips for a heartbeat before he drags his gaze back up to meet mine. We're very close, all alone in the cottage's front room, and he smells wonderful—like pine and woodsmoke.

"Everyone in the Hayes family?" he echoes with a dangerous smile. "Would that include little old *me*, Blythe?" He leans closer, so close I can feel the heat of him through his jacket. "What kinda novel would I belong in, do you reckon?"

"Ew," Caden announces loudly, materializing out of the shadows. "I thought you came here for the internet. Flirt in your own house, Wyatt."

"We weren't—" both of us protest, but Caden goes entirely still in a way that sends fear skittering down my spine. I watch as he throws his head back and takes a long, deep breath. For a long moment, I don't understand. I sure as shit don't smell anything.

But I'm also not giant and muscly and jumpy around the full moon.

"You're a fucking werewolf," I say with glee.

"Yeah," Caden replies in a low voice, not looking at me. "Could you be quiet so the werewolf can concentrate?"

I almost say "sure" out loud before realizing how stupid that is, so instead I just nod, probably too vigorously. Caden creeps toward the window by the front door, and it does not escape my notice that someone that big shouldn't move that quietly.

Beside me, Wyatt's hand slides to his belt, where I'm pretty sure he carries a hunting knife. In the dead quiet, I hear the porch steps creak. A simple, common thing, I know, and yet the sound still stirs an ancient kind of dread in me. I shrink back against Wyatt, my spine bumping into his chest. This isn't really the moment to examine the feeling that explodes in me when he protectively slips one hand around my bicep, so I stow it away for later.

Over the thudding of my furiously beating heart, I hear the distinct sound of paws padding across the porch, the click of nails clear as day. But Fern wanted to go with Fallon when we dropped her off at her house. There shouldn't be any kind of dog here. I squeeze my eyes shut and hope that Caden is expecting a werewolf buddy.

A low growl slips under the door at the same moment I catch the glow of a predator's eyeshine through the window. I don't need to peer past Caden's heavy, cream-colored curtains to know what's prowling on his porch.

It's the hellhound, and apparently it's still hungry.

Chapter 16
Wyatt

The sound of the hellbeast on the porch slices a shard of fear through my gut that I'm unfamiliar with. I can't remember the last time one of Them made me truly afraid. As though by instinct, my fingers close tighter around Alice's arm, and I realize where the sharp depths of this feeling came from.

Her. I'm afraid for *her*.

I'm afraid I can't protect her, not here. Not with what I've got on hand. Inwardly, I swear up a storm. It'd take a bigger gun, and much bigger rounds of silver bullets than what we've got here, to even have a *hope* of slowing a hellhound down. Killing one—well, I'm not even sure that can be done. Creatures of the High are often like Them, nigh on impossible to kill.

Cade's moved to the front door, his arms spread wide at its frame as he leans forward, breathing too hard for my liking with Alice in the room. My little brother will be a good wolf someday. He's got the temperament for it. Calm, calculating, fiercely intelligent, with a heart that contains oceans. But he's not even a year out from the change—and he's a danger to everyone in this cottage right now, but especially Alice, as her scent is new to him.

"Cade," I breathe. "Calm down."

"Can't," he growls, and that's no euphemism. The change is upon him. "Get her to the cellar—into my cell."

"Don't want to leave you," I murmur, keeping my voice low and soft.

Next to me, Alice is remarkably calm. I can't tell if she's good in a crisis or doesn't get how much danger she's in. But she's still and quiet, breathing evenly.

Cade glances back at her, a faint moonstone glow to his eyes. "You're not scared," he says with a wolfish whine.

"No." She smiles, brave as can be. "I'm fairly certain I'm safe with all the Hayes kids."

Cade's eyes flash to me. "Can we keep her?"

I chuckle, and some of the tension drains off. But the click of nails on the porch and the hiss of unearthly beastie snaps the three of us taut again.

"Lock her in, Wyatt," Cade growls. "Not for me, but it. It's hunting, and the only thing it could want here is her."

He's right. I know he's right. But I don't want to leave him. Not like this. Not alone. That thing gets through the sparse wards, and my little brother is dead.

I'm torn—Alice or Cade? A few days ago, this would have been an easy question to answer, but the fact that I'm hesitating even a little is worrisome. How has Alice Blythe made room for herself in my heart so easily?

"Also," Cade says, sounding a little guilty, "I may have done a deal with Blackstone."

Blackstone is a warlock, arms dealer, and so much trouble that he's not worth tangling with. Any other time, and I'd give my brother the dressing-down of his life for messing around with that end of the demimonde. But if Cade's got good news for me, I'd welcome it right now. "Yeah? What've you got?"

There's a scratch at the door. We all freeze. We don't have time to talk about this.

"I'll find it," I say, pushing Alice toward the back hall. The choice has been made for me. I can protect them both this way. "Door to the basement's down here."

She protests, but just a little. "Wha—"

"No questions right now, Blythe. Gotta save your life first."

She looks up at me, those hazel eyes wide. And for what just might be the first time in Alice Blythe's life, she gives in. "Alright."

I hustle her into the back hallway of the cottage and push the heavy basement door open. It's hewn from old white oak that Cade and I reinforced with iron and silver rebar on the interior. It was supposed to be a "just in case" measure. For if he got out, or something nasty got in. I never imagined we might test it with something as strong as a hellhound.

"Lock the door," Cade says from the hallway. His voice is low and dangerous.

I push Alice towards the stairwell and nod to her to get going. Thank all the old gods, she just goes, flipping the light on nonchalantly.

The cottage is silent for a long moment, eerie and too still. The birds have gone quiet outside, and the day's grown darker somehow. All the hallmarks of not one, but a whole damn pack of hellhounds.

Caden's body convulses, and he grips the doorframe to his bedroom. "I don't have long," he grunts. "Can't hold back much longer. Gun's on the workbench."

I nod, turning swiftly back to the stairs, taking them two at a time. When I meet her at the bottom, she's already got the lamps switched on in the basement. The knotty pine panels on the wall that once seemed so comforting to me now look like eyes, watching.

"Get in there," I murmur, grabbing the iron keys off the door. I pull two rifles from the wall and grab several boxes of silver bullets, handing them to her. "What do you know about loading a gun?"

Alice stares blankly at me, shaking her head. "It's been a long time..."

After a quick breath, deep as I can take it, I nod and do the work for her. My fingers fly. She won't be able to reload, but hopefully she won't need to. "Anything that comes down here that's not Cade or me, you shoot it 'til you run out of ammo. And don't come out 'til Fallon comes to get you."

"Fallon?" she whispers, realizing that if Fallon comes for her, it means neither of us are able.

I nod, unable to meet those gorgeous eyes. "Or a big black cat with glowing eyes. The cat-sìth are safe enough for us, especially Cat. You don't have to be afraid of him. He's Fallon's and he can open any lock for you."

From upstairs, the stillness is broken by a long, vicious growl. It's Caden; the shift is complete. I shove the guns toward Alice, grab the keys from the hook outside the door, and lock her in before tossing the keys to her. "Back in ten, tops," I say with a grin I don't feel in the slightest. "Don't come out 'til you get the all-clear, promise?"

Alice nods slowly. I can't tell if she's afraid or just stunned, but I don't have time to think about it. I turn back to the workbench and find the gun Caden bought from Blackstone. It's a thing of beauty, but I don't have time to admire it. I just load it without another look back at Alice.

If I look at her, I'll have to deal with the way my heart's beating out of my chest, a raptor in a cage, demanding that I stay right here and make sure she's safe. But that's not how this works, and I damn well know it. She'll be safe because I'll make her safe, and no other way.

"Be right back, Blythe," I murmur as I head for the stairs.

"I know you will," she replies, her voice only shaking a little. "I trust you, Wyatt."

I pause, my heartstrings plucked by the confidence in her words just a little too hard. I can't turn around. I just nod and take the steps back upstairs two at a time, just like I came down, slamming the door shut behind me. It locks, and it won't open 'til me, Fallon, or Cade go back down.

We had the new witch in town, Willa Proctor, help us with this one. She's uncommonly good with warding, a rare talent for modern witches. Fallon had all kinds of wild theories about why that is, and I'm not sure why I think of it now, but it does seem a little strange.

I shake off the random thought as I reach the top of the stairs. My brother stands in wolf form, a hulking sable beast with glowing golden eyes, staring at the front door. Cautiously, I approach. Caden and I have been working on this for a year, but we've never tested it under stressful conditions.

Keeping my voice low and steady, I let him know I'm behind him. "On your left, bud."

He glances behind him, irritation like a living thing in his expression. I can't help but chuckle a little. Even in wolf form, Caden is still my little brother. Still irritated as fuck with the way I act. I place my hand on his back.

And all holds. Caden hasn't lost himself to his wolf. He recognizes me. Hell, he even leans against my thigh, like Fern would, though he's nearly twice her size. Even in this tense atmosphere, I breathe a sigh of relief. He really has made progress.

If we make it through this, I hope this will help open the

door to healing his agoraphobia. This is a huge step forward for him.

But my relief is short-lived as something heavy slams against the door.

A slow split cracks right down the center.

"They're through the wards," I grit out through clenched teeth. "Fall back."

The smell of sulfur seeps through the crack, and then there's another heavy thump. No footfall, no noise, just the thump of hellbeast against the wood, as though the hound came from nowhere at all. The door splits apart as Caden and I jump aside, falling back to opposite sides of the front room.

I barely have time to get behind the couch to set up the rifle as three hellhounds burst through the breach in the cabin door, splintering it apart in a cascade of wood and slavering jaws. The one closest to me has a white scar on its shoulder that I recognize. It's the one from the Stardust.

Inwardly, I swear up a storm. I can't believe I've put Alice in this kind of danger. Why else would They be here? The three beasts still as Caden growls at them. I desperately want to open fire, to eliminate the creatures before They have a chance to find Alice.

But there are rules to our profession. Ancient rules that exist between us and the Courts to keep some semblance of peace. Mere destruction of property is not enough for me to shoot one of the hellhounds, even if it is Alice at stake. They have to attack first, or I risk starting a war so unholy it would swallow Blackbird Hollow whole.

Caden, too, remembers just in time, the growl dying in his throat as he lowers his head just slightly to the beasts. The stench of Them is absolutely vile. I've only come this close to one of Them one other time, and I don't remember the hounds smelling so badly.

But we were just children then. Perhaps I've forgotten. My heart races as we wait. The one in the lead is missing one of its six glowing eyes, a massive scar slashed across its face. It sniffs the air, almost delicate in its grace, its skull pulsing with the same glowing fire as its eyes, suddenly visible through the fur on its face.

It keeps its terrible jaw shut, letting out a huff—smoke billowing from its mouth. Caden and I both freeze, watching, waiting. I've read about this, but never thought I'd see it. The smoke sinks to the floor, taking on a life of its own, almost as though it's got a mind—a sentience. The hounds watch it undulate before shooting forward, into the back hall.

They let out an unearthly bay, a call to something primal, something deeper, and rush after the seeking smoke. Toward the basement door. *Toward Alice.* Caden and I spring into action as the hounds lope forward, following the smoke.

In a moment that shocks me, They bypass the basement entirely, headed straight for Caden's bedroom. A ruckus breaks out as They tear the room apart. I frown, not understanding until I hear more wood splintering.

My brother's behind me, but I hold out a hand to him, signaling for him to get back. "Protect Alice," I hiss, moving as stealthily as I can.

The beasts aren't behaving as They should. If They were tracking Alice, They'd be barreling against the basement door about now. Instead, the hounds are tearing Cade's room apart. *But why?*

I step forward, making my footfalls as light as I possibly can, keeping back as far as I can and still see what They're up to. They've destroyed Cade's bed and are tearing at the floorboards. The room is filled with the stench of not just sulfur, but rotting flesh. And then I see it: a flash of red.

Before I can get my eyes on it completely, one of the

hounds has it in its mouth. The scene is chaotic as the hellhounds home in on Their prey. The putrid scent of death and sulfur fills the air as the wet sounds of death crowd out any other noise. The hounds move with a speed I cannot easily track now, and I understand what little chance we ever had against Them.

Even with Blackstone's gun, there was no stopping these beasts. The one missing an eye stops and turns toward me, gore dripping out of its maw. Inside my head, a rough voice I can hardly understand says one word: *Powrie.*

Redcaps. There are redcaps hiding under Caden's house. It all makes sense. His bedroom was once a screened-in sleeping porch, back when this place was someone's summer house. It's the only part of the house not built over the basement.

The hellhound's head snaps back around as one of the horrific little creatures pops its head up, trying to escape. I take aim, but I needn't have. The hellhound has it snapped between its jaws before I can shoot.

They came for the redcaps, not Alice. But why? It hardly makes sense. Why would the creatures go after Their own kind? The Hunt has always been a bit of a mystery to us, but maybe I was wrong to dismiss Cade's theories.

I'll have to chew on that later. I can see with my own two eyes that They've nearly cleaned the redcaps out. There's no telling what will happen next, but I don't want Them going back through the house, back by Caden and the basement door.

I slip out into the hallway, leaving Blackstone's gun on the kitchen table as I move faster out the back door and around to the French doors on the porch. I yank the doors open and step aside, calling out, "Feel free to exit here, kind sirs."

Through the side-panel windows that flank the doors, Caden appears in the doorway. He whines softly at the sight of his bedroom. That same rough voice blasts through my mind, making my ears feel like they're bleeding. I realize it's not the voice I don't quite understand; it's the language. I can just make it out, but barely. *If you will not lead a pack, Caden Hayes, join the Hunt.*

Caden does something I don't predict: he bows to the hounds' leader, the one with the missing eye, dipping his great, furry head low. And then I hear Cade's voice clear as day in my head, though he too speaks Their language. *My duties are here.*

The three hounds stare at him, then at the open doorway. Tense silence fills the space between us, and I wonder if it was a mistake to leave the gun in the kitchen. But then They're gone, disappearing in a whiff of smoke, the smell of sulfur and ash the only thing left behind.

Caden whines at the destroyed floor as I make my way back across the bedroom. I can't make heads or tails of what just happened, but I want Alice to stay in the basement 'til I'm sure They're not coming back. I can't just leave her worrying, though.

I open the basement door and call down, "They're gone, but you stay there for a spell while I take stock of things."

Alice hums some sort of answer that sounds vaguely noncommittal, but I need to move quickly. I leave Caden staring at his destroyed bedroom, still in wolf form, and take off to check the perimeter. There's not a warding or sigil on this earth that would keep one of the High or Their minions out, but the redcaps shouldn't have been able to get in.

The place where the ward was broken is obvious. There's a trail of bright green moss spreading from the forest toward the windows of Caden's house, and using my tiny bit of the Sight, I can see where the wards were disturbed enough to let the redcaps through.

Wards and sigils are funny things. They work alright enough with the malevolents, but they're less useful for keeping things like pixies or other forest neighbors out sometimes. Still, Willa Proctor's wards were the best I'd seen. They should've held.

I shake my head as I turn back to the cottage. Too many strange things are happening in Blackbird Hollow for my liking. As I approach the house, my heart stops. Through the open French doors, I watch Alice walk into Cade's bedroom. My heart thumps, three wholly terrified beats of my caged beast of a heart.

Why can't that damn woman do as she's agreed? Too brave for her own good, and now all the good luck of the past ten minutes might be swept away in the heat of a bad moment. Every muscle in my body is ready to spring. Ready to throw myself between my brother and this slip of a woman I just met.

Caden turns swiftly, scenting her, and I don't know whether to stay still or run toward them. But my little brother's glowing eyes are soft as he tucks his huge head under her right hand reassuringly. Caden not only instinctively recognizes that Alice isn't an enemy—he *knows* her.

Her eyes meet mine, and a small smile banishes all desire to scream at her to get back. "We're good," she whispers, and though her voice is soft under the sounds of the forest coming back to life, I hear Alice Blythe loud and clear.

We're good. *We are.*

Chapter 17
Alice

If someone told me just a few days ago that I'd be standing in the splintered ruins of a bedroom, petting a goddamn werewolf and trying not to get choked up about everything that just happened in the past hour or so, I would've laughed.

Laughed, and then, beneath the nonchalance and aloofness I've so often worn as a guise, I would've *hoped.* I would've hoped wildly and unreasonably for it all to be true. I blink away tears and let out a long, shuddering breath, gently patting wolf-Caden's enormous head. Wyatt's gone from looking at me like I just stepped on a grenade to gazing at me like—

No. I won't go there. I won't read into the expression on his face. I won't tumble into those dark, fathomless eyes. Because if I don't get my hopes up, then I won't get hurt.

"Can he change back?" I ask, instead of voicing all the messy, half-formed things rattling inside my head.

"Nope," Wyatt says with a shake of his head, navigating over the destroyed floors with ease. "Not 'til after the full moon. But this is the calmest he's ever been with the change." He pauses, glancing down to meet Caden's eyes. "Sorry. Not tryin' to talk about you like you're not in the room."

Caden lets out a dramatic huff and turns away, his claws clicking as he pads down the hallway, apparently dismissing us.

"You alright?" Wyatt asks. I startle, not realizing he'd come to stand at my side. When I look over at him, his eyes are narrowed with deep concern. For *me*. My stomach flutters.

"Fine," I reply, not trusting myself to say more. Instead, I glance out the window, where the forest is waking up from its unnaturally quiet nap. A fox trots across Caden's yard, and the afternoon is brighter now, that strange mist and unnatural dimness lifting as though it had never been there at all.

As if Wyatt hadn't locked me away in the basement with a wild look in his eyes. As if this man I barely know hadn't seemed ready to fucking die for me, if that's what it took.

I draw in a shuddering, uneven inhale. "Does your brother drink?"

He takes half a step back, brow creased in confusion. "I mean, not during the change," he tells me. "Probably not the best idea."

Laughter overtakes me, drawing the remaining tension out of my body. "No," I laugh. "Sorry. I mean that *I* could use a drink. Do you think he's got anything here he wouldn't mind sharing?"

"Oh," Wyatt says, his eyes lighting up. "Sure does. More local brews and fancy IPAs than a single man or wolf could ever drink. I'm sure he won't mind if we borrow one or two."

And that's how we end up in Caden's backyard. The youngest Hayes sibling's cottage sits at the top of a gentle hill. The back patio's situated at its crest, the yard sloping away from the cottage until mossy, light-dappled ground gives way to the thicket, then the woods. He's got those old-timey lights strung up on the trees ringing the little patio area and an assortment of battered, mismatched outdoor furniture. I sink into a chaise lounge with faded cushions that feature flamingos drinking margaritas, which is the kind of energy I probably need after all that excitement and, you know, mortal danger.

Wyatt collapses into the plastic Adirondack at my side, and Caden curls up on the stone patio in the sun. I wonder if he and Fern ever play when he's in the change. I wonder if that's a weird thing to ask.

"What's proper werewolf etiquette?" I ask as Wyatt hands me some locally brewed concoction with an illustrated label featuring a jack-o'-lantern ringed by pixies. "Like, it's still *him*, right? He's not reverted to some kind of...dog-like intelligence level?"

Caden raises his head from the sun-warmed patio and shakes his head at me, which answers that question. "Still him," Wyatt tells me after taking a very, very long pull of his beer—nearly a chug, if I'm honest, though I can't exactly fault him. "But the change is hard at first. So much wolf, so little human. It takes time to level out. It's why I was worried. Your scent is new to him, and I didn't know how he'd react."

Wolf-Caden quite literally grumbles in response, standing and stretching just to curl back up, this time facing away from us like a surly cat. I find myself smiling. I don't know what it is precisely with the Hayes kids, but I just...instantly like all of them. And I very rarely instantly like people. Even less do people like me in return. But I feel as if we're all the weird little puzzle pieces that got lost underneath the rug, and somehow we just *fit* together. It's too absurd to say aloud, so I don't, but the feeling thrums pleasantly in my throat.

I look back at Wyatt to find his brow furrowed as he chews on the inside of his cheek. "You okay?" I ask, reaching over and placing my hand on his forearm without thinking. It feels so good. So natural. In the bright autumn sunshine, there's no doubt in my mind that he blushes, which makes my stomach flip in turn.

"There's just..." He presses his lips together and drags a hand through his hair. "Look, we hedgeriders never presume to know everything. Our traditions are good, and we make sure to pass down as much info as we can. But the Wild Hunt? That's High Court shit. It's not something we usually deal with, so we don't know as much about it." He pauses again, meeting my gaze. "I have no idea why They went after the redcaps like that. I've never seen 'em go after Their own."

On the other side of the patio, Caden raises his head to yip —what I take as agreement. "Huh," I say, turning the information over in my head. "I mean, you're the experts. The Fe— *Them* existing has all been theory to me for a while."

Wyatt raises an eyebrow at me. "But?" he asks, like he can read me that easily, which makes me flush.

"But," I say, setting down my beer because I know I'm about to start talking with my hands, and I've found it's best not to have a beverage in them when that's happening. "Let's think about it. In folklore, the Wild Hunt is often a harbinger of bad shit, or associated with dead souls. Okay. But what else? In Welsh folklore, there's this idea that Gwyn ap Nudd, Their leader, helps keep imprisoned demons from harming humans."

Wyatt abandons his beer, too, his eyes bright as he follows my theory. I can see the thoughts flickering in his gaze, but he waits until I'm done to speak. "What if the Hunt's actually got a function?" he says, his voice rising with excitement. "Beyond just doing fucked-up shit for fun. Because, if I'm honest, that's what a lot of Them do here."

"It would be unwise to anthropomorphize Them," I say, leaning on the edge of my flamingo-patterned chair. "But that doesn't mean the Hunt isn't doing *something*. Sure, there's the kidnapping and the death and blood. You know, the fun stuff.

But what if They're more like the Gwyn ap Nudd myth?" I twist at the waist, gesturing back toward the house and the utterly ravaged bedroom. "What if the hellhounds came to take care of the redcap infestation? Like, if the redcaps somehow infringed on some rule or law. I mean, Fallon said They don't usually come this close to town, do They?"

My voice is growing louder and louder, and I know my face is probably getting red, the same way it always does when I feel like I've unraveled something. But Wyatt just looks over at me with utter concentration, as if the things I'm saying are completely worthy of his time—even though he's the hedgerider, and he's been doing this his whole damn life.

"We gotta talk to someone who knows more than us," he says, steepling his fingers. Then his gaze slips to his brother, and his expression falls. "But Cade's the one who normally sets up our liaisons with experts. He handles all that, the chat rooms and message boards."

Disappointment echoes through me as I lean back into my seat. Sure, I know a few message boards, but with my six-month absence, I'm not getting anybody to agree to meet. "Which means," I huff, "we're gonna have to wait 'til after the full moon."

Caden glances over and throws his head back, mocking us with a deeply mournful howl. Wyatt snatches some acorns off the ground, tossing them at his brother, but he's laughing the whole time. And, I realize with a deep feeling of contentment, so am I.

By the time I email my parents and we use our opposable thumbs—which Caden currently lacks—to clean up the bedroom as best as we possibly can, dusk has begun to darken the horizon. A chill climbs up my spine as I slide into the passenger seat of Wyatt's truck, but I'm perfectly cozy. I've got my hands stuffed into the corduroy-lined pockets of my coat, and the smell of the truck's cabin is familiar, comforting—sun-warmed leather, damp soil, pine trees.

"I would've happily stayed and done more," I tell Wyatt as he climbs into the driver's seat.

"I know," he replies, flashing me a smile. He puts the truck into reverse and backs out of the driveway, gravel crunching beneath the tires. "But with the moonrise, Cade was getting more uncomfortable. More unpredictable. It's for the best that we headed out, even though he was incredible today."

"So were you," I say before I can stop myself.

He turns to look at me as we reach the end of the driveway, the truck idling on the dirt road. "Weren't too bad yourself," he breathes, his muscular forearm flexing as he grips the wheel tighter.

"Minus the puking," I reply, because god forbid I be normal and cool. But Wyatt just chuckles, shaking his head as he shifts the truck into drive.

"I nearly passed out the first time I dealt with a redcap," he tells me, flipping down his visor as we drive into the setting sun. "The smell is what gets you. And you, darlin', got hit with a double whammy: hellhound *and* redcap."

We're talking about something undeniably disgusting, but Wyatt Hayes just called me "darlin'," and that seems to be all my mind is capable of processing. I manage to get out some half-assed response and then launch into a completely unnecessary story about when an undergrad student forgot to put a specimen back in the big freezers, and I arrived at the lab on a sweltering May morning to what I christened "stench-ageddon." I wonder if the rest of the department still calls it that, still tells stories about it, even though they fucking abandoned me.

I swallow hard, directing my mind back to the present, and as we amble down the hill toward Wyatt's house, a thought strikes me. "What if it's not the hellhounds taking the hikers, then?" I ask.

He frowns, considering it. "We don't have much else in this neck of the woods that would be snatching people without a trace," he says. I like the way he doesn't immediately dismiss my idea, just makes me aware of the contradictory evidence.

"Redcaps would leave a crime scene, I'm guessing?" I ask.

"Sure would," he drawls slowly, like he's lost in thought. "Worse than the hellhound did today."

I nod, my mind racing, and turn to look out the window. I catch a view of Blackbird Hollow's main drag at the bottom of the hills, lights twinkling like fireflies.

My heart swells with a fierce kind of nostalgia for my grandparents' farm. Hell, I even feel it for that musty little apartment we lived in afterward. We stayed because all the predictions said the entire town would be underwater with just one more big storm, and that made it cheap as hell. Besides, my mom worked at the post office and my dad was the foreman at the only factory in town. Where else were we supposed to go after losing so much? Everything had already fallen apart, and that village by the river was the only place my parents had found where people were trying to put things back together.

Tears cloud my eyes, which is so stupid, but—god, I wish we had found Blackbird Hollow back then. After the last of the Catastrophes swept through, and like nearly everybody else, we had nothing but the clothes on our backs. I wish we'd walked a little farther. Tried a little harder. Spared a thought about the hills to our north, the rolling fields and green orchards. Everybody said these places were dangerous, rough, and that it was better to stay closer to the big cities.

But as we pull up to Fallon's driveway, the rambling antique house lit from the inside, impossibly cozy against the surrounding dark, I can't imagine anything further from the truth.

"I've never felt this safe in my entire life," I find myself saying, pressing my forehead against the cool window. "You'd think that wouldn't be the case, with the hellhounds and the redcaps. But I do. I've never felt as safe as I do in Blackbird Hollow."

I hear his sharp intake of breath from the other side of the cab, and it should probably make me reconsider, but I don't.

"With *you*, Wyatt."

Like a child, I squeeze my eyes shut, hoping I didn't just absolutely ruin everything. When I hear his door open and then close, my heart shatters a little. It would've shattered a hell of a lot more had my own door not been pulled open.

Framed by the last rays of the setting sun, Wyatt stands there, his chest rising and falling rapidly as he devours me with his gaze. "Guess we're throwing caution to the wind, then," he breathes. "I like it."

And then his hands are in my hair, his thumb stroking my jaw. For once in my life, I don't think, I don't anticipate, I don't analyze. I just follow the light, the warmth, reaching for him with both hands just before his mouth crashes into mine.

Chapter 18
Wyatt

Alice Blythe tastes like forgotten memories and hope. She feels like a crackling fire after a snowball fight, and a steaming bath after a long day in the woods. Her arms wind around my neck as she slides out of the truck, her body fit tight against mine. My heart races past my mind, which is screaming for me to slow down.

Just as Alice makes the sweetest sound I've ever heard, the screen door slams, and puppy footfalls have us jumping apart. When my head snaps back to look for Fallon, she's nowhere in sight, but I can hear her cackling in the house.

A low laugh rumbles through me, reminding me that I've still got Alice clasped tight to my chest. She sighs, and I want to know everything about the nuance of her breath. Is that a happy noise? A wistful one?

Fern pushes her nose into Alice's hand, giving her the biggest doggy smile as she sits on my foot. It's clear she approves of me kissing Alice, and from the sound of laughter in the house, Fallon does too.

As I draw back a touch, I see Alice's eyes have gone wide

and stunned, and I wonder if I got all my signals crossed. What if she meant that she felt safe with me like a big brother?

I take half a step back from her, just to give her a little breathing room. But I'm no chickenshit with lovers. One deep breath, and I ask her outright. "Did I read that wrong? Should I not have kissed you?"

Slowly, her head tilts up, and those big hazel eyes of hers blink twice. She has uncommonly long lashes, and the pink flush in her cheeks makes her prettier than I thought possible. Not that I've been thinking about how pretty she is every minute of the day since I met her.

"No," she says, then seems to realize I asked her two questions. "I mean yes."

She's either completely blown away by my kissing skills, or she's trying to figure out how to file a sexual harassment claim with Hedgerider HR, which we absolutely do not have.

"I'm gonna need you to be a touch more specific," I whisper, not wanting my eavesdropping big sister to hear us.

Alice nods but still doesn't answer. She just bites that bottom lip, her eyes narrowing a bit.

I take a deep breath and another step back. My heart's got to racing in a way that signals anxiety rather than excitement. I need her to say something or to go for a very long run.

Her hand shoots out, and she grabs my hand before I can take another step backward. "No, you did not read that wrong. Yes, I wanted you to kiss me. And..." Alice pauses, staring at our shoes and Fern, whose tail thumps powerfully on the crushed gravel of the driveway. "I think I'd like you to do it again sometime soon."

She's so damn adorable, I can't help but laugh. I squeeze her hand. "That can be arranged."

"Thank you," she says as she lets go—somewhat reluctantly,

I notice. Then she grimaces. "You're going to give me shit later for thanking you, aren't you?"

I throw my arm around her shoulders and press a kiss to the top of her head. She smells incredible, but I can't let myself think too far ahead just yet. "Damn right I will, Blythe."

Alice leans against me a little as we head up the front walk. Fallon saunters out with three crystal glasses and a bottle of the good whiskey, grinning, pushing the screen door with her hip. She sets her supplies down with a flourish on the bent willow table that matches the couches on the covered porch.

"Thought we might celebrate the momentous occasion of my brother getting the first tiny bit of action he's seen in, what, five years?" Fallon smiles, and it's all jokes, but the sparkle in her eyes tells me it's good fun. She likes Alice.

"Five years?" Alice murmurs as she takes the glass Fallon offers her. "That *is* quite a while to go without any action."

I plop down on the chair opposite the bent willow couch and grab my own glass of whiskey, shaking my head. I'm trying not to think too hard about when the last time she kissed somebody might be, or if she's still carrying a torch for someone.

The only thing to do with women like this is to give as good as I get and be gracious about the fact that they'll win every time. "Let it be known that I declared right here and now that, if given the chance, the two of you will make each other worse from here to eternity."

My sister grins as she drags Alice down on the couch next to her, spreading the quilt she keeps out here over the two of them. "Your concerns have been noted."

Fern sticks her head under their blanket, and there's a commotion of coaxing her up between them. When the three of them are squished in together and have stopped cackling like a band of wild hyenas, I lean forward and set my drained glass down on the table.

"We might want to order a pizza," I muse. Fallon raises an eyebrow at me. She doesn't order the pizza; I do. "Which, of course, *I* will do. But Blythe and I have had quite the afternoon we need to tell you about."

"Better get extra cheese then," Fallon chirps. "And Alice can give me the broad strokes of what happened."

I nod, slapping my thighs with my hands before pushing out of the chair. "Any other requests?" I lock eyes with Alice. "We typically get sausage—they do the crispy kind at the Slice o' Heaven, with mushrooms and grilled onions."

Alice shakes her head. "That sounds good."

As I open the screen door, Fallon calls to me, "Wanda dropped off a bag of barbecue potato chips she whipped up in the cauldron this afternoon. Bring those out." Before I can respond, she adds, "Maybe some beer? One of those real hoppy IPAs Cade left here."

I nod, and as I kick my boots off by the front door, I hear Alice ask, "Now, does she clean the cauldron before making the potato chips, or are there...like...spell remnants in it that make the chips better than any I've ever had?"

Fallon responds without missing a beat. "The latter. Obviously. Wanda's a witch."

"Obviously," Alice replies as I stand there listening like a weirdo.

When the two of them giggle like they're sixteen, I head for the phone. A hollow ache in my chest slows me down. If Alice decides to leave Blackbird Hollow when all this is over, I'm gonna get hurt.

But Fallon wasn't kidding about it being five years. After the last disaster in my romantic life ended, I swore off lovers for a while. But Alice could never be *just* a lover. I've known her for five whole minutes and I already know that. When she leaves—if she leaves—I'll break.

I don't have to know her for a week, a month, or even a year to know that. I knew it the moment she swept into the Stardust, the chill wind rustling behind her. Never would've believed in any sort of emotion past lust at first sight, but whatever this is, it's not just lust.

I don't think I can hold back my heart. It might not even be good to, at this point. I lean against the kitchen wall for a minute, listening to the soft sounds of the two women on the porch discussing redcaps and the High Courts. They talk in loops, feeding on each other's ideas, saying ridiculous things and laughing while they tease out their theories.

I like the way they talk to each other. The way I fit so easily into their dynamic. And Caden's gonna click with the vibe too, because Alice is already on our wavelength, like she's the missing thread we needed all along.

Whatever's blowing our way is bad. It always is with our line of work. But I can't think of a single wrong thing about Alice Blythe coming here. Even if she leaves, I can't imagine feeling different.

With that settled, I take a single deep breath and dial Slice o' Heaven.

An hour and a half later, and I've got a fire going, the three of us are stuffed full, and all's mostly well with the world. After we ate, Fallon brought out the distilled herbal concoction she makes every spring that drinks like a bottled meadow. It hasn't got a lick of alcohol in it, which means she wants to talk things through.

Now, she's lying on the fluffy old sheepskin rug we found in the garage the year we moved in, staring at the crown molding like she does when she's got an idea brewing. Alice and Fern are stretched out on the cracked leather chesterfield, like two peas in a pod, with Alice giving that spoiled wolfdog far too many belly rubs.

Cat appears out of nowhere and jumps into my lap as the fire pops. Fallon sits up to scratch the giant cat-sìth on the head, before wrapping her arms around her knees. "I've been puzzling out what we've seen of the Hunt over the years," she says, caution in her voice as she glances my way. "And I'm not sure I remember much that's useful to us. Just the stuff we've already talked about."

I nod. I know where this is going, but she's gotta say it.

Alice turns her head away from Fern to look between my sister and me. She feels it, then, the tension in the air. I can feel the question behind her teeth, just itching to get out: *What's going on?* But she doesn't ask. She just waits.

"What do *you* remember about the first time?" Fallon asks, her voice small and soft.

I blow out a breath, stroking Cat's back as he makes biscuits on my chest. He's immediately irritated with me and disappears, reappearing next to Fallon. "We really gonna do this tonight?"

Alice sits up a little, and to my surprise, Fern doesn't stir. She really does feel comfortable with Alice.

From the floor, Fallon nods, still staring at the ceiling. "We were living in California when our parents died, which is also the first time we came across the Hunt. Wyatt'll remember better than me...I wasn't myself at the time."

She swallows hard, but can't seem to manage more. Alice is alert, but quiet. I like the way she listens but doesn't throw out a bunch of preemptive platitudes. Alice is obviously deeply acquainted with sorrow, and she's better than saying empty shit to grieving folks.

"Am I alright to explain this to her?" I ask Fallon, keeping my voice gentle as I can.

It says a lot that she'd bring this up in front of Alice. I don't want to step on her toes, but I know how hard this is for her to talk about. Fallon nods, closing her eyes as Cat lies across her chest, purring loudly.

Alice sits up, pulling the cream afghan over her criss-cross applesauce legs. I can't think about Alice's legs, what they might look like bare in the summertime, stretched out over an inner tube on the lake.

I have to clear my throat to remind my blood to run someplace other than straight to my cock. I grew up with no question in my mind about respecting women, but the thoughts running through my mind since that kiss are anything but respectful. Another sharp breath, taken straight through my nose, helps me to refocus.

And my sister's face, eyes squeezed tight against the story of how we got here. Nothing kills a hard-on like remembering this shit. I take another drink of Fallon's herbal spirits, wishing they had just a bit more bite. But maybe it's best to tackle this tale straight-up.

I stare at the coffee table for a long time. It was one of the first things I made when I started working wood, and Fallon's cherished it ever since, piling it high with old art books she's gathered over the years and her favorite poetry. There's a dog-eared copy of Mary Oliver's *Devotions* that makes my teeth ache to look at.

Fallon may look like our Mama, but she's not a damn thing like her. Nothing has ever made me more conflicted than my gratitude that she's everything our mother could never be. Fallon actually loves us.

And that's why this story's so hard to tell.

"When Fallon and I were ten and eleven, and Cade was naught but a babe, our parents had settled for a spell in New Big Sur. There were kelpies there for the first time in centuries, and we stayed to help the locals figure out how to navigate Them. Then the phoukas moved in and people got confused between Them."

Fallon smiles from the floor, probably remembering how she and I spent hours telling the NBS Elementary kids about all the Fey horses they couldn't ride. It'd been a surprisingly infuriating conversation that led to talk of unicorns, which always gets Fallon pissy.

Alice leans forward to look at Fallon, and the movement's so tender that I almost have to stop to collect myself. She's intuited that this conversation's a sensitive one, and she cares. Best to rip the bandage off, then.

"Seemed like we were gonna stay there forever," I explain. "Maybe our parents got too comfortable, I'll never know. But we came home one day to the little house we'd rented for three years, and it seemed like every inch of it was covered in blood. Cade was in his crib, his jammies soaked through, but perfectly intact.

"Our parents were nowhere to be found, but there was a trail of blood, like they'd been dragged. I stayed with the baby, and Fallon went after them." I pause for a moment. Fallon's face has gone pale, but her eyes stay resolutely closed. "She didn't come back. It took me two days to get someone to watch Cade so I could go after her. Found her in the woods with them, practically catatonic. Best I could get out of her was that our mother was still alive when she found her."

This was the hard part to tell, because Fallon hated how bitter it made me. "She didn't bother to tell Fallon who'd attacked them. Just told her she'd fucked up coming home so late, and that she didn't get to be a little girl anymore. That she had to take care of us and teach us 'what little she knew.'"

That part was the worst, because I knew it wasn't an exaggeration. Our mother was always on Fallon's back, always making her feel like she'd never live up to the standards of a hedgerider matriarch.

"I had no idea what was in the woods, what could've killed our parents, or what might still be lingering. But the forest was far too quiet. As I got Fallon to her feet, the Hunt rolled through. What we do know about Them is that They mostly take folk on holy days for the Courts. Samhain, equinoxes, and the like."

Alice nods when I pause, her eyes sad as her gaze rests gently on my sister. It gives me the push I need to keep going. "So I wasn't afraid They'd take us, but I *was* afraid. Fallon wasn't there, not really. She was just...gone. I was afraid of what might happen if the Hunt saw her."

"Why?" Alice breathes when I can't continue right away.

I meet her eyes, trying to keep my heart in my chest rather than jumping to my throat. "Because once They've chosen someone, They never stop hunting them. And she was soft, vulnerable, and I didn't know much about the Hunt at the time."

From the floor, Fallon whispers, "You should've seen him. He puffed up his chest and yelled, 'You can't take this girl! She's my sister!'" She grins up at Alice, as though she can reassure her that this whole tale ends up just fine.

And I guess, to look around now, that's how it might seem. But I'll never forget the terror I felt as the hounds passed us by, the sound of Their baying as They caught the scent of Their quarry.

My heart stops. "It was April eighth, and the hounds were baying."

Fallon sits straight up, locking eyes with me. "Their wounds."

Alice slides forward on the couch, questions in her eyes.

"We've tried to match the wounds we saw for years, but nothing we know of has ever caused that kind of damage," I tell her, hoping to fill in the gaps Fallon and I just did.

Alice nods, her eyes thoughtful. "And April eighth isn't anywhere near one of Their holy days?"

"Right," Fallon assures her. "All the old-timers we've ever talked to have told us what we saw wasn't possible... That because of how I was—after—that we must've got it wrong."

She and Alice share a knowing look. They both understand what it's like to not be believed, and it's another brick in the wall of the sisterhood sprouting up between them.

My head shakes slowly, like I can't stop it. "The Hunt paid us no mind. They were after something else. It was like we weren't even there. All these years, I thought we got it wrong, Fallon."

My sister's eyes brighten. There's nothing she loves more than a lead. "This is it, Wyatt. I can feel it. We're gonna find out what happened to them." She turns to Alice, and the look that passes between them is solemn. "You got here right on time, Blythe. Almost like Fate has her hand on us."

Alice blushes deeply. "I'm not sure abou—"

"No," I interrupt. "Fallon's right. Shit's falling into place."

It's a selfish thing to say. I don't know that for sure. But I know Alice wants to belong somewhere, and I want her to decide it's here. It's too soon for me to want that, but I can't seem to keep my damn mouth shut. I should, but with her I'm reckless. That's something I'm gonna have to rein in if I want to keep her safe.

Chapter 19
Alice

I want with all my heart to belong here. I didn't know you could be homesick for a place that isn't your home and that you haven't even left—but that's the best way I can describe the feeling curled up beneath my breastbone, bitter and sweet.

Last night, after the fire died and Fallon fell asleep on the big sheepskin rug, Wyatt stepped out to check the wards around the house. I sat there, Fern's giant head on my lap in the lamplit gloom, and tried to imagine going back to the city. Back to OrthCon and my studies. Back to Amir's internet café or my shitty apartment that's probably Sector-bugged to hell and back.

And I just couldn't do it. I've watched a hellhound tear a redcap apart. I've seen a real-life werewolf. I've been mocked by pixies and accepted by the wolfdog curled up next to me. I've been befriended by Fallon Hayes, the badass hedgerider matriarch who's been through some serious shit—and, as such, doesn't *take* any goddamn shit.

And, of course, I've been kissed by Wyatt Hayes. He tasted like bonfires by the river and the hot cider my grandmother used to make every autumn. It's been a while since I've kissed anyone, but I know for a fact it's never felt anything like *that* before. And I know that I've never even dared to dream of a romance with someone like him—stupidly hot, yeah, but also kind and thoughtful and so fucking brave. I only met him a few days ago, but somehow he already knows more about me than most of my friends back at the university. How do I walk away from that?

I let out a long breath and reach through the shafts of early morning sunlight to trail my fingers along the spines of the books in Fallon's library. The Hayes' library, technically—a collection of every single piece of family hedgerider lore, records, and information that dates back at least a hundred years. It's unprecedented in most academic fields given the Catastrophes; nearly everything that wasn't digitized is lost to us.

There's plenty of empty shelves in the library, which I was delighted to discover resides in the turret I've admired every time we've pulled up the driveway. Two kids can only carry so much, after all. The original collection they brought from that cottage in New Big Sur only fills about a shelf—no more than twenty-five books. But they've added so much in the time they've been here, and for some reason, that makes my heart swell with pride.

"One hot coffee," Wyatt announces, startling me out of my reverie as he strides through the antique French doors. He's holding two steaming mugs, dressed in his usual jeans and flannel button-down. I try to drag my gaze away from his broad shoulders and the curve of his mouth. I remind myself that Fallon showed me the library—just past the big formal dining room—so I could put my degrees to use. *Not* so I could make out with her brother.

I'm really good at multitasking, though.

"Thanks," I say with a smile, reaching for the mug. He sets his down first on a low shelf, and then twists mine around so I can grab it by the handle—to protect me from the searing heat, I can't help but notice. Butterflies fill my stomach.

"Find anything interesting while I was gone?" he asks, meeting my gaze over the brim of his coffee mug.

"Everything in here is incredible," I tell him, and I absolutely mean it. I gesture to the leatherbound journal I set aside on the scuffed table tucked up against the bay window. "I found some mentions of the Chosen."

He flinches and then sets his jaw. "I don't think the Hunt's ever marked this many folks in the same spot," he says, reaching for his mug. There's shadows under his eyes I don't remember seeing before, and I don't think he shaved this morning. "What do you think the Chosen have to do with what's going on here?"

I shrug. "I'm not sure," I admit, twisting the sleeve of my sweater. "I guess I'm just trying to understand Them better. So if there's any accounts of observed, repeated behavior the Hunt's demonstrated, I'm interested."

He watches me carefully, and I want to say something—*anything* to alleviate the concern I can see weighing on him. But I can't find the words, or maybe I'm afraid, so I take a big gulp of my coffee and then spread my hands.

"In my extraterrestrial research," I begin, "abductions are obviously a commonly reported phenomenon. The thing is... alien abductees normally come *back*."

He nods grimly, taking a step toward me to lean against the bookshelf. "But the ones that get taken by the Hunt don't."

I nod, probably too aggressively, and wave my hands in the air. "And that's easy to explain away, right? When people do come back from their time fucking around in Faerie, or whatever, of course Sector's gonna get to them first and make up some story about aliens. When they don't come back, well...no body, no crime."

Wyatt narrows his eyes, which I can't help but notice glimmer like rain-damp river stones in the morning sunshine. "Where you going with this, Blythe?"

It's so stupid, but my heart clenches that we're back to Blythe and not Alice. Maybe it's just because we're brainstorming right now, and he likes a clean separation between hedgerider business and Wyatt business. I don't know. I'd like to know, though, if he'd let me.

"What makes the Hunt choose someone?" I ask.

He studies me like the answer is hidden in my messy, unbrushed waves or the depths of my eyes or, fuck, the inner workings of my soul. "I wish I knew," he replies, his voice hoarse, worn rough with sorrow.

A shriek cuts through the peaceful morning, and I jump, my heart leaping into my throat. I turn, following the sound, and find Fallon just outside the big bay windows that wrap around the turret.

"Fuck you, lesser celandine," she shouts, oblivious to us. Despite the cool morning, she's dressed in biker shorts, a giant t-shirt with holes, and that gorgeous sweater she clearly treasures. She stoops and begins to aggressively tear something small and green from the front beds.

I look back toward Wyatt, raising an eyebrow inquisitively.

"She uses gardening to get her rage out," he says with a sigh, but the twinkle's back in his eyes. "Sometimes it gets a little loud."

I let out a laugh, glancing through the window. Now armed with a spade, Fallon is down on her knees, stabbing the offending weed—they just look like buttercups to me, but I'm no gardener. The moment she digs up the roots, she flings the clump of soil and plant behind her with an impressive amount of fury. Fern trots around the yard, occasionally jumping into the air to snatch the weeds like a frisbee.

When I turn back, Wyatt's taken a seat at the table that reminds me of the alcoves in my favorite part of the university library. My heart pangs as I slide into the chair across from him, reaching to close the hedgerider journal I'd pulled.

"Okay," I say, steepling my fingers. "What else do you have on observed, repeated behaviors?"

He meets my gaze with a nod and then climbs back to his feet, moving toward the shelves. "Hey, you don't have to fetch it for me," I say, shooting up and following him.

"Just how I was raised," he mumbles, digging his knuckles into one eye as he scans the shelves.

"Wyatt," I say in a soft voice, reaching out to brush his forearm. "Are you okay?"

He glances over at me, finally meeting my gaze for more than a few seconds at a time. "Yeah," he replies with a forced smile. "Just tired."

I don't know what makes me say it, but the words are tumbling out before I can stop myself. "You don't have to answer this," I say, my fingers still curled around his soft, wash-worn flannel shirt sleeve, "but I need you to know that telling me about what happened in New Big Sur is a hard fucking thing. I have a feeling you think that trauma's all Fallon's. She was the one who found them. She's the one who heard your mom's last words."

Something breaks in Wyatt's expression, and I want to wrap my arms around him and hold him forever. Or just as long as he needs. As long as he wants me to. That'd be alright, too. I'm used to having an expiration date.

"But you're the witness, Wyatt," I continue, fighting back a lump of emotion in my throat. "You have to carry that memory for her. With her. You were both too young for any of that, and you don't have any less of a right to be fucked up by it just because Fallon was the one who went after them."

He tilts his head, examining me, giving me the saddest smile I've ever seen. Then his hand cups the side of my face, and he leans forward with a sigh, settling his forehead against mine. "Thank you, Alice," he breathes, his other arm wrapping around my waist.

"For what?" I whisper, those two syllables all I can manage to get out, my throat choked with tears.

"For being you," he replies. "And for being here." He pulls away slightly, his fingertips tracing my jaw with a whisper-light touch. I shiver, and I think maybe he would've kissed me if we weren't both distracted by a loud squeaking sound coming from outside.

I twist to look out the window and find Fallon pulling an ancient-looking wagon piled way too high with pumpkins. The wheels make a horrible noise against the stone-paved walkway that winds around the house. We both watch wordlessly as the front wheels hit a small bump, spilling at least ten little pumpkins onto the lawn.

Fallon, of course, screeches and then curses vividly. I laugh, because I can't not—it feels like a big, warm blanket wrapped around my shoulders. "You're so lucky you get to watch *The Fallon Show* whenever you want," I joke, looking back to find Wyatt pulling a few books from the shelves.

"Lucky is one word for it," he snorts, shooting me a sideways glance, one brow arched. He's already ridiculously handsome, but when he gives me that silly little smile, I feel like I'm going to melt right into the gorgeous old hardwood floor.

"I think I told you I'm an only child," I muse, taking the books he hands over to me.

"You did," he says. I'm sure he hears the words I'm not saying. But he doesn't push. Doesn't pry. He knows how heavy personal histories can get in this world, how uneasily those gory stories lie beneath their headstones.

But with Wyatt, I feel like I can safely dig mine up. I know he'll catch me before I tumble into an open grave.

He pulls one or two more books from the shelf and then turns to face me. I should go back to the table. I should dive into research. But I feel safe, just like I said last night, and if he was willing to tell me about his parents—about Fallon, about New Big Sur—then I want him to know this, too.

"I grew up southeast of here," I say, clutching the books tightly against my chest, their soft leather-and-paper smell like a security blanket. "My grandparents' farm. Not too far from the coast, but safely inland enough to not worry about flooding."

Wyatt watches me carefully. "Why don't we sit, Alice?" he asks. I blush, because I'm "Alice" again. "Feels like you're 'bout to tell me something that might be a little easier with a warm mug in your hands."

"Yeah." I nod, tucking an errant wave of hair behind my ear. "Yeah, okay." We pile the books in the center of the table, and then I slide into my chair. He pushes my mug closer to me, and I oblige with a choked laugh, wrapping my hands around the warm ceramic. It *does* help. I examine the mug's artwork—a faded, vintage-style ad for a resort town that's been underwater for a few years now.

"So you grew up southeast of here," he says gently. The sunlight streaming through the window gilds his dark hair like he's some knight in shining armor from an old story. Not that I need saving. But someone to ride into battle alongside? Absolutely. I'm tired of doing it alone.

"On my grandparents' farm," I say, looking down at my hands. "My mom had moved away, but when things got bad, she thought it made sense to go back. She'd just married my dad, and they were living together in one of the big Northeastern cities."

The ones that are just rubble now, I don't have to tell him. He knows. He's not interested in pretending the last fifty years didn't happen or rewriting them into something less awful. And, god, I didn't realize how much I needed that.

"The farm must've been so appealing," I continue. "Crops, fresh water, enough space and fresh air to ride out the pandemics." I pause, my fingers tightening around the mug. "For a while, it was good. I mean, as good as anything was gonna be."

He nods, all his attention on me, but it doesn't feel scary or judgmental. It's not even heavy. It's like my favorite sweater on a cool day, wrapping me up in soft warmth, keeping the cold and the dark at bay.

"I was born there," I say, looking up to meet his gaze. Memories flicker through my mind, and I almost smile. "Pretty fucking idyllic, honestly. Because my whole life was just the farm. I didn't really know what was out there, and the Fe—those of Them we had nearby were pretty tame, in hindsight."

I pull in a long, jagged breath. "But everything bad just kept spreading. I didn't realize how many nights my parents and grandparents were spending wide awake, always two of them on patrol at all times. They'd help anybody they could, of course, but as the years went by, less and less people wanted help, and more people just wanted to take whatever they could."

I don't need to explain that to Wyatt, either. He knows. Without a word, he reaches across the table and wraps his fingers around my wrist. Easy as that, just like he's settled right in between my ribs, somewhere near my heart.

"And the government, they...they didn't want to help. They *wanted* people to raid and loot. They wanted the excuse to crack down even further," I continue, squeezing my eyes shut. I've only told one old boyfriend this story, and honestly, I hope he's forgotten all about it. I don't want him to know me like that anymore. But I desperately want Wyatt to. So I open my eyes and meet his gaze, even though tears stream down my face. "We ended up being right in the middle of Zone 1."

His gaze widens, and then his jaw clamps down. "Christ, Alice."

I laugh, because I have to, raising my hand to roughly wipe away tears. "Yeah," I croak. "My grandpa was convinced the soldiers would let us stay if we just explained ourselves, if he showed them the deed and the photo albums, if he made them understand how long his family had worked that land. But of course they didn't. Whoever was in charge saw fertile land that was actually still producing crops, and the big creek on the property that hadn't dried up, and they decided to take it. My grandfather refused to hand it over, and one of the soldiers shot him."

I swallow down more tears, my hands shaking. I keep my eyes open, because if I close them, I'll see it, and I'd rather not. It's cruel that I can remember that moment so clearly, but not the barn kittens or what the apple trees smelled like or the taste of my grandma's strawberry-rhubarb jam.

"It was chaos after that," I continue, letting out a long, shaky exhale. "I don't know how my mom got us out, but she did. My grandma came with us, but she didn't make it to the town where we've been living. Just too heartbroken."

Wyatt says nothing, because he knows words don't mean shit against the weight of something like this. Instead, he gets up and comes to kneel beside my chair, and then wraps his arms around me. I bury my face into his flannel, the scent of woodsmoke and pine sap clinging to the fabric.

When I was a kid, I never understood my mom when she

told me that my grandmother was too heartbroken to keep going, keep walking for miles and miles to find somewhere safe. The grandmother I knew could manhandle the big, mean billy goat without breaking a sweat. She could pick apples for days and then hike all the way to the closest towns to make sure everybody had something to eat. It made no sense to me that someone so strong could just fade away over a broken heart.

As I press myself tighter to Wyatt, the memory of our kiss still on my lips, I'm terrified that I'm beginning to understand.

Chapter 20
Wyatt

After her story about her family's trip out of Zone 1, things between Alice and I settle into something comfortable for a few days. It's like she let a big breath out, and her shoulders came down from around her ears. I can feel myself pulling back a little, but I try not to let it show.

It worries me how fast this is all happening—whatever this is between me and her. It worries me, because I've seen what it's like when civilians get immersed in hedgerider life. It's fun at first for the ones who've always hoped there was a bit of magic in the world, but the longer time wears on, the more they understand: this shit never ends.

The Courts, the lesser Fey, the weird stuff that's harder to explain. It all just keeps on coming. And once it starts, once you see, it's hard to stop seeing. It follows you forever. And I have to wonder if Alice has thought of that. If that's what she wants.

On Sunday morning, I'm washing the dishes when Fallon announces we're out of coffee. This is a five-alarm emergency in our family, and I don't have any at home to go grab. Alice offers to drink tea, to which Fallon replies, "You drink tea if you want to, Blythe. I'm off to town for magic beans."

And then she grabs her keys, whistles to Fern, and poof, she's gone. It's remarkable how fast she can move when she's motivated. Alice and I are alone in the kitchen. I move about, making her the cup of tea she mentioned. It's hard to tell what might distract Fallon in town. With that thought, I double the leaves in the teapot. No reason for me to go without.

"Wyatt?" Alice asks from the table. "Is everything okay with us?"

"Sure," I say from behind the sink.

I peek out to see her frown. Girl's got a mean little frown, and I love it. That's the trouble right there; there are things about the way I feel about Alice Blythe that my mind's already calling love. But how am I supposed to say that without scaring the ever-living shit out of her?

As I set the kettle on to boil, I blow out a big breath. "I'm scared, Blythe. That's what's wrong."

"Scared?" she asks, like it's impossible that I'd ever be frightened. It puffs something up in me that she thinks of me that way, but it scares me, too. What if I disappoint her? "Of what?"

I can't quite look at her. "You. This." She's quiet. So damn quiet, I know she knows there's more, and she's waiting. I remind myself not to be a chickenshit about love and turn to face her. "I'll say it plain. I'm scared this will get old. That you'll stay for a few months and realize that hedgeriding never ends. That it's bloody work and people you love will die doing it. And then you'll leave."

She arches an eyebrow, but her breath comes even and slow. Alice is one cool cucumber when it counts. "Does something I've said or done make you think that's the kind of person I am?"

"No," I reply. "Not a bit. But you asked what's wrong, and I'm telling you what I'm scared of. I know the difference between fear and truth, but that doesn't mean I'm not scared of you leaving."

The words hang between us, but Alice doesn't look away. And then she smiles like sunshine. Like it's her birthday and I gave her the best gift at the party. I don't know what's happening, exactly, but I know Alice well enough to know that she wouldn't smile like that if she was gonna break my heart right here and now.

"And why," Alice asks, getting up from the kitchen table, "should it scare you that I might leave?"

She's standing so close to me now, looking up at me with those serious hazel eyes, that I could reach out and touch her. And I'm not one hundred percent sure, but I think she's coming on to me. "You know why, Blythe."

There's a cruel little smirk on her face when she shakes her head, and now I'm certain. Alice is about to change the game, and I'm here for it. "Nope. Not a clue." She seals her fate by tapping my chest as she says, "You're going to need to enlighten me."

"Oh," I breathe, new air filling my lungs. If Alice wants to play this way, I'll play. There's not many I'd be willing to tease like this with. In fact, she might be the one and only. "Do I?"

She nods, stepping closer. This little dance we're doing is a tricky one, but she's right. She hasn't once given me the impression she's the love 'em and leave 'em type. And it's not like she's *exactly* a civilian. She was getting a goddamn PhD in Extraterrestrial Biology, after all.

If she wants to be enlightened, I can do that for her. Maybe we both need a little reassurance of where we're at.

Before I can think another thought, I've got my hands around her waist and I'm boosting her up onto the kitchen counter, my hands sliding up her bare thighs. She makes a breathy little noise that tells me this is exactly what she was bargaining for when she got up from the table.

She presses her hands to my chest, pausing. "I want to see what's here. Between us, between me and this town, and what I can bring to the table with what's going on here. But I can't promise I won't leave someday, just like you can't promise you won't leave me. We're just not there yet."

I like her answer. It doesn't set up promises to break. It's real, and realistic. It's honest. "So, you wanna see what's between us, do you?"

She smacks my chest, and I nestle between her legs, dragging her against me hard enough that she can feel just exactly what's *between us* at the moment. Alice gasps, and her mouth is on mine in an instant, her hands in my hair, her back arching into me as she wraps her legs around my waist.

And then we're making out like teenagers left alone in the house for a hot second. I've got my hands up the back of her shirt, and she's not wearing a bra, which just about makes me lose control. I don't want to go too far too fast. Not with Alice.

But she's moaning in my mouth, her tongue dancing with mine as she deepens the kiss. I wind my hands through her waves, pulling the hair at the nape of her neck so I can trail kisses down the column of her throat, nipping at her when she whimpers, pulling her hips tighter against mine.

"Wyatt," she breathes in my ear as she tilts her hips into just the right spot that has to be giving her an accurate perception of how much I want her. "God, that feels good."

She's only wearing a tiny pair of boxer shorts under her giant t-shirt, and it would be so easy to slip my hand inside them. But I am determined not to fuck this up by doing too much too soon.

The kettle whistles, startling us both so much that we bang

heads. She screeches. I swear. I yank the kettle off the burner, and the two of us dissolve into laughter. Alice laughs harder as I return to my previous position, this time to hug her.

She wraps her legs around my waist again and smiles up at me, but there's something a little sad in her eyes. "I don't have anything to go back to, Wyatt. And I'm not saying that to obligate you in any way. If things don't work out here, I'll just figure something out."

I pull her a little closer, hating that she thinks I'd feel like she's a check on my to-do list. "You're not a chore. Whoever made you feel that way needs their kneecaps forcibly removed."

I gesture around the kitchen to the signs of her and Fallon coexisting not just peaceably, but amicably. There's books everywhere, scrunchies and hair claws, and I can't tell whose is whose, 'cause I've seen them both in all of them. There's a whole flock of wool sweaters and, frankly, too many shoes at the back door. There's notes with both their handwriting on the table, and some with mine, too.

"I don't know if you've noticed, but you've fit neatly into our life here pretty quick. Honestly, I think that's what's scared me."

She nods, wrapping her arms around my neck a little tighter. "It scares me a little bit, too. But after everything—" She chokes up a little, and I know she's thinking of the tales we've told these past few days. "After everything, I think we all deserve a little happiness."

"We do," I agree.

The sound of Fallon's Jeep coming up the gravel driveway has Alice laughing again. But we don't spring apart like kids caught at something. Alice tousles her hair a little, but she stays on the counter as I dump the dry tea leaves back into the canister. If there's gonna be coffee, we don't need the tea.

Alice slides down from the counter, on my wavelength without speaking, to fill the coffee pot with water. When Fallon walks back in with Fern and a bag of coffee, she tosses it to Alice, smacking her ass as she strides by. "Did you get in his pants while I was gone?"

"Just a little," Alice replies, snapping Fallon's bra strap as she passes her.

"I oughta pull your hair," my sister says with a grin.

I take the coffee from Alice as Fallon hugs her around the waist. "I like having you here, Blythe. There's too much testosterone around here. With you, me, and Fern, we've finally tipped the scales in the right direction."

Alice leans back against Fallon and grins at me. I grab the old Insta-Photo camera off the shelf above the bulletin board and snap a photo of them. We only have one package of the photo paper left, but I want to remember the two of them like this. Fern jumps up at the last second, and I'm pretty sure she's in the shot. It's all just fine. I've got a photo of my girls, and when it's done drying, it's going on the fridge with all the other family photos.

Caden shows up at six on the dot, with a case of beer, a cheesecake, and three loaves of freshly baked bread. He bows a little to Fallon as he deposits them on the kitchen counter, with a "Milady" for her. She pinches his cheek and tells him to get out of her kitchen.

It's only on Sunday dinners that Fallon insists on it being *her* kitchen, but that's well enough. My little brother has a hug for Alice, another for Fern, and then he looks at me and asks, "So, what do you need help with?"

I punch his arm, but I do have a job for him. "Wanna help me with the old chalkboard?"

"The one me and Fallon stole from the old schoolhouse?" he asks with a disbelieving laugh. "We still have that?"

Alice looks up from where she's been allowed to chop the lettuce for salad. "There's a story there."

"Have Fallon tell it to you while we get it out of the basement," I say, pulling on Caden's arm.

On the stairs, Caden grumbles good-naturedly. "What are you gonna do with it, anyway?" he asks.

"It's got a corkboard on the back, remember?" I say as we reach the bottom of the cellar stairs.

"Not really," Cade says, pulling the cord for the light on the ceiling.

"Alice is good with a pinboard. Figured we could use it for the investigation." Caden nods, but he's got an odd look on his face. "What's up?"

"Nothing," he answers.

I shake my head. "That's a something-face. Spit it out."

He sighs. "Look, this could mean a lot of things, and I've got a theory, so don't freak out."

I cross my arms over my chest. "That is not a good way to keep me from freaking out, but go on."

He rolls his eyes at me, and the kid could be ten, not twenty-five. "There's some Sector code attached to Alice's emails." He can tell I'm about to say something, because he just keeps going. "It's not like what I've seen attached to their internal stuff. It's something else." He pauses to take a quick breath before concluding, "Wyatt, they're tracking her."

My heart goes from beating wildly out of time to a slow, steady beat, before my blood pressure starts to rise. "Why are they tracking her?"

"That's not the question you need to be asking, bro."

"I hate it when you call me that."

Caden rolls his eyes again, and for half a second, I wish I thought slapping him might help things. "Fine—that's not the question you should be asking, Wyatt Hayes, Boss of Me."

"Cut the shit," I snap back.

"She emailed her parents from my house, Wyatt," Cade says, gripping my shoulder. "I've got my shit pretty locked down, but it's possible they know she's here. The truth is, we're not gonna know 'til they make a move. We need to know how they've tried to track her before."

I push Caden toward the heavy oak-framed chalkboard looming in the corner. "Grab your end, *little bro*. Alice is gonna want to put all this on her pinboard of doom."

Caden shakes his head and lifts the whole damn thing like it's nothing at all, then practically sprints up the stairs with it.

"Show-off," I call after him. Damn werewolf strength. But the kid's got a point. We need to know just exactly what Alice's history with the government is. With the Hunt moving in and Sector on our tail, the threats are coming in hot and fast.

"Always be prepared," I mutter on my way up the stairs, remembering the crap Mama used to say. "Or trouble will find you with your pants down."

The woman was wrong a whole hell of a lot, but when she was right, she was right.

Chapter 21
Alice

Fallon's telling me about the time seven-year-old Caden accidentally made a bargain with a lesser Fey, and somehow Wyatt weaseled out of it by stealing the corkboard from the old schoolhouse, which is situated on a site sacred to Them, and of course made Caden come along as penance. I'm so absorbed in the tale that I almost slice off my finger instead of chopping lettuce, but luckily I manage to finish prepping the salad without any bloodshed.

"Wait, Fallon," I say, laughing, dumping the lettuce into one of those old-fashioned salad spinners, "how the fuck did stealing a corkboard satisfy the deal?"

"Weren't you listening?" she demands, throwing her hands up in the air. Fallon is a terrible storyteller, but I'm sure as shit not going to tell her that. Not a single shred of her recounting was even in chronological order. She turns to face me, crossing her arms over her apron, a simple black garment with one line of text embroidered in white: "I'LL FEED ALL YOU FUCKERS."

"Yeah," I tell her delicately, beginning to spin the lettuce. "I *was* listening, but—"

My sentence is broken off by Caden's arrival in the room. He's holding one end of a massive vintage chalkboard and walking backward into the big, open kitchen. It's gotta weigh a ton, but he's carrying it with one hand, while Wyatt's gripping it for dear life on the other end.

"Don't even know why I'm helping you with this," he teases Caden as he sets his side down with a grunt. "Aw, fuck. It's facing the wrong way."

"I got you, Mr. Hayes," Caden says, his tone sarcastic, as he grasps the board and begins to turn it so the corkboard faces out. I should be focused on dinner preparations so Fallon doesn't go for my jugular, but the wide, beautiful expanse of empty cork draws me in like a riptide.

"You're such a nerd," Caden laughs, looking at me. "Lit up like a damn Solstice tree over a corkboard."

I giggle, popping the lid off the salad spinner. It feels good to be teased like I'm one of them. I have a strong feeling that if any member of the Hayes family is super nice and polite to you, it means they don't like you very much. But being ribbed on like this? Perfection.

"Before you fill it up with all those ideas in your terrifyingly massive and beautiful brain," Wyatt says, walking over to the counter, something serious weighing his tone, "we gotta talk."

I freeze, my heart climbing into my throat. I thought we'd ironed things out, more or less. Had Caden suggested things were moving too fast between us? Or that there just wasn't enough room in Blackbird Hollow's hedgerider unit for me? I swallow and push my racing thoughts away—no, he wouldn't bring up something like that in front of everyone, I don't think. And he sure as hell wouldn't have kissed me like *that* if he just intended to throw me to the curb.

"Okay," I say, abandoning the salad for now. Beside me at the stove, Fallon's paused her sautéing, peering over her shoulder at her brothers with a guarded curiosity and some degree of worry.

"When you emailed your parents," Caden says, settling down in one of the mismatched kitchen chairs and folding his hands on the table, "I found Sector code on your account."

I stare at him, my mouth parting but no sound coming out.

"Now, we don't think you're some traitor or spy, Alice," Wyatt says, and he means it. "I just wanna make that clear from the get-go."

Fallon snorts. "Of course she isn't." She says it fervently, like it's more a hope or a prayer than a statement. My heart clenches.

"Makes sense that Sector would keep an eye on someone like you," Caden says with a shrug. In the kitchen's lamplight, he looks so young, and yet he wears seriousness as easily as a high school jersey. "And I've got things pretty much handled, so hopefully that email won't blow your cover. But...I gotta know if they've made attempts to track you before."

"We need to understand your history with Sector a little better, Alice," Wyatt adds, his expression open, though his brows are furrowed. "And I'm sorry to be asking you about what might otherwise be private. It's just, if we wanna work together here—"

"Yeah, you need to know," I say with a nod. "Look, I'm really sorry about the email issues, Caden. I would've never asked to use your computer if I knew."

The youngest Hayes sibling shrugs, nonchalant. "Shit like this is bound to happen."

"I should've told you everything already," I say, guilt gnawing at me. I dig one hand into my hair, fingers curling into my scalp. "God, I'm sorry. I just got so wrapped up in everything. It's been such a whirlwind. It's like the rest of the world stopped existing."

Beside me, Fallon's gone back to sautéing without a care in the world. "Now, I know my brother didn't dick you down so good you forgot about the entire world, Blythe," she says.

I turn bright red and let out a sound that's somewhere between a stutter and a laugh.

"Fallon," Wyatt implores from where he's leaning on the kitchen island, his eyes fluttering closed as he steeples his hands. "I'm begging you. For just thirty seconds—"

"Mr. Rabbit!" I shout, clapping my hands to my mouth. All three Hayes siblings look at me like I've lost my mind. "I'll answer all your questions about when Sector and I crossed paths. But right before I came here, they bugged my apartment."

Wyatt's eyes widen in alarm as Fallon sucks in a deep breath, but Caden's cool as anything, just nodding along as I speak. I'm gesticulating wildly now, the lettuce long forgotten on the counter behind me. "I have this stuffed rabbit from when I was a kid," I explain. "They put some kind of a listening device on his eye."

"And where is Mr. Rabbit now?" Caden asks, one brow arching.

Wordlessly, I raise one hand and point upstairs, where he's perched on Wyatt's old nightstand. In the bedroom where I've been sleeping for more than a week now—the one that's already begun to feel more like home than the apartment I leased for a year.

The one I might have dangerously jeopardized because of my admittedly intense-ass crush on Wyatt Hayes. *Fuck.* I should've thought to have someone else check over all my stuff before I even came into the house.

"Alice," Fallon says, clicking off the stove and setting the pan off to the side. "Go get Mr. Rabbit."

"Yes, ma'am," I say with a nod, fleeing the kitchen for the stairs.

A few minutes later, I'm tearing around the corner, my socks nearly slipping on the worn hardwood floor. Mr. Rabbit is clutched to my chest as I reenter the kitchen to find all three of them gathered around the table. The chairs are pushed to the side. A pair of scissors, a needle, sewing thread, and a pocketknife are lined up with military-like precision at one end. Wyatt's dragging one of the big old floor lamps toward the table, as far as the cord will stretch.

"Oh, no," I whisper defensively, wrapping my arms around the plush toy. "I already had to gouge out his eye. You wanna *cut him open?*"

Wyatt switches the lamp onto a brighter setting as Caden snaps on a pair of latex gloves. "We're gonna take good care of him, I promise," Wyatt tells me as he approaches, holding his hands out. "And anything we gotta do, we'll fix him. I swear we will."

I'm caught between laughter and tears as I nod, handing Mr. Rabbit over to Wyatt. Gingerly, he places the plush on the table face-up. With a serious frown, Caden leans over Mr. Rabbit.

"Scalpel," he says. Wordlessly, Fallon hands him the pocketknife, which Caden snaps open. I shuffle closer to Wyatt, who immediately wraps his arms around me. When Caden brings the edge of the blade to Mr. Rabbit's rounded belly, I turn my head into Wyatt's chest. His large, warm hand cups the back of my head as his brother cuts open the last remaining piece of my childhood. I can't bear to watch Caden rifle around in Mr. Rabbit's stuffing, so instead I breathe in Wyatt's scent—clean laundry and fir trees with a dash of bonfire smoke.

"Abdomen is clear," Caden says. "Needle." I turn to look over my shoulder, though I'm covering most of my vision with my hands. Through my fingers, I can just make out Fallon threading a needle. She snaps the thread with her teeth and then ties the end into a knot before handing it to Caden.

"See?" Wyatt murmurs into my hair, one hand rubbing my back. "Gonna fix him right up."

I don't know why we've all collectively decided to make an absolute production out of this, but I appreciate it so much. If I cry about a stupid plushie, I know no one in this room would mock me for it, and if I burst into hysterical laughter, I have a feeling the three of them would follow me. I suck in a deep breath as Caden pierces Mr. Rabbit's soft little belly with the needle, deftly weaving the wound closed. His sewing is all tiny, fastidious stitches, his eyes narrowed in concentration.

"He was top of his class in sewing in home ec," Fallon tells me solemnly.

"Only the best for Mr. Rabbit," I say with a nod, leaning back against Wyatt as Caden finishes his stitches.

"Now for the cranial cavity," Caden says, looking up at me.

"Not the cranial cavity," I gasp, my eyes widening.

Caden winces. "You may not want to watch this," he says, tying off the thread and handing the needle back to Fallon. "Scalpel."

Then Mr. Rabbit is face-down on the big table, either end littered with notebooks and hair claws and coffee mugs, though the circle of light from the big lamp halos a section that's bare and empty, save for the stuffed animal. Caden takes the scalpel from Fallon and then steadies himself, taking a deep breath. The next moment, he's slicing into the back of Mr. Rabbit's head.

"Oh, no, I don't want to watch," I whisper, turning back into Wyatt. I let him hold me as Caden finishes up his exploratory surgery. What feels like ages later, Mr. Rabbit is given a clean bill of health—no bugs, though he's got more new scars than I want to acknowledge.

"I'll knit him a sweater," Wyatt promises as I take the plush back into my arms. "Then you won't be able to see any of the scars."

"Do you knit?" I sniff, shoving tears out of my eyes with the heel of my palm.

"Yes," Wyatt says at the same moment Fallon replies, "Poorly." They exchange glances over the kitchen table as Caden rolls his eyes, and I find myself breaking into laughter. Tears stream down my face, too, and I cuddle Mr. Rabbit against my neck, feeling silly and sad and utterly at home. Wyatt finds a way to tuck the stuffed animal into the neckline of my sweater so I can continue making dinner without putting him down. I chop vegetables for Fallon's lettuce as Caden minces more garlic for the roast chicken she's making, and then I tell the Hayes siblings all about my run-ins with Sector.

The blog, of course. The threats. The enrollment at Orth-Con. We're all standing around the kitchen island, beers in hand, as we wait for the chicken to finish roasting.

"So they've been interested in you for a while," Caden concludes.

"Seems that way," I say with a shrug.

"Ever approached you for recruitment?" Fallon wants to know, examining me.

I shake my head. "Nah," I say. "I think I'm probably too insane, even for them. It's always just been about keeping my nose clean."

Fallon nods, her gaze going toward the stuffed rabbit still tucked into the neckline of my sweater. "Sorry again. About Mr. Rabbit," she says softly.

I shrug. "We had to make sure. I don't want Sector interfering any more than you do."

I feel a little better now that Caden also went through the contents of my bag. The entire Hayes family knows what kind of underwear I wear, so I'm glad that's out of the way. Wyatt wants to check in with Marion tomorrow and see if anything sketchy happened with the room I was planning to stay in. "And if any of them bother you again," he adds, his expression suddenly a storm cloud, "you just let me know."

"Aw, you gonna defend your lady's honor?" Fallon teases from the oven, where she's bent double, checking the roast on the chicken.

A blush creeps across Wyatt's high cheekbones. "Something like that."

"If Sector fucks with Alice," Fallon says, her voice muffled, "they're fucking with all of us. Hope they damn well know that."

My eyes blur with tears for the second time today, which is too many. It's not that I'm, you know, not in touch with my feelings or whatever. It's just that things are really, really fucking hard. If I start to let myself feel too much, then I'm afraid *all* of it will come crashing down, like it did earlier when I told Wyatt about my grandparents' farm. I don't know how to let myself feel everything until we're living in some kind of utopia, which I doubt will happen in my lifetime. Otherwise, it's too hard to handle everything about this world *and* all the things I feel. I'll explode.

"Yes, they sure as hell are," Wyatt murmurs from behind me. One hand curls around my waist, and he speaks the words from the back of his throat in a way that makes my breath catch.

A golden silence descends on us as Fallon pulls the chicken from the stove. It smells wonderful, and the skin looks perfectly crispy, coated in all kinds of spices that make my stomach rumble.

"Oh," Caden says, perking up on the other side of the counter. "By the way. I've got it all arranged."

I look at him quizzically and can feel Wyatt doing the same. Caden waves a hand. "Sorry, sorry. I mean with learning more about the Hunt. Got you lined up with a professor over at the college."

"Good," Fallon says with a nod, pulling out a long carving knife from the block. "Wyatt and Alice, you two should go. Better cover that damn corkboard if it's gonna take up so much room in my kitchen."

I glance over at the empty board, just waiting to receive all my theories, no matter how insane or far-fetched.

And for the first time in my life, I won't be following this thread alone.

Chapter 22
Wyatt

Three days after Mr. Rabbit's surgery, and one short drive to Three Ravens College later, Alice and I are sitting in Professor Adelaide Waterhouse's office, waiting while she brews a pot of tea. Alice is reading the professor's notes, which are upside down to her view from across the desk.

Dr. Waterhouse is related to our Widow Harkness in some distant way—one of her ex-husbands' nieces, I believe—and was thus approved by the coven as a resource for our investigation. She'd only meet with us in person, so we made the drive. I was surprised to find that she wasn't a middle-aged scholar, but rather some sort of genuine academic prodigy. From the dates on the multiple degrees that have been shoved into a box on the small couch by the deep casement window, it looks like she's been out of school for at least three years.

By my reckoning, that makes the redhead witch who enters the office carrying a tray of tea supplies just about Caden's age. Her thick, round glasses are perched atop her head, her wavy copper hair sticking out every which way. She's got the shine that all witches have, that inexplicable sparkle of magic sticking to her like a burr on wool.

Much to Alice's obvious chagrin, she sets the tray down on the notes my girl was trying to read on the sly. "Fix your own tea," she mutters absently. "I don't know what you want in it."

Alice cocks her head to the side a little, arching an eyebrow, but she does as the professor asks. I don't actually want tea, so I stay put. The woman in question doesn't sit, instead pulling a wooden step stool from nowhere discernible, only to climb atop it and drag a series of black notebooks down from one of the top shelves of her built-in bookcases.

The shelves in question are stuffed full, and it takes me a moment to see the traces of magic on them. Nobody's getting anything out of there that she doesn't approve of. Adelaide Waterhouse is a tiny thing, height-wise, but voluptuous and fierce, with a sharp seriousness to her that feels familiar and alien at the same time. I wonder if I've run into her before somewhere.

Doesn't seem like she'd take teasing particularly well, but she's got that certain something that makes me think she'll help us if we approach this right. We won't be able to joke with her the way we do with Alice, but that's alright. It's good to know how to handle valuable contacts like her. I wonder why Caden didn't brief me better.

"Your brother says you're looking for information about the Hunt," the professor says, matter-of-factly. The way she says "your brother" makes me think he's been exasperating her. That's not much of a surprise. "And from what I can parse out, the lot of you are woefully misinformed."

She stares straight at me when she says this. Alice gives me a pointed look, a mean little smile on her face, like she's getting off a little on me being the one in the dark for once.

Dr. Waterhouse points a delicate—and slightly accusatory

—finger at Alice. "And *you*. You punched a Wallingford at OrthCon. Got yourself kicked out over it."

Alice startles at the professor's tone, and it takes all the willpower I've got in me not to snicker. The professor is quite severe, and I hope to all the gods in heaven and below that Caden never meets her in person, because she's whatever the wolf equivalent of catnip might be for him.

"Yes," Alice admits with one of her wicked smiles. "I did punch that fuckface Aston Wallingford, and I'd do it again."

The professor sits primly in her seat. "Good. Glad you got out of that ridiculous program. You should've come to our folklore program in the first place. I've spoken to the Chair about you; she's also my coven leader, and if you so desire, your application will be fast-tracked for spring."

Surprise lights Alice's face. "What?"

"LuvCroissants1212 and I are old friends," Dr. Waterhouse says, conspiratorially. Alice pales a little at the name but doesn't comment. One of her friends from the cooking blog, I surmise. "So, I've vetted you a bit. Also, I summoned your transcripts. You have potential. Let me know if you're interested."

Alice takes a deep, shuddering breath, all the sass gone out of her countenance, and I wonder what she's thinking.

But the good professor has already moved on. She taps her teacup lightly with a long, unpolished nail, pursing her lips slightly. "Now, you've been operating under the notion that the Hunt is some infernal device of the Courts to steal souls to amuse Them, yes? Running around willy-nilly kidnapping people."

Willy-nilly. I'm tucking that away for game night. I shrug. "Sure, along with all the maiming and killing and eating folk whole—that's about the size of it."

The professor shakes her head, pulling a notebook from her little stack. She pulls her glasses down onto her nose and flips the pages until she murmurs, "Here it is," and flips the open notebook around. There's a hand-drawn sketch of the region, vertical lines passing through various towns. One goes straight through Blackbird Hollow.

"These are ley lines. Once the Hunt roamed freely—Their purpose with the Courts was vague to us. There are stories, of course, that paint Them in a variety of lights. But there's really only one observable fact to pay attention to, in my opinion."

Alice leans forward, rapt in her attention. "Which is?"

"They travel the ley lines now, persistent and constant, practically relentless in what looks like an organized, gridded search to me, which is a stark departure from Their past behavior. In the past decade, either Their aims have changed, the world has—"

"Or it's a combination of the two," Alice breaks in. She leans back in the old Windsor chair, shaking her head. "Something about the world's changing, and so is the Hunt."

Dr. Waterhouse nods. "That's my feeling. Conditions have changed, and Their behavior *appears* to be less erratic, less random."

Alice crosses her arms in her lap, leaning forward again. "So what do *you* think the Hunt is doing? Off the record, of course. What's your unofficial hypothesis?"

It warms me to see Alice in her element like this, batting ideas about with an equal. I hope she'll take Dr. Waterhouse's offer and join the department here. Brick by brick, the shape of a new life for her forms in my mind, and I'm selfish enough to hope she sees my place in it. That she can stay in Blackbird Hollow and have some semblance of the life she was hoping for in the big city.

"My best guess?" The professor narrows her sky-blue eyes, steepling her fingers. "There's always been a pattern to it; we just didn't understand it. They're not wreaking havoc. They're on a mission. The only reason it's seemed random in the past is because whatever They were chasing was behaving erratically. And now? Well, the Hunt goes where its prey does." She stops abruptly, like she was going to say more but thought better of it.

Alice shakes her head. "Please say whatever it is you're thinking. We need to know as much as we can if They're coming through Blackbird Hollow."

"And They are," Dr. Waterhouse says, a definitive edge in her voice that sends a chill through me. "Think," she says quietly, tracing her finger up the ley line that goes through Blackbird Hollow and Three Ravens. "What does Blackbird Hollow—this whole area, really—have that other towns around here don't?"

Alice looks at me. She's out of her depth here, but I'm not. "Witches," I growl. "We've got more witches than any other county in the tri-state area." I follow the line of the professor's finger. "And more of Them. That's because of the ley lines, isn't it?"

Adelaide Waterhouse nods. "We're all attracted to these lines of power. The world used to be full of magic; the ley lines radiated it out, sending it in a reciprocal loop between Faerie and here. But they don't radiate anymore. They just pulse, so we go to the pulse, rather than letting magic come to us."

"And why do you think that is?" Alice asks.

Dr. Waterhouse takes another notebook from her stack, but she doesn't open it. She just holds it to her chest. "You ever just have a *feeling* about something, Miss Blythe? The evidence is all scattered, not adding up to much, but in your gut, you know a thing?"

Alice nods furiously. "Yes."

The professor nods back. "I thought so—"

She's about to say more, but there's a knock at the door. A raven-haired young person sticks their head in, their brown eyes worried. "Dr. Waterhouse, please come. Janice tried playing Metallica to the—*you know*—and something's gone *very* wrong."

Bluecap emergency, Dr. Waterhouse mouths to us as she stands, handing the notebook to Alice. "You can look my notes over, but this is probably going to take a bit." She pauses by the door. "Mr. Hayes, please tell your brother to come see me if he needs help finding relief from the pain after the change. I have ideas."

Before I can ask how she knows about Caden's condition, she's gone.

Alice's eyes go wide. "Are they doing *experiments* on Them here?" she whispers when the professor's footsteps in the hallway die off.

I shake my head. "Not likely. But some of Them, like bluecaps, are curious about witches and hedgeriders. They're attracted to our lineage, and if we're interested in Them, too... well... Odd collaborations do happen."

Alice nods, opening the black notebook the professor handed her carefully. She spends a few minutes glancing through it, shaking her head. "So no one really knows where the source of magic is?"

I shrug, not quite understanding where all this is leading, but I trust Alice. And if our coven trusts Dr. Waterhouse, I trust her too. I'm here to flesh out information that Alice doesn't have so she can use her big brain to puzzle all of this out. "Old timers used to assume it was Faerie itself. Caden could tell you the particulars of why that theory fell out of favor, but more recent experts like Dr. Waterhouse think maybe it comes from someplace between our realms."

Alice's head bends over the notebook, her mouth twisting up in concentration as she scans through the pages, turning back to previous sections occasionally, then skipping ahead as she nods—to herself or to the book, I'm not certain. "Waterhouse thinks there's a leak—leaks, plural—in wherever that place is. Wherever the energy we call magic comes from, she thinks it's bursting at the seams."

"Is that all?" I laugh, wry and frustrated. It's always something with this job. "What's that have to do with the Hunt?"

Alice shakes her head. "She doesn't say it here, but..." Her face scrunches up again. "We call Them the Hunt for a reason. What are They *hunting*?"

I lean back in my chair, staring at a fairly recent water stain on the professor's ceiling. That can't be good for the plaster. "Well, if Dr. Waterhouse is right, they're hunting witches, and some of Their own kind." I see the connections a little clearer now, but not much is certain. "Like the redcaps, and the way the hellhounds spoke to Caden."

Alice closes the notebook, placing it carefully back on Dr. Waterhouse's stack. She glances at the tea tray, and then the door. "Cover me, okay?"

She's gonna take a peek at those notes. That's probably a little rude, but this is an investigation, after all, not a social call. I nod, getting up to lean against the door. There's no warding on the top of the professor's desk to stop Alice from snooping.

"Stay out of her bottom left drawer," I caution as I cover the door. "She's got it spelled to set off the fire alarm if anyone other than her fusses with it."

Alice stares at me for a second. "You can see that?"

I nod. "Lots of hedgeriders have a touch of the Sight. Comes in handy."

She doesn't remark on that comment, but nods, lifting the tea tray. Her eyes move quickly over the pages of notes underneath, then she sets the tray back down in exactly the same spot it was in when she lifted it.

"She's doing some kind of ritual to honor the dead on

Halloween," Alice says, pulling a little notebook out of her pocket and jotting something down.

"You gonna join her?" I ask with a smile.

Alice smiles back at me. "Nope. That's not what I was interested in. She made a note in one of the margins—everything else is well organized. It's basically a recipe and a grocery list, all written in the same pen."

She lowers her voice to a volume barely above a whisper as she comes over to me, placing her hands on my chest and leaning in real close. "But on the bottom of that second page, she scribbled something down fast, in pencil."

She beams up at me, like I'm gonna give her a gold star. I tip her chin up with my fingers, snaking an arm around her waist to pull her against me. We've barely been alone since Sunday dinner, and while I could sneak into my old room at night, it doesn't feel like we're there quite yet. But here, alone in the professor's office? I'm not above a little hanky-panky.

But before I give her a gold star, I need to ask what she saw. "You gonna tell me what she wrote down or not?"

Alice's eyebrows go up in surprise, like she's already forgotten. "Oh, it says 'Silverwood Springs.' Ring any bells?"

"Not a one," I breathe, my voice going rough as she leans harder into me. I press my hand into the small of her back, feeling the soft curves of her long body melt into me.

She leaps up on her tiptoes to kiss me, her arms twining around my neck. Heat spreads through me, and I want her out of here, into the truck, where we can make out like feral teenagers. She moans in my mouth as my hand slides up under her sweater, meeting bare skin.

A little higher, and I get the treat of knowing that she's only wearing one of those silky little bralette things. I pull on the back of it, and she gasps, wrapping one leg around my thigh, tugging me between her legs as I pull her harder against me, deepening the kiss that's turned feverish and desperate in a matter of moments.

Footsteps in the hall have us jumping apart, both of us red in the face. But they pass and we both laugh, though I don't think either of us is quite ready to abandon the moment.

Alice checks her watch. "We told Fallon we'd be home in an hour. Do you think the professor is coming back?"

The way she says "home" is like a punch in the gut. I want her to stay so godsdamn bad, I fear I'll be ill if she goes. "No, probably not."

A little smile—one of those that I recognize means she wants to get into some kind of trouble—spreads over Alice's face. "Then by my count, we have at least a half-hour to fool around in the truck." In an instant, she's got her fingers wound through mine. "What do you say? Up for a little action in the truck?"

"Yes," I agree. "Fuck yes."

I open the door, and as we step into the hallway, the same student from before pops out of a room down the hall, covered in some kind of disgusting-smelling goo. "Mr. Hayes?" they shout. "They weren't bluecaps, and they're *angry*. Can you help?"

I glance down at Alice, shaking my head. "I'm gonna deal with this fast." My hand slides down to her ass as I bend toward her ear. "I promise not to come back covered in whatever that is."

"Stay horny," she whispers, grabbing my ass right back.

As if I had any other choice.

Chapter 23
Alice

With my temple resting against the truck's sun-warmed window, an alien feeling of contentment blooms in my chest. Though the day is chilly, the truck's been baking in the sun for almost an hour now, and the temperature inside is perfect. It's the kind of coziness that might've lulled me into drowsiness were I not so amped up about ten different things.

First, Dr. Waterhouse's theories. It felt good to toss around my thoughts with another academic, and it felt even better to have our theoretical knowledge backed up by Wyatt's real-life experience.

Second, her offer of a spot in the folklore doctorate program. I'd actually wanted to apply to Three Ravens right out of my undergraduate degree, but then Sector had shown up. My options were OrthCon or a black site. Or worse, maybe. I guess there are too many like-minded weirdos up here in Stonehaven County, and Sector wanted to keep me away from it all.

Third, and perhaps most pressing—at least judging by the

way I've got my legs crossed tight, my hands tucked under my thighs—is how feverishly Wyatt kissed me back in Dr. Waterhouse's office. He makes me feel like a teenager sneaking away from the bonfire to kiss my crush in the twilight gloom of the tree line. He makes me feel like I have some kind of purpose, some kind of a future, some kind of a life that consists of more than being underestimated and having to constantly beg people to consider that I might actually be onto something, not just batshit insane.

I press my forehead against the warm window and pull in a deep breath. I understand the things I'm thinking and feeling fall under the umbrella of what's commonly identified as love. This isn't infatuation—at least, I don't think. I wouldn't have been able to wait this long to sleep with him if that were the case. But I've been holding off, I guess, even though I really, *really* want to have sex with Wyatt Hayes. Of course I do.

But with him, it'll mean something. Like a declaration or an intention. A promise that I'm going to stay. Or that I want him to ask me to stay. I swallow hard, pulling my knees up to my chest, shins pressed against the dashboard. I'd make that promise right here, right now. But I don't know if he's there, and goddammit, I'm too much of a coward to ask. I don't know what I'll do if he says no, or if he just isn't sure yet. So, like an adult, I'm just avoiding it entirely. Besides, he seems pretty damn content with making out like high schoolers, at least based on how tight his jeans get below the belt every time.

I groan, cranking the window down for some cold air. I can't be thinking about *that*, not when I don't know how long I'll be waiting or if he'll be covered in the same goo as the student-researcher.

"Honestly, I'd probably be all over him even with the goo," I admit to myself with only a twinge of shame, grinning like a madwoman. I catch a glance of someone walking toward the truck, and my heart slams against my ribs.

But it's not Wyatt. It's a student, I think, in a dark green skirt that flows like wind in the summer leaves. She strides through the parking lot, her gaze locked on the woods behind me. A tiny spike of anxiety strikes me, and I glance over my shoulder into the tree line, but there's nothing there. I turn back just as the woman draws even with the truck. I can't help but notice she's incredibly beautiful: tawny brown skin kissed by the sun, long locks of golden hair, and big, dark eyes. When the light hits her hair, a strange, spring-green shimmer runs along the strands.

She doesn't seem to notice me. I get it; if I were going out into the woods to collect a sample in the middle of my research, I wouldn't notice an entire mariachi band set up in the parking lot. I lean against the window, curious as always. I think about calling out to her, apparently hungry for another discussion with a fellow academic. Once I get started, it's hard to stop.

But then the driver's-side door opens. I startle, turning to find Wyatt sliding into the truck. He's mercilessly goo-less, and all thoughts of the student-researcher in the flowy skirt evaporate from my mind.

"Oh, thank fuck," I murmur, drinking him in—the flannel shirt rolled to his elbows, the sharp line of his jaw covered in dark stubble, the mischievous quirk of his mouth. "I was worried you'd be covered in bluecap slime."

He pulls the door closed behind him and slides closer to me. "Suppose then I'd just have to strip for you," he says with a grin. "You'd hate that, I'm sure."

I laugh, reaching for him. "I can't imagine a worse fate," I reply, shuffling over to the middle of the wide bench seat. He captures my waist with both hands, pulling me into his lap, and I'm all too happy to oblige.

"Spriggans, not bluecaps," he tells me in a low, breathy tone, his chest hitching as I move to straddle him, gripping his broad shoulders. "Should've known. Typical spriggan humor."

For once in my life, I don't give a single shit about Them. I have no urge to ask questions about spriggans or pull my notebook from my back pocket. I only want to drown in the deep, dark forest of Wyatt's kiss. He traces the side of my face with one hand as I press myself closer to him, arching my back. I take fistfuls of his flannel in both hands and kiss him before my mind betrays me.

He tastes like bonfire smoke and caramel coffee. I gasp against his lips, threading my fingers into his dark, tousled hair. One of his hands slips beneath my sweater, flattening against the small of my back. My body responds immediately, my hips grinding against him, and I'm left with little doubt that Wyatt wants me as badly as I want him. His tongue slides into my mouth, and desire roars through my body like a wildfire.

Before I can think better of it, I'm pulling off my sweater, tossing it into the back of the truck's cab.

"Gods, Alice," he growls, his dark eyes sliding down my body, lingering on the skimpy bralette.

"Like what you see, Hayes?" I ask, trying to shove his flannel off his shoulders.

He answers me with a low, breathless sound, wrapping both hands around my waist and pulling me even closer. His mouth meets my collarbone, his fingertips sliding beneath the strap of my bralette.

I shrug my shoulder, letting the silky strap tumble down around my bicep. The sound of his sharp, hungry inhale summons even more damp heat between my legs. When he kisses the curve of my breast, his lips impossibly soft and his breath hot against my skin, I whimper.

"More, Wyatt," I beg, wrapping my fingers around his hand and dragging it to the waistband of my jeans.

He laughs against my skin, pulling away just enough to meet my gaze. Mischief glitters in his dark brown eyes, making me think of the smoky quartz clusters a roommate used to keep lined up on her windowsill: deep and fathomless, all sharp corners and hard angles until the sun hit them just right. Then, nothing short of magic.

And that's precisely what it feels like when Wyatt unbuttons my jeans and slides his large, powerful hand beneath the band of my underwear. He's barely touching me—and not even touching me where I'm begging to be touched, not quite—but I still let out a cry. With anyone else, I might be self-conscious about it, but not with him.

"You're insatiable, aren't you, Alice?" he asks, wrapping his free hand around the back of my neck and dragging my mouth to his. I tumble into his kiss, driving my hips against his fingers.

"You knew what you were getting into," I gasp against his lips. I feel him smile, and then his fingertips press against the place I've been daydreaming about him touching me for too long. Desperately, I fumble at his belt buckle.

"Not so fast, Miss Blythe," Wyatt drawls as his slow circles at the apex of my thighs come to an agonizing halt. "I've been thinking about this for longer than I think is wise to tell you. I don't want any distractions."

I heave a deep breath. His hand slides down my neck to my collarbone and then lower, cupping my breast in his fingers, his thumb brushing my nipple. I can't honestly think of the last time any guy I hooked up with was more concerned about my pleasure than his own.

"How are you so perfect?" I ask. I mean to say it playfully, in that arch tone I'm so accustomed to using, but it comes out far too honestly. The words scrape at the side of my throat as I gaze down at him—the flush in his cheeks, his hair tousled by my fingers, his lips swollen from the intensity of our exchange.

Wyatt looks up at me with surprise, one eyebrow raised. If he says something clever, I miss it, because he increases the pressure at my core and pleasure surges through me. I'm putty in his arms, melting further and further into his strong embrace, not a single thought in my mind. Well, except for one:

I could absolutely fall in love with Wyatt Hayes.

Suddenly, he goes stock-still beneath me. The breath I pull in to ask what's wrong answers my question—the taste of sulfur fills my mouth, and I gag, reaching over to crank the window back up.

"Not a godsdamned moment of peace," Wyatt snaps, pulling me closer against him as he peers over my shoulder through the windshield.

I yank my sweater on—I'm not getting caught with my not-so-proverbial pants down by a fucking *hellhound*—and zip up my jeans with shaking hands.

"I don't see it," I bite out, my heart hammering in my chest.

"Me, neither," he says, staring out into the sunset-gilded parking lot.

"That's actually...worse?" I offer just as the truck rocks with impact. I scramble for the pistol I know he keeps in the glove compartment at the same time he starts swearing, yanking down the sun visor where the keys are stowed and slamming them into the ignition.

Clutching the pistol to my chest—where it'll do a ton of good; great job, Alice—I tilt my chin back in what feels like slow motion, looking up at the cabin's roof. Indents punch into the metal, like something heavy is crouched above our heads. Wyatt notices at the same time, his entire body preternaturally still as he takes in the situation with an emotionless expression.

The truck creaks, the cabin rocking again. Sulfur chokes me. "Is it..." I whisper as quietly as I can, pointing at the roof. He doesn't turn my way, but he gives me a sharp nod. Summoning my bravery, I let out a long breath and then, slowly as I can, set the pistol down on the bench seat between us.

That gets his attention. Wyatt's eyes meet mine as the cabin roof groans beneath the weight of what I presume is a hellhound. "Bullets," he whispers, lifting his chin in the direction of the glove compartment.

"They didn't want to hurt us at Caden's," I tell him in a low, strained voice.

He narrows his eyes at me in confusion. When he understands, his gaze widens, but he doesn't look at me like I'm completely insane—which, honestly, I wouldn't blame him for in this scenario. I'm going off a hell of a hunch, and nobody likes testing a hunch in real time.

"But the redcaps would've," he whispers. God, I love how quickly this man can put the pieces together. And from his demonstration, I'm also fairly confident he's gonna be good at making me orgasm. Two points for Wyatt.

"So what's the *real* threat?" I reply, trying not to think about how close I was to coming for him, because it sort of seems like we should deal with the otherworldly creature first. It's the hedgerider way of life, I'm learning.

Wyatt leans forward onto the dash, careful to keep away from the windshield, though I'm pretty sure the terrifying beast straight out of folklore knows we're in the truck. I search the parking lot, too, fighting against the glare of the setting sun.

"Fuck," I whisper. "Wyatt. Do you see them?"

"Sure do," he replies. "Ten o'clock."

Across the parking lot—it's more eleven o'clock to me, but whatever—is a dark SUV with tinted windows. I can't make out the license plate from here, but I'd be willing to bet even Caden wouldn't be able to run 'em. About fifteen or twenty paces ahead of the SUV, and moving toward us fast, are four Sector agents. Well, I assume they're Sector despite their entirely innocuous appearances that, quite frankly, I would've never been able to discern from the general populace of Blackbird Hollow. But something gives them away pretty easily.

The guns.

Not hunters' rifles or even the big rock-salt shotguns the Hayes give out to the more reasonable locals this time of year. No—fucking *machine guns*, half the size of the people wielding them. My mind goes blank, my mouth dry, my heart throwing itself against the cage of my ribs.

Last time I saw guns like that was back on my grandparents' farm. The government isn't even supposed to *have* weapons like this anymore, not after the Treatise and then the Reformation.

But their sights are trained on us all the same.

"Wyatt," I say.

"Yeah," he replies. "Bullets, Alice."

"Right, right," I say, shuffling through the glove compartment with both hands. Before I manage to locate the ammo, the cabin creaks, and then the entire truck shakes. A loud, metallic bang rings out, and for a long, terrifying moment, I'm pretty sure one or both of us has been shot.

But I'm wrong—so deeply wrong. Instead, there's a hellhound crouched on the hood of Wyatt's truck. The setting sun gilds the unnatural arch of its spine and turns the dripping pools of its saliva into molten gold. The sound of its growl—slithering and raw, unlike the sound of any earthly mammal—slinks into my ears. Dread rattles me. Until I realize the hellhound is facing away from us, placing itself between us and Sector. Almost like it's...

"Have I fucking lost it?" I whisper.

"Nah," Wyatt replies, though he's still loading the pistol's chamber. "Well, maybe a little. But no. The hellhound seems to be *protecting* us."

"Huh," I say, blinking slowly. "That sure wasn't on my bingo card."

Chapter 24
Wyatt

It's cold comfort, but even with the fancy guns Sector's packing, they don't stand a chance against the hellhound on the hood of my truck. Problem is, neither do we—the pistol's not gonna be much help, and there's no way I can get to the rifles fast enough to do much good if Sector opens fire. I can't remember the last time I was caught so unaware.

I can, but I don't want to. This is what happens. This is why they leave.

I asked Alice to go for the ammo to give her something to do while I assess our situation, but I'm coming up blank. The place in my brain where I'd usually have strategy on strategy and already be moving onto action is full up on fear. Fear that we've gotten ourselves tangled in something bigger than I want Alice—or myself—involved in.

Sector doesn't hunt the Hunt. Sector doesn't fuck with Them, or us. They just watch, useless and impotent. They *monitor the situation*. Their definition of monitoring is a touch more active than mine. I assume they're still running experiments on Them in their black sites. They did before

Reformation, and just because they were supposed to stop doesn't mean they did. We've always assumed they just got quieter about it.

But something's different now. My mind goes straight to Alice. Of course it does—because she's so godsdamn special to me, of course I assume she's that special to them, too. And after Mr. Rabbit, I've gotta wonder.

The little plushie was clean, but he hadn't been just before Alice left the city. My heart rate increases as all the possibilities of what's going on here run through my head.

The hellhound crouches down, slavering as it lets out a puff of sulfurous smoke. Alice has fished ammo out of the glove compartment, but the otherworldly sound of a pack of hell-hounds baying makes her jump so hard that the bullets spill from her hands.

Everything happens at once. The agents take aim—at us or the hellhound, I have no fucking clue. The pack shows up on the heels of the thickest mist I've seen crawl out of the forest in all the time we've lived in these parts. I push Alice down as Sector opens fire. Not a single bullet hits the truck. But the sound of growling grows louder, the smell of sulfur so thick in the air now that every breath triggers the worst of my gag reflex.

"Stay down for me," I mutter as I turn the ignition. The truck roars to life.

Alice grabs my hand. "Don't leave."

I glance over at her from our mutually crouched positions. "Darlin', we've gotta go."

She shakes her head, her honeyed waves swaying. "We need to see what happens here."

Alice really is missing a few integral marbles for her jar, but from a strategic standpoint, she's not wrong. We came to Three Ravens for information on the Hunt, and we're being offered up a prime morsel of it, complete with firsthand evidence.

I sigh at the sounds of those absurdly large guns. "Fine. Just a peek."

We both raise ourselves up just enough to peep over the dashboard. One agent's reloading, and the other appears to take aim again, but they're not gunning for any of the sixteen hellhounds that stand between us and the agents. They're aiming straight into the woods.

And then I clock it. The truck's position, facing toward Old Main, backed straight up to the forest. Like always, I parked as far back as I could, under the canopy of trees. The place where I feel the safest—the most at home.

Is it possible the hellhounds aren't protecting *us*? Are they protecting something in the forest? I spin in my seat, searching the dark wood for something, any scrap of evidence that this isn't about Alice—but there's nothing behind me. Nothing I can see now, anyway—and apparently neither can the agents.

"They're packing it in," Alice hisses, hitting my shoulder with an insistent little fist.

The touch brings back the memory of her skin under my fingers, and I flush hot at the thought. Apparently, now that the danger's passed, my body's going to take the opportunity to remind me that I nearly got to third base with Alice just ten minutes ago.

One long, deep breath centers me somewhat. Enough that I turn back, and sure enough, the agent who'd been reloading has started the car. Before I can gather my thoughts enough to say something, they're peeling out of the parking lot with a dramatic squeal.

The mist rises, thick as split pea soup, and the hounds fade into it, their scent of rotten eggs receding as they do. In moments, it's like nothing happened at all. Even after a lifetime of dealing with this shit, I find it surreal that I can be in the thick of it one moment, and the next...everything's normal.

And my new normal means that I think about Alice every second, even during an encounter like the one we just had. My head's spinning with myriad adjustments. I've always been adaptable, and now that my heart's all the way in with Alice, my mind's rapidly shifting to make room for her.

Her and her big brain that needs both time and space to process.

I stay quiet for a few stray moments, scanning the parking lot for more trouble and finding none. I watch as the last of the mist curls back into the forest, birdsong slowly returning as the air clears. Next to me, Alice is still, her eyes narrowing like she's thinking hard.

"What're you putting together, Blythe?"

She shakes her head. "Nothing. That's the trouble. That was strange, wasn't it?"

I nod. "It was."

There's something she's not saying, and I wonder what she's made of all this that I don't see yet. Caden does the same thing occasionally when he's chewing on a theory. It never does to rush him, and I don't want to pressure Alice if she needs the space in her head clear to work things out her own way. The voice in *my* head that reminds me not to be chickenshit at love also reminds me that trusting someone means giving them room when they need it, so I don't pester Alice into telling me what she's pondering.

I lean back in my seat a little, stretching my shoulders. "You like fruit?"

Alice raises an eyebrow. "Is that code for something?"

I chuckle as I take the truck out of park. "No. Just wondering if you like citrus. Barnes Whitney drives down to the Groves periodically, and we haven't picked up our crate yet."

Alice's face lights up. "There's *citrus* in Blackbird Hollow right now?"

I nod. "Yeah, Fallon asked me to pick up our crate on the way home. Marion's got ours at the Stardust, if you want to stop by. I'd also like to ask her about what we just saw."

Alice nods. "That's a good idea." She grins. "You said citrus...does that mean there might be limes?"

I grin. "Key limes, if we're lucky. You might not guess it, but Fallon makes a killer key lime pie."

Alice smiles a smug little smile at me, tweaking my nose with her index finger before pressing the sweetest kiss to my lips. When she pulls away, she's still smiling. "That's where you're wrong, Wyatt. I believe the Hayes kids can do just about anything."

But *she's* wrong there. If I was as powerful as all that, her smile wouldn't stop at her lips. Something's eating at Alice, and as I pull the truck out of its parking spot, I realize that much as I want the fabled trust we're building, I don't have the guts to ask her what it is.

Chickenshit, that little voice warns from deep within. And it's not wrong. I am chickenshit, because I don't want to ask her what's on her mind, only to find out she's already having second thoughts about me. If Alice is gonna disappear, I don't want to see it coming.

I want to be happy 'til the happiness runs out. And if it does—hell, if the past serves as a pattern—*when* it does, I'll face the music. Until then, we have citrus to procure, and a town to protect from the Hunt.

Barnes Whitney leans against his ancient pickup in the parking lot of the Stardust. He's a tall Black man, lean, with an elegant, poetic temperament. As I park, he waves, pushing off his truck and adjusting the canvas jacket he's worn since we were teenagers. It's a comforting sight after the past hour's events.

Alice claps, gasping as she slides out of the truck. The back of Barnes's old Ford is *full* of crates of various citrus. Barnes grins as Alice is drawn into the orbit of the sunshiny fruit. His cousins run one of the groves down south, and we're lucky to have a direct line this far north. Not everyone has access to citrus these days.

"I'm headed up to Mill Creek," Barnes says as Alice rests her chin on the sidewall of the bed of his truck. "So I'm all loaded up."

Alice nods. "I've never seen this much all together. What's it like in the Groves?"

Barnes winks at me as I point to the main office, stepping aside just enough for me to see that there's a rifle resting on the bench seat of his truck. I nod to him. Barnes is good people. We've worked together on a bunch of jobs. Some of his people grow citrus, and others hunt monsters. Barnes is a bit of everything, and manages to also be a bit of everywhere, too, bringing bits and bobs of things and news alike back with him every time he comes home.

Alice is safe with him, but I press a hand to the small of her back to let her know where I'll be. "I'm gonna go chat with Marion real quick."

She nods, but her stream of questions about the Groves falls from her tongue like the jewels from old tales. Barnes is as drawn into her questions as she is to the load of citrus, and I leave the two of them to chat about fruit.

Inside the motel's lobby, Marion is painting a tiny wooden dog. She glances up at me as the bell on the door rings. "Your crate's by the old Harkness House."

I glance at the miniature street she's moved to the front of the lobby. She's reconstructed all of the houses from our childhood that had to be torn down for one reason or another. Sure enough, there's a crate labeled "HAYES" in Fallon's big, bold lettering. But I don't move to pick it up.

"You hearing anything weird about redcaps?" I ask, leaning against the counter. The tribe's bound to have better information than even Caden's got access to.

Marion shakes her head. "Not much more than you, probably. Something weird's going on."

I nod. "You think this is all the Hunt?"

She shrugs. "That's more your area."

I watch her dip her tiny paintbrush into the red paint and give the dog a tongue. When she sets it down, I ask, "What about the hikers that went missing? Hear about them?"

Marion shakes her head slowly. "Strangest thing. There's not a damn thing to find out—about any of them."

My forehead creases, the muscles in my shoulders drawing together, tight and tense. "Well, that's not right."

Slowly, Marion nods, setting the paintbrush down. "The only thing that's unique about them is the fact that there's not a *single* special thing about any of them. They were all as average as can be for visitors to the area. Bland. Rich but not too rich. White. A variety of ages."

We know all this already, but the tribe's got different access to government resources than we do, and I've always known that Marion's got her hand in more than she lets on with their affairs. "Too clean?"

Marion nods, pursing her lips. "Not even a parking citation."

I shake my head. "Impossible. They were all from the cities."

"I know," Marion says, and her tone's ominous. "Someone

made very, *very* sure there was nothing to find, about any of them."

That sure sounds like Sector, but Marion and I both know that there's forces worse than Sector out there. Ones that would know how to make it look like Sector pulling one of their more "advanced" routines. This is the kind of 3D chess that I despise, fucking with real people's lives for what always turns out to be heinous means. Humans at their worst really aren't much different than the High with Their eyeball ice cubes.

The bone-deep ache that says it doesn't matter how much we reform, that we'll always circle back to this nonsense, swells within me. The only thing to do in a moment like this is care *more* about the people right in front of me.

I glance out at Barnes, who's watching Alice's hands flutter around as she talks about something. She's speaking rather passionately, and I wonder what she's telling him.

"What about her?" I ask, knowing Marion. "You find anything odd about Alice?"

The corner of Marion's mouth quirks up into a smile. "She's on Sector's radar. Little bit of a thorn in their side, always just a bit too close to truths they don't want average folks knowing. That blog of hers was a problem."

I nod slowly. "So nothing suspicious?"

Marion shakes her head. "Not about Alice."

There's a tone Marion's got—it's her tell, and years of game nights have me tuned into it. "What is it?"

Marion sighs. "The person she's been messaging most with for the past few years, love_cookies210, they don't exist. No other internet activity whatsoever. Kind of odd."

"Indeed it is," I breathe out. It lines up too close to the missing hikers and their nothingness. Lots of pieces falling together, but none of them fit yet. "You thinking Sector?"

Marion shrugs. "Nothing we could dig up, Wyatt. Your

girl's good, but someone's got an eye on her. Sector, or one of the *other* agencies."

The feeling that whatever's coming our way is closing in on something that's too intimately tied together for my liking descends upon me like a summer storm, fast and violent. I stare out the big front window at Alice.

Barnes is holding his side, he's laughing so hard, and she's got tears streaming down her cheeks as she cackles. But I know how fast a storm can change directions, and Alice is a force of nature.

I wonder how long I've got 'til she decides to bolt on me.

Chapter 25
Alice

"Alice!" Fallon laughs, throwing back her dark, glossy waves. "What makes you think you have a *choice*? I'm the head bitch in charge, if you haven't noticed."

I sigh, resting my elbows on the farmhouse table that's become deeply familiar to me. Old protest songs leak from the boombox on the vintage credenza. The corkboard at my back is far from empty after our visit to Dr. Waterhouse and our... *encounter* yesterday afternoon. As always, the space smells of rich spice and wool sweaters, which soothes me. And even though Wyatt ran home to grab some supplies for Halloween, his pine-and-woodsmoke scent still lingers in the air and on my skin like a comforting blanket.

"I'm just not sure if I'm up for it," I admit, curling my fingers into the pockmarked surface of the table. "Yesterday was...a lot, Fallon."

She frowns at me. Apparently, saying no to a girls' night out with Fallon is a serious offense, at least judging from how violently she starts zesting one of the limes. "If you're not okay with hedgerider life," Fallon warns me from the counter, her voice low and firm, "then you gotta cut my brother loose, Alice. That boy is falling *hard.*"

My head snaps up at that. "No, no, Fallon," I say, desperately backpedaling, making incoherent gestures with my hands. "The hellhounds, Sector, a friendly little shootout in a parking lot? I can handle that. It's..."

Fallon frowns at me then, putting the zester down and striding over to where I'm seated at the table. There's an empty glass of fresh-squeezed orange juice in front of me—I could drink a hundred more, but I'm trying to be reasonable—and my notebook is open, my fingers cramping from a desperate attempt to collect all my theories.

"Okay. So if it's not that, then what exactly is it? You've been weird all day," she says, powerful hands gripping the back of the chair opposite me. I stare at the tattoos exposed by her rolled-up sleeves for a long moment, searching for the right words.

When I don't find them, I bite down on my tongue, roughly dragging a hand through my hair. My skin goes hot, heart pounding furiously in my chest. I don't know how to tell her what I'm feeling. That yesterday reminded me of the past, of my grandpa back on the farm. Of the fact that I've never truly been able to shake the feeling it's my fault, somehow.

Maybe if I hadn't been there, my grandpa wouldn't have defended the farm so fiercely. Maybe if he hadn't seen that rare slice of land as the only way his daughter and grandchild could actually survive the days to come, he might have just complied with the soldiers. Maybe then he would've left with my grandma, and maybe we would have found somewhere safe. Maybe then the sound of bullets and the sight of those guns wouldn't have sent me into such a spiral.

I've hidden it fairly well, I think. Barnes and the citrus were a good distraction, but once the adrenaline wore off, the dread seeped in. "Look, something happened when I was a kid," I finally say, looking up to meet her eyes. "The agents with the guns yesterday afternoon just reminded me of it. I'm a little shaken."

Understanding dawns on Fallon's face, so vulnerable and impossibly gentle that my throat catches. "Oh," she says softly, draping herself over the back of the chair. "I get it, Alice. I'm sorry. I didn't realize."

I shrug. "Of course you didn't," I reply, pulling the sleeves of my thick oatmeal-colored sweater over my hands. "I didn't tell you."

"Do you wanna talk about it?" Fallon asks, something mischievous flashing in her gaze. I raise my brows expectantly as she stands up straight, her hands pressed together in front of her chest. "Over drinks? At girls' night? We can get drunk and cry and maybe vandalize one of my ex's cars!"

Despite myself—and the sour pit of despair in my belly—I laugh so hard I snort, which sends Fallon into a bout of laughter, too. I have to admit, it feels *good*. It feels good to be around people who have been through shit. It makes it easier. A lot of the people at OrthCon lived through the Catastrophes and the Reformation, sure. But they weathered those years from behind the gates of sprawling compounds. Some of them were even able to leave the country, only returning when things got better. We aren't the same.

But the Hayes kids? They get it, just like Fallon said. And they all seem to understand that sometimes I need gentleness, and other times I need gallows humor.

"Besides, Alice, you should know stuff like that doesn't usually happen," Fallon adds as her laughter fades. "Sector doesn't usually intervene. At least not like that."

I falter, chewing on my lower lip. Wyatt said the same thing last night. Neither one of them seems to understand that their statements only make me *more* worried. What if I'm the problem? What if it's me being here in Blackbird Hollow that's causing Sector to intervene more directly—with outlawed weapons, nonetheless?

"Yeah," I reply with a forced smile. "Well, yesterday was free exposure therapy, I guess."

Fallon snorts, turning back to the counter. "You're fucked up, Blythe."

"Takes one to know one, Hayes," I shoot back.

"Let me finish up with this pie," she says over her shoulder. "I think it might actually break Caden if I promise key lime and don't deliver. Then we're having a godsdamn girls' night. You need it."

"Are you sure that's a good idea?" I ask, though I've never seen Fallon walk anything back once she's made a decision. "With Halloween tomorrow?"

She turns to me then, a wicked smile on her face. "That's *exactly* why it's a good idea. Get us loosened up. And, if the Wild Hunt takes us, at least we had one last party before the end."

THE TEQUILA barely burns as it slides down my throat, which is a pretty good sign that I'm drunk. I still slam the lime wedge between my teeth to cut the harsh flavor, my eyes watering. Beside me, Fallon cheers gleefully.

"See?" she asks, punching my shoulder. "Girls' night fixes everything!"

I laugh, leaning onto the wide bar. Rock music blares from the speakers in the corner. Every single person in this place knows Fallon, and apparently a lot of them know about me, too.

"Why is the blonde girl giving me the stank eye?" I ask

Fallon, looking over at her and gesturing at a corner table with a nod of my head.

She peers around me, her eyes narrowing. "Oh, she's been sweet on Wyatt for *years*," Fallon cackles, rubbing her hands together in delight at the same time my stomach twists. "She's gotta be pissed that some city girl came in and scooped him up."

"How would she know that already?" I ask incredulously, taking a gulp of the local cider.

Apparently the folks in Blackbird Hollow have decided Wyatt and I are an item, even though we sure as hell haven't had that talk ourselves. Though I did almost go for it this morning, sitting out on the porch with coffee, the mists rolling in and the foliage gleaming bronze-bright, the whole thing like a movie scene. But just as I'd opened my mouth, I remembered the guns and the bullets and the plainclothes agents. I remembered that there was a distinct possibility I'd brought more attention to Blackbird Hollow just by being here.

"Small town, babe," Fallon replies with a roll of her eyes, interrupting my thoughts. "Everybody's all up in everyone else's shit."

"Do you still wanna vandalize one of your ex's cars?" I ask, my words slightly slurring. The music pounds thickly in my ears, and I'm too warm in my barn coat.

"We haven't even cried about our traumas yet!" Fallon says, slamming her fist onto the bartop a bit too strongly. The whole thing shakes, and other patrons look over at us. "Don't rush the schedule, Blythe. I've got this down to a science."

"I trust you." I laugh, but I actually mean it. Being here in the locals' bar—a place called Lucky's that serves a late-night brunch on Sundays, when Janey closes the diner up early—underscores how much I feel like a puzzle piece finally slotted into its right place. And that's what makes me turn to Fallon, my heart racing as I open my mouth.

"Fallon," I say, reaching across the bar to grip her wrist. "I'm fucking terrified."

She meets my gaze evenly, though her eyes widen slightly. "About Samhain? The Hunt?" she asks, all her attention on me, that dark gaze no longer roving the bar for potential threats.

"No, not really," I say, my tongue too big for my mouth, the alcohol and the fear pounding through my veins. "Well. About everything."

Without hesitation, she looks at the bartender and gestures before taking me by the hand and leading me to a booth tucked into a corner. The music is a little quieter here, and I feel less visible, less like the new animal exhibit in the zoo.

"So," Fallon drawls, resting her hands on the table, "you're terrified. About everything. Tell me more."

And, fuck, I do. I probably tell her too much. About my grandfather's farm, about watching him die, about my grandma, about how yesterday brought back all of those fears. Maybe it's the alcohol, but I can't deny how comfortable I feel with Fallon. How I can't understand how I lived without her for this long—or Wyatt, for that matter.

"I'm just afraid that there's something Sector doesn't like about me being around hedgeriders," I tell her, raising my hand to chew on my fingernails, but Fallon snatches my wrist and shoves my hand back into my lap. "And I'm so, so scared that something is going to happen to you or Wyatt or Caden if I stay. Even though I want to stay. I can't imagine not staying. But I also can't live with myself if something happens."

Fallon listens patiently as I talk, handing me a handkerchief from the pocket of her leather jacket when tears stream down my face. This probably isn't the fun, rowdy girls' night she imagined, but I can't keep this bottled up any longer.

"It's easy to forget how new you are to all of this," Fallon says, her tone light but serious. "You fit in so well. I forget that you don't know some of the basic stuff about our world."

After making sure I'm okay, she launches into an impressively detailed conversation—especially considering how much tequila I watched her consume—about hedgeriders and Sector. About the Hedgerider Council, which is run by "stuffy old white guys in the U.K." but also has a local committee headed up by folks here.

"It's not something I'm deeply involved in," Fallon says with a shrug, "but trust me, Sector can't just kill a hedgerider, no matter the circumstances. There's a lot of diplomacy behind the scenes."

"Can't imagine why they don't involve *you* in diplomacy," I say dryly, earning a wide grin from Fallon.

"Activity has certainly kicked up since you arrived," she concedes, crossing her arms. "And are they paying closer attention to us because you're here? Maybe. But it's not entirely because of you."

I let out a long, jagged exhale. I feel about fifty pounds lighter and take what feels like the first deep breath since yesterday afternoon. "As long as you're sure," I say, dabbing my eyes with Fallon's handkerchief.

Bad night for her to manhandle me into a makeover. I never would've pegged Fallon for having the time to get good at makeup, but shit, she's *excellent*. I don't want to ruin her artistry. Not to mention that Wyatt will be picking me up later, and now that I know I'm not an active danger to the people I'm beginning to care about very, very much, I'd like to look hot as hell.

"I'm sure," Fallon says with a smile. Her expression falters, something soft and vulnerable crossing her sharp features. "Alice?"

"Yeah?" I say, unsure.

"Thanks for caring this fucking much," she says, her tone choked. Maybe it's just the dim lighting of the bar, but I'm pretty sure that her eyes are shining with tears. "We have a great community here, we really do. We take good care of each other. But sometimes—well, I'm kind of difficult."

"I hadn't noticed," I say with an arched brow.

She snorts, rolling her eyes. "Sometimes it sort of feels like people tolerate me because of what I can do. Because I can handle Them. And sometimes I wonder if they'd kick me to the curb if I weren't useful."

I sit back with surprise, examining her. "Fallon, I think people here love you more than you understand," I say, meaning every single word. "Look, I haven't been here very long. But folks admire the shit out of you. Maybe not all of them. I'm sure you've been given plenty of reasons to feel the way you do. But I don't think the people who are afraid of getting cut on your sharp edges deserve to feel the warmth of your company."

Thanks to all that hedgerider training, Fallon moves so fast that I barely register when she throws her arms around me. But I hug her back fiercely, burying my face into her leather jacket. Then we're both crying, cradling each other in Lucky's battered pleather booth, bathed in the skittering purple lights.

"Right on schedule," I say, making Fallon laugh. We pull apart, smiling shyly at each other, before Fallon recovers herself and sits back in the booth, one arm thrown over the back, looking like a queen surveying her kingdom.

"I want you to understand how frequently Sector is here," she says suddenly. "For every agent you see, there's at least one more that even I can't clock." I lean forward on the table, watching as Fallon gestures around the room, identifying agents.

"Obvious," she scoffs at a white man in his thirties wearing a dress shirt and tie, clutching a beer bottle. "Not so obvious," she continues, this time gesturing to someone who *looks* like they belong—worn-in clothing, no fancy haircut—but who isn't really engaging with anyone. Just watching. Finally, Fallon lifts her chin in the direction of a femme-presenting person in a vintage dress spinning around on the tiny dance floor, holding court with three or four people vying for her attention.

"No way," I exclaim.

"Yes way," Fallon says with a nod. "See what I mean? There were *always* a ton of Sector agents here. You just didn't notice them before." With that, she stands, sliding out from the booth. "Alright, ponder your lesson. I gotta piss."

I laugh at her abruptness and take another sip of my beer. I'm exhausted and wrung out, but I feel like I can breathe again. Nervousness and excitement flutter in my belly as I think about seeing Wyatt soon. I glance down at my outfit, hoping he'll like it. Fallon dug out a black tube top from her closet, insisting it would look cute with my loose, mid-rise jeans. And I *do* look cute, especially with the subtly shimmery body lotion she dabbed on my collarbones and shoulders.

Movement in my peripheral vision makes me look up; it's only been a few moments since Fallon left. Instead of the tall, lanky hedgerider, there's a woman in her early sixties with silvery-blonde hair sliding into the booth next to me. I startle, leaning away. She's dressed in nondescript, tailored trousers and a nice blouse.

Which means she's absolutely not from Blackbird Hollow, and I swear she wasn't in this bar just a few minutes ago.

"This seat's taken," I tell her. In the large, shadowy room, she looks a lot like my grandma—the same round face and warm eyes, a similar shade of blonde shot through with silver.

"It's nice to meet you," the woman says, ignoring my words. I look at her, bewildered, my heart climbing my throat.

"Are you Sector?" I ask, narrowing my eyes at her. "Because you sure as shit look like Sector. And if you are, you should get the fuck out of here."

"Oh, Alice," the woman says, reaching across the table to pat my hand before I can yank it away. "Your friend's coming back from the bathroom, so I'll have to tell you more later."

"Later?" I spit at her, adrenaline coursing through my veins, all the fear and dread from earlier surging back in as though it had never really left.

She stands then, brushing imaginary lint from her pants with one hand. "I thought you'd be more excited to meet me. After all, we've talked for years," the woman says with a smile as I stare her down. "Alice, I'm Cookie."

Chapter 26
Wyatt

I'm early to pick the girls up from the bar. I check my watch. Got about an hour 'til I can safely go in for a beer and check on things. Fallon's a stickler about her own timetables, everyone else's be damned, but she'll throw a shit fit if I head in there early and spoil her night out with Alice. Fern was deep in a nap at home, so I haven't even got my dog to talk to.

I dig around under my front seat. There's a Sweet Valley Twins book in here somewhere. Fallon picked up a plastic bin of them from an old barn a few years ago, and Caden and I have been making our way through them. My fingers wrap around *If I Die Before I Wake*, and I grin at the haunted house on the cover. Looks kinda like our house, now that I think about it. The twins are trapped in a dream with a half-monster named Eva, and I can't wait to see what happens next.

As I kick my feet up on the dash, a prissily dressed white woman in her sixties comes out of the bar. She gives me a Sector kind of feeling, which isn't particularly odd. But the way she stands in the golden pool of light under the bar's striped awning, scanning the parking lot, catches my eye. What's she looking for?

I follow her gaze until it reaches my truck. When she sees it, her looking around pauses, and her eyes slide straight to mine. At first, she frowns for half a second, and then the slipperiest, most conniving smile I've seen in a long-ass while spreads over her face. On the surface, she looks like someone's granny, but that smile. That's something else entirely.

And not a supernatural something else. A completely human, downright evil sort of expression. I toss the twins aside, and I'm out of the truck before I can think a second thought. Before I can get across the parking lot, an old silver station wagon pulls up, a white man who looks like the perfect pair to the woman standing under the awning at the wheel.

As she gets into the car, she grins at me, her pale gums showing, eyes practically maniacal with some kind of secret joy. I break into a sprint, but can't make it in time. The car pulls away, speeding out of the lot before I even have a chance to stop them.

Fuck Fallon's timetable. Girls' night is over. I push the wooden door to Lucky's open. Joan Jett & the Blackhearts are playing on the jukebox, and I find Alice staring blankly at the wall as Joan wails about love hurting. Fallon's headed back from the bathroom, and when she sees me, I can tell she's about to yell.

I point at her and shake my head. "Don't start. We're going. Now." I turn to Lenny at the bar and point at them next. "You put whatever they had on my tab, and I'll be by after the first to clear the grindylow infestation from your end of the lake."

Lenny nods, their freckled nose scrunching a little with a frown. "Deal. Coupl'a slices of key lime pie would be appreciated as well."

I glance at Fallon, who nods. "Sure. Why not?" Then she sees Alice and the blank stare. "Wha—"

"Sector, while you were in the ladies'," I hiss as I take three long steps across the ancient wood floors to pull Alice up out of the booth. "Come on, sweet girl. Let's get you home."

Alice looks up at me, her skin too pale, her eyes wide with fear. "Cookie was here."

"Fuck," I spit out, my voice too harsh for the state Alice is in. I pull her into a hug, and I feel her legs turn to jelly. She's panicking, so I scoop her into my arms. A couple of wolf whistles let out from around the bar, and there's a round of applause.

Fallon blows kisses as we make our way to the door, but Alice doesn't say a word until we're outside. "The things I told her... I..."

I hush her a little. Fallon makes eye contact with me. "Cookie? The internet friend?"

I nod. "Looks like she's Sector."

"Fuckity, fuck, fuck, fuck," Fallon barks. She was drunk as a skunk coming out of that bathroom, but she's stone-cold sober now. That's a talent she's had as long as I can remember. "Take her to your place. I'll see what I can find out."

I nod and hold my sister's gaze. "Stay safe, you hear? Nothing crazy tonight."

Fallon grabs my shoulder, serious for once in her godsdamn life. "I promise. You just take care of our girl."

Alice peeks at her over my shoulder. "I ruined girls' night."

Fallon kisses her forehead. "You didn't, baby girl. Not even a little. That dumb bitch Cookie did, but maybe a hellhound'll gobble her up."

Alice sniffles. "I told all my secrets to a secret agent. That wasn't very covert ops of me."

"The booze is hitting her," Fallon observes.

"Thank you, Madame Obvious," I reply.

"That's Mademoiselle Obvious, to you," Fallon corrects. But there's not much humor in her words. Not much snap. She's as worried as I am. "Get on home. I'm gonna use the payphone and call Cade. He can come help out."

A month ago, I doubt he would've, but now, for Alice? I bet he will. "Okay," I agree, and we part ways into the night.

I get enough out of Alice on the way back to my house to figure out what happened. She and Fallon had a big heart-to-heart, and then that Sector bitch showed up and revealed herself to be Cookie.

Alice won't hear that it's possible that's a lie—that Sector lies like they buy bad suits for field agents. She's sure she's given up all her secrets to someone none of us can trust, and she's beating herself up for it—somewhat incomprehensibly, which tells me she's had tequila. She pushes her boots and pants off as we walk into the house, which confirms the tequila diagnosis.

Fern whimpers when she sees Alice stumble, but I manage to get her onto the couch and covered up with a quilt before she has any adverse effects from her night out. With my dog's supervision, I surmise she's had just enough to need a nap, but not enough to want to vomit. After a glass of water, Alice promptly passes out, Fern guarding her like it's a full-time job. I slump into a chair, my mind failing to process the way the night ended.

Since I can't manage that, I build a fire and stick one of Janey's frozen pizzas into the oven. I've spent a lot of nights with drunk folks. Alice is gonna wake up half-sober and starving. I pour myself a glass of cheap whiskey, doubling my usual, and shoot it down fast, something an awful lot like fear chasing me. It burns going down, but I pour another and send it to my belly just as fast.

"You trying to catch up?" Alice asks from the kitchen doorway. She only looks half-drunk now. I take another double shot of whiskey, half for courage, half to get on her level. She smells the air. "I'd kill for some pizza."

"No need for murder," I murmur. I want to reach out for her, but her eyes have that same guarded look as when she first got here. "What happened at the bar?"

She shakes her head as I down another double. "Not a lot more than what I already told you. Some woman who looked *way* too fucking much like my Nan told me she's Cookie...and she implied that we'd talk again."

I let a long breath out, relieved. The woman was Sector, or one of the agencies that runs Sector; they're like a fucking wasp's nest. "Okay," I reason. "Well, that's good then. We can find out what she wants."

Alice huffs angrily. "Don't try to convince me this is a *good* thing, dammit."

I'm not sure exactly why she's so mad. But maybe it's not "Cookie" that's got her in a tizz. "Why's this eating at you so much?"

Alice throws her hands up in the air, shaking her head. Like I'm the slowest creature on the planet. It stings a little. "Because I've been talking to a Sector agent for...I don't even fucking know how long. Because I thought Cookie was my *friend*."

And Alice hasn't had many friends. I've got a better handle on this now. I nod. "Okay. Well, good news there."

"What?" she growls, leaning against the counter, crossing her arms tight over her chest. It's then that I realize she's standing in my kitchen in nothing but a tube top and a pair of black cotton panties, and that the whiskey's catching up to me. My cock has a mind of its own and jumps at the thought of her half-naked and apparently a little pissed at me.

But now's not the time for thoughts like that. Now's the time for getting her to see what's happening here. Alice is all up in her head, her big old brain working overtime, telling her stories that aren't all the way true.

The kitchen timer goes off. I pull the pizza out of the oven and set it on the stove to cool before turning back to Alice. "You said she looked like your Granny, right?"

Alice nods but doesn't say anything else.

"Well, that's good news," I continue. "If that's so, then it's likely you haven't been talking to the woman you saw in the bar. Bad news is, it seems like they've probably read a good amount of your messages with Cookie, if not all."

I'm scrambling, putting the pieces together as I go, but I've gotta get her to see this wasn't something she did. It was something done *to* her. "So the secret part stands. But I don't think that was *actually* Cookie. Somewhere out there, there's a little weirdo with a stringboard just like yours, who probably loves you."

I think I've done a pretty good job of summing things up in a convincing way, but Alice just glares at me. "You don't get it."

I reach out for her hand. "Maybe not all the way, but I do understand why you feel like shit right now."

She snatches her hand away from me, shaking her head and gesturing at the fridge. "No," she breathes. "You grew up with all *this*. You have no *idea* why this fucks me up."

I stare at the fridge, almost twenty years of photos covering it—just like there are up at Fallon's and more at Cade's. It's all evidence of the life my siblings and I have had here. School dances. Pumpkin carving. Even a few school plays. Proof that despite how shitty things have been, we've been here, while Alice was out there.

I grab Alice's hand again, gripping harder this time. "Tell me then, sweet girl. Tell me why it fucks you up."

She shakes her head at me, angry tears falling on her cheeks. "Can't you even fight with me?" she sobs. "I'm trying to have a fight with you, Wyatt."

This isn't drunken crying—she's not that drunk. It's something deeper. Some essential wound that Alice needs healed. But I can't help if I don't know why it hurts. I pull her closer. "Why?"

Her forehead falls into my chest. "Because it would make it easier if I could hate you right now. If I could convince myself this isn't where I belong."

I take a long, deep breath, hearing the depth of her words. My mind wants to overanalyze, but I don't let it. Instead, I push Alice away from me 'til she's looking up into my eyes. "I'm not making it easier for you to leave this place, Alice Blythe. You go if you want to. If you don't like it here. If you don't like the town, the people, whatever. Go if you want to go."

Her eyes widen, like she's a little shocked by my words. I move my hands to her shoulders, the strength of my grip increasing as I bend toward her, my eyes narrowing. "But you're not leaving here because you baited me into a fight. You leave, you leave because you *want* to. Because you don't want me, or this life. Not because I'm pushing you out of anything. I'm not. I'd pull you all the way in if you'd let me."

She stands staring at me for half a second, and then she's in my arms, her bare legs wrapped around my waist, all silk skin and soft curves, her hands in my hair. "I want you, Wyatt. I want you so fucking much."

"You sure about that?" I ask. "I'm not one to take advantage of your state."

"Not that drunk anymore," she whispers, her eyes clear.

"Thank the gods," I growl, pushing her onto the counter as our mouths crash into each other.

She yanks the tube top off in a move so elegant, it nearly

takes my breath away, then pushes my t-shirt off before pulling me back into her arms. When we're skin to skin, she lets out a gasp, her back arching.

"Tell me more about how you want to pull me in," she murmurs, bringing my hand between her legs. "Tell me how you want to be inside me."

I chuckle. "That's not exactly what I said."

She looks up at me, those gorgeous eyes of hers heavy-lidded with desire. "But that's what you want, isn't it?"

Every bit of me heats at her words, my fingers moving lightly over the tiny bit of remaining fabric between us. "I think you know what I want, sweet girl."

Alice whimpers as I increase the pressure of my touch.

"I want you in every way possible, for as long as you'll have me."

Her lips are plush and a little swollen from kissing me as she moans. "Please," she pleads. "Please, I need you. Don't make me wait any longer."

I slide a finger between the elastic of her panties and where she's begging me to touch her. The warmth of her core is just millimeters from my fingers, but I don't give her what she wants.

"I need to know this is what you want, Alice."

She looks up at me, tilting her hips so her body meets my teasing fingers. She's wet, and I almost lose control, but I need to hear her say it. "I need you inside me," she insists. "Now."

There's no choice, then. What Alice wants, I'm going to give her. As I sink deep inside her, she moans. "Lift your hips for me," I prompt her as I free both hands to pull her offending panties off.

She does as I ask, and I reward her with a kiss so deep, I wonder if I've lost myself, if I've already disappeared inside Alice Blythe. She's unbuckling my belt, and though I try to stop her, try to tell her we should go slow, she shakes her head. "We can go slower the second time," she pants. "I'm on birth control. I've been tested, and neither of us have fucked anyone in so long it's probably a little embarrassing, right?"

I laugh, but nod. "Yes, and I've been tested too. Every year at my check-up. All good."

She pushes my pants down over my hips, my underwear going with them to the floor. "You want me to fuck you here on the kitchen counter?"

She looks around, as though she's just realized we're still in the kitchen. "No. Take me upstairs to your room, Wyatt. To *our* room."

"Anything you want, sweet girl," I whisper as I throw her over my shoulder.

She squeals happily as I march her upstairs.

Chapter 27
Alice

I wrap my legs tighter around Wyatt's waist as he stretches over me, flipping on a bedside lamp. Then he's haloed in golden light, his collarbones like carved marble, the expanse of his muscular chest making my breath catch.

"You still sure?" he breathes into the crook of my neck, his lips pressing against my skin as he increases the pressure at the apex of my thighs. I arch into him, gasping his name as pleasure nearly devours me. "Are you sure I'm what you want?"

I slide one hand around to his face, cupping his sculptural jaw in my hand. "Yes," I manage to exhale, breathless. His deep brown eyes meet mine, and there's more there—a story for another day. Words won't do for tonight. I need to *show* this fiercely kind, compassionate, and incredibly gorgeous man that I want him more than anything. "Are *you* sure you won't get tired of me?"

His mouth trails down my neck, breath ghosting my collarbone, before kissing the top of my breasts. At the same time, he slides a finger inside me, and I cry out, grinding my hips against him. "I can't ever imagine being tired of you, Alice Blythe," he near-growls, his lips brushing my nipple.

I wrap one thigh tighter around him, desperate for more, my heart pounding. "Prove it," I gasp.

He laughs softly, pulling away to meet my gaze, one of those dark brows arched. Slowly, his thumb still working in quickening circles at my core, he slips another finger inside me, sliding in and out. "Oh, sweet girl," Wyatt murmurs, bringing his mouth back to my breast. "When I'm done, there won't be a doubt left in your mind that I want every last part of you."

Desire rockets through me, white-hot and hungry. "Then give me more," I beg, bucking my hips into his hands. "Give me all of you. Now."

"You sure know how to make a man feel wanted," he replies with a chuckle, reaching over to the nightstand and grabbing a condom from a drawer. I whimper when he pulls away from me, but as he rocks back, I'm treated to a perfect view of him: broad shoulders and a tapered waist, all wiry, coiled muscle from hard work. My gaze drops to his cock as he pulls the condom on.

"Fuck," is all I manage, biting my lip.

His eyes slide to me, the rest of his body still, amusement playing on his lips. "Like what you see?" he asks with an arched brow. Before I can answer, his gaze roams my body, bare to him in the lamplight. His cock jumps, and an intense jolt of pure need spears through my chest.

"Don't make me wait any longer," I whimper, reaching for his forearm. He laughs and leans forward, drowning me in a kiss that makes me forget the rest of the world exists. I can feel the evidence of his desire against my damp wetness, and it's all so fucking perfect that I moan into his mouth.

"I love it when you make that sound," Wyatt growls, sliding his arm under my waist and pulling my hips flush with his. I tangle my hands in his mussed hair, capturing his lower lip between my teeth.

"I need you inside of me," I tell him. "Or I'm gonna scream."

"Oh, darlin' girl," he laughs. "I'm gonna make you scream either way."

And then—*finally*—he's inside me, filling me to the brim. My entire body throbs with pleasure, my chest heaving into his.

"Wyatt," I pant, digging my fingernails into his shoulders as he moves against me, sliding one hand between our hips. Deftly, he finds my clit, his circles harder and faster now.

"Fuck, Alice," he moans in a low, hoarse voice that takes my breath away. "You're godsdamn perfect, you know that? Like you were made for me."

I'm soaking wet and trembling with need. "Harder," I demand, sliding my tongue into his mouth. "Fuck me harder."

He obeys without protest, entwining one hand into my tangled waves and then driving his hips into mine so hard that my head bangs into the bedframe. I barely fucking notice, my mind fuzzy with pleasure and unbridled joy—okay, and probably the tequila, a little.

"Shit," Wyatt says, reaching down to grab a pillow from the floor. He still slides in and out of me, pulling a strangled cry from my mouth, as he props the pillow up behind my head with one hand. "You alright?"

"*Much* more than alright," I tease with a laugh, looking up at him. "You're such a damn gentleman." I can't believe he's real. I can't believe that in this shit world, Wyatt Hayes even *exists*, let alone wants me—wants me this bad, his eyes glittering with desire, mouth swollen from my kiss.

"Oh, Blythe," he breathes as he plants both hands on either side of my head. He moves in and out of me slowly, the muscles on his abdomen rippling. Pleasure and pressure mount low in my belly. "I'm not always such a gentleman." He pauses, considering me with what might be adoration in his eyes. "You make me into a wild thing."

I grin at him. "Show me, Hayes."

With a velvety groan that makes my head spin, Wyatt does exactly that. He drives into me hard—hard enough to make the headboard bang against the wall. I barely hear it, so utterly lost in him. My entire world is little more than the feeling of his warm, tan skin against mine, the taste of him in my mouth, the thick, hard length of him inside me.

I should go slower, I know—it's been a long time. But I don't care. I want him like this, half-feral, both of us a bit mad with desire. I want to know I'm not the only one who's been delirious and distracted by thoughts of finding myself in bed with him.

"Been thinking about this for so long," Wyatt admits, like he's read my mind, panting against my jaw as he drives into me again and again. I realize distantly that I can barely hear him over the sound of my own moans, high and breathless, barely sounding like myself. "I dreamed about being deep inside you, that smart little mouth saying my name over and over."

Pleasure gathers in me like a stormfront, electricity crackling. I wrap my fingers around one of his wrists and try to pull his hand back between my legs. He laughs and rolls us over, putting me on top. I spread my legs wide to take him all the way inside me, drawing a deep breath. He grips my hips hard, fingers pressing into my skin—and, fuck, I love it. I try to memorize it: Wyatt Hayes beneath me, his mouth parted in a breathy moan, his chest rising in a short, hard breath.

I push my hair off my shoulders, my skin growing damp, and roll my hips, beginning to ride him. I start off gentle, trying to get my bearings, a little embarrassed by my lack of muscle memory. But then he meets my gaze.

"Thought we weren't goin' slow, love," he murmurs. "Ride me hard, Blythe."

It's impossible not to give this man what he wants—especially because he rarely asks for anything at all. I wish he'd ask me for everything he's ever desired, because I would do my goddamn best to make sure every single thing came true. But for now, I just grin, rolling my hips harder against him. A wave of pleasure sweeps through me, and I greedily fuck him harder, my breasts bouncing, drawing the most wonderful sounds from his mouth.

Wyatt slides his hands from my hips to my breasts, playing with my nipples until I cry out, the tension in my core almost too much to bear. "You take my cock so well," he groans, driving his hips up into mine.

"Wyatt," I pant, pulling one of his hands to my core. He obliges, pinching my nipple as he works his fingers against my clit. It's all a perfect symphony of pleasure, like nothing I've ever experienced before. "I think you might've been made just for me."

"I think so, too," he replies, returning his hands to my hips, where he grips me so hard, I cry out. "Now, are you gonna come for me, Alice? Shatter for me?"

"Yes," I whimper, grinding against him, pulling a breathless groan from his mouth. "God, I love how you feel inside of me."

Wyatt grins, a tumble of dark hair falling across his forehead. "Show me how good it feels," he commands, his voice gone low and rough. "Come all over my cock, sweet girl."

His words send me tumbling over the edge, and I cry out, his name dripping like honey from my tongue, my body gone boneless and trembling as I crest the towering wave of pleasure. My vision goes near-black, and then I find myself lying on Wyatt, our chests pressed together, his arms wrapped around me. We're both breathing hard, a slick sheen of sweat coating our skin.

"Best damn day of my life, Blythe," he chuckles, pressing a kiss to my forehead. But I can feel that he's still rock-hard inside me, so I push to sit up, my brow furrowed.

"Not yet," I tell him with a grin. "Tell me what you want. You pulled me all the way in. Now tell me what I gotta do to pull *you* all the way in."

He pushes a damp wave of hair away from my forehead. "I think I'm already there," he murmurs. "Think I've been there for a while."

I raise a brow at him, sitting back to ride him again—slower this time, pulling myself all the way up before sliding back down. He lets out a hoarse, husky sound, his fingers clutching my hips. I grin with triumph.

"Tell me, Hayes," I say, riding him harder now, watching his attention stray as my breasts bounce.

This time, he doesn't hesitate, rolling me back over with a ferocity that makes me weak. He gathers me up in his arms, pulling my legs tightly around his hips. "I'm gonna bury myself inside you, Alice," he whispers against my neck.

"You better," I reply, nipping at his ear. He groans in response, tangling his hands in my hair, and then fucks me so hard that if he had neighbors, they'd absolutely hear me screaming his name like I'm in a goddamn porno.

"Fuck, Alice," he rasps, his head tilted back in pure ecstasy, the golden lamplight tracing the sharp line of his jaw. "Gods, you feel so good."

"How long?" I manage to gasp. "How long have you been imagining this?"

He pauses, leaning down on his elbows to capture my mouth in a long, lingering kiss, his hips moving slower now.

"Since you walked into the Stardust office. Since day one and every moment since."

It's more than pleasure rekindling itself in my body now. It's the feeling that I could grow old with him. No, we don't know what the future holds—but right now, tangled up in Wyatt's sheets, his mouth on mine, I know with a fierceness that if we both continue wanting each other, nothing will ever be able to tear us apart.

"Fill me up, then," I tell him, biting down on his lower lip until he rolls his hips harder into mine. "Show me everything you've been saving for me."

With a near-feral sound that sends anticipation shivering through my body, Wyatt sits back up, his hands gripping my waist. "Lift those lovely hips for me," he growls, sliding his palms to the crooks of my knees as I obey his command. My back arches as he increases his pace, and I reach for him, digging my fingernails into his shoulders as he fucks me as hard as I've been wishing he would.

"Alice," he cries out, so much feeling in the two scant syllables of my name. I feel his cock pulse inside me, pushing deliciously against my throbbing walls. I savor every second—his parted mouth, eyes locked on mine, filled with something that I know could be love, one day, if it's what we both want.

To my surprise, the pleasure in my core flutters, and another orgasm rises inside of me, sweeping my body with warmth. I bite out his name as he buries his head in the crook of my neck, one hand stroking my hair, powerful fingers so impossibly gentle.

He rolls to the side, immediately pulling me into his arms. I settle my head on his chest, his skin damp. Drawing in a deep breath of his smell, all bonfires and deep pine woods, I close my eyes, utterly spent and beyond satisfied. Tomorrow morning, I hope I'll get to see more of Wyatt's space—of his room, of his home, of the knick-knacks he's chosen for his bookshelves and Fern's favorite spot on the battered Chesterfield I passed out on earlier.

I want to *know* him, and I want him to know me just as deeply. Tears fill my eyes, and I feel so silly for it, but...I haven't been close to many people in my life. Beyond my startling lack of lasting romantic connections, I've just always struggled to fit in.

But here, in a handsome stone farmhouse high in Blackbird Hollow's hills, tucked in Wyatt Hayes's arms, I feel like I fit perfectly.

Wyatt mumbles something, breaking my reverie as he presses a kiss to my temple. My heart lurches as he gets up, but he's back in a few moments with a towel, in case I want to clean up a little, and a giant mason jar filled with water. Then we're back in bed together, our limbs winding together, his mouth finding mine unerringly, even in the nighttime gloom.

His lips trail over my collarbone, my breasts, my belly, my hips, and then my thighs. "Tryin' to memorize all of you," he says in a rough voice against my skin, shifting further down the bed. "But you see, Alice, I'm missing a crucial bit of information..."

I lift my head to look at him quizzically, only to find him sliding between my legs. "And what's that?"

He slips his hands around my thighs with a devilish grin, his gaze dropping to the damp, aching place at the apex of my legs. "What you taste like, sweet girl."

Chapter 28
Wyatt

Halloween dawned red and blurry, the sun barely making the effort to cut through the blue haze, but I rolled over when Fallon opened my front door, calling softly to Fern that it was time to go out. I'm grateful for her help, and the privacy. We have a policy about mission days—sleep as late as possible—but Fallon can't ever manage it. However, I can, so I tucked Alice under my chin and fell back asleep.

Now, I wake with a start, adrenaline running through me, my dreams a blank space in my mind. Alice is sprawled out next to me, her arm thrown over my chest. I made her drink a ton of water, and she ate half a pizza before we slept, but we could still use a donut or two to stave off any lingering effects of a girls' night with Fallon.

I slip out of bed, grabbing a worn Slice o' Heaven t-shirt from my old Eastlake dresser. The clock next to the bed says it's almost one. Alice stirs a little, her eyes bleary.

"Hey," she whispers, her voice somewhat hoarse.

I can't help but be pleased by that fact. I did have her making a racket last night. "Go back to sleep for a bit," I urge her. "We've got a big evening in front of us. I'm going to get donuts."

"Okay," she murmurs, soft and sleepy, rolling over to the edge of the bed to slip her hand into mine. "You're not sneaking away, then?"

I crouch down to push her blonde waves away from her face. "I'm not going anywhere but the bakery, sweet girl."

She makes a happy noise, and then her breath evens out. She's actually relaxed. When I open the door, Fern bounds in from the hall, climbing right into bed with Alice, who hugs her close.

Fallon's sitting on my back deck. She's wearing a near-ancient sweater, the pastel yarn woven into a pastoral scene with a bunch of sheep on it and a pair of track shorts so tiny I can barely see them.

"Put some damn clothes on," I mutter at her. "You'll catch cold."

"You're not the boss of me," she spits back.

"Fair enough," I reply, heading back into the house, my sister close behind.

In the kitchen, Fallon fills a twenty-ounce mason jar with water and slams the whole thing down before sighing. "There's *nothing* on that Sector woman. I went out to see Marion, and there's nothing on CCTV whatsoever. She knew her angles. Car went right outta town, too, then disappeared somewhere between Big Hill and the Roadhouse." Fallon clears her throat. "You know what that means."

I hold back the urge to deny what we both know. It would feel better to pretend like Sector wasn't overly interested in Alice, but it won't do any of us a lick of good in the end. "Yeah."

Fallon shakes her head, the same gritty determination in her eyes that's taking root in my chest. "Been a while since they wanted someone from around here."

She's right. Sector hasn't courted anyone from Blackbird Hollow in over a decade. They came after a few of the more powerful witches when Caden was in high school, but they were so roundly turned out that they didn't come back. Well, they didn't come back with those kinds of intentions, anyway. We probably got too complacent. Can't do a thing about that now.

"What're we gonna do?" I ask.

Fallon sighs. "I went out to Cade's last night, after I talked to Marion. I've got feelers out."

I rest my shoulder on the side of the fridge, feeling worn through all of a sudden. There's too many things happening at once, and I'm near-certain I'm missing something vital about all this. "What kind of feelers?"

Fallon sighs as she gets coffee out of the cabinet. She knows her way around my kitchen as well as I know hers. "The official kind."

My eyebrows raise, shock running deep through me. "Council feelers?"

The sound of the coffee grinder obscures whatever my sister says, but she nods, her expression grim as I've ever seen it.

The Hedgerider Council was absolute shit when our parents died. They did nothing but remind Fallon that she was duty-bound to keep up the family business and sent an amount of cash so meager it was gone in an instant. We've hated them ever since—steered clear of them as much as we could. There's only a few ways they'd make Alice official, and it's too soon for anything that serious, but if she were Council-official it *would* stop Sector from coming after her.

"You want her to stay," I breathe.

Fallon narrows her eyes at me as she dumps the coffee grounds into the machine. "Yeah, I do. She makes you all gooey and easy to deal with, and..." Fallon trails off, the pain in her eyes nearly killing me. "She gets me. It's not hard with Alice, like it is with other people."

I reach out and squeeze Fallon's shoulder, feeling the wiry muscle under her sheep-patterned sweater. "If they ask, you tell them I'll comply with whatever their terms are. Can't say how Alice will react to that, but it doesn't have to be a whole thing."

Fallon chuckles. "Yeah, I'm sure Alice will see marrying you as a casual event." The humor drains out of her smile. "But I get the feeling an engagement might do the trick. We're sure as shit not getting her Fey-blessed."

That would require a trip under the hill, a bid to the Courts, and we're all as likely to die or go mad as we are to come back with protection for Alice. So we're definitely not doing that. They'll suggest it, though. The Council is full of bastards like that. Ancient councils are fucked-up business, after all.

I blow out a big, deep breath. "Well, we haven't had a betrothal in the family since Mama and Pa. If that's what it takes and Alice agrees, it'll keep her safe for life."

Hedgeriders can get a divorce, but once you're in, by blood or by marriage, there's no getting out. Fallon makes a noncommittal kind of noise as the coffee maker bubbles to life.

"What's that about?" I ask.

She glances at me, a prim little smile on her face. "Nothing."

"You don't have nothing-face," I reply, following her to the front porch.

"I'm going to make some eggs," she says. "So if you're going to get donuts, get at it."

"Fallon." I grab her sleeve. "You need to tell me if there's something about all this you see as an issue."

She shakes her head. "There isn't."

I think back, carefully examining my words to ferret out what I might have missed. What I might have said to make her react like this. It's a game I'm good at with Fallon. My heart skips a beat.

"Who is it?" I growl. If the Council wants Fallon married off, I'll be damned if I let that happen. "Who're they trying to force on you?"

She sighs. "Nobody."

My sister's not big on outright lies, unless she's running a mission. But she sure ain't telling the truth right now. I don't ask another question. I just stand and stare at her.

She looks up at me, then shakes her head. "It doesn't matter, Wyatt. I'm old as the hills and he's never come looking for me. Doubt there's much chance that he'll come this way now."

Old as the hills. Is that really how she sees herself? I get it, though. Having to grow up as fast as we did fucked us both up. Still, this is all new information for me. "Mama and Pa already arranged something...*before*?"

My sister lets out a sharp bark of a laugh. "Of course they did. I'm the Hayes heir. Their union joined together two of the most important bloodlines in the North." She shakes her head. "Did you think Mama wouldn't trade me off like cattle at her quickest convenience?"

Her words are harsh, but she's right. I'm not sure why I never wondered. Maybe we've been out here, away from other hedgeriders, for too long. Slowly, I shake my head. "If he ever does show up...whoever he is—"

Fallon throws a hand up in the air. "He ever shows up, and I'll deal with it myself. Don't worry about me. Worry about Alice."

I'VE GOT an order in for hot donut holes and a half-pint of Mac's hollandaise, but the diner's bustling and there's a bit of a wait, so I head across the town square to talk to Willa Proctor, who's working in the community garden with Sally Laveau.

"Willa," I call, just as she lifts a pumpkin into the wheelbarrow next to her. It's huge, too big for her to lift on her own, probably, but Willa's got a way with magic.

She looks up at me as she sets the pumpkin down, dragging the back of her hand over her pale forehead, leaving a streak of dirt. "Hiya, Wyatt," she drawls.

She's from out west somewhere, though I've never heard anyone say exactly where that is. Fallon hoped we'd hit it off when she moved here, but we never did. Not romantically, anyway. Willa's just about as gun-shy as I was 'til Alice showed up.

Today, Willa's dark brown hair is pulled back in two thick braids. She's wearing a cotton floral dress and a pair of heavy work boots. As soon as she sees my expression, she asks, "What's wrong?"

"Your wards," I explain. "Out at Cade's. They let some redcaps through."

"Shit," she breathes out, but there's not a scrap of panic in her eyes. "Tell me what you saw."

I nod, recounting the scene to her as best I can. Her amber eyes are solemn and attentive as a hawk's, her sharp features drawn with concern. She looks ancient and impossibly young all at once, like all the most powerful witches. I take a moment to wonder if we've all missed something about Willa. If there might be more to her than just her uncommon talent for wards.

"Mossy footprints?" she asks, shaking her head. "That's not redcaps or pixies. Nor's it likely to be the hellhounds."

"Not exactly footprints," I muse. "Sort of, but...I don't

know, not really *formed*. Just made me think of footprints, I guess."

She nods, glancing at Sally, who shakes her head. "That's one of the High. Hard to say which one." Sally's eye catches sight of Belle, who's pulling carrots. "Stay in that row, baby girl." She winks at me. "Don't want her pulling up the mandrake just yet."

Willa smiles at the little girl before turning back to me. "I'll get out there tomorrow, after the Hunt's gone, and take a look."

"Thank you," I reply, though there's something in Willa's voice that hesitates, like she's unsure about something. I glance down at the giant gourd in her wheelbarrow and grin, sure I've sussed out the source of her uncertainty. "Can I help you get this monster pumpkin somewhere?"

Willa laughs. "No, I've got it. It's for the gym."

I nod, frowning a little as I follow her across the square. We're all on edge today. "It was a good idea to do trick-or-treating there tonight—should keep our kids and the leafer kids safe. Wanda says you thought of it."

Willa smiles faintly, but her eyes are sad. "Kids are precious. Can't have 'em snatched up."

I wonder what that sadness is about for the briefest of moments, but as we pause to cross the street, Willa's hand skims across her belly, and the sadness in her eyes intensifies. Sorrow pangs in my chest. Too many of us have been through too much.

Barnes Whitney waves from across the street, shouting that Janey's got my order ready.

"Good luck tonight," Willa says as we part ways. Her fingers brush my arm as she passes. It's a friendly gesture that leaves me warm and a little sleepy-feeling. I blink a little as she says, "I'll call tomorrow evening and let you know what I find out about your footprints."

"Thanks," I reply, before jogging in the opposite direction. I have the nagging feeling that I've forgotten something, but I'm not sure what it is. There's probably just too much going on today.

Barnes waits for me. "Got everything ready for tonight. We need an extra gun or two? My cousin Julius came up with Mona last night."

Barnes's cousins are worth ten of the folk around here when it comes to dealing with Them, and Julius's wife Mona was a sharpshooter in the last of the conflicts out West. "I'd sure appreciate it. You all head out to the house in a couple of hours and we'll get you fitted with the right ammo. Cade's got a couple of new toys."

Barnes raises an eyebrow. "Blackstone?"

I nod, glaring a little. "Sure thing. Kid's got a death wish, but it's convenient this time."

He grins, shaking his head. "We'll keep 'em in line." With a clap on my shoulder, he squints at me. "We've got this, Hayes. This time tomorrow, we'll be out at Lupine Falls getting the bonfire started."

I nod, but there's a tight sort of feeling in my throat. Mama always used to say that nothing's over 'til it's over, and I'm afraid she's right.

Janey sticks her head out the door of the diner, a paper bag in hand that smells like maple donuts, bacon, and buttery goodness. "Mac fried up some bacon, and put some of those crumbles into the butter for dipping, the way Fallon likes."

"Thank you, Janey," I reply as she blows me a kiss.

Barnes nods to me. "See you in a bit."

"Sounds good," I say, turning back toward the truck.

The sun feels like it never rose all the way today, and there's a tense feeling in the chill air, like time's about to stop. I feel a little relieved that Julius and Mona showed up, but the only thing that gets us through tonight is to keep moving. It's time to get this show on the road.

As I pull up to my house, Caden and Fallon are out front with Fern and Alice. Fern dances around, while Fallon laughs so hard that she has to wipe her eyes, and Cade's face is red, while Alice moves her hands, describing something I can't hear just yet.

Her eyes sparkle with delight that they're laughing, but she's not giggling at her own tale. There's nothing that looks like the tension she held in her face last night about Cookie, but there's a tightness to her movements I've come to recognize as worry lurking beneath her skin. But then her gaze snags on the truck, her eyes going straight to mine, and she looks almost peaceful, her shoulders relaxing the tiniest measure.

And in that moment, I know I'm done for. All I've ever wanted is for someone to look at me like that. To look at me like I'm just the thing they were waiting for. And my heart nearly bursts, because I was waiting for her, too.

Chapter 29
Alice

I shove one of the last remaining donuts into my mouth as I push the door of Wyatt's truck open, my half-full travel mug of coffee in my other hand. Fern's right at my heels, jumping down onto the cracked blacktop. The air is thick with the smell of woodsmoke as I draw in a deep breath.

I shut the door and tip my head back, looking up at the large building—an old factory with a hardware store on the first floor. Like everything else, it's closed up tight. Main Street yawns wide and empty at my back, the sweep of dusk curling around Blackbird Hollow like a giant's fist.

Halloween night is here. The Hunt is coming.

"Do you feel it?" Wyatt asks me from the other side of the truck, where he's gazing down into the valleys that spill out below Main Street. He's got his head tilted to one side, hands in the pockets of his jacket, the last scraps of the sunlight outlining him in gold, and for a moment, he looks immeasurably ancient. Or maybe just...not entirely human, like there's something else running through his veins, something that's different from the rest of us.

When he turns to look at me, he's just Wyatt again. I consider his question, opening my mouth to say no. But then a nameless feeling stirs in me, and I press my lips together, gazing into the hills. For once, no porch lights twinkle. No smoke curls from chimneys or bonfires. Instead, it's just darkness. I know that everyone's doors are locked, lined with rowan and iron. The wind comes blowing again, wild and crackling with energy. For a moment, I do feel it. Not because I'm a hedgerider—because I'm *human*.

And we've always been afraid of the things that come in the night.

"Actually," I finally say, turning back to him, another shiver creeping along my shoulders, "yeah, I think I do."

"Don't really know whether that's a good or a bad thing, to be honest," he tells me. He pauses, gesturing to the factory's roof, which'll serve as our post for the evening. "Ready?" he asks.

He offers me his hand, and I gladly take it, our fingers lacing together. I don't think I believe in things like fate or destiny, or even soulmates. But it's hard not to feel like we weren't made from the same stardust. Or some shit like that.

Fuck. I'm in *love*, aren't I?

I set my jaw and follow Wyatt through a side door into the old factory. As we begin to climb a set of enormous metal stairs, the same two sentences echo through my brain, over and over again:

I just found him.

And I'm damn well not gonna lose him.

"Alright," Wyatt mutters, settling into the camp chair next to me a little less than an hour later, the muzzle of his gun resting on the roof's ledge. "We're as ready as we'll ever be."

I take a deep breath, surveying Main Street from our vantage point, perched a few stories above ground level. The leaf peepers and weekenders seem to be cooperating. Even the Archer Inn's outdoor dining patio, which flanks the side of the elegant antique building, is bare of any tables and chairs. Above us, dark clouds roil in front of the quarter-moon, looking ominous as all hell.

Luckily, it's only an illusion courtesy of the town's witches, cast to help convince out-of-towners to stay the fuck inside. On a night this quiet, I should be able to hear oldies like Type O Negative or Concrete Blonde blaring from Lucky's just a few doors down, but it's utterly silent. Besides the leaves driven into wild dances by the wind, there's no movement at all. For a town usually so full of life, it's deeply eerie.

The handheld radio crackles to life, scaring the shit out of me. "You sure we shouldn't swap?" comes Falllon's staticky voice. "Alice and I need to have a girls' night debriefing. Also, if you get all horny while the Hunt's here and end up distracted, that'll make us look bad."

I burst into laughter, snatching the radio before Wyatt grabs it. I can't put into words how grateful I am for her dry, flippant humor right now. "We're good, I promise," I tell Fallon, looking across Main Street to where I can just make out her form on the roof of the Archer Inn. "Could we add a girls' night round-up into the 'we survived the Hunt' debriefing?"

There's a pause, and then Fallon's voice returns. "No, Alice, don't be absurd," she replies gravely. "We can't just tack something so silly onto a huge, important discussion."

I nod, tucking a stray lock of hair back into my braid. "You're right," I reply, turning to Wyatt. "We might have to postpone the debriefing on the Hunt."

Fallon's cackle echoes through the handheld radio at the same time Wyatt rolls his eyes.

"The devil made you both on the same day," he grumbles, doing a bad job of hiding his smile as he checks the chamber of his gun—for the third time, I can't help but notice.

I open my mouth to shoot back, because the humor feels so good right now, but then Fern gives a low warning growl from where she's lying between us. In the dim moonlight, I watch her slowly rise. Her coat stands on end, tail held stiff and straight as she sticks her head over the half-wall at the roof's edge. Time seems to grind down, impossibly slow, as she takes a long, deep inhale, like she's searching for a scent in the air.

The moon breaks through the witches' clouds, turning Fern into something that looks remarkably like a silver wolf. My breath catches. Then she throws her head back and howls—long, mournful, more human than any dog I've ever heard, and yet so incredibly *in*human it makes the hair on the back of my neck stand up.

Without a word, Wyatt cocks his gun. The rifle in my hands is filled with salt capsules, but he's got pure iron loaded in his chamber, anointed with Wanda's faesbane oil—a highly guarded recipe that's been in her coven for hundreds of years, since They came to these shores.

Everything seems to hold perfectly still, and then the radio resting next to my knee crackles. It's Caden's voice this time, not Fallon's—deep and resonant, perfectly calm.

"They're here."

Some strange, heady mixture of eagerness and terror floods me, my heart slamming into the delicate skin of my throat. I peer over the half-wall, scanning Main Street, which more or less follows the ley line. I don't have Caden's wolf-vision, though, so I don't see anything yet but shadow and lamplight.

"You good, sweet girl?" Wyatt asks me, his voice uncharacteristically strained.

"I'm good," I tell him, my finger resting on the salt rifle's trigger.

He snorts softly at that, letting out a long breath. "I'm damn lucky that you're a little crazy."

I'm about to reply, probably to say something that's more than a *little* crazy, like declaring that I think I want to spend the rest of my life with him—but then movement catches my gaze. In my peripheral vision, I watch Wyatt go completely still—and it's at the same moment that Fern appears to stop breathing entirely.

There's something coming up the hill.

"Something wicked this way comes," I murmur, leaning my shoulder into the butt of the rifle. It's been a while since I shot one, but Fallon gave me a refresher earlier today. I feel ready. Or, at least, ready enough.

A kind of rumbling crackle fills the air, and my heart flutters wildly. Then a strong scent slams into my nose; it takes me eons to realize it's utterly mundane. Gasoline. My mouth falls open, brows knitting together as I watch what looks like a bunch of motorcycles pull into town. If not for the sheer amount of Them, and if not for the days of preparation that went into all this, I might be willing to overlook the sleek bikes and gleaming, studded leather, the pitch-dark helmets and hungry revving of the engines. If I were anywhere else, on any other day, I might watch these motorcyclists ride by without more than a curious glance.

But I'm *here*, perched on a roof next to a hedgerider, and I know too much now. My breath is shaky as I pull it into my lungs, desperately trying to understand how something that looks like simple motorcycles can cover so much ground this quickly.

"Hold steady," comes Fallon's voice, incredibly calm, over the radio. "They're just passing through."

It's a reminder and an observation, I realize. They're making no attempts to stop, as if all the iron and rowan are propelling Them forward, keeping Them faithful to the narrow, glimmering ley line.

With one hand, Wyatt reaches for the radio. "Sector," he says. "Archer Inn."

I grit my teeth, glancing toward the building across from us, on the other side of Main Street. My eyes hunt through the nighttime gloom until I find the outlines of two undoubtedly besuited people. They're cloaked in the shadows of the fancy burgundy awning, but they're there. Outside. As the Wild goddamn Hunt comes roaring up the street.

"Are they fucking insane?" I ask, weirdly breathless for not moving at all.

Wyatt makes a low noise of disapproval from the back of his throat. "Was hopin' they'd observe from inside," he grumbles. "That's just reckless."

"I hope it's that woman from last night," I say, surprising myself with the malice in my tone. "And I hope They fucking take her."

He glances over at me, his smirk outlined by the moon and all the more enticing for it. "You know, if you look at Them out of the corner of your eye," he tells me, studying me closely, "you'll be able to see. Really see. If you want to."

I sit up straight in my camp chair, staring at him quizzically. I glance down at the motorcyclists drawing ever closer, and then back at Wyatt.

He arches a brow before returning his gaze to the sights of his rifle. "I think we both know you want to, Blythe."

"Of course I do," I whisper in response, twisting my torso around, trying to catch the Hunt in my peripherals. For a few moments, I'm unsuccessful, cranking my head back and forth. It's only once I narrow my eyes and glance away, about to ask Wyatt for further instructions, that it finally works.

My stomach drops. A primordial sort of fear unfolds in my veins, like this terror had been stitched to my ribs my entire life and I just never needed it until now.

"Good god," I gasp, squeezing my eyes shut before I can stop myself.

"The High Fey," Wyatt murmurs with what might actually be a hint of reverence. "In all Their glory. All Their horror."

Gone are the motorcycles gleaming in the moonlight, a sea of anonymous black visors. Even the scent of gasoline seems to morph in my nose, becoming something strange and wild: rain-drenched stone, a splash of mead, a curl of woodsmoke, and dark, lingering spices I can't name.

My heart slamming against my sternum, I peer into the darkness from the corners of my eyes. My mind desperately tries to explain what I'm seeing, commanding me to turn my head and realize that They're not so terrifying, not really.

But I hold myself at that defiant angle, chin tipped up, as I watch the Wild Hunt. At the front, a long-limbed Fey with streaming copper hair dressed in a diaphanous gown rides some kind of chimera—a panther-like body with too many eyes, set spider-like onto its forehead, and the vicious tail of a scorpion.

Creatures that I think must be kelpies flank the lead rider. If I keep Them in my peripheral gaze, if I resist the urge to look away, I can hear the sound of those wet, backward hooves on the pavement instead of revving engines. Upon the kelpies' wide, long backs are people that I distantly recognize as human. For now, at least. I do not know what the Wild Hunt does with the ones They take. I let out a shaking breath, watching the kelpies' greenish, corpse-light eyeshine in the dark, something poisonous-looking dripping from Their fanged equine mouths.

I am not sure that I *really* want to know.

Behind the chimera and its kelpie-guard is a long line of elegant terror. Some of Them look like us, minus the too-tall bodies and pointed ears, but there's something so viciously inhuman in Their faces that it makes my entire body quiver with fear. A monstrous horse with spider-legs and swiveling bat's ears patrols the left flank of the Hunt, red eyes flashing in the moonlight. Six black warhorses walk abreast in a perfect line, their riders pale as death. As They draw closer, I can see the riders' eye sockets are all empty and sightless, Their mouths crudely sewn shut with thick, dark thread. I glance down to find Their hands are stitched to their mounts' necks. Queasiness floods my stomach, and I squeeze my eyes shut.

Fallon's voice sparks to life over the radio. "Wyatt, we got a runner. Not one of ours."

Her words set in, and my eyes fly open. It would be a lie to say I'm not grateful for the way there's only a large horde of motorcyclists in front of me again, though the smell of gasoline doesn't return—it's still all rain-damp stone and dark spice and woodsmoke. Wyatt's already speaking quickly into the radio as I lean over the half-wall, desperately searching the street.

A small child costumed as a tiny bear cub runs from the back of the Archer Inn, where there's a few guest cabins at the edge of the woods. I suck in my breath painfully, fingers curling around the trigger of the rifle.

"Hold," Wyatt tells me, throwing out his free hand to grip my shoulder. My heart leaps into my throat, every vein in my body pounding as I watch the little one toddle toward the Hunt. The child can't be more than three or four, their face filled with guileless joy beneath the hooded bear-cub onesie.

"No fuckin' way," Fallon says over the radio.

I'm pretty sure Wyatt and I both stop breathing as we

search the street below us, looking for the source of Fallon's comment.

One of the Sector agents, a bland-looking woman in her thirties with mousy hair and a dark suit, leaves the shadows of the awning and walks to the end of the sidewalk. My hand grows clammy against the rifle's trigger, my blood pounding so hard I feel faint. Even though the child wanders closer to the Wild Hunt, the Sector woman stays perfectly still. In the moonlight, I see her cross her arms, eyes narrowed.

"Oh my fucking god," I spit. "She's *watching*. To see what happens when someone gets taken."

Wyatt grunts his agreement as Fern whines. "Stand down, girl," he says to her, his voice heavy.

My mind runs ragged and wild, and I'm pushing up out of the camp chair before I realize what I'm doing. But the salt cartridges in my rifle won't do shit against the Hunt. I should've let Fallon give me real bullets. It's not like she didn't offer. I just didn't trust myself.

"Wyatt," I hiss between my teeth as a gleaming white horse turns away from the Hunt's pack, its cloaked rider reining it toward the child. A hand reaches out, beckoning with too-long fingers. The sound of the little kid's giggle—enticed by a glamour, I'm sure—sinks into my blood like lead. My gaze jumps to the Sector woman, who's walked a few more steps into the street, nothing but clinical interest on her face.

"I can't get a clean shot. I've gotta go down," comes Fallon's voice over the radio. I look toward Wyatt in horror, terrified that I'm going to watch the Wild Hunt steal Fallon *and* the little one. But then his brow furrows, and I think I know him well enough to know he's just made a decision by the particular set of his jaw.

A second later, he turns the muzzle of his rifle away from the Hunt and shoots the Sector woman in the leg. She screams and drops to the ground, her limbs thrashing like a deer struck by a car. My ears pound and I bite down on my tongue so hard that I taste blood.

The Hunt moves like a tide. No longer flowing along the ley line, waves of Them break off and swarm the Sector woman. I realize with a start that even though I'm looking straight at Them, I can *see* Them for what They truly are.

Crowns of bone glint in the lamplight, stained with old blood. Severed fingers decorate the long, tangled manes of desiccated horses that shouldn't even be standing, let alone carrying a rider. The cloaked figure on the gleaming white horse throws Their hood back, revealing one of the most impossibly beautiful faces I've ever seen. They smile, showing Their teeth, mother-of-pearl sharpened into a thousand knives.

There are other things, too. Things I don't have language for, things that my mind won't let me look at for more than a moment or two.

So I happily glance away, blocking out the tortured screams of the Sector woman as the Hunt drags her away. Instead, I search for the rounded ears of the little one's bear costume. Relief surges through me when I find them being shepherded out of the street by an ivory-skinned woman with two long, dark braids. The zippers on her leather biker jacket glint in the lamplight as she takes the child by the arm, pulling them gently toward the sidewalk. There, Fallon's waiting on the ground level of the Archer Inn. She takes the child into her arms before disappearing behind the faesbane-dressed doors.

I collapse against Wyatt, Fern shoving her wet nose into my cold hands as I bury my face into his shoulder. "Fuck," I whisper, my mind a tangle of horror and relief.

"Hopefully that's as exciting as things get tonight," he says, though there's something guarded in his tone. "I didn't—look, I hope you don't..."

I pull away to glance at him, my adrenaline running so high that for a long moment, I have difficulty understanding his words, let alone the look on his face. Until, all at once, I do, thinking about our conversation all those days ago—days that feel more like a lifetime.

"You did the right thing," I tell him, reaching up to brush a lock of dark hair out of his face.

He smiles at me, the curve of his mouth just as dangerous as the Wild Hunt in the streets below. "I don't have any question about that," he says, raising one brow. The confidence in his expression falters. "Only if you—"

"You did the right thing," I repeat, my fingers trailing to his collarbone. "And it didn't bother me at all." I pause, trying to actually take stock of my feelings, and apparently decide to blurt out, "It was pretty hot, honestly."

His smile returns, and slick heat floods me. I lean in, my hand taking a fistful of his jacket, before the radio crackles again.

"Do you guys see Willa?" comes Fallon's voice—panicked, for once.

Wyatt and I both whip back around to the street, leaning over the roof's edge. The witch who shepherded the kid to Fallon is still in the street. Her body faces the safety of her coven, who have gathered on the porch, but her head is turned toward the Hunt. Her eyes are narrowed, her lips moving ever so slightly, like she's reciting a spell.

"Wanda, can you come in for me?" Wyatt asks. In my peripheral vision, I can see his hands shaking on the radio.

I hear Wanda's rich voice, completely calm and heavy with authority, but all I see is Willa as she turns to fully face the Hunt. I'm no expert, but I don't think she's in a thrall—her face is still hers, none of that moon-eyed glassiness Wyatt warned me about. She bites down on the inside of her cheek just as a motorcycle pulls over, idling. The rider pulls Their helmet off, revealing long, tumbling silver hair. In the lamplight, I see an impossibly beautiful and fiercely masculine face turn toward Willa, Their jawline sharp as a knife. My breath catches.

They—he, maybe—calls out to Willa. She stares at him, unafraid, her gaze moving slowly from the crown of his head to his heavy boots resting on either side of the motorcycle. I'm no lip-reader, but it's almost like all the adrenaline crystallizes my hearing and my vision.

"Oh," I swear Willa says. "So it's time?"

The Fey on the motorcycle grins at her. It's unabashedly flirtatious, the corners of his mouth curving into an expression that would be more at home in a romantasy novel than in the feral, hungry tides of the Hunt.

"Yes," he growls—*actually* growls—the single word a deep, dark rumble from the back of his throat.

Willa's clearly nervous, but in the back of my mind, I realize that she's dressed like...like she's going somewhere. Her leather jacket's zipped closed with a bandana tied around her neck, and she's wearing black cowboy boots instead of the usual work or hiking shoes I see around town. Well-worn deerskin gloves are tucked into her back pocket like she's got a job to do. Almost as if she's seen the Hunt before. Almost like she's been waiting for this night—but in a much different way than the rest of us.

She walks, stiff-legged, toward the silver-haired Fey, whose gaze devours her in a way that makes me blush from all the way up here on the roof. When Willa reaches him, the Fey wraps one arm around her waist and pulls her against his broad chest. Beside me, Wyatt inhales sharply, bringing his rifle up to shoot. But then we both watch the Fey whisper something in Willa's ear. She *relaxes*. The ledge's concrete bites into my hands as I search her face for evidence of thrall.

Instead, the dark-haired witch looks straight up at us and *nods*. Then she turns to the Archer Inn, giving Fallon and Caden a wave, before turning her gaze back to the coven gathered on Widow's porch and making some complicated gesture with her hand that I don't recognize.

Finally, she turns back to the silver-haired Fey. The moment holds taut for far too long, but then he pulls her up onto the motorcycle, sliding one muscular arm protectively around her waist. With his large, long-fingered hand, he tips her chin up in a strangely gentle movement and examines Willa's face, smirking down at her.

She says one word, clear as day: "Okay."

And then she's gone, the silver-haired Fey rejoining the last of the Wild Hunt as it winds through Blackbird Hollow like a funeral procession. From across the street, Fallon leans over the edge of the inn's roof and yells, "Get it, girl!" at the top of her lungs.

I sit back in my chair, my mind buzzing. For a while, no words come out, but then I turn to Wyatt, my brow furrowed.

"I thought you said that They *weren't* fuckable."

Chapter 30
Wyatt

"Woman," I breathe, unable to decide between laughing and shaking Alice Blythe silly. "You will be the death of me."

My heart races, hardly believing the scene that just played out before us. Hardly believing we survived this without a real fight.

Willa leaving with the Hunt was a wild card that none of us could have anticipated, but... Suddenly, I remember the way Willa acted in the garden. The way she'd been hesitant with me about agreeing to come out to Cade's to check the wards. Had she known all along the Hunt was coming for her? She was certainly dressed to leave.

My mind runs over the details. The sleepy, forgetful feeling I'd gotten when she touched my arm. The way our conversation slipped through the cracks in my mind, almost immediately. I doubt very much that Willa would have let us go to all this trouble if she'd known exactly what would happen here, but she'd known something the rest of us did not. And I had to admit, our plan was executed perfectly.

Too perfectly, probably. I glance at Alice, who's still smiling at her Fey-fucking joke. Godsdamn it, I love it that she finds herself amusing. But my mind can't sink into the moment, into the relief that the town's preparations saved us. That we weren't needed. There's a puzzle piece missing, and I can't tell what it is.

A crackle comes over my walkie. It's Barnes. "The first of the procession has crossed the county line."

The first of Them. That's it. In all the excitement over the little bear cub and Willa, I never spotted the hellhounds. With the amount of Them in these parts recently, there should've been a whole pack. Where the fuck are They?

I switch the channel on my walkie to the one Cade and I use in private. "You sense the pack, bud?"

Alice's eyes widen as my realization sinks into her, too. Her instincts for this life are sharpening. She stands up, craning her neck to and fro, shaking her head at me. She can't see Them.

"No," Caden responds, his voice slow, pondering. "But remember, Dr. Waterhouse's research indicates that They may not stay as close to the Hunt proper as we imagine."

Alice sucks a nervous hiss of air through her teeth, returning to her chair, but she doesn't sit. She's still looking at the dark, shadowed forest, like she might somehow be able to track the hounds at this distance.

She plucks the walkie from my hand, bringing it toward her face. "It's possible They cast a wider net because of Sector's presence, right?"

"Sure is," Cade responds. "And we've still got everything locked down."

The wind shifts, cold as winter, sending the scent of home-fires and pine forest into my nostrils. Not even a hint of sulfur. Fallon comes on next, apparently having returned the bear cub to where he belongs. "Best thing to do now is get everyone inside and keep 'em there."

Mona comes on over the group channel, her voice a slow Southern drawl, rich and warm. "The rear-guard is passing through. Couple'a hellhounds at Their backs."

Cade responds to her. "Good. The rest of the pack?"

Julius replies. "Not yet; probably sweeping the woods, if I had to guess."

Something a little like relief flows through me. None of ours are in the woods tonight, and the coven did their best to keep the leafers out of the way. We might just make it through this unscathed—without too much drama or fanfare—and why shouldn't we?

Barnes and Julius aren't hedgeriders in the sense that they were born into European hedgeriding families. They, and Mona, are known as Hunters here in the Northern Territories. They know the demimonde as well as we do, probably better in some ways. They don't just deal with Them; they deal with the Earthbound. The stuff people used to call cryptids, monsters, and demons. I trust them to help us with this.

Julius, apparently, takes the walkie from his wife. "Where're we drinking?"

"Yeah." Alice laughs. "Where *are* we drinking?"

I click the walkie on. "Lucky's roof. Let's do a quick sweep to make sure folks are staying put, and meet there in an hour."

The walkie static partially obscures Mona's response as they cross out of the county and the coven's enhanced reach. "—see you there. Keep the kids inside for the rest... Be safe."

"Roger that," I respond, filling the blanks in on my own.

Down on the street, Wanda steps off the dark front porch of the herbal shop. She stares at the place Willa disappeared, shaking her head.

"Come down with me," I urge Alice. "I wanna know what the *hell* just happened to Willa."

She nods, slipping her hand into mine. I can't deny that she looks happy, but there's something jittery about her. Like all this has amped her up too much and she can't quite stop moving. She follows me down the iron steps of the fire escape, Fern close behind, and when we get to the last step, I turn to help her down as Fern leaps past her.

Alice slides against me, her mouth meeting mine in the alleyway, hot and needy. Her heart thumps against my chest, and my hands slide under her sweater on instinct. I need to touch her. Need to know she's still here, still safe. It still feels like we got off too easy. Like someone might steal her from me. Her skin's a little damp, like she flushed hot during the Hunt's ride through town. That doesn't surprise me much. I got the same way.

The weight of her pushes me against the brick wall as she deepens the kiss, her tongue dancing with mine. She's here, she wants this. She's not going anywhere. Not tonight, anyway.

And then the walkie crackles, Caden's voice coming over the speaker. "Where'd y'all get off to?"

I laugh against Alice's mouth, and she giggles, pressing her forehead into mine. That laugh is better than the kiss, even—for my heart, anyway. It's a breathless little sound, and then four little words slip out that send my emotions into the stratosphere. "I love it here."

Fern thumps her big, furry butt down on both our feet, wedging herself between us, somehow leaning into us both. It's a powerfully comfortable feeling having the two of them where I know they're safe. I want to gather them both up, tuck them into my jacket so I know where they are at all times.

But that's not how love works. I learned that when Fern was a pup, better than I ever learned with my siblings. Animals are good teachers. If I kept Fern too close, she got restless. When I let her run, let her do what her instincts told her to, make her own doggy choices, she always came back to me. Always wanted to come home because I showed her early on that I'd always be her safe place.

My sweet girl's got a bit of that same spirit, I reckon. She needs to know how deeply she's wanted—needed, even—but if I hold too tight, it'll break her.

"I love you being here," I murmur back, wondering if her declaration is the first step to telling me she loves me. Mine certainly is. I want to tell her so bad it practically aches in my chest.

I've always had a home with my siblings. We might have worked things out in an unconventional way, but when we left California, Fallon and I made a pact to do shit differently than my parents did. So this isn't the family I never had; it's more. An expansion of what Fallon and I built here in Blackbird Hollow with Caden.

This town has always been our soft landing. Our happily ever after, or so I thought. But with Alice in my arms, Fern sitting on my feet, the Hunt past us and leafer season almost over, time seems to have spun out into something else. Something more like whatever *after* is like in the old tales. I never knew I wanted this so badly. After the shit I've messed up in the past, I assumed I'd given up on romance. But now...now I want it all with Alice.

And I wonder if I can have it.

The walkie crackles again. "Are you two getting it on in the alley?" Fallon asks, sounding scandalized. "I haven't had a debriefing on Bang Zero yet. Slow down so I can catch up on the gruesome details of your sex life."

I let out a string of curses my sister can't possibly hear from across the street but will most definitely sense because we are just that close. I grin at Alice and roll my eyes a little as she shrugs, as though to let me know she finds Fallon's complaint perfectly valid. Her arms tighten around me in a hug, though, and I can smell the fresh scent of her shampoo.

She smells like citrus and green things. She smells like she belongs in my bed on Sunday mornings, on the back porch in the evenings, and right beside me as long as I live. But much as I want to tell her that, I know this isn't the right moment.

Under my hands, she shakes a little. The Hunt rattled her, as it should, and the night's sure as shit not over. We'd all do well to stay wary. I press the button on my walkie. "Heading over to talk to Wanda."

"On my way," Fallon replies.

Cade says something in the background I can't hear, but it sounds like he's hungry. He's always hungry these days. Part of the change.

Alice's hand finds its way into mine, and we walk out of the alley with Fern, finding Wanda still staring at the spot where Willa got taken.

As we approach, the air changes. It's colder the closer we get to Wanda. Feels like spirit activity, though that's not my area of expertise. I kinda wish Barnes were down here so I could ask him.

But it's not the temperature that sends fear skittering through me like a novice hedgerider. It's Wanda's eyes. They've gone milk-white and cloudy, like someone stirred a bit of Blackbird Hollow's signature mists into her peepers.

The witch is standing stock-still in the street, her tan corduroy dress the only thing moving in the damp breeze that sends leaves shuddering toward us like rogue tumbleweeds. Her fingers are stretched toward the ground, like she's searching for something.

Alice lets go of my hand, whispering, "Wanda, are you alright?"

My heart thumps hard several times. Then Wanda blinks, her eyes going back to their usual luminous brown. She nods as the air warms. "Yes. I wanted to find something out."

"What?" Alice asks, her voice gentle.

Fallon and Caden approach as Fern tucks her head under Wanda's hand. Wanda blinks a few more times, then draws in a big, deep breath, drawing her thick green sweater tighter around her. "I wanted to know just what manner of Fey the One who took Willa was."

"And?" Fallon asks. "Besides the hot kind, what was he?"

Alice snickers. Caden and I both roll our eyes, but they're not wrong. He was gorgeous in a deadly, horrific kind of way. *Not my type*, I think as the moonlight catches Alice's hair. *Not anymore.*

Looking at Alice in the Samhain moonlight, I am positive that I will not have a type that isn't Alice Blythe for the rest of my life.

"Unseelie Court," Wanda murmurs. "But more than that. Wherever the Hunt's living these days, They're living in proximity to something weird. Something *bad*."

Fallon and I exchange a glance. Fallon puts a hand on Wanda's arm. "Do we need to go after Willa?"

Wanda shakes her head. "No, she'd been having dreams. Portents." Her eyes avert from my sister's. "There's stories about faery brides..."

Alice and Cade both shake their heads at the same time. He gestures to her, as though to say, *Ladies first*. Alice nods, and something deep in me warms. The two of them are already so in sync, they're operating like family. "But faery brides are One of Them that marries a human man."

Wanda smiles gently, clearly appreciating Alice's body of knowledge, while having plenty of her own. The older woman's eyes are soft as she answers. "Yes, of course. It's different when the woman is a witch, though. It goes the other way... They come for her in the night, speak words to her that only she can understand..."

It sounds like the lines of an old tale. One I don't recall, but that Wanda apparently knows well. I think she might say more, but she simply shrugs. "She went of her own accord. Whatever he said to her, she went knowing what she was getting into. And she saved that child. Gods only know what They do with the little ones."

Wanda's voice goes quiet at that last sentence, sounding small and afraid. Like hedgeriders, witches have the Sight. We can all see exactly what They are more easily than humans can. It's the Fey blood running through us, however distant. It lets us see more than we could otherwise. I wonder a little at how easy it was for Alice. Typically, it takes those not of the bloodlines more than one try to see Them clearly.

Fallon slings an arm around Wanda's waist. The older woman leans her head against my sister's shoulder. Fallon might not think it, but she does have friends.

Wanda hugs Fallon back, then smiles. "I need a drink. Will you walk me to Lucky's?"

Fallon grins back at her. "Now that's a plan."

Wanda looks at me. "We need some ice, I think. Can you get some on the way back from your patrol?"

"Sure," I agree, then glance at my brother, who looks like he might gnaw his own arm off. "We have food?"

Wanda shrugs. "They made pizza at the kids' event with Janey. And someone was going to go pick up s'mores..."

Alice smiles. "We can do both."

Caden wrinkles his nose, looking for all the world like he's ten years old again. My heartstrings pull a little. "They wanna go make out."

My heartstrings snap like a wet towel to the ass, and I roll my eyes. Little brothers are always gonna little brother, apparently.

Wanda chuckles, slipping out of Fallon's grip to loop her arm through my brother's. "Then we should let them. You and your sister can help me gather some wood. We can have a little fire."

As Fallon heads toward Lucky's with Caden and Wanda, she turns and makes eye contact with me. "Me and Cade'll do the north end of town. Keep your wits about you."

Fallon whistles for Fern, who looks up at me. I nod to her, giving her permission to go with her auntie, but she doesn't move. She whines at Alice, and my heart clenches. Alice crouches down, and my dog, who hasn't ever truly loved anyone who wasn't a Hayes, shoves her head so hard against Alice's chest that she almost knocks her over. But Alice leans into my big girl, steadying herself as her arms wrap around Fern's neck.

She sprinkles kisses all over Fern's face, telling her she's a good girl, calling her "my sweet baby-puppy." And then she whispers, "Go with Auntie."

And Fern does it.

My heart jumps into my throat. I feel like I'm gonna sob, scream, or make sweet love to Alice Blythe right here on the street. I don't know what to do with the emotions welling up inside me. This is the kind of thing I've pushed down for so long, wishing for it but knowing if it ever came my way, it'd be the one true thing I was scared of.

But I can't push it away anymore. Alice is the one for me. She has been from that first moment at the Stardust, and if I have my way, she will be 'til the day I die. I love Alice Blythe, and there's no going back to whoever I was before she got here.

My girl has her rifle strapped to her back like a pro, and I take her hand in mine. I'll tell her everything tonight, when we're alone at home. My house—our house, if she wants it to be. "Let's go on a little monster hunt, and rustle up some grub, whaddya say?"

"I go wherever you go, sweet boy," she murmurs, her kaleidoscope eyes soft.

Her fingers close around mine as mist creeps down from the hills. We walk forward together, Alice Blythe and I, swallowed by the darkness, bathed in the warmth of this new, fragile love between us.

Chapter 31
Alice

The evening air is bitingly cold, tinged with winter, but Wyatt's hand in mine makes me feel like I'm standing in front of a bonfire. Even though we've seen none of Them in the past half-hour's search, my skin is still flushed hot from witnessing the Wild Hunt.

Okay, and probably something else, if I'm honest.

"I love having you here." Those words from his mouth, spoken like he'd never said anything truer in his entire life. I take a big step up from the road and onto the old brick sidewalk, trying to shift my focus to the task at hand. But all I can think about is Wyatt Hayes. Adjusting the strap of my rifle, I glance over at him, admiring the line of his jaw in the lamplight.

"See something you like, Blythe?" he asks me in a drawl from the back of his throat.

"Maybe," I reply with a noncommittal shrug. "Guess you'll have to find out after we make sure there's no silver-haired Fey on motorcycles lurking in the alleys."

"They're damn lucky They wanted Willa and not you,"

Wyatt replies, arching his brow as he peers into a pocket garden between the grocer and a sprawling bookstore that I haven't gotten to check out yet.

His words register, and I pause, damp leaves circling my feet like hounds as a cold wind blows down from the hills. "Oh yeah?" I ask slyly, pressing myself into him.

He goes still, his eyes sliding away from the darkness of the park to meet mine. "Ah-ah," he replies, wagging one finger at me. "You're startin' a dangerous game with that."

I grin up at him, and any hope I had of being a responsible adult who makes sure the town is safe from monsters before thinking about other things is gone. "What would you have done?" I ask, pressing my free hand into his chest. His heart seems to beat into my palm, and my knees go weak. "If They tried to take me?"

A long, shuddering breath goes out of him as he turns to face me, sliding both arms around my waist. The moonlight and the illumination of the streetlamps cast half his face in a luminous glow that makes me wonder just how much Fey blood he has—because how could a regular human be this goddamn beautiful?

"I would've gutted every last one of Them," Wyatt replies, resting his forehead against mine. His fingers slip under my sweater exactly where I need to be touched—where I'm *yearning* to be touched after what I've just seen. I tell myself it's only because I've just watched old folklore come to life and parade through the streets with its teeth bared, and not because of how much I've fallen for this man.

His mouth brushes my brow, then both sides of my jaw, hands sliding down to my jeans. "Would've hunted 'Em right to Faerie's godsdamn door if I had to," he murmurs, the words rough around the edges.

I grab the collar of his jacket with both hands and haul him down to me. He meets my kiss hungrily, pressing a husky groan against my lips. I let out a gasp and pull him closer, as close as I possibly can. I know he's afraid. I know there's things in his past —and mine—we haven't yet discussed, but I don't want to push him. He'll tell me when he's ready. It won't change how I feel, anyway. I only want to know what he carries so I can help shoulder the weight.

Because I think Wyatt Hayes has been carrying around enough pain for at least ten people, and he does it without complaint. He can be the handsome-as-hell, flannel-wearing, kinda grumpy, Fey-fighting man of little words to everybody else in this town. But not with me.

With me, he can be whoever he wants, whenever he wants. Because it's the core of Wyatt—his crackling warmth, his kindness that only fools mistake for weakness, his fierce protectiveness—that I think I might be falling in love with, not the rest of it. As I slide my hands under his shirt, fingers brushing the hard muscle of his stomach, I acknowledge that I'm also pretty into the rest of it, too.

He cups my face in his hands as he gently pulls away, looking down at me, his chest rising in a short, hard breath. "Let's get that ice and s'mores stuff," he says, looking deep into my eyes. "Drop it off. Make our excuses. Then I'm going to take you home, Alice. My home." He pauses, his mouth parted, and I guess something in my eyes tells him to keep going. "Yours, too, if you want it."

"Okay," I whisper. Heat uncoils between my legs, and something I don't think I've ever felt before strains in my chest, like a flower blooming on the first day of spring, tender petals pushing against ice-cold snow. "I would like that very much."

"Alright," he says with a soft smile, taking my hand in his again. Then he leads me up a set of stone stairs and into an antique building with decorative details that make me think of a gingerbread house. A gilded sign on the front window reads "*The Sweet Shoppe, Gifts, Sundries and Gourmet Foods*." Inside, there's a second set of doors, much more modern than the exterior, my reflection in the glass surprising me.

Wyatt raps on the door in a specific pattern, and then a stout woman with short, dark hair and a kind, round face appears. She cracks the door open, narrowing her eyes at us.

"I heard everything on the radio," she says. "But I'm gonna have to check, alright?"

Wyatt nods. "As you should, Mrs. Cheng."

Mrs. Cheng steps back inside and flips a switch, filling the space with overhead lights. I blink in the sudden brightness as the woman reappears in the doorway. I can now see she's dressed in a floral-patterned house dress, a long wool cardigan, and hot pink Wellingtons that go to her knees.

Unceremoniously, she flicks a lightly scented oil at us—Wanda's faesbane, probably. When neither of us begins to scream or bleed or do whatever the Fey would, she nods grimly and reaches into the pocket of her cardigan, retrieving two long iron nails. Without a word, Wyatt holds out his hand, gesturing for me to do the same. She drops one nail into his hand, then mine, and watches us closely.

"Oh, good," Mrs. Cheng says a few moments later. "That would've been awkward. Come on in. I heard there's a party at Lucky's." She pushes open one of the doors, revealing a glimpse into a lovely shop with towering shelves and large crates of every variety of snack known to man.

"Yes, ma'am," Wyatt replies. "Getting stuff for s'mores."

"And ice," I say.

"Ice is out back," Mrs. Cheng tells me, turning to walk back into the store, the wide floorboards creaking pleasantly with her steps.

"I'll go grab the ice," Wyatt tells me, raising our still-entwined hands to his lips, brushing my knuckles with a kiss.

"No," I say with a sudden fierceness. "I'll go get it."

He looks at me, eyes hooded by concern. "Alice, I think it's best—"

"Swap guns with me," I say, raising my eyebrow at him. "I'll be fine." I'm struck with a burning desire to prove to him that I can handle this life. That even with hellhounds still prowling, I can go grab ice from out back. How is this ever going to work if he feels like he's gotta keep an eye on me every second of every day? That's not sexy. Or practical.

Wyatt watches me, saying nothing, though I can see worry etched around the corners of his eyes.

"How am I gonna live here if you're afraid something's gonna grab me every time I'm out of your sight?" I ask him after a few beats of silence, crossing my arms.

He lets out a long sigh, dragging one hand through his hair. "Not every night is Samhain," he replies slowly. "With the Hunt passin' through."

I pull my rifle strap over my shoulder and hold it out. "Hand it over," I say, gesturing to his iron bullet-loaded rifle. "It's right out back."

With a little smile, Wyatt relents, something in his shoulders releasing. We swap guns as I beam triumphantly at him the entire time. I need him to know I'm not going anywhere. Something tells me that weighs on him a little too heavily. I want to make his burdens lighter, not become one.

"Be careful, sweet girl," he tells me.

I stand up on my tiptoes to give him a quick peck on the lips, and then I turn and jog down the stairs. I take a tight turn into the alley, passing the little park. Out back, a streetlight illuminates a gravel parking area, hemmed by a side street and a fence that just barely holds back the dark of the woods.

Beside a massive lilac bush, an icebox is tucked up against the cedar shake siding, its old-fashioned advertisement faded. I sweep my eyes around the perimeter, taking a deep breath. No sulfur. No strange lights. No delicate finger of dread tracing a chill up my back.

I slide the rifle around by the strap so it's resting on my back and then trudge toward the icebox. With a grunt, I slide it open and reach inside. I've just wrapped my fingers around a bag when my skin prickles, like someone's watching me. Setting my jaw, I yank the bag out and whirl around to face the parking lot.

There's only darkness. I let out a sharp breath, reminding myself that just on the other side of the wall at my back, Wyatt's probably picking out marshmallows and Mrs. Cheng is ready to throw down with her bottle of faesbane. I put the bag of ice on the ground for a second, pressing my cold hands to my face.

"Easy, Alice," I whisper to myself, waiting for my heart to stop beating so fast. But if anything, the uneasiness intensifies, my skin gone clammy under my sweater. I'm about to grab for the handle of my rifle when someone steps out of the shadows and into the streetlight.

The fucking Sector agent from Lucky's. The one who looks like my grandma. The one who claims to be Cookie.

She's in a different—but still stupid—suit, ugly shoes crunching on the gravel as she walks over to me. Look, I know she's human, and Fallon was pretty clear that we do our best to only shoot Them, not people, but I'm fucking exhausted. I grab for my rifle and level the muzzle at her.

"I didn't know we were on such bad terms," the agent laughs. Her smile is like my grandma's—but only in the sense that Sector might've peeled my Nan's face off her skull and made a mask out of it.

I scowl. "Thought you'd clear out of here after the Hunt went through."

She's annoyingly calm despite the fact that I'm literally pointing a gun at her. Tucking her hands in her pockets, she comes to a stop a few steps from me, smiling up into the sky as if there's some inside joke I missed. When her eyes finally meet mine, they're ice-cold.

"We have multiple interests, Alice," she says. "The Hunt is one of them, yes." Watching me closely, she pauses and then takes another step forward.

"Nope," I say, my finger curling around the trigger. "No closer."

She stares at me with a hard expression, like she's trying to gauge whether or not I'll actually shoot a person. To be honest, I'm not sure, but if there's any reason to do it, it'd be for Blackbird Hollow. For Wyatt.

"You are right about one thing," she says, infuriatingly casual. "My team is headed out soon. And we'd like you to come with us."

Moments pass slowly, my exhausted mind trying to make sense of her words. "What?" I finally sputter. "Are you fucking insane?"

She spreads her hands, making me jump, but there's only open palms and a false imitation of peace. "Our offer," Not-Cookie says, "was for you to stay enrolled at OrthCon in the Alien Biologies Program."

"Kinda hard since aliens aren't even fucking real, you hag," I spit, my balance regained. I think about yelling for Wyatt, but this agent is *my* problem. I'm clearly what brought her here. So I'll handle it. I owe the Hayes that, at the very least. "If you people cared so much about me staying there, you probably shouldn't have let me get expelled."

Not-Cookie lets out an exasperated sigh. "The point is that

you're not enrolled," she says, her mouth curling into something almost...maniacal. "Which means we can do whatever we want to you. Per the terms *you* agreed to, might I remind you."

I narrow my eyes at her. "Babe, remind me—which one of us has the gun right now?"

The Sector agent who looks too much like my grandma, who claims to be one of the only friends I've ever had, drops all pretense of even being a goddamn person in one fell swoop. The second those words leave my mouth, her entire expression changes, and she steps back, bringing her fingers to her lips and letting out a short, harsh whistle.

To my horror, two—then three, then four—besuited agents creep out of the shadows surrounding the parking lot.

And all of them have handguns trained on me.

"I'm honored you thought you'd need five agents to take down a pasty academic," I find myself saying. My heart suddenly leaps into my throat, my blood pounding, as if my body has just realized I'm in danger.

She shrugs. "We thought the Hayes boy might be with you. Since you've grown so *attached*."

That startles me further. "If you go near the Hayes family, I'll fucking kill you," I snarl, meaning every word of it. I lean into the butt of the rifle, wondering how many shots I can get off before an agent takes me down.

"We want you, Alice," Not-Cookie says with a terrifying smile. "Your mind. Your talent. If you work for us, there will be no funding restrictions. You would have your own lab, your own team. We need to understand more about the Fey. You are uniquely positioned to help us do that. You can even stay in touch with your beloved little hedgeriders."

My mind spins. "You had to corner me in a parking lot and point a bunch of guns at me just to offer me a *job*?" I ask incredulously.

"You pointed a gun first," Not-Cookie says, sliding her hands back into her pockets.

"That's fair," I grumble.

"And it's not an offer," she continues, stepping toward me, right up to the muzzle of my rifle, letting the metal press against her suit jacket. Her heart is just beneath—if she has one. Up close, the woman who is not my grandma looks absolutely *unhinged*—just as mad as the swarms of the Hunt did with Their mother-of-pearl teeth and bloodstained crowns. "It's very sweet you think you have a choice."

I'm too startled to even remember I could pull the trigger. But somewhere in the back of my head, my mind is running a thousand calculations. It would put all of Blackbird Hollow in danger if I killed a Sector agent. If we have a shootout in the parking lot. Would the violence draw the Hunt back to us? Or, even worse, the hellhounds?

"I'm not going anywhere with you, you insane bitch," I laugh, glancing around at the other agents, who have unfortunately closed in on me, their faces expressionless.

"And who, exactly, is going to stop me from taking you?" Not-Cookie asks with a fake pout, her startling light-blue eyes sliding down to take in the rifle's muzzle against her chest. "A 'pasty academic' who's never killed anyone?"

"My boyfriend is right inside," I spit, gesturing to the grocery store. "And he'll absolutely fuck you up."

Not-Cookie throws her head back and laughs as if that's the most amusing thing she's ever heard. "Stupid girl," she sneers. "The Hayes don't have the power to save you. They sure couldn't save themselves back in New Big Sur."

"The Hayes saved this whole *town* tonight, asshole," I reply, but my voice shakes as I flinch from the realization of just how much Sector knows about the people I love. I shift my weight, and the gravel crunches beneath my feet, loud as an explosion in the tense parking lot.

Not-Cookie leans away from my rifle, looking thoughtful. "Since you're so sure," she says, suddenly sly in a way that makes ice slink into my gut, "how about this? You come with us, no fuss, or we storm that grocery store, and then the Hayes house, and then whatever squalid little hovel they've holed up in, and we'll see who comes out on top."

My hands shake against the rifle. I feel like I might throw up. "You can't do that," I say, my gaze darting to the other agents, but all their expressions are cold, distant. "The Hedgerider Council—"

"Those old have-beens?" She laughs, the sound becoming more like a howl. "They're all the way across an ocean, Alice. What do you think they'll really be able to do? Do you think we haven't killed hedgeriders before? Wiped entire towns just like this one off the map?"

All at once, moving faster than a woman of her age should be able to, Not-Cookie grabs the muzzle of my rifle, shoving it to the side, and leans into my face. She's so close, I can see the white outline of a scar under one eye.

"Come with us," she snarls, "or you'll see just how weak and useless a family like the Hayes really is."

This time, I'm the one laughing. The sound of it surprises me, as does the way it comes bubbling up from my throat with a wild, reckless abandon. "For one last time, bitch," I spit. "If you try to take me, you'll find out *exactly* how terrifying the Hayes are."

Chapter 32
Wyatt

Mrs. Cheng is chatting me up something fierce. Telling me all about how she likes the looks of Alice Blythe, that it's time I settle down and get married, have a baby Hayes or ten. She *actually* suggests that Alice and I need to have at least ten babies, and it takes a whole mess of effort to keep from laughing. It's best to take Mrs. Cheng seriously. She's fierce as all get out, and I do actually value her opinion on most things. But ten babies sounds like a lot.

"It's not as if you'd have to have them all at once," she says with a sly smile as she places the bag with the s'mores supplies on the counter.

"You pulling my leg, Mrs. C?" I ask.

The woman reaches up, lifting onto her hot-pink tippy-toes, and pinches my cheek. "Every time I get the chance, kiddo."

A lump forms in my throat. I pat her hand. "Thanks for that."

She nods. There's a faint sound of voices out back, so slight I might not have noticed them if Mrs. Cheng was playing her usual nineties alt-rock playlist. But tonight, it's quiet, and I hear the tone, though not the words, and I don't like it one bit. Mrs. Cheng hears them, too, and pulls what might be conservatively termed a bazooka from under the counter.

"Blackstone?" I ask.

Mrs. Cheng winks at me as we move toward the back room. There's a secret door that pops out just down from the ice machine, obscured by a giant lilac bush that Mrs. Cheng has lovingly tended to for nearly twenty years.

I shake my head. "Not you too. Can't anyone in this town buy arms from someone who isn't a total sleaze?"

"He's got the best guns," Mrs. Cheng assures me. "And a cute butt."

I sigh deeply. Women who outwit me at every turn, Fey-fucking jokes, and warlock arms dealers with cute butts—this is my life. There's no point in telling Mrs. C to stay inside. She won't. Plus, I'm not completely opposed to having backup.

As we near the door, the sound of voices gets louder, and I can hear my girl sounding less than pleased.

"This door gonna squeak when I open it?" I whisper to Mrs. Cheng.

She rolls her eyes at me. "Who're you talking to, Middle Hayes? I am the queen of WD-40," she snaps.

Mrs. Cheng hasn't called me "Middle Hayes" since I was little. Makes me feel like I've got a mom on my side. Mrs. Cheng lost all her kids, in an incident she won't discuss, before she came here—but, unlike my own mother, she's got an instinct for parenting. I think she'd be a mom no matter what happened to her in life.

"Alrighty, then," I whisper and push the door open.

We step outside, and Mrs. Cheng shuts the door, silent as can be, behind us. We press ourselves against the brick wall, taking stock of what's happening. From the sound of the conversation, it's gotta be the Sector agent we've been calling Not-Cookie Grandma.

Mrs. Cheng peeks through what appears to be a peephole in her lilac bush. Of course she's got a peephole in her landscaping. Why would I expect anything less? She throws up her hand, wiggling all five fingers. There's at least five agents out there then. Great.

I hear the end of one of Alice's sentences. "The Hedgerider Council—"

She sounds worried now. I nudge Mrs. Cheng out of the way so I can take a peek. There's Not-Cookie-Grandma. I glare at her from Mrs. C's peephole, then take stock of the agents. Two are pointing their guns wrong. One's got the safety on still.

"Those old have-beens?" Not-Cookie-G laughs. "They're all the way across an ocean, Alice. What do you think they'll really be able to do? Do you think we haven't killed hedgeriders before? Wiped entire towns just like this one off the map?"

She sounds fucking unhinged. But she's wrong. Sector hasn't done shit like that in nigh on thirty years. She's lying to my sweet girl. Trying to scare her into giving up. Anger rises in me as she grabs Alice's rifle and leans in to menace her. I'll give it to the broad, she's quick.

"Come with us, or you'll see just how weak and useless a family like the Hayes really are."

Alice laughs at the same time Mrs. Cheng and I do. Her words cover up the sound of us stifling our laughter. "For one last time, bitch. If you try to take me, you'll find out *exactly* how terrifying the Hayes are."

I smile to myself, warmth flooding me. *That's my girl.*

Mrs. Cheng nods to me, and I step out first, aiming the salt-filled rifle at the back of the agent with a gun on Alice, the only one who's got a chance of actually shooting her. I point the muzzle at the back of his knees and pull the trigger. The man goes down, howling like a baby as the salt sprays across his legs. It's gotta hurt like a son of a bitch. I kick his gun out of the way as the rest of the agents turn.

Alice's eyes leap to mine. I smile at her. "You telling my baby lies, Agent NCG?"

The elder agent frowns at me, clearly trying to puzzle out what I've just called her. It gives Mrs. Cheng time to grab Alice's arm and pull her back toward me, into the lilac bush. But the remaining agents and Not-Cookie-G advance toward us.

In one smooth motion, I swap guns with Alice. "Now, you know damn well that Sector hasn't wiped shit off shit since Reformation was in its infancy. Let's not overstate things."

Not-Cookie-G glares at me, but then her mouth quirks into a smile. "Do you think you can shoot enough of us before we kill her?"

"Thought you were gonna kidnap me," Alice hisses. "What happened to that?"

Not-Cookie-G shrugs. "You know what they say—if we can't have you, nobody can."

I suck in a breath of cold night air. It's been a long fucking day, and I hate this shit. I hate bandying idle threats and talking. Because that's what these threats are. Idle. At the end of the day, maybe we got too good at hiding who we really are from Sector. They sure do have an overblown idea of themselves, though.

My eye snags on the mist curling around the downed agent's legs. He's sobbing on the ground, but quietly at least. One second he's there, whimpering away, and the next he's gone, a bloody streak all that's left. The sound of his screams disappears into the forest.

"Well, shit," I mutter. "Looks like we're gonna set fire to the raindrops."

"That's not how that song goes," Not-Cookie snarls as six huge hellhounds step out of the forest. On each of Their backs rides a beautiful, naked woman. Their limbs are far too long, Their skin the faintest shades of iridescent green in the moonlight. Various leaves trail through Their long hair, eyes glowing fluorescent.

And when They see me, They all grin, looking like a pack of devils with Their sharp teeth.

"Wyatt Hayessss," the nymphs murmur in unison. "You've brought the enemy to our door. We shall grant you a boon."

Alice's eyes light up, but Mrs. Cheng shakes her head, waggling her pointer finger at Them as dry leaves rustle around her feet, greening up in the presence of the forest Fey. "No boons."

Soriya Cheng, a voice says as the biggest of the hounds steps forward, its jaw dripping with venom. It's got a missing eye. The one from before. What are the Wild Hunt's hellhounds doing here, with the Hunt already gone, being ridden like godsdamn horses by a half-dozen tree-nymphs? *Go home, child.*

I glance down at Mrs. Cheng, who grumbles, "I didn't even get to shoot a dirty little Sector goofball."

Another time, perhaps, the hound replies, its horrible voice almost affectionate. It tracks that Mrs. Cheng would have befriended an alpha hound. *Rest well, dear one.*

"Yeah, yeah, you too." Mrs. Cheng shrugs as she pats my arm. She hands me her bazooka. "Put it back where it belongs when you're done and lock up."

"For heaven's sake," Not-Cookie snarls. "Is this what Blackbird Hollow's best amounts to?"

Alice—my little shit starter—growls like a full-blown werewolf, shoots the agent aiming wrong in the leg with salt, and in a second, the nymphs are down off the hounds' backs. The forest looms closer than it should, the trees taller suddenly. The air goes cold, the ice machine stops humming, the lights in the alley wink out.

The agents start to shoot, and I throw the bazooka at Alice. "Kill Not-Cookie." She frowns for half a second. "It'll be a blessing for her."

Alice lifts the gun, and for an instant, Not-Cookie seems to understand just what a miscalculation she's made. Hedgeriders aren't at war with Them; we're straddling the line between our worlds. Sector's always confused us with Hunters. That's the problem with letting incompetents run things.

The nymphs laugh, gleefully. "Kill her if you can, Alice Blythe," They sing. "We'll bring her back and suck her dry, feed her blood to our roots, her entrails to the wind."

"Gross," Alice whispers, then shrugs. "But y'know? Sure. Feed her entrails to the wind or whatever."

One of the nymphs steps forward, touching Alice's bazooka. Foxglove springs out of it. "Poison, just like you," the creature whispers, admiration shining in her eyes. "I wager you taste like datura with a hint of salt."

The nymph's eyes slide to mine as the remaining agents begin to realize just how fucked they are. The hounds are closing in on them, and Their rancid breath must be pouring down their necks. The mist's thicker than ever as the nymph that rendered Mrs. Cheng's bazooka useless asks, "What does she taste like, Wyatt Hayes?"

I lower my gun and slide an arm around Alice's waist. "She tastes like she's *mine*."

Alice's fingers dig into my arm as the nymph's lip curls slightly. Not-Cookie uses the moment to her advantage, drawing an enormous bowie knife from a sheath beneath her jacket. She shoves it through the nymph's abdomen, and all hell breaks loose.

The hellhounds pounce. The Sector agents open fire, and I

start picking them off. Not-Cookie lunges for Alice, still trying to take her rather than running. And then half a dozen more agents swarm out of the alley, dressed in expensive tactical gear, helmets, and automatic rifles.

I shove Alice back toward the lilac bush. "Get inside."

"Not a fucking chance," she shouts back.

And then she shoots that bazooka, her eyes locked with the injured nymph's. They both nod, as though they've agreed upon something. To my amazement, instead of bullets, red honey locust thorns fly out of the bazooka, long and sharp as the dickens. The injured nymph throws her hands out, as though guiding the thorns, straight into three of the original agents' eyes. They fall immediately, and the nymph snarls, leaving Alice and me behind to jump into the fray.

I cover Alice, kneecapping as many of the tactical agents as I can. It's the place where their armor's weak. As they stumble, the hounds and the nymphs take them. The trees are too close now, obscuring the moon. It's hard to see.

But Alice and I are the only ones affected by the darkness. The tactical agents wear night vision helmets, and Fey creatures see just as well in the dark as They do in the light. The red and green of Their eyes flash in the near-pitch darkness.

I reach for Alice, but she's right behind me, tucking herself into my side. The two of us shoot into the dark, and I think we're probably making some headway when she screams. She's there one second, and the next, she's gone, the bazooka falling to the ground.

The scent of petrichor fills my nose. "What would you give for forest Sight?" a nymph sings in my ear. It's not the one Not-Cookie stabbed, but another, this one younger.

Her voice is terrible, the song of dying years and wolf winters. Long fingers wrap around my arm, keeping me from struggling. I smell pine sap and leaf mold. Petrichor and the wintergreen of willow bark.

She has me pressed against her, but instead of feeling the soft curves of a voluptuous body, I feel the hard bark of a tree. We haven't come across nymphs too often—They usually keep to themselves. You don't bother the trees, you don't meet wood nymphs. It's simple, and I don't fuck with trees that aren't already fallen.

"I'd give just about anything right now," I whisper, "but I think you said a little somethin' about a boon."

"So we did." She laughs, then shoves her fingers into my back, slicing through skin, muscle, and down to bone like a hot knife through butter. I scream, but she's as good as her word. To be Fey-touched is to feel pain, and I'll carry the wound for the rest of my life, but even as her power burns through me, I know it's doing some good, along with the harm.

As her Fey-fingers touch my spine, I see with the eyes of the forest. It's not just night-vision; it's something more. Something bigger. Like I'm every tree, every mushroom, everything in the godsdamn circle of life. And it is all so beautiful, all so precious, I want to cry.

And there's my girl, being dragged off thrashing by Not-Cookie-Grandma.

The nymph snarls. "Let us take our revenge."

I nod at the creature, who now looks more tree than woman. But she is far more beautiful this way. I can't explain it, but I've never seen something as pure and good as this nymph. Cruel? Yes. But I have always loved the forest. Always loved the trees. Always loved these woods, dangerous as they are.

"I don't know what you're taking revenge for, ma'am," I offer, "but I'm with you."

She moves like the wind, and whatever she did to me doesn't hurt any longer, and I can move with her as we follow them into the forest, catching up with hardly any effort at all. The nymph grabs Not-Cookie by the hair, I grab Alice by the arm, and we force them apart. Alice rages like a feral beast, slipping out of my hands and onto the forest floor, scrabbling for the bowie knife that Not-Cookie dropped. There's just enough moonlight to find it, and when she has it in her hands, she moves.

Before I can stop her, she's shoved it in the woman's gut. "That's for the nymph," she snarls.

My heart sinks as a part of me mourns for her. I never wanted her to have to harm a human. But the nymph who gifted me forest Sight smiles triumphantly with a love I didn't imagine her kind capable of.

Before Alice can do anything else to the woman, the nymph swallows Not-Cookie whole. I don't know how else to describe it, but it's like her entire body becomes a gaping maw, and then Not-Cookie-G and the nymph both are simply gone, an ancient ash tree standing in their place.

Alice yanks on my arm, dragging me back toward the fight. "We've gotta finish them off," she huffs. "Take the rest of them out."

But when we make it out of the forest, there's not a single Sector agent left. In fact, there's no one behind the store except the hound with the missing eye and Mrs. Cheng. They appear to be talking.

The hound turns to me and Alice. *You would be wise to keep your wits about you and set a watch for the forsaken.*

I swear under my breath. "I don't know what the fuck that means."

You will, the hound promises, and then lopes off into the mist.

"Do you know what that means, Mrs. Cheng?" Alice asks, a little out of breath from our run through the forest.

Mrs. Cheng shrugs. "Who ever knows what that one's on about? He's a good enough pup, but a hellhound all the same. They speak in riddles."

"Mrs. Cheng," I ask, trying to keep the impatience out of my voice, but it's been a wild end to a stressful day. "Are you some kinda expert on hellhounds?"

Mrs. Cheng just smiles at me. "Middle Hayes, you don't know the half of what I'm an expert on." And then she giggles, pointing to an overflowing grocery sack next to the smaller bag of s'more supplies. "Thought you could use some extra snacks after all that. Bring my bags back to me tomorrow, please," she chirps as she heads back into the store.

Alice looks up at me, her eyes wide. "I don't know whether to laugh or cry?"

I curl my arm around her head, kissing the top of it. "Sweet girl, I feel the same."

She leans against me, shuddery laughs fluttering against my chest. "I need to lie down on the bathroom floor and scream." *I know the feeling.* "You have one of those at your house?"

"Sure do, sweet girl. Let's get our dog and go home."

I look down at Alice, and she throws her arms around my waist. "Don't let go," she sobs into my chest. "Don't you ever let me go."

"I won't," I promise as I hold her as tight as I can without hindering her breathing. "Now that I've got you, you're mine forevermore."

Alice doesn't say another word, but she doesn't need to. She's staying. I know it.

Alice Blythe is staying in Blackbird Hollow forever, and my heart might burst for how happy I am.

Chapter 33
Alice

Fallon's the first to turn around as we drag ourselves through the heavy door and onto Lucky's roof. It's a delightful scene. They've got lights strung up on the stucco walls and a little firepit with a crackling flame.

Wanda and Barnes are doubled over laughing about something. Mona and Julius are slow dancing to "Drive" by Incubus, which is impressive. Caden's sprawled on a blanket with half a pizza in his lap, feeding the crusts to a very pleased-looking Fern. I recognize some of the witches of Foxglove Coven from the preparations in the gym, gathered by the edge of the roof. They have their arms linked and appear to be singing to the moon. Marion's sitting up on the half-wall with a beer in her hand, her dark hair glinting in the firelight as she explains something to Janey and Mac with lively enthusiasm.

My heart swells so big that for an irrational moment, I'm scared it's going to burst right through my chest. Tears spring to my eyes, and I roughly shove them away with the back of one hand, plunking the bag filled with s'mores goodies onto a worn plastic table.

"The hell happened to you two?" Fallon demands as she stalks over, her eyes wide.

To my surprise, Fern abandons Caden—and, even more surprisingly, the pizza crusts—to bound over to us. She shoves herself between Wyatt and me, her tail thumping hard against my legs.

"Oh," I say with a strangled laugh.

"Sector. Not-Cookie-Grandma. Hellhounds. Nymphs," Wyatt says with a heavy exhale. He turns to look at me. "Did I miss anything?"

"Mrs. Cheng has a bazooka," I add, feeling like that's important.

"Yeah, I know," Fallon says, crossing her arms. "About the bazooka, I mean. We got a two-for-one deal."

"Can we *please* find a better place to source our damn guns?" Wyatt demands, exasperated, as he hands Fallon the bag of ice. She passes it off to Caden, who wordlessly dumps it into the battered cooler tucked against the wall.

"You're both alright, though?" Fallon asks, stepping closer, clearly going into hedgerider matriarch mode. "'Cuz you look like shit."

"Thanks," I snort, stepping forward to pull her into a tight hug. "We're okay. I just want a bath."

"Believe it or not," she whispers into my ear, like it's some kind of secret, "Wyatt's got a hell of a clawfoot tub at his house." She pulls away from me, though her hands still grip my shoulders, to give me an exaggerated lusty wink.

"What is wrong with you?" Wyatt demands, sinking down to let Fern kiss his face, which is a very important part of her routine.

"You didn't get bit by anything, right?" Caden asks us in a weary tone, looking over his shoulder from where he's crouched next to the cooler, loading more beer into it.

“A nymph shoved her fingers into my spine,” Wyatt offers.

Fallon blanches, and Wanda’s suddenly at her side, expression sharp with interest. “A nymph did *what* now?” she wants to know.

“Nope,” I say with a hard shake of my head. “Tomorrow. We’ll tell you all about it tomorrow. Promise. Or go ask Mrs. Cheng. I’m surprised she’s not here.”

Worry prickles me, but then the heavy door at my back bangs open. I jump a mile into the air, whirling to find Mrs. Cheng coming around the corner. Her face is red, her arms full with a big cardboard box.

The rest of the party goes quiet as she drops it onto the ground. Then she puts her hands on her hips and surveys everyone. “I thought we should have fireworks,” she finally says, gesturing to the box.

“Fuck yeah,” Caden exclaims, jumping to his feet with unabashed glee. For a moment, I see the little kid he used to be, and emotion chokes off my throat.

For so long, I’ve only had my parents, and—even though I understand why, and even though I know they love me—they left me, too. I squeeze my eyes shut, tears falling freely from my lashes. These past few years, I’ve had no one.

Out of nowhere, the memory of seeing my neighbor in their yard, everyone gathered around the firepit, comes barreling into my mind. That unbearable loneliness I felt wraps its arms around me in a stifling embrace. I clamp down on my jaw, not really wanting to fall to my knees and sob at the “yay, we survived the Hunt!” party, because I feel like that would ruin the vibe.

When I force my eyes open, I see Julius dipping Mona low—to “Save Tonight” by Eagle-Eye Cherry this time, which is somewhat more appropriate. To Fallon smiling at Mrs. Cheng. To Wanda gleefully accepting a bowl of mac ’n’ cheese from

Janey's outstretched hands. To Wyatt kneeling so Fern can kiss every inch of his face.

The loneliness dissipates like I never felt it at all, like I never knew its name better than my own, like my family was just always *here*, waiting for me to have the courage to take the leap.

"Your turn. Gotta keep the baby happy," Wyatt says, brushing my arm as he rises.

With a tear-choked laugh, I let myself fall to the ground, burying my face in Fern's fur as she yips excitedly. My body aches terribly, and I have a feeling it might hurt even more tomorrow. I'm worried I'll dream about that Sector agent's grin, about how she dragged me with such surprising strength, about how I shoved a knife into her gut without a second thought.

But not tonight, I tell myself as I rise to my feet. "Hey," I whisper to Wyatt, lacing my fingers through his. "We got our dog. Take me home, please."

"I JUST THINK Fallon could've done without the 'ew, you're old married people, go home and have your old married people sex' comment, y'know?" Wyatt tells me as he strips off his jacket, tossing it into the woven hamper in the corner.

"I think expecting Fallon to have a filter is a foolish endeavor," I reply with a laugh, peering out the large bay window into the darkness of the forest that curls around Wyatt's cottage like a half-moon.

"Nah, sweet girl," he says, suddenly beside me, his hand on my elbow to pull me away from the window and into him. "You can have all the daylight hours you want to look out the windows. Not at night, though." He reaches above me to pull the curtain closed.

"Oh, is that true, too?" I ask, turning to look at him. "That you shouldn't look out the windows at night?" I dozed off on the drive home, Fern draped over me like a heated blanket, and my mind came back to life a little. Enough that I'm tempted to search for a notebook—but then the light from the crackling hearth in Wyatt's bedroom catches the curve of his bicep. I realize he's shirtless and we're finally alone all at once.

"Do you ever just turn that beautiful brain off?" he asks with a laugh, sliding his arms around my waist.

I lean into him, our bodies slotting together like the last two pieces of a puzzle, finally whole. "No," I reply, tilting my chin to look up at him. "Do you think you could distract me?"

His mouth curves into a smile that makes heat simmer low in my belly. "Is that a formal request?"

I barely manage to nod before he scoops me up into his arms. I let out a shriek, Fern answering with her own excited bark. I wrap my arms tighter around his neck as he leaves the cozy bedroom. I take one last look over his shoulder at the antique headboard of dark wood, the Eastlake dresser topped with framed photos, the little marble fireplace, and the battered chestnut leather-covered Eames chair in the corner. The bed's dressed with a vintage quilt that I swear looks just like something out of my Nan's cedar chest.

I bury my face in the crook of his neck to hide my smile, as though I'm seeing it all for the first time. I am, sort of; I could barely take my eyes off Wyatt last night, if I'm honest. If he'd taken me back to a leaking storage unit with inflatable furniture in weird colors, I would still happily make it my home. But *this*? It's like we've gone hunting together for years, pulling old furniture out of abandoned buildings or bartering in the early-morning sunshine of a flea market for the perfect pieces.

It's like it's always been ours.

Wyatt flips a light switch and then leaves the narrow hallway, ducking into the bathroom. Gently, he places me onto a wooden bench as I gape at the space I didn't even register last night.

"Are you kidding me?" I whisper as Fern shoves her head between my knees. I absently stroke her head as I peer around, taking in the tall ceilings and gleaming tile that climbs halfway up the wall. Rich green ornamental trim separates the tile from a cottage-style floral wallpaper that reaches to the ceiling. Across from me, a sturdy, antique oak nightstand with tall, spindly legs has been converted into a vanity with a farmhouse-style sink set into it. Warm light glows from the frosted glass sconces on either side of a carved mirror as Wyatt cranks the faucet on the tub.

The goddamn tub.

Adorned with brass filigree above its clawfoot feet, the massive ceramic tub sits in the corner, its spout filling the room with steam. In the corner, a wooden plant stand hosts a big pothos vine that trails down to the floor, draping across a braided oval rug.

"You have good taste, Hayes," I manage as Wyatt turns around to face me. His jeans hang low on his hips, the sharp V of his muscles making my breath catch. With a smirk, he prowls over to me.

"I sure do," he says just moments before sliding his hands into my hair and bringing his mouth to mine. I moan into the intensity of his kiss, hooking my fingers into his belt loops to pull him closer. I'm so tired, and there's part of me that just wants to throw myself on the bathroom floor and scream.

But I kinda like this better.

He gently pulls my sweater over my head, leaning away for a few moments, his eyes trailing down my body. "I don't think I have any real injuries," I assure him as I glance down at myself. But then I notice a wicked bruise on my shoulder and a raw, red mark encircling my wrist—from where Not-Cookie had dragged me, I realize.

"I'll be doing the lookin'-after, Blythe," he tells me, the skin around his eyes crinkling as he kneels before me. "You just relax for the time being."

"A nymph shoved her fingers into your spine," I protest, reaching around his waist to skim my hands over the small of his back.

"Sure did," he agrees, unbuttoning my jeans. My mind goes blank and white with need. "And I'll let you take care of me real soon." His eyes meet mine, glittering in the warm light. "But I'm a firm believer in 'ladies first.'"

"Fern," I say, looking over at her. "I think there's a squirrel somewhere."

Her ears perk up at the word, her head canting to one side. "Go check the wards, girl," Wyatt laughs, pointing to the door. Her claws ringing out on the tile, Fern wheels and takes off down the hallway. I reach over and shove the door closed.

"Finally alone," I breathe, tracing my fingers along his stubbled jaw.

"You like it here, Alice?" Wyatt asks me, gesturing to the space. "The house, I mean?"

I want to play coy, to tease him, but I can't stop my mouth from splitting into a grin. "I *love* it."

His breath catches, and then mine does the same as we both realize we're creeping closer and closer to saying those first two words with a very different third one. My heart thumps against my breastbone and I feel like my entire body has been filled with effervescent warmth.

He kisses me again, and I throw my arms around his neck, lifting my hips as he pulls my jeans down my legs. Slowly, I trail one hand down his chest, sliding lower until I find where he's hard and wanting. I play with him, pulling a low groan from his mouth.

"Take my damn pants off, Blythe," he rasps with a laugh, moving my other hand from his neck to the fly of his jeans. I laugh, too, happily unbuttoning his pants and pushing them down to his knees. He undoes the clasp on my bra, slipping it off my shoulders as his hands run up my sides to cup my breasts.

With a contented sigh, I wrap my thighs around his hips, pulling him closer. He trails his lips down my neck, peppering my skin with open-mouthed kisses that would leave me weak in the knees if I were still standing.

"I'm yours, Alice," Wyatt murmurs against my collarbone, his fingers dipping beneath the elastic of my underwear. "As long as you'll have me, I'm yours."

Before I can answer, his mouth is on my breast, his fingertips pressing against my clit. I let out a gasp, my back arching. "You're stuck with me," I tell him, reaching into his boxers.

"Gods," he exhales as I stroke him. "Nobody's ever touched me like you do."

"And if somebody else ever tries, I'll fuckin' kill 'em," I reply, meaning it as a joke, but it comes out with a fierceness that surges up in me like a tide.

"I've got no doubt about that," he murmurs, shimmying my underwear down. I lift my hips eagerly, pulling his mouth back up to mine. Then I'm drowning in his kiss, in the caramelized bonfire smoke of him, the crackling warmth that feels so much like home.

Like I've *finally* come home.

Chapter 34
Wyatt

Breakfast on the back porch occurs more at lunchtime than breakfast; Alice calls it "brunch" as she sips her coffee, her plate of eggs, bacon, and fried potatoes practically licked clean. I love it that my girl can eat.

The air's starting to turn, the golden warmth of autumn leaching off, winter lurking at its heels. Snow'll dust the hills before we know it. My mind's already torn ahead to Solstice, wondering if there's childhood ornaments somewhere we can go pick up for the tree, and wondering when Alice's parents will come home.

I have a conversation I need to have with her pops. The thought bounces around in my mind, no longer frightening or tinged with anxiety for the future that hasn't arrived yet.

Alice will stay. We will fall in love properly, deeply, in all the ways that make the kind of marriage my parents never could've hoped for. We'll make a life they never would have dared dream about, and when the time is right, I know in my soul that I'm gonna ask for the hand of the woman next to me.

She wipes her lips with a gingham cloth napkin, smiling at me. "What're you thinking about?"

I grin. "Guess."

She waggles her eyebrows at me as Fern zips around the yard, enthusiasm and puppy bounciness returning to her body now that the Hunt's passed us.

"Not that," I laugh. "Well, not before...but now..."

Alice laughs too, setting her plate on the deck, snuggling into her chair, and pulling the thick quilt I keep in a basket by the door over her. Her eyes are a little sleepy as she smiles. "Well, I've gotta say, you look a lot like you love me."

The words pierce my very soul, and I answer without hesitation. "Well, I do, sweet girl. Maybe it's too soon to say, but I do love you."

She smiles, warmth infusing every inch of her, but she doesn't say it back. Instead, she takes my hand and squeezes. "Will you let me just luxuriate in that for a while?"

Her question is tentative, like I might be angry with her. But I know Alice Blythe like I know my own soul. She loves me too; that's plain as day. But she's never had enough love to go around for herself, the stress of not belonging chasing her like a pack of hungry hyenas.

I squeeze her hand back. "You luxuriate as long as you like, darlin'."

She brings my hand to her lips and kisses my knuckles, whispering, "I knew you'd say that."

Emotion chokes my throat. No one's ever seen me quite as clearly as Alice does. I may have belonged with Fallon and Caden, and here in Blackbird Hollow, but now I'm seen. Known. And it's the best thing I've ever felt.

Inside, the phone rings, and I'm tempted to let it go unanswered. But this soon after last night, I can't.

Alice lets go of my hand and grins. "Better go get that."

An hour later, Caden, Fallon, Fern, Alice, and myself are somehow all squeezed into the cab of my truck, bouncing along a dirt road, deep into the forest. Everyone's talking at once, and I can't make out the multiple threads of conversation and drive at the same time.

I catch snippets of gossip from last night's celebration on the roof, theories on Fey anatomy, and something incomprehensible from Fallon about puffer vests being the avatar of the apocalypse. It's fucking chaos, and I love it.

As I take a turn down what can only be described as a game trail, I spot flashing lights in the mist. We've crossed into tribal lands, and the guardians are here, just where Marion said they'd be. She's sipping coffee out of an ancient insulated mug, which she raises to me as I slow the truck.

When the five of us spill out of the cab, Leonard Gill and Debbie Kingbird both rise out of crouches just beyond the SUV with the flashing lights. All three of them laugh at us. A couple of horses look up from where they're grazing on the other side of the small clearing.

Debbie snorts. "Fuckin' Hayes kids—what is this, a clown car?" The chief's brown eyes sparkle with affection, despite the bark of her words. She extends a hand to Alice. "Good to meet you, Miss Blythe. Marion's had a lot of interesting things to tell us about you."

Alice returns the handshake, bowing her head slightly in deference as she notices the beaded badge embroidered on the chief's barn jacket. "I hope some of them were good."

Leonard chuckles, elbowing me as he comes to stand next to me. He's got about four inches on me, and thirty years, silver threading through his braids. "Glad y'all could make it out. This is your area, for sure, not ours."

Chief Kingbird nods. "You can take it from here, Marion."

Marion smiles. "Sure thing."

The Chief and Leonard make their way across the clearing, avoiding a circle of mossy lumps in the center, and mount their horses. As they disappear into the forest, Caden stares at the circle. Alice goes to stand next to him, and they murmur to one another in nearly indecipherable tones.

Marion pours two more cups of coffee from a thermos on the hood of her SUV and hands them to me and Fallon. "Thought the two of you could use some decent coffee."

Fallon nods, breathing deep as her eyes move around the clearing. "Two more hikers taken?"

Marion nods. "We tracked them to this location, and it's like they just disappeared."

Fallon points to the new moss growing on two trees, all the way across the clearing. "They disappeared into those trees."

My heart thumps slow and heavy as I realize what's happened. "Nymphs. The hikers that've gone missing. It's the nymphs, not the Hunt."

Marion nods as Caden makes his way over to the trees our sister's already spotted, Alice right at his heels. They're so deep in conversation, I doubt either of them hears us. Marion leans against her old blue SUV, using one hand to dig around in her big leather bag. It's something she tells me was once known as a "Birkin," and she's quite proud of having come across it at a flea market.

She pulls out an ID badge that pictures a handsome white man, just about my age, with a hard look in his eyes. The name reads "Brett Turner." I swallow hard. "He's dead?"

Marion nods toward the trees that Alice and Cade are giving a thorough going-over. "Or whatever happens to them in the tree." She turns the ID over, and a notorious HBL logo is emblazoned on the back. HB Lumber used to be a fracking company pre-Reformation. I sneer at the ID.

Marion pushes a piece of paper toward Fallon, who glances over it, her eyes narrowing in rage. "It just never fucking ends with these people, does it?"

I glance down at the tribal document regarding Mr. Turner, who is apparently a lawyer for HBL. He's got a record of harassment and worse, but HBL's been buying him out of the trouble he's made for himself time and time again.

Marion stares at the trees. "Whatever those nymphs have done," she says in a steely voice, "you don't stop them from continuing to do it, you hear?"

Fallon nods. "Wouldn't dream of it."

Marion puts a hand on my sister's arm, sighing with relief. "I knew you'd understand, Fallon." My stomach twists suddenly at the look that passes between them. There's something I don't know. Some hurt Fallon's endured that I don't know about.

My sister's eyes lift to mine. "It was a long time ago, bub." I want to hug her tight, but she just holds my gaze. "I don't talk about it."

"Alright," I murmur. "But if you change your mind..."

"I know," Fallon whispers. "Wyatt, I *know*. And I am alright."

The funny thing is, I believe her. I glance at Marion, and from the way she's looking at my sister, I know she's the reason Fallon's okay now. Fallon looks at the printout again, taking a sharp breath. "Every one of the ones that went missing were HBL?"

Marion nods. "Every single one over the past decade. And the Chief did a bit of digging of her own. HBL can't get an accurate survey of the land, because everyone they send out disappears."

Fallon chuckles. "Bet they wish it was legal to use those fucking satellites now, don't they?"

Marion snorts. "No drones, no satellites... They'll figure it out eventually, but the nymphs have given us time to sort out what to do next."

Across the clearing, Cade's got his hand pressed to one of the trees that ate the folk from the lumber company. A sound that's somewhere between a giggle and a windchime tinkles through the clearing, and suddenly we're surrounded.

The forest is full of nymphs, Their sharp teeth gleaming in the low autumn light of the afternoon. Alice gasps as one approaches her, touching her hair. "I know you."

The nymph smiles dreamily. "You were in the parking lot at Three Ravens the other day. Such pretty hair."

Another half-dozen or so surround Caden, Their eyes hungry. "You're so beautiful," one of Them says. Another chimes in, "Would you like to dance with us?" while yet another chirps, "We like to watch you bathe."

"Hey," I bark out. "That's not polite."

The one who made the comment about watching Cade in the bath frowns. "It's not?"

"No," Alice says gently. "You should ask before doing things like that."

"Can I watch you bathe?" the nymph asks, her wide green eyes feverish with lust.

My brother's cheeks go red as Marion snickers. "Um...no?"

The nymph looks crestfallen, but another speaks up. "What about an orgy? You'd like an orgy, wouldn't you?"

Caden swallows as Marion, Fallon, and Alice all fall to pieces with laughter, and Fern sniffs the nymphs that have clustered around Caden. "I..." My brother looks at me, panic in his eyes.

I have to chuckle, setting my mug down on the hood of

Marion's SUV. "Good neighbors," I say softly. The nymphs turn. "Caden is not of a persuasion to engage in the kinds of activities you describe at this time."

"Would later be better?" one asks me eagerly.

It takes everything I have not to laugh. "No, I think this is a state that will last for all his natural life."

"Oh," They all say in unison, disappointment blooming over the clearing like azaleas in spring.

Most of Them disappear, fading into the forest, but the one who spoke to Alice lingers. She wears a crown of willow on her brow, her hair the colors of autumn leaves and her eyes a deep well of concern. "Do not worry," she says with a smile as she searches all our faces. "The tree-killers will never prosper here. This is now our home."

Marion clears her throat, and the nymph's eyebrows leap up. "We have made the necessary arrangements with..." The words the nymph speaks next are not understandable to me. She speaks in a Fey language that predates time itself, but Marion seems to comprehend her, nodding as the nymph explains herself.

Finally, Marion speaks. "That will be fine, then. None cut the trees here unless they've sickened or have already fallen."

The nymph smiles. "We know you need fuel for your winters. We will gather wood in both your territories as tithe for our presence here." She walks toward Fallon and takes her hands in her too-long fingers. "Dear little sister, we mean your charges no ill will. Only those that do harm will be eaten."

Fallon nods. "See that it stays that way."

The willow-crowned nymph smiles, her razor-sharp teeth showing, before her eyes turn my way. "And you, Wyatt Hayes. Would you like to keep your forest Sight? Or would you prefer I remove it?"

The way she says "remove it" sends prickles down my

spine, to the spot where the nymph dug into me. Miraculously, there's no evidence on me that someone shoved nymphy fingers into me, but I can't be sure the removal would be so kind.

Alice steps forward, her eyes narrowed with a kind of fierce concentration that makes me proud. "No deals. Your sister gave him the forest Sight to meet her own ends. Those ends were met. The bargain is closed."

The willow-crowned nymph nods. "What a clever girl," she says as she fades from sight. "Remember to set a watch for the forsaken."

Her words echo through the clearing. Fallon spins toward me. "What's that mean?"

I shrug. "Don't know. The alpha hound said it too, though."

Marion shakes her head as Caden, Alice, and Fern all gather around the hood of the SUV with us. "There's something happening on your end of things that spells trouble. Too much activity down the ley lines, all going to and fro someplace out West. You have a problem brewing."

Fallon sighs. "When's it ever been any different?"

Marion shrugs, looping her arm through Fallon's. "Never ever, girly. What're you wearing to the Hallows tonight?"

Fallon grins as Alice looks helplessly at me. "Are the Hallows the big party Lizzie was talking about the other day?"

"Yes, sweet girl." I smile, thinking that feels like ages ago. "We gotta find you a costume."

"Not *we*," Fallon insists, pushing between us. "You ruined girls' night, and I haven't had my essential debriefing yet."

Marion smiles. "You two wanna ride back with me? I heard Widow Harkness has a chest of old dresses we might raid from her modeling days."

And just like that, the three of them are piling into Marion's SUV without so much as a fare-thee-well. Caden laughs as

Marion maneuvers the vehicle around my truck and they speed off into the mist.

"Well," he says. "What're you wearing tonight?"

"Why?" I ask. "Are you actually gonna come?"

Cade smiles. "Yeah, big brother, I am. If we've got more trouble on the way, it's time I get back to living life."

I sling an arm around Caden and hug him. Despite the fact that closing this chapter of trouble has only meant opening another, I'm happy as can be. "Let's go work out what to wear to the Hallows," I say, whistling for Fern. "It's gonna be a hell of a good night."

Chapter 35
Alice

I'm returning Widow's avocado-green phone to its receiver on the floral patterned walls of her kitchen when I hear Fallon screeching my name from the top of the stairs.

"Stop hanging out with my brothers instead of me!" she shouts. "Hang up on Caden!"

I break into laughter, glancing around the corner to find her angrily gesticulating at me from halfway down Widow's grand carved staircase. "I just did," I reply, reaching for my coffee—served in a dainty vintage teacup, saucer and all. Then I pad through Widow's gorgeous foyer to the base of the stairs.

"Sorry. My parents emailed. Caden wanted to let me know right away that they're alive and stuff," I say as I begin to make my way up the stairs.

Fallon's head tilts to the side, hair falling across her shoulders like a shining curtain as she examines me. "Shit," she says, drawing the word out. "Caden being considerate of another human being? My family sure is under your spell."

I link my arm into hers as we begin to climb the remaining stairs together. "I left my entire life behind to hang out with you guys forever," I remind her. "If anything, you're the ones casting spells here."

"Didn't someone already explain this to you?" Widow asks me from where she's suddenly appeared on the second-floor landing, still garbed in a long, embroidered silk robe that pools around her feet like water. "It's the town. It's Blackbird Hollow. Pulls the right people in. Pushes the wrong ones out. It's why so many folks leave. Can't take the ley lines, that feeling in the air." She winks at me. "But people like *us*? We can't get enough."

I smile at the witch, pausing when Fallon and I reach the second floor. The bay window on the other side of the landing steals my attention. Blackbird Hollow is framed like a painting, glowing golden in the afternoon light. My heart swells. "Yeah," I agree before taking a long sip of coffee. "This place is pretty damn magical."

"You know what else is magic?" Fallon asks, one eyebrow raised. "Widow's closet." With that, she wraps her fingers around my forearm and drags me into the first door on the left. As I pass over the threshold, a gasp slinks from my lips.

The rest of Widow's antique home is all dark, shining wood and soothing earth tones, decorated with paintings of rivers, quilts in faded floral flannels, lovingly restored rattan furniture, warm off-white walls, and pops of stormy blue-gray. Glossy, oversized fashion books crown worn catalog cabinets, and ancient pharmacy shelving adorns the light-soaked kitchen.

I was expecting more of the same, but as Fallon pulls me into the space, I instead find an explosion of color and texture. The walls are painted a rich merlot, just barely visible between the frames of artwork decorating the room. At the far end, pale green curtains in a brocade pattern drape around a tall, narrow window.

The entire wall to my left is lined with garments in every

imaginable hue and fabric, skirts and trains spilling out onto the wood floor beneath my feet. Marion's seated at a fussy vanity with an elegantly shaped mirror, holding what looks to be a slinky flapper-style dress up to her chest.

"Isn't it wonderful?" Fallon asks me in a reverent whisper, trailing her hand along the wall of garments. She stops, fingers running down a slipper-pink sleeve for a second before moving on.

"And we're just allowed to...look at any of these?" I ask in bewilderment. There must be at least a hundred pieces of clothing here, if not more—and they all look like once upon a time, when the world was different, they would've been *incredibly* expensive.

"You're allowed to do more than look," Widow assures me, coming through the door with a pleased smile on her face. "Pick anything you'd like to wear tonight. I finally got it all unpacked and hung up. Might as well make use of it."

I pause, glancing at Widow's frame—tall, willowy, perfectly proportioned. "I'm not sure if anything would actually fit me, though," I bemoan.

At the vanity, Marion twists in the velvet chair, beaming over her shoulder at me. "You're in Blackbird Hollow now, Alice," she grins. "Widow or someone else in the coven will make sure whatever you want to wear fits perfectly."

"*Magic*, silly goose," Fallon reminds me from further down the garment rack. I can't hide the excitement bubbling in me as I set my coffee cup down onto the vanity and dive into Widow's literal fashion archive, oohing and aahing as I go. I find about five different drop-dead-gorgeous dresses in less than a few minutes, but I'm not sure if any are really *me*.

Marion and Widow are deep in conversation about how to make the slippery, jade-green dress fit Marion's stature appropriately when I hear Fallon give out a quiet little gasp. It's so unlike her that my head snaps in her direction immediately, something like worry rising in my throat.

But instead of a monster or even just a nymph peering through the window, Fallon's cradling a dress. It's somewhere between pale blue and ivory, embroidery shimmering in the light of the crystal-trimmed sconces by the vanity. If I'm honest, it's not something I would've ever expected Fallon to pick. Not with the billowing sleeves and yards upon yards of floating tulle fabric. I thought maybe the paneled leather dress I passed a few hangers ago might be more her taste, or even the slinky aubergine number with dark velvet ribbons. But the gown in her hands is like starlight condensed, the kind of dress that's Faerie-made for a princess in a faraway, ethereal land.

"Ahh," Widow observes, looking up from Marion's chosen dress. "Is that the one, Fallon?"

Her head snaps up, meeting my eyes, and then she looks at Widow, mouth parted. "Oh, I—*could* I?" Fallon asks with such tenderness, one hand gently skimming the gown's poofy skirt. "Really?" The last word is a wistful whisper, more a wish than anything else.

I don't know exactly why, but my eyes suddenly brim with tears. Maybe I'm thinking about the little girl that Fallon never got to be. The dress-up trunk her Nan never dragged out from the cellar. The butterflies she never chased through the creek in a vintage wedding dress, five sizes too big.

"Of course," Widow replies with one of her dazzling smiles. "I think that would look absolutely lovely on you. Come, I'm nearly done with Marion's alterations."

Fallon pulls the dress from the rack, tracing the gossamer-thin lace trim along the plunging neckline. Her gaze darts to me. "It's not really me, though, is it?" she asks, a hard glint appearing in her eyes.

I swallow, somehow knowing that if she sees my tears, she'll shove the dress back without a second glance. "It's *so* you, Fallon."

"We're going to be late." I frown, checking the time on the ridiculous clock hanging above Fallon's dresser. It's shaped like a white duck wearing a handkerchief around its neck, two little ducklings adorning either side.

"I'm not gonna let a fucking duck tell me what time it is," Fallon shouts from the bathroom, her voice muffled, referring to the clock that she personally chose for her own house. "We'll get there when we get there."

I make eye contact with the big duck that holds the clock in its belly. "'A queen is never late,'" I remind it, peering into its beady little eye.

"'Everyone else is simply early,'" Fallon finishes for me, looking pleased as she floats out of the bathroom, dressed in Widow's ballgown.

I stare at her, no better than a man. Fallon is always beautiful, like the rest of the Hayes, but tonight she's...*magnificent*. Between the gown and her makeup—a wet, silvery look that makes her appear ten years younger and also somehow ancient at the same time—I'm speechless.

"My bestie is a hottie," I manage.

"Yeah, well, so is mine," Fallon replies, reaching over to place two hands on my shoulders and gently turn me to face the big mirror leaning against the wall in the corner of her bedroom. "Like, *godsdamn*. Look at you, Blythe."

I laugh, blushing, but I look. The woman framed by the carved wood is very different from what I usually see in the mirror. She's on the taller side, looking elegant instead of gangly for once, a golden kiss of sun to her skin thanks to the past few weeks with the Hayes. Her hair is down, the waves encouraged for once instead of subdued, softly framing her face.

Shimmery gold and green eyeshadow brings out her hazel eyes, complementing the creamy off-white dress that looks like it was made for her. Delicate beading beneath the bust glimmers, highlighting her waist, and the layered skirt offers a peek of her long legs.

"Hell," I manage.

"I may have done too good a job," she observes from behind me. "My brother's gonna be distracted tonight."

My blush deepens at the idea of Wyatt seeing me all dressed up. It's silly, I know, but it's not something I've ever really gotten to do. However, I certainly *have* watched that scene a hundred times on all the old VHS tapes: the girl entering the party, everyone going silent because she looks so beautiful, but she only wants one person's attention.

I draw in a deep breath.

He said he loved me.

Wyatt Hayes loves *me*.

"Yeah," is all I can force out, my blush deepening. It's so unlike me, and I'm half-annoyed at myself because I'm here with Fallon right now, and I want to focus on her. But she just smiles down at me, something tender in her eyes.

"I'm so happy the two of you are happy," she murmurs, wrapping her arms around me. I close my eyes and lean my head on her shoulder, pulling in the smoky, slightly floral scent of her. "Mostly because this makes it more likely you'll stay forever."

"If I came here and it was just you," I say, "I would've stayed, too, Fallon. I hope you know that. You would've been enough for me. More than enough."

She says nothing but squeezes me tighter with her powerful arms. I draw in another deep breath, trying to take a snapshot of this moment in my mind. You never know you're living in the good old days until they're over. No matter what happens, I want to remember this. Want to be able to close my eyes and smell it, feel Fallon's arms around me, and know without a single doubt that I belonged somewhere.

When she pulls away, she's carefully pressing her fingers to her lower lids. "We should've said the sappy things *before* makeup," Fallon laments, reaching toward her dresser and opening the top drawer. "Too bad. Here. I have a present for you."

She hands me a battered box with a cream ribbon tied around it. "It's a welcome gift. A 'thanks for saying you'll stay' present. But before you open it, you have to promise that no matter what, we'll be buried next to each other."

I nod seriously, reaching out for the present. "Yeah, okay. Easiest promise I've ever made." I pause, looking up at her. "If I die first, you have to do my makeup. I wanna look good in the forever box."

Laughter bursts out of Fallon, bright as the sunrise. "Sure, Blythe," she says before her eyebrows knit together. "But I'll be really sad if you die first. I'm gonna have to forbid you from doing that. Sorry. Matriarch privileges and all."

"Well, I don't want *you* to die first," I protest, handing the box back to her. "So I can't accept."

"Hmm," Fallon says, crossing her arms and refusing to take the gift. "Okay, how about this: we gotta die on the same day."

"Only if you promise we'll also die in the same hour," I counter.

Fallon offers a crisp nod. "Deal. Okay, open your present, you fucking weirdo."

I snicker, pulling at the cream ribbon and then lift the top off. I part a few layers of tissue paper, only to find myself staring at Mr. Rabbit. Confusion stirs in my mind, but then I gasp.

"He has new eyes!" I exclaim, setting the box down on Fallon's dresser and pulling the stuffed animal out. "And a sweater!"

Two gleaming black buttons are sewn onto Mr. Rabbit's face, a perfect pair, replacing the one I had to cut off due to Sector's bug. A little green knitted sweater covers his upper body, hiding all the cuts Caden had to make. Two tiny felt letters spell out BH, letterman jacket-style. My vision blurs with tears as I clutch Mr. Rabbit to my chest, my lower lip quivering.

"You're gonna ruin all that makeup I did," Fallon says, but there's no venom in it.

"Your fault," I manage, my voice wavering as I try to blink through the tears, staring down at Mr. Rabbit. "He's perfect."

"Wyatt made the sweater," she explains. "Cade did some plastic surgery to make the stitches as invisible as possible. I found the buttons and cleaned him up. He needed some more stuffing and a good bath."

"I don't know how to thank you," I say in a strained voice, hugging Mr. Rabbit closely. "For everything."

Fallon smiles at me, an echo of that softness I saw in Widow's dressing room returning to her face. "You can thank me," she says, a near-feral grin taking over her features, "by not letting those tears ruin your makeup. And by having a damn good time tonight, Blythe. I think we've all earned it."

THE FOREST CLEARING is awash in firelight, staining the edges of everything in a golden-orange hue that feels like comfort distilled. I keep my arm linked with Fallon's as we make our way up the hill, leaving her Jeep behind in the meadow. Fern races down the hill toward us, yipping happily, though she's strangely polite about not jumping on our dresses, instead settling for running in laps around us.

Leaves crunch underfoot and the air smells crisp, laced with woodsmoke. An old hip-hop song I don't recognize rises on the wind as we grow closer, the scent of hot apple cider filling my nose. String lights swing from the tree branches that lean in low over the clearing, illuminating the pixies flitting through the air. As we draw closer to the bonfire, I can just make out a few nymphs dancing on the far side of the meadow. The moment I look at Them directly, the beautiful creatures are gone, leaving only the weathered trunks of ancient trees in Their place, but I can hear Their bell-like laughter echoing through the night.

"Welcome to your first Hallows, Alice," Wanda greets us, breaking away from the crowd to offer me and Fallon mugs of cider. I take one, gratefully wrapping my hands around the warm ceramic. I'm glad Fallon insisted I grab a leather jacket from Wyatt's old room. I'm not sure how great it goes with the dress, but she insisted the overall look was very *Buffy*.

"Thanks," I say to Wanda. "Hope it's the first of many." I peer around her shoulder, telling myself I'm not looking for Wyatt. "I have to talk to the tribe if I wanna stay here, right?"

Fallon laughs next to me as Wanda smiles, arching one brow as she glances behind her to where Chief Kingbird and Marion appear to be passionately—and very drunkenly—playing a game of Jenga on a plastic table. "You do, yes," Wanda replies, turning to meet my gaze. "But I think you'll be just fine."

Warmth floods me despite the evening's chill, and I nod happily, taking a long pull of the cider. It's perfect. I wonder if it's coven-made, too, in that well-seasoned cauldron that makes everything else of theirs I've had taste so goddamn good.

"We're gonna go find Wyatt," Fallon says to Wanda, shooting me a sly smile. "But we'll catch up later, yeah?"

The tall witch goes still, her features slack. Her mouth parts slightly, but no words come out as a pale wispiness floods her eyes. Panic clutches at my throat as Fallon's fingers wrap around my wrist. "Just root work," she explains in a low whisper. "Sometimes spirits are demanding."

I nod, remembering that Wanda had done the same thing last night, even though it feels like a thousand years ago. We don't have to wait long. Wanda's eyes clear a few seconds later, her attention settling on me.

"I normally only speak with my own ancestors," she tells me, examining my face, "but I just had two very polite white folks ask if I could tell their granddaughter how proud they are of her."

For a moment, I don't understand, and I probably stare at Wanda like an absolute idiot. "Your Nan and Poppop," she says softly, reaching out to place a hand on my shoulder. "Grace and Ron, right?"

Emotion closes my throat off, and I fight to find the right words.

"Oh, you're definitely gonna ruin her makeup," Fallon quips from beside me, shooting Wanda a playful glare.

"They're...my grandparents are *here*?" I manage to ask, voice quivering.

"Of course," Wanda says with a gentle smile. "The ancestors are always with us. Yours are very, very proud of you, Alice, and love you dearly."

"Thank you," I manage, my voice small and worn. "Thank you, Wanda."

The witch pulls me into a tight hug, smelling of vanilla and brown sugar and spice, and I probably would've burst into tears if I didn't catch sight of a familiar face.

"There she is," Wyatt says as Wanda and I pull apart. His smile is wide and dazzling beneath the brim of his flat cap. He's dressed in shades of green—an olive blazer with a brown-and-moss plaid vest layered beneath and army-green corduroy pants. A red bandana is tied around his neck, drawing attention to his stupidly perfect face.

"Why do you look like a little boy about to go work on the railroad?" Fallon demands, glancing at Wyatt with a frown.

Wanda cackles with laughter, squeezing my shoulder one more time before Janey appears, pulling the witch into a dance around the bonfire. Wyatt glances at me with a mischievous smile and then looks at his sister with a shrug.

"Barnes picked it out," he says pointedly.

"Barnes?!" Fallon echoes as she raises her chin, clearly searching the Hallows partygoers for the impeccably dressed, soft-spoken man. "Well, I guess even the best strike out now and again." Then she smiles, gesturing to me. "In more important news, do you see how beautiful Alice looks tonight?"

I've literally slept with this man twice—three times, if you count this morning—but I still feel myself turn red when his gaze sweeps back to me. It's all smoldering heat and something not unlike adoration. "Yes," Wyatt replies, a murmur from the back of his throat, rich as a crackling bonfire. "Yes, Alice, you look beautiful. Just like always."

"Gross," Fallon says, even though I can see her smile. "Alright, I'm getting out of here before you two start making out."

Wyatt tips the brim of his cap at Fallon as she strolls away, a vision in pale blue and glimmering gold thread. Then he steps close, sliding his hands around my waist.

“Thanks for Mr. Rabbit,” I tell him, tipping my head back to look up into his eyes.

“Did you like his sweater?” he asks playfully, resting his forehead against mine.

“I loved it,” I reply, our lips brushing. “I want one in my size.”

“That can be arranged,” he replies, pulling me against him.

I arch into him, sliding my hands up to grip the lapels of his jacket. Then his mouth is on mine, and I lose myself to it—to this tender thing blooming between us, to the glorious bonfire surrounded by people I can easily imagine myself loving, to the nymphs in the tree line and even the pixies flitting through the air like fireflies.

There's cheers when Wyatt dips me low, his large hand open on the small of my back. I laugh against his mouth as he pulls me back upright, breaking the kiss to cradle my face between his fingers.

“I only came here because I thought I didn't have a home to go back to,” I tell him. “Funny how things work.”

One of his dark brows arches. “How's that?”

I shrug. “Because I ended up coming home anyway.”

A smile overtakes his features as he gazes down at me. “Hey,” he murmurs. “You look beautiful. And you also look a lot like you—”

“Love you?” I ask with a laugh. “That's because I do, sweet boy. I love you, Wyatt Hayes, and I'm afraid you're stuck with me for the foreseeable future.”

He raises one of my hands to his lips, brushing a delicate kiss onto my knuckles that makes my knees weak. “I wouldn't have it any other way.”

Then he laces his fingers into mine and leads me closer to the heat of the bonfire, where our family is already dancing in the light.

. . .

THE END

THANK you for reading *Welcome to Blackbird Hollow*. Your authors regret to inform you that the road has not run out, the story's not over, and we've got more shenanigans to share. *Greetings From Blackbird Hollow* is on its way, and in the meantime, if you'd like to read about a *very* important day in Alice & Wyatt's near future, scan below to claim your free bonus epilogue!

Author's Note – Allison

Getting to write this book with Victoria was the highlight of my decade—hell, maybe my life. I can't even express how many times we've whispered and screamed to one another about just how easy this was, how magical. But that's us, all around. The universe is the only one who knows all the ways you've saved me, Victoria. In this life and the next, I love you.

Blackbird Hollow is an expression not just of magic, but of the way I hope the world still is in some places, and can be again someday. A place where people may not always agree about things 100%, but they'd ride at dawn for one another if anything threatened their community.

Community is more than pretty words. It's hard work. It's gardens and shopping small; it's pulling together in hard times. It's showing respect to one another and giving back as much as we take, but doing both, because doing just one throws everything off.

Blackbird Hollow is romance, sure, because romance (in my humble opinion) is the best vehicle for exploring all kinds of love. But it will always be a love letter to the places I've grown into myself, and all the love I've found along the way. There's not enough room to name names, but you all know who you are.

And to the readers, you make it all worthwhile. Protect what's good with all you've got, babes. The town that slays the Fey together stays together. Remember that.

Author's Note – Victoria

The first day Allison and I corresponded also happens to be the same day as my wedding anniversary to my beloved partner. It would be silly of me to write a book like this—or any of my other books—and not believe in portents. So I'm going to go ahead and say that the first email landing in my inbox on October 23 was no coincidence.

In a lot of ways, *Welcome to Blackbird Hollow* is an expression of Allison and I's love for each other: imperfect but resilient, messy but unyielding. It's a model of how we both think that love—*real* love, the tough stuff, the kind with sharp teeth and scraped knuckles—might just be able to turn things around.

I think I'd like for you, dear reader, to understand that I belong with Allison in the same exact way Alice belongs in Blackbird Hollow. And I think I want you to take this silly little romance book and let it guide you to the people you belong with, too. It'll be messy and weird, even without faeries interfering. But it'll be worth it. I promise.

I'm not sure if I believe in past lives, but on the days when the wind blows a strange way and I get that same tingle up my back that the Hayes kids do, I can't help but feel *so* sure that Allison and I have known each other since before time began. That in every universe, we've created art that helped people, even in the tiniest of ways. That maybe we were made from the same stardust, or some shit like that, like Alice would say.

And if you've read this far, I think you were made from that same primordial matter, too. You belong with us in Blackbird Hollow, and I'm so glad you found this book.

Now go plan your Hallows party with your people.

Also By Allison & Victoria

Allison Carr Waechter

The Immortal Orders Trilogy (Complete)

At the White Wolf (Standalone Novella)

Behind the Iron Gate (Fall 2025)

The Aethereals Duology (Complete)

The World of the Orphium Maere

The Consulate

The Swan

The Angel (Coming 2026)

Victoria Mier

The Fatebound Duology (Complete)

Between the Rival Courts (Coming 2026)

Holy Wrath (Standalone)

Together

Welcome to Blackbird Hollow

Greetings From Blackbird Hollow (Coming 2026)

www.ingramcontent.com/pod-product-compliance
Lightning Source LLC
Chambersburg PA
CBHW020912310726
48980CB00011B/842/J

* 9 7 9 8 9 9 3 0 4 1 4 1 4 *